APARAJITO

Bibhutibhushan Bandopadhyay was born in 1894 in Muratipur, a small village about hundred miles north of Calcutta. Bandopadhyay attended a local village school. In 1914 he was admitted to Ripon College, Calcutta, from where he graduated in 1918. He took up teaching as his profession and continued as a teacher for the greater part of his life. He died in 1950.

His first publication was a short story which appeared in a Calcutta journal in 1922. From then on he wrote regularly. He is credited altogether with fifty published works, seventeen of which are novels and twenty collections of short stories. His greatest work, however, and that which brought him fame, is *Pather Panchali*. *Aparajito* is the sequel to that famous novel. The noted film-maker Satyajit Ray, made three films based on these two novels, which have come to be known as the Apu trilogy.

Born and brought up in Delhi amidst people from various parts of India, Gopa Majumdar learnt the art of translation quite early in life. She has translated many of the famous Bengali writers, but is best-known as the translator of Satyajit Ray's works. Among her other well-known translations is Ashapurna Devi's celebrated novel, *Subarnalata*.

In 1995, she was given the Katha Award for translation.

In 2001 came the prestigious Sahitya Akademi Translation Prize for *Aparajito*. Gopa Majumdar lives in Britain at present, and is actively involved in promoting Indian literature abroad.

APARAJITO

(THE UNVANQUISHED)

Bibhutibhushan Bandopadhyay

Translated from the Bengali by
Gopa Majumdar

HarperCollins *Publishers* **India**
a joint venture with

New Delhi

Published in 2003 by
HarperCollins *Publishers* India
a joint venture with
The India Today Group

First published in 1999
3rd impression, 2008

HarperCollins *Publishers*

A-53, Sector 57, NOIDA, Utter Pradesh - 201301, India
Hazelton Lanes, 55 Avenue Road, Suite 2900, Toronto, Ontario M5R 3L2
and 1995 Markham Road, Scarborough, Ontario M1B 5M8, Canada
25 Ryde Road, Pymble, Sydney, NSW 2073, Australia
31 View Road, Glenfield. Auckland 10, New Zealand
10 East 53rd Street, New York NY 10022, USA

Printed and bound at
Thomson Press (India) Ltd.

In memory of
Satyajit Ray
who gave Apu's dream to the world

CONTENTS

Foreword: *A Glimpse of the Master*   *ix*

Translator's Note   *xiii*

Pather Panchali: *A Synopsis*   *xix*

Aparajito   1

Glossary   473

FOREWORD

A Glimpse of the Master

Reading the works of Bibhutibhushan Bandopadhyay
is like looking at the universe. It evokes the same feeling of
wonder and awe. He is one of those rare authors who can
grasp life in its entirety, not just the whirlpool of the period
he lived in. This adds a touch of magic to his works. His
vision soars to the bright evening clouds. Then comes down
the next moment to the stillness of night or speeds towards
the approaching dawn. Yet, in the next instant, he is not there
any more, but has made a journey to the farthest corner of
creation, taking his readers with him. Bibhutibhushan was a
wayfarer roaming the highways of the physical universe, but
his heart was bound in an unbreakable bond with the simple
joys and sorrows of earthly life.

His father was Mahananda Bandyopadhyay, a village story-teller and singer, Though an educated man, Mahananda was not financially successful in life. Bibhutibhushan saw a great deal of poverty when he was growing up. His father travelled through villages, telling stories, singing ballads from the epics and mythology, writing plays, setting an ideal of nomadic freedom before his son. This is perhaps how the seed was sown. Bibhutibhushan travelled all over India, particularly the Saranda forest ('The Land of Seven Hundred Hills', as described by Colonel Dalton) in Bihar. To him, every bush was afire with the wonder of nature and the invisible power behind it. He was, in his own way, fully conscious of the cosmic backdrop against which life played its role. This special trait in his character earned him the unique place he enjoys in Indian literature: Added to this was the simplicity of his language and sincerity of his feelings. Anyone who has read his works knows that what he said came straight from his heart, from a deep faith in what he felt to be true. In this day and age, when many of us are forced into a never-ending rat race, Bibhutibhushan's language, his vision and his very positive philosophy of life bring a sense of deep peace and tranquillity.

Aparajito, Bibhutibhushan's second novel, a sequel to *Pather Panchali*, was serialised in *Prabasi* and was published in two volumes in 1932. Bibhutibhushan perhaps faced quite a lot of difficulty with this novel, because here Apu, the famous hero, is in the big metropolis Calcutta, working hard to earn a living and to acclimatize himself with the ways of city life. The peaceful Nischindipur is gone, Apu finds himself gasping in the claustrophobic atmosphere which bewilders him. He never really understands the city. While working as an accounts clerk in the house of a big landowner, he hankers for a small piece of blue sky, the verdure of the open fields, for the magic of the open emptiness of the horizon. The author himself felt this problem, as this was his autobiographical novel. The grim struggle for existence could not daunt Apu. His love for nature and for simplicity kept him going in spite of all the hurdles and pitfalls.

This struggle for existence and yearning to go back to his roots are two main features of *Aparajito*. The peaceful village Nischindipur, where Apu and Durga grew up is gone for ever, but the desire to go back remains. As the novel goes on, readers are mesmerised by the simple style of the author. As one of the Western critics said of him: novelists in the Western countries can teach us about violence, sex, alienation and psychological problems, but this Bengali author can teach us about the basics of human life and society. This was possible for Bibhutibhushan because he maintained no double standards. Many of his contemporaries described him as a saintly person, and truly he was that. In his works he shows us the way to conquer sorrow and fear.

Bibhutibhushan's interests in life were varied. His personal library, at least partly, still exists. It contains books on astronomy, physics, botany, world literature in general, anthropology, philosophy and all the earth sciences. He used to take a few books with him when going out for a late afternoon stroll, find a comfortable place under a big tree, and read till it was dark. Books accompanied him to bed, too. Often he read till the small hours.

We can see reflections of his extensive reading in his works. In *Aparajito*, he warns us against the indiscriminate deforestation and resulting environmental hazards sixty-five years ago, a time when almost nobody was aware or concerned about pollution. Not only an avid worshipper of nature, Bibhutibhushan was also a pioneer of conservation of environment. He wanted to save what he loved.

Like André Gide and Rabindranath Tagore, Bibhutibhushan maintained a diary regularly. The last entry was made only three days before his death. In 1924, while on a sojourn in Bihar, Bibhutibhushan wrote in his journal about the theory of relativity and time dilation. It was only eight years after Einstein's publication of the theory of general relativity and Bibhutibhushan had already read and grasped it. His acquaintance with the ever-expanding frontiers of knowledge gave his works a special depth and class. Combined with this was his positive humanism, love for everything and everybody.

It is for this reason that his works will be remembered and read for ever.

Barrackpore   Taradas Banerjee
December 1998

xii

TRANSLATOR'S NOTE

⋙◆⋘

When Bibhutibhushan Bandopadhyay began writing *Aparajito* as a sequel to *Pather Panchali* in 1932, he could not have imagined that his second novel would be deemed equally successful not only in literary circles, but—years later—by the whole world, who would watch the story of Apu's life on the silver screen. Any mention of the Apu trilogy made by Satyajit Ray, even today, makes Indians feel proud. Ironically, though, the story that the world has seen has only been the one told in the films. It is true that Ray did not make any major changes, and kept to the main plot, exactly as Bibhutibhushan had described it. He even used the same lines the characters spoke in the two novels. But he did take the liberty to combine the last few chapters of *Pather Panchali* (*The Song of the Road*) with the first few of *Aparajito* (*The Unvanquished*) when he made the second part of the trilogy.

He had to, not only because it was his right and privilege as the film-maker, but without doing so, the story would have lost its continuity. When he made the last film, *Apur Sansar* (*The World of Apu*), again, for his own cinematic purposes, he stopped at the point where Apu is reunited with his son. If the film makes such an impact, it is largely because it ends at that precise moment.

This is the story that millions have seen. But what about the story originally told by the author? Apart from those who have read the original novel, how many know what he actually said? What happened to Apu after he left his father-in-law's house, happily carrying his little son on his shoulders?

Pather Panchali was translated in 1968 by T W Clark and Tarapada Mukherji. So Bibhutibhushan's story of the young Apu was related to non-Bengalis thirty years ago. However, they, too, chose to end the book with Apu's departure for Kashi (Varanasi), when he is about ten years old. By this time, his sister, Durga, is dead. What happens to Apu and his parents in Kashi is not included in the translation. The reason given by the two translators is this:

'... The climax surely is reached when Opu and his parents leave Nischindipur; and what follows, if the reader goes on with it, is something of an anticlimax.... For Opu the road goes on; but Durga, his home and his village, are now finally left behind. As the train draws away from the station the last chords of the symphony are struck, and the rest should be silence.'

Strangely enough, in the intervening years, no one translated *Aparajito*. To tell the truth, the idea of translating it might not have occurred to me, either, if I had not come across a book published last year. It was *The Vintage Book of Indian Writing: 1947-1997*. One of its editors was Salman Rushdie. What he said in his introduction is now well-known, and much has been already said on the subject. It is not my intention here to add my own comments. What did surprise me, however, was one sentence that may have escaped the attention of many. When talking of 'vernacu!ar-language writers who would merit a place in any anthology', Mr Rushdie mentions Bibhutibhushan, and adds in brackets, for the benefit of the uninitiated, the words 'the author of *Pather Panchali*, on which Satyajit Ray based his celebrated Apu trilogy of films'. With a start, I realised that even the famous and knowledgeable were capable of making a mistake. As a matter of fact, Mr Rushdie had made almost the same mistake that I myself had made in my early teens. Having seen the three films at a film festival, I had gone to my school library and demanded the Apu books. On being handed *Pather Panchali* and *Aparajito*, I had asked, 'But where's *Apur Sansar?*' The librarian could only smile at my ignorance. 'Three films. Two books. Read them. You'll know,' I was told. I was to discover subsequently that there was, in fact, a third book called *Kajal*, which was the story of Apu's son, but it had nothing to do with Ray's films.

Mr Rushdie, I realised quickly, could not be blamed. How was he to know about the existence of the second novel, when it was not available in translation? But perhaps the time had come to rectify the matter. I had translated a few short stories by Bibhutibhushan three years ago. Could I not do *Aparajito*?

'Go ahead,' said the chief editor of HarperCollins India, beaming kindly. 'Go ahead,' said the author's son, Taradas Bandopadhyay, sounding quite cheerful. Thus encouraged, I picked up a pen and sat down with the novel at my desk. And there I remained seated for several weeks, simply chewing my pen instead of writing with it. Go ahead? *How* was I going to accomplish that?

It soon became clear why the novel had not been translated before. Perhaps there had been dozens of translators before me, who had tried and failed. How could I hope to succeed?

The main problem was the language. It seemed to have flowed from Bibhutibhushan's pen as spontaneously and with as much vigour as a waterfall from a mountain. It was as complex as it was simple. Most of it was pure poetry, rhythmic and lyrical. At times, there was great rhetoric. At others, he used very ordinary colloquial expressions. The lyricism in his language is at its height when he describes nature. And no matter where he places his protagonist, there is always an underlying philosophy of thought: Apu has a special sensitive insight, a deep awareness of the 'extraordinary' hidden in all things ordinary, all around him.

It was obvious that I was required to tread with extreme caution. So I began, at first, by trying to retain every word, and every sentence, just as it appeared in the original. In so doing, one thing became apparent. While it reduced the risk of my critics accusing me of 'rewriting' the text of a well-known classic, it did very little to enhance readability. What was eloquent and beautiful in the original, in a painstakingly faithful translation, sounded not just stilted, but archaic, fanciful, or positively melodramatic.

Then I discovered other problems. The novel had been serialised in a magazine before it was published as a book. As is normally the case (certainly in Bengal) with a book that is published after serialisation, no one thought of editing it at the time. Some of it, therefore, sounded repetitive and, at times, somewhat rambling. There was also the assumption (again, a common problem with a sequel) that the reader had read *Pather Panchali*, and was familiar with all its characters. A few pages were devoted purely to such characters. Apu himself did not feature in them at all; nor were the events described linked in any way to his own story. It dawned upon me that those readers who had not read *Pather Panchali* would certainly find it difficult to understand the relevance of these pages. A certain amount of editing seemed inevitable.

Related to the question of structure was the number of chapters. There are twenty-six chapters in the original, but not all of them are of equal length. Two of the longest had to be broken to give each chapter in the translated version more or less the same length.

While I was still struggling to sort out some of these major problems, a friend visited me one day, and said, 'Translate *Aparajito* into English? Oh, don't be absurd. You can't do it. You mustn't!'

'Why not' I asked, much taken aback.

'How can you have Apu and Sarbajaya and everyone else speaking in English? How will you describe in English all the details of their life in a village in Bengal? Will anyone understand it?'

I told my friend to mind his own business, but soon realised the truth behind his words. It was not just the spoken lines that had to be transferred into English. That was difficult enough. But there were names of plants, animals, birds and even food, for which there was either no English equivalent at all; or, if there was, it was not in common use. For instance, while it seemed logical to use 'mango' instead of *aam*, and 'woodapple' instead of *bel*, it was awkward to use 'rose-apple' for *jaam*. A way round this problem was to use Hindi words in some cases, which I thought might be comprehensible to a large number of Indian readers, and many non-Indians. So, when dealing with items of food, I used 'paneer' for *chhana*, and 'puri' for *luchi*. But where plants and birds were concerned, many original Bengali names had to be retained. There is a glossary, compiled with non-Indian readers in mind, but that does not include English names for all the local flora and fauna described by the author.

What, then, is the final result? I have finished translating the novel, I have done some necessary editing, I have tried hard to prevent a complete 'anglicisation' of Apu and his world. But have I succeeded? Has justice been done to Bibhutibhushan's beautiful language? Have I been able to convey the depth of his vision?

The reader must find the answer. Should anyone attempt to find fault with my efforts, they may well find their job not altogether difficult. But, for what it is worth, here is the missing portion of Apu's life. For all those who may have seen the three films and wondered what could have happened to Apu and Kajal, here is the answer.

I cannot thank Taradas Bandopadhyay enough, not only for so readily giving his permission for this translation, but also for his continued support and encouragement. Had he not given me total freedom, and approved whatever changes I suggested, I could not have found the courage to complete my task.

My heartfelt thanks also go to the following:

Sandip Ray, for allowing the use of the photograph from the film 'Apur Sansar' for the cover.

William Radice, without whose generosity, help and advice, I could never have crossed the many hurdles that came my way.

Santipriya Bandopadhyay, who never failed to respond to my desperate queries with both promptness and calm reassurance.

Renuka Chatterjee and Shoma Choudhury of HarperCollins India, for all their understanding and cooperation; and

Ian Baker, who stood by me like a rock throughout this whole exercise, with unfailing patience, good humour and admirable composure.

I am deeply indebted to you all.

London   Gopa Majumdar
October 1998

PATHER PANCHALI: A SYNOPSIS

❧

Harihar Roy lives in a village called Nischindipur.
With him live his wife, Sarbajaya; daughter, Durga; and son,
Apu. An old cousin called Indir Thakrun lives with him, too,
but she dies when Apu and Durga are quite young.

A Brahmin, Harihar makes a living by working as the
family priest for various people. His job takes him away from
home for long periods, but his income is both small and
irregular. In his absence, his wife Sarbajaya has to fend for
herself and her two children, fighting poverty and the snobbery
of her wealthy neighbours. Little Apu and his sister Durga,
however, are wholly untouched by the horrors of poverty.
Their love of nature shields them from it; their joy in simply
being able to roam freely in the woods, or by the riverside,
wipes out all the disappointments and deprivations life heaps
upon them.

Then disaster strikes. Durga dies when she is only thirteen. By this time, it is clear to both Harihar and Sarbajaya that nothing can be gained by continuing to live in Nischindipur. They must find a new life, in a new place. With this in mind, they sell their few possessions and leave for Kashi (Benaras). Apu is only ten at the time.

For a short while, things appear to improve. Harihar reads from the scriptures, and tells stories from Hindu mythology at Dashashwamedh Ghat. He has a few competitors who also do the same job, but even so, he starts to bring home more money than he could in the village. The rented room they live in is both dark and damp, but it is here that Sarbajaya finds contentment. Apu starts going to a school, and all is well.

In only about a year, the family is torn apart again. This time, things are much worse. Harihar, the sole breadwinner, dies after a brief illness. Sarbajaya is left alone to take care of herself and her son, in an alien land, without friends and without any money. A few kind neighbours help but, naturally, that cannot last for ever. Her pride does not allow her to go back to Nischindipur. Even if she were to return there, she knows she cannot live in her dilapidated old house.

After a month of grim struggle, there is an offer of a job. A family from Burdwan (in Bengal) while on a visit to Kashi announce their need for a Brahmin lady to help with their cooking. They want to take their new cook with them when they return to Burdwan. Sarbajaya and Apu must be uprooted once more, but their only other option is starvation. They leave for Burdwan happily enough.

Their new home turns out to be a large and wealthy household teeming with maids and servants. Sarbajaya joins the kitchen staff as an assistant cook. She and Apu are given a small room, close to a stable. The arrangement is far from satisfactory, but at least mother and son have a roof over their heads again.

While Sarbajaya spends most of her time in the kitchen, Apu roams in the big house, watching its inhabitants from afar. He is too shy and timid at first to approach any of them. However, when there is a wedding in the family and many relatives arrive from other towns and villages, he meets a girl called Leela. She is younger than Apu by a couple of years. Her father is one of the owners of the house, but he lives in Calcutta. Though Leela cannot stay for more than a few days, a friendship grows between the two children chiefly because both Leela and her mother (known to the staff as Mejo Bourani) are kind, affectionate and devoid of snobbery. That Apu is the son of a kitchen assistant does not seem to bother either of them. Leela does not hesitate to invite Apu to her study, show him her books, and even visit him in his poky and smelly little room. She gives him her own fountain pen, despite Apu's protests, just because he has never seen a pen that does not need to be dipped in ink. When she returns to Calcutta, neither she nor Apu realise that theirs is a friendship that will last an entire lifetime.

After her departure, Apu tries to befriend the other children in the house. He discovers quickly that they are not sweet and kind like Leela. One day, Apu is unjustly blamed for another child being injured, and is severely punished. He tries hard to keep this news from his mother, but it does reach her ears. Both feel humiliated, but there is little that they can do.

Eventually, in time, they come to terms with their situation. Apu's heart yearns for the carefree days of his childhood, spent by the side of the river Ichhamoti; he misses his sister and other playmates, a girl called Ranu in particular. But he knows in his heart that life is not about looking back and holding on to grief. A feeling of optimism, inherent in Apu's attitude and approach to life, removes all pain. The future will be his, he realises, if he can only look ahead.

Pather Panchali ends with this message of hope. When *Aparajito* opens, Apu has spent three years in Leela's house in Burdwan. He is going to school, and life has settled into a routine. Fate, however, is simply waiting to disrupt it.

ONE

It was quite late in the afternoon. Even so, there was a fair number of beggars gathered outside the front gate of the Roychowdhuris. It was Biru Muhuri's job to ensure that each of them got an adequate supply of rice, but the beggars had a strong suspicion that Biru was in league with Jamadar Shambhunath Singh. The two of them, it was generally believed, often conspired together to deprive the poor of the portions that were rightfully theirs. Every Sunday, the beggars fought with Biru, and it always ended with irate chowkidars trying to push aside a number of the more aggressive ones. Then either the old cashier or the chief clerk emerged from the house to arbitrate. No one could remember a single Sunday when the weekly business of giving food to the poor had been concluded without strife.

Inside the house, too, two of the kitchen staff were quarrelling. It came to an abrupt end as the cook, Mokshada, quickly heaped her own plate with food and disappeared. Sarbajaya had been a silent onlooker. She was younger than most of the kitchen assistants. It was partly for this reason that she stayed out of quarrels in the kitchen. There was also the fact that, having come from a village, she did not fit in with those used to the wealth and comforts of life in the city. However, it was to her that Mokshada had been complaining against another maid called Shodu. Sarbajaya never took sides, and was quite adept at uttering soothing words to whoever happened to address her. She was therefore viewed with kindliness by all. When Mokshada left, Sarbajaya served herself lunch and went back to the little room she lived in. This was not the room in which she had spent the first two years. Not that it made any difference, for it was as small and its floor as damp as the other one; but at least it was not close to the stables as the first one had been, which was a relief.

Shodu entered her room even before Sarbajaya had had the chance to place her plate on the floor.

'What was Mukhi telling you about me?' Shodu asked furiously, 'She's a bad lot, that woman, I'll tell you that for nothing. Tell her she can go and complain to Boro Bourani—or whoever she fancies—but *I* will speak to Bourani, too, and have Mukhi thrown out of the house. You mark my words, I'll get rid of her very soon!'

Sarbajaya smiled, 'No, Shodu Mashi, please don't upset yourself. You don't really think I took her seriously, do you? She is like that, she always speaks without thinking, but she doesn't really mean any harm, you know. Besides, I have been working here for three years, and I've known you since the day I arrived. I know what you're like, and believe me, I've never heard anyone speak ill of you. Even Mukhi didn't say anything much, honestly!'

2

Mollified, Shodu looked around and said, 'Where's Apu? He hasn't gone to school, surely? It's Sunday today!'

Sarbajaya had not yet had her bath. She never got the chance to bathe in the morning. By the time she finished her chores in the kitchen, it was almost always past the lunch hour. Now she began to pour coconut oil from a bottle into a bowl and said, 'No, Apu has gone to visit a friend. He goes to his house on holidays. My son is quite mad, really—he doesn't even seem to mind the hot sun in the afternoon. Why are you still standing, Mashi? Please sit down.'

'No, I did not come to stay,' Shodu replied, 'I won't keep you from your meal. I just wanted to hear what Mukhi had to say about me. Tell her when you see her in the kitchen, not to meddle with me. I know a lot about her, things she wouldn't like repeated. In fact, I may look meek and mild, but if I decide to open my mouth ... speak to her, won't you, and tell her to watch her tongue.'

Shodu left. Sarbajaya began oiling her hair. Then the noise of footsteps made her look at the door and exclaim, 'Just look at you! Your face has turned red from roaming in the sun. Come in and sit down ... Apu, what am I going to do with you?'

Apu made straight for his bed and, pulling a pillow to himself, lay down. Then he fanned himself furiously for a few minutes. Finally, he looked at his mother and said, 'Haven't you had your bath? It's past two o'clock!'

'I am just going. Do you want to eat anything?'

'No,' Apu shook his head.

'Why not? Aren't you hungry? I've got a nice dish of paneer here. All you had this morning with your rice was a little daal and fried brinjal. Come on, you must be hungry.'

Apu raised himself. 'Show me what you've got!' he demanded. Then, without waiting for a reply, he climbed down from his bed and started to lift the lid from Sarbajaya's plate.

3

'Don't, don't touch it!' Sarbajaya shouted. 'Give me a couple of minutes. I'll share this with you as soon as I've had my bath.'

Apu laughed. 'Why can't I touch it? You sound as if I'm an untouchable. I am a Brahmin, Ma. You must not talk to me like that.'

'A Brahmin?' Sarbajaya scolded him, 'When do you ever do your daily puja, or anything else a Brahmin is supposed to do? Brahmin! You ought to be ashamed of yourself.'

A little later, when Sarbajaya returned from her bath, she said, 'You can eat from my plate. I won't take long.'

Apu smiled again, 'Eat from your plate? Never. No Brahmin eats off a used plate!'

Sarbajaya paid no attention and began eating. After a few minutes' silence, Apu spoke softly, 'I've heard about a job, Ma. It'll mean working at the station. I'll have to stand on the platform and sell stuff to the passengers as they get off the train. I should be paid five rupees *and* something extra for food. I heard someone mention it. I can do it without giving up school.'

Sarbajaya knew Apu went about asking people if they could get him a job. If he got something with a steady income, it would not be a bad thing. But she did not like to hear Apu talk of going out to earn a living. He was only a young boy. How could she let him go out every day, in the scorching sun or pouring rain, to fend for himself in a big city where danger lurked in every corner? No, she could not bear to think of it.

So she made no immediate reply, except to say, 'Come, sit here and finish what's left. Yes, I've had enough.'

Apu got up and began eating. 'Won't that be nice, Ma?' he went on, 'Five rupees is quite a lot of money, isn't it? They'll raise my pay afterwards, so they said. My friend Satin was telling me of rooms that are going to be let ... they're

4

near his house, he said. Two rupees a month for one of them. It will be small and may only have a tin roof, but we'll manage, won't we? Here they make you work so hard all day, it's just not fair. I can go to the station straight after school, and have something to eat there. That should be all right, shouldn't it?'

Sarbajaya said, 'I'll make you rotis. You can take them with you.'

Ten days passed after this conversation. Neither Apu nor his mother raised the subject. Then, suddenly, the senior Mr Roychowdhuri fell ill. His illness took a serious turn, and for the next couple of weeks he remained in a critical condition. No one in the house spoke of anything except his illness and whether he was making any progress. Two weeks later, when he was reportedly out of danger, Apu returned home with a smile on his face and said to his mother, 'I have spoken to a shop where they make kites. If I help with the pasting and sealing, they will pay me seven rupees a month and give me two new kites every day. It's a huge place, Ma, they send their kites to Calcutta! They told me to go there on Monday.'

Sarbajaya knew this smile, this gleam of hope in his eyes. She knew it very well indeed. When she used to live in the village with her husband, she had seen the same look in his eyes, heard the same tone in his voice—many, many times during the fifteen years she had spent there. Things were going to change, the bad days were over, good times were just round the corner! When they sold all their possessions and left Nischindipur for good, even then Harihar had had the same dreamy look on his face.

Less than four years since his death, Apu was speaking exactly like his father. Sarbajaya tried to ignore the warning signs. She had ceased to have a home of her own, but a very feminine desire to set one up and run it in her own way often

5

caused her pain. Now, when Apu spoke with such enthusiasm, she wanted to believe he was right. No matter how thin and brittle the ray of hope, her heart yearned to clutch at it. Besides, how could she wipe out the joy in Apu's face? How could she crush his youthful eagerness under the weight of her own age and experience?

'Very well,' she said, 'that's good news. Go and see them on Monday and let's see what happens. Oh, by the way, did you know Mejo Bourani is coming soon? They were talking about it in the kitchen.'

Apu's eyes lit up. 'When, Ma, when?' he asked anxiously.

'Later this month. Boro Babu isn't well enough to look after things, so Mejo Babu is going to do that until Boro Babu gets better.'

Apu opened his mouth to speak, but shut it again. He could not bring himself to ask his mother if Leela was going to come with her parents. Of course she'll come, he told himself firmly, if both her parents were going to be here, Leela certainly would not be left behind.

The next day, when he returned from school and walked into his room, his mother said, 'Have something to eat first. Then I'll show you what I received today—a letter!'

'A letter? Who's sent you a letter?' Apu sounded amazed. No one had bothered to write to them since his father's death. In the two-and-a-half years they had spent in this house, they had never received even a postcard. Why, he'd almost forgotten that there were such things as letters and post offices! 'Show it to me!' he demanded.

Yes, it *was* a letter and that, too, in an envelope. His mother's name was written on it. Apu took the letter out and began reading it quickly. Then he cast a puzzled glance at his mother and asked, 'Who is Bhavtaran Chakravarty?' Looking at the sender's address, he added, 'he's written from Kashi!'

6

'You met him once when you were about seven. He spent three days with us in Nischindipur. Don't you remember? He bought a doll's house for Durga.'

'Oh yes. Yes, I do remember. Didi said he was your uncle. How come in all these years ... ?'

'He's my father's cousin. He always travelled a lot, mainly to holy places like Gaya and Kashi. He never settled down for long in his house in the village either. I visited him only once. His village was called Monshapota. His daughter and her husband used to live in that house, but I believe they are both dead now.'

'Yes, that's what he has written,' Apu glanced at the letter again. 'He says he went to Nischindipur to look for us and then learnt we'd gone to Kashi. How did he get our address, Ma? He must have asked the Rama Krishna Mission.'

Sarbajaya smiled, 'I was about to lie down for a little nap after lunch, when Khemi came and said there was a letter for me. I couldn't believe it ... and he says he'll take us away from here. Does he say when?'

'No, he only says soon. Won't that be just lovely, Ma? I hate the way you have to work here all day. We could live on our own again ... in our own home!'

It had not quite sunk in. Sarbajaya could barely allow herself to believe the promise her uncle's letter held for her. An end to working as someone else's servant, being free, being able to run her own life ... but no, there had been so many disappointments in the past. She did not dare hope, or make plans. Nevertheless, mother and son spent a long time chatting about the possibility of starting life afresh. Then Apu said, 'There's going to be a puppet show near my friend's house. Can I go, Ma?'

'All right. But make sure you come back before they close the main gate here.'

Apu left instantly, his feet barely touching the ground. He had not known such happiness for a long time. Free ... ho would soon be free. But what about Leela? She was going to arrive any day. Would she speak to him again? Or would she act all grown-up and not look at him at all?

The puppet show started quite late and Apu could not leave before it finished. By the time he came out, it was so late that he knew the gate at the Roychowdhuri's house would be locked. It was extremely unlikely that one of the chowkidars would condescend to unlock it for the son of an assistant cook. Where could he go? Suddenly he felt afraid. He had never spent a whole night out on his own. What was his mother going to say?

He looked a little helplessly at the dispersing crowd. Then he spotted a small paan shop that was still open, selling paan and lemonade. He slowly made his way to it and found an upturned wooden crate by its side. He sat down, lost in thought. He couldn't tell when he fell asleep, but when he opened his eyes, it was daylight and there were people on the streets.

He returned home a little later. To his surprise, he found two carriages standing outside the gate. As he entered the compound, he saw a few children dressed and ready to go out.

'Where are these people going?' he asked one of the maids as he walked towards his own room. 'Are they going to the station? Is Mejo Babu arriving today?'

'Yes, so I've heard. A letter came yesterday, I believe. Only Mejo Babu and Bourani are coming. Leela has her exams, she won't come until Christmas.'

Apu felt a sharp stab of disappointment. Leela was not coming! It mattered little if she came during her Christmas holidays. He was not going to be here. He had wanted so much to see her before he left. Leela had not visited this house for such a long time.

'Where were you all night?' Sarbajaya demanded the moment he got back. 'I could not sleep a wink!'

'Well, it got very late, so I thought the gate would be locked and I couldn't get back anyway, so I went to my friend's place ...' Apu broke off and started laughing. 'No, Ma, the truth is that I slept on a crate near a paan shop!' he confessed.

'Oh my goodness, what do I do with you, you horror? You slept out in the open? All night? What if you caught a chill? Or something worse happened? You must never go out in the evening, do you hear me? Not for a puppet show, or a play, or anything.'

'It was not my fault, Ma. I could hardly break open the gate, could I?'

It took Sarbajaya a while to calm down. Then she said, 'I wish you were here last night. My uncle turned up soon after you left. He'll come back again this evening, he said. He's staying here with some friends. He ... he wants us to leave with him the day after tomorrow!'

'Really? So soon? What else did he say? Tell me everything.'

Sarbajaya explained what her uncle had told her. Bhavtaran Chakravarty had no one left in his family. He wanted to leave his property and other possessions in Sarbajaya's care, so that he could live permanently in Kashi. Having actually spoken to him, Sarbajaya could no longer hide her joy. She had already got together the few household goods she had collected over the years. 'Look at this lamp!' she said, pointing at a large oil lamp, 'I can light it in the kitchen of our new home. Do you know how much oil it can take in? All the oil you can get for two paisa!'

❧❦❧

That afternoon, Apu had just settled down to have his lunch when, suddenly, a shadow fell across the threshold. Apu looked up quickly and turned into a statue.

9

Leela!

Leela entered the room a second later, smiling. But she stopped short as she took a proper look at Apu. Was this the same young boy she had played with more than a year ago? He was even then a handsome boy, but now ... his face, his hair, his eyes ... did Apu always have such beautiful, expressive eyes? Leela felt a little shy. To cover it up, she said quickly, 'How tall you've grown, Apurbo!'

Apu was thinking exactly the same about Leela. This could not be the same girl he had met a year-and-a-half ago. How lovely she looked! Leela was easily the most beautiful girl he had ever seen. He could not take his eyes off her.

Then they both felt a little awkward. 'How come you are here?' Apu said finally, 'I asked only this morning, and was told you were going to stay back for your exams.'

'So you thought of me, Apurbo?'

'Thought of you? Of course I thought ... no, I mean ... you just disappeared, didn't you?'

'Disappeared? Me? What about you? I wrote to Grandma before Khokamoni's annaprashan and asked her to send you to our house. All the others went, why didn't you?'

Apu knew nothing about this. No one had told him. 'Who is Khokamoni?' he asked.

'My little brother. Didn't you know about him? He's almost a year old now.'

Apu felt a little sorry for Leela. Clearly she had no idea that the friend she had invited with such enthusiasm was a complete nobody in this house. Who would even dream of including the child of a servant among the family?

'It's been a year and a half since I last saw you,' he said, changing the subject, 'which class are you in?'

Leela sat down on his bed. 'I am not going to talk about myself until you've told me what you've been doing. I hope your mother is well? You, too, are going to a school, aren't you?'

'Yes, I'll soon be in a new class,' Apu replied, tilting his head a little proudly, 'I stood first in my class last year. They gave me a prize!'

Leela looked at him again. It was past three o'clock. Why was he having his lunch so late? She could not help asking him about it. This embarrassed Apu. He normally had something to eat before going to school quite early in the morning. But it was always a meal of just rice and daal, served with a marked reluctance by the cook to him and some other workers whose jobs took them out of the house. It was never a full meal and Apu began feeling hungry even before his classes finished. When he got back home in the evening, absolutely ravenous, he always pounced upon the food Sarbajaya left for him on her own plate. Today being a holiday, he was eating a little earlier than usual.

He could not find a suitable reply, but Leela understood. The very modest furniture in the room, Apu's very ordinary clothes hanging from a rack, the very simple meal he was eating so hungrily, all pierced her heart. She did not speak.

'Did you bring all your books?' Apu went on. 'You'll have to show me each one.'

'Yes, I got some specially for you. I bought *Stories of the Sea* because I know how much you like stories. I'll get it and all the others when you've had your lunch.'

Apu gobbled up the last few mouthfuls. Leela did not fail to notice that not a single grain of rice was left on his plate. A strange feeling rose in her heart and seemed to suffuse her whole being. She had never felt anything like this before for anyone she had known. A few minutes later, she left Apu and returned with the books she had brought for him. Apu was both pleased and surprised to see that she had guessed what kind of books he'd like and chosen all the right ones. *Stories of the Sea* was full of astonishing facts—apparently, there were mountains under oceans, volcanoes, and something

11

called coral that was formed by sea creatures but it looked like vegetation, and a whole continent submerged under the sea ... Apu could hardly believe it.

Then Leela showed him her old drawing book. She had always been very keen on drawing. 'Remember I had once drawn a plant with flowers on it? Look, I've drawn so much more since then,' she said. Leafing through the pages. Apu thought her drawing had improved a lot. He himself could not draw even a straight line. 'These are good, really good,' he said. 'Do they teach you drawing in school, or do you do it simply as a hobby?' Then it occurred to him that he had not asked her anything about her school. 'Which class are you in?' he said. Leela began telling him about her school, and they chatted for a while.

'Won't you go and see my mother?' Leela asked.

'Yes, later. I'll go and see her in the evening. I think that will be better.' After a short pause he added. 'I haven't told you, Leela ... we are going to leave this place.'

Taken aback, Leela stared at him. 'Where will you go?' she asked, her eyes wide with wonder.

'My mother has an uncle, you see. He tracked us down recently and now wants us to go and live in his house,' Apu explained briefly.

'You can't go away, just like that!' Leela exclaimed, but stopped herself from protesting further. There would be no point in saying anything to Apu. He was hardly the decision-maker.

Neither of them spoke for several minutes. Then Leela broke the silence by saying, 'What will happen to your studies? A village like that might not have a school. Apurbo, why don't you stay on here? At least you can continue to go to school.'

'I know. I'd be quite prepared to live here alone, but Ma ... no, she could not live anywhere without me.'

'There's something else. You could come with us to Calcutta and live in our house. I can tell my mother. She won't mind. It's quite easy to travel from our house. We've got electric trams in Calcutta now. Even six years ago, they used to be drawn by horses, now they are run by overhead electric wires ... you'll see what I mean when you come with us.'

This sounded like a very good idea. Leela and Apu chatted at some length, then Leela went back to her own room.

Sarbajaya's uncle arrived in the evening. He saw no point in further delays. Two days should be enough to pack their meagre belongings. 'I will collect you on Wednesday and we can leave the same day,' he said before he left. Apu toyed with the idea of telling his mother about Leela's proposal. In the end, however, he could not bring himself to do so.

Their train pulled into the station at Ula as soon as dawn broke. They had to disembark at Ula to go to Monshapota. Bhavtaran Chakravarty had arranged for a bullock cart to meet them at the station and take them to his house. Apu had not been able to sleep very well during the night. He had just dozed off when he heard Bhavtaran call his name and quickly opened his eyes. Their train was standing at a station. A few coolies had already removed some of their luggage.

A few minutes later, they settled themselves in the bullock cart and it began moving. Bhavtaran began smoking a hookah. He was about seventy, tall and thin and clean-shaven. All his hair had turned white.

'Are you sleepy, Jaya?' he asked.

Sarbajaya smiled, 'No. I slept on the train, and so did Apu. You're the only one who didn't get any sleep.'

Bhavtaran started to cough. 'I never thought I'd find you,' he said, upon recovering somewhat. 'When my daughter died last year—her husband was already dead—I had no one left to turn to. At times I even had to cook for myself. So I thought of Harihar. I have a little rice field, and in our village there aren't too many Brahmins. Harihar could easily have managed as the village priest. And I could then go and live in Kashi. So I went to Nischindipur to look for you. I had no idea you had left it and were, in fact, living in Kashi yourselves! When your neighbours told me where you'd gone, I went there as soon as I could. I've been going to Kashi for ten years, I know a lot of people there, so it wasn't really all that difficult to track you down finally. When Harihar died, I was in Kashi. If only I'd known before ... !'

Apu leant forward eagerly, 'Did you go to our house in Nischindipur, Dadamoshai? Does it still look the same?'

'No, I didn't see your house. I got all the news from others in the village. When no one could give me your address, I came away. Your neighbour, Bhuvan Mukherjee, did ask me to stop for a meal, but all he had to say was how foolish your father had been, and a lot of other unpleasant things.... Anyway, I did find you in the end, and that's what counts. I think you'll be able to manage quite well. I have a few disciples who will look after you. A family of telis live next door, they're wealthy enough. They'll come to you to help them with their pujas ... I'll show you everything. Then I'm sure you can cope on your own.'

By this time they had left the village behind and were cutting across a field. Trees and large bushes dotted the way. The sun was now fairly high in the sky, bathing the world with its golden light. Apu saw clumps of wild basil by the road. The grass was still wet, glinting as it caught the sun, as if a spider in the land of fairies had spun little silvery webs everywhere. There was a faint smell too—not the smell of

14

a particular flower or plant—but simply the sweet scent that rose from the dew on the grass, the crops in the fields, the abundance of wild plants and the light morning breeze.

Apu had not seen such greenery for a long time. A wave of joy rose within his heart, strong, sharp, wonderful. This was not surprising, for it took very little to delight him. Sometimes despondency could hit his young mind just as easily, but it seldom took him long to shake it off.

It was noon by the time they reached Monshapota. Sarbajaya parted the awning that covered the rear of the cart, and took a quick peep at the place where she was going to start her new life. It seemed to her that the village was a bit congested, there were more houses than trees or fields. A few men were chatting among themselves outside a house. They looked curiously at the cart entering the village. A fishing net hung across bamboo poles in the courtyard. Perhaps this was where all the fishermen lived.

The cart trundled on for a few more minutes before coming to a stop. Sarbajaya saw a courtyard, a medium-sized cottage with a thatched roof, two smaller huts standing separately, a guava tree in the courtyard and a well on one side. A large tamarind tree stood behind the house, spreading its leafy branches and leaning over its roof. The courtyard had been fenced in with bamboo trellis. Bhavtaran climbed out of the cart. Apu helped his mother get out.

In the evening, Sarbajaya received her first visitors. They were her next door neighbours, the wife and other female members of the teli family. The wife was very dark and very fat. With her were two of her daughters-in-law, a daughter and some small children. Each woman had thick and heavy gold bracelets on her arms, which impressed Sarbajaya greatly. She brought out a couple of reed mats, spread them on her little verandah and said a little shyly, 'Please sit down.'

15

The teli's wife bent down and touched her feet. The other women followed suit.

'I saw you arrive, Ma Thakrun,' said the fat lady with a smile, 'I would have come sooner, but just didn't get the time. One of my sons returned from town, we have a shop there, you see. Then my granddaughter wouldn't leave me. By the time I could put her to sleep, it was past two o'clock. She's had a rather chesty cough for some time, so the kaviraj prescribed something for it. Peacock feathers, he said. They must be burnt over a slow fire in a bronze pot, then crushed and mashed with honey. It isn't easy to get that done, I can tell you ... Hajri, do you know if your brother remembered to get some honey?'

Hajri, the youngest amongst the women, nodded and started to speak. But her mother stopped her and went on, 'That's my daughter, Ma Thakrun. I got her married in Behrampore. My son-in-law works in our shop. They are pretty well-to-do, but his mother died and his old father married again and told him to get out! Can you believe that? So my husband said....'

One of the other women spoke this time. She was one of the daughters-in-law. In her early twenties, she was the prettiest in this group and not dark like the others. Perhaps she came from the city. She pouted slightly and said, 'They've only just arrived, Ma, they must be tired. I think we should make arrangements for a meal. They cannot be expected to cook right away, and it's getting quite late.'

At this moment, Apu returned to the house. He had gone out almost immediately after setting foot in his new home to see what the village was like. The sight of so many women made him stop short in the courtyard.

'Who's this?' asked Sarbajaya's garrulous visitor. 'Your son? Is he the only one you've got? Just look at him. Doesn't he look like a young prince?'

Suddenly finding himself the centre of attention, Apu started to beat a hasty retreat, but his mother called out to him.

'Stop, Apu! He's very shy—and yes, he's all I've got left. I had a daughter, too, older than him. But she ...' Sarbajaya's voice trembled.

'... is no more?' said her visitor and her daughter-in-law simultaneously.

'No. She was such a beautiful child, and so quiet, absolutely lovely. She was only thirteen when ...' Sarbajaya stopped again.

The teli's wife sighed. 'What can you do, Ma? It's all God's will, isn't it? Anyway, we are all very pleased to have you. There are no other Brahmins in this village, we have to fetch a priest from the town each time we want a puja done. Once a fellow called Chatterjee ... what was his first name, now? Never mind ... this Chatterjee came to live in our village. He came alone, but said his wife and children would be joining him soon. But months passed, there was no sign of his family. Then, last year ...' here she had to stop for a moment, for some of the women had started giggling. Smiling a little herself, she continued, 'A woman—only a cowman's daughter, mind you, not a girl of high caste or anything—used to clean his house ... and to think *I* had sent her there because she used to work for me, too ... well, last year he ... I mean, they ...' her remaining words were drowned as the other women dissolved into giggles. Trying to follow the general drift, Sarbajaya exclaimed, 'You mean they ran away together?'

'Yes! *And* he took all the pots and pans and plates I had given him from my own house. I just wanted to help him out, after all he was a Brahmin, and look how he ...!'

The laughter continued. The lady rose eventually, leaving Sarbajaya with renewed words of welcome and offers of assistance to get a meal underway.

TWO

More than a week had passed after their arrival. Sarbajaya had arranged her new home to her satisfaction, delighted at being able to bring to fruition all the little dreams and desires she had kept locked in her heart for more than four years.

It gradually transpired that Bhavtaran Chakravarty, while a good man and affectionate enough, was rather tightfisted. The teli family paid him an allowance annually to do what was required for the worship and upkeep of their family deity. It was this allowance that was going to pay his expenses in Kashi. If Apu could take over the business of the puja, they could live on the food the telis would provide regularly, and Bhavtaran could keep his money. Bringing Sarbajaya and her son had not, after all, been an act of pure generosity.

Sarbajaya herself did not mind. She was quite happy with the arrangement. Under dual pressure from his mother and her uncle, Apu soon began to act as the village priest. The word spread, and he began to be called away to houses far away to perform the necessary rites for a Lakshmi Puja, or some other ceremony.

On such days, he would rise early in the morning, have a bath and leave wearing a silk shawl he had once been given. In his hand he would clutch the manual all priests used that held the necessary instructions. This was something he had never done before, but he found himself enjoying it. Problems arose when he had to refer to the manual again and again, thereby revealing his lack of experience. How did one chant the right mantra to make sure Shiva was satisfied? How was he to hold the bell in one hand and use the other implements to invoke the gods? Apu was not quite sure; nor had he learnt to cover up his mistakes by making things up as he went along.

This caused him great embarrassment when one day he was rather unexpectedly called by the Sarkars who lived some distance away. Their own priest had had some disagreement and left in a huff. Apu was the only Brahmin in the area. Nirupama, the oldest daughter of Mr Sarkar, was getting everything ready for the puja. She was considerably surprised to see a fourteen-year-old boy, wrapped in a silk shawl, manual in hand, looking suitably grave. 'Can you do the puja?' she asked frankly. 'Are you sure? They said you were related to the old Mr Chakravarty. Is he your uncle? What's your name?'

Apu felt shy and awkward. He answered her briefly, and got to work. In a few minutes, Nirupama caught him out and began laughing. 'No, no, no!' she said, not unkindly, 'you should not offer the tulsi leaves without first washing the idol. There, put it down—no, not on the floor. Look, there's a marble slab. Yes, put it down there. Now pour water into the copper pot....'

19

By the time Apu finished, his face had turned red and he was sweating profusely. All he wanted to do was go home, but Nirupama and the other women made him have a meal, then packed sweets and other foodstuff for him to take home.

⁕

A month passed. Bhavtaran had already left for Kashi.

Apu tried to settle down in Monshapota, but found himself comparing it with Nischindipur. Monshapota did not have a river, or wide open spaces. There were, to his mind, far too many people and too many houses. Where were the trees Nischindipur had abounded with, the flowers, the birds, the deep chhatim woods where the sun used to spread its last rays every evening, suffusing each branch with a reddish golden hue?

His priesthood flourished. The Sarkars called him often. Everyone liked him for his good looks, and shy and quiet manners. Sarbajaya was well pleased with the food that Apu always brought back with him. 'You have got a lot of rice today!' she would exclaim. 'And so many sweets! Who gave you sandesh?'

'The Sarkars. And look at these, Ma. I got these from the Kundus,' Apu would reply, pointing proudly at a bunch of bananas.

Never before had Sarbajaya handled such good things. This was a dream come true—a dream she had often dreamt in Nischindipur when she was penniless; when the broken roof of her house had leaked profusely during heavy rains, when she had had to face endless humiliations from snooty neighbours and others in the village. She had dreamt of a better future then, sitting quietly on silent afternoons, her eyes noting the trembling leaves in a bamboo grove, her ears hearing the distant call of a dove. Even when the shadows lengthened near the long wall by the woods, she had continued to spin colourful webs in her mind. Now—thank you, dear God—it had started to look as if those dreams would stop being just a distant memory. She could—she did—dare to hope once more. Perhaps her worst days were over.

❧

Apu continued to handle his new job with enthusiasm. On the days that he was supposed to do a puja, he would wake early in the morning, and gather flowers and great quantities of young leaves from woodapple trees. He would then take these with him, together with a notebook in which he had written all the rules of various pujas. Even if he made mistakes, his eagerness and devotion always made up for his lapses.

A few months later, however, when the rainy season was well under way, Apu made a sudden announcement, 'Ma,' he said, 'I'd like to start going to school again.'

Sarbajaya gave him a startled look. 'School? Where would you find a school?'

'There's one in the next village.'

'The next village is miles from here. You couldn't walk there every day!'

Sarbajaya brushed it off for the moment, but when Apu made repeated requests over the next few days, she got annoyed and said, 'I honestly cannot see why you are asking me. If that's what you want to do, go ahead. You are so like your father. He never listened to me, either. Go to school! If you spent all day in school, who do you suppose would do the work you are now doing? We've managed to settle down after so many years, Apu, do you think it's wise to spoil everything when things are going so well?'

Apu did not reply. His mother was right. After Bhavtaran's departure, quite a lot of responsibilities had fallen on Apu's shoulders. It was not just the priesthood. There was a plot of land which Bhavtaran had rented out to some farmers to grow rice. Apu had to collect the rent on time and make arrangements for the harvest. All this was in addition to his priestly duties, which—as it happened—he still enjoyed.

One evening, he was returning from the house of the Sarkars after a Lakshmi Puja, carrying his things in a bundle. It was dark, but there was bright moonlight. The evening air felt quite cold. He heard a woodpecker hammering at a coconut tree, and saw another tree—a wild plum—covered with fresh blossom. The uneven ground in a vegetable patch was glistening in the moonlight. The ditch next to it looked jet black. His imagination running riot, Apu tried to picture the higher ground as a bear, the lower as a reservoir, and the next rising slope as a mound of salt. He was in a very good mood. 'They gave me an orange!' he thought. 'I can have it when I get back home.'

Suddenly, out of the blue, memories of Nischindipur came rushing back. He had dreamt such dreams by the bank of the Ichhamoti, on similar moonlit nights, and on hazy afternoons. What was going to happen to him now? How could he spend his entire life in this little village, doing nothing but acting as their local priest?

A couple of days later, he raised the subject of going to school again. So what if the next village was miles away? He could walk every day, he would not mind. What he did mind was the thought of never getting out of this village, never seeing the world.

Sarbajaya repeated her previous remarks. She had no idea what going to school meant. She had got what she wanted. If Apu continued to have a steady income, she would have him married in a few years. Then her happiness would be complete. However, a couple of months later, Apu rebelled once more and this time he was adamant. Sarbajaya failed to stop him from walking to the next village and getting himself admitted to their junior school.

For a whole year thereafter, Apu walked the four miles to his school—and back—enjoying every minute of it. He never forgot the joy of those days, the kind of joy he had not felt since leaving Nischindipur.

The road was lined with trees, some large like banyan and mulberry. There were bushes everywhere, thinning out occasionally to give way to open spaces under a bright blue sky. At school, Apu often felt as if he had come to a foreign land. He sat restlessly for the last bell, setting out eagerly for his homeward journey. The shadows were longer now, tall palms swayed their branches to bid farewell to the evening sun, birds called out, preparing to roost; a strong breeze rustled through the crops in the fields ... there was freedom in the air, every little thing he saw brought a message of hope.

But what gave him the greatest joy was speaking to other travellers. This was the first time in his life that he was travelling alone. The world was still new to him, there was so much to see, so much to learn. Although he was usually shy, he did not hesitate to run forward to catch up with whoever he happened to spot—usually a farmer returning home, with a hookah in his hand—and start a conversation: 'Where are you going, Kaka? I can go with you as far as Monshapota. Where do you live? Shikrey? I have heard of it, but have never been there. Is it a big village?' Apu's questions were endless. The people he spoke with were ordinary village folk, they did not mind answering him. When he looked back, Apu could not recall how many stories he had heard from different people, how many glimpses he had been offered into the simple lives of these villagers. Always passionately fond of stories, he listened intently to every tale, as image after image rose in his mind to make these stories come alive.

One particular story made a deep impression on him. Apu's companion—a complete stranger, as always—had told him how he had run into a woman from his own village. She was no ordinary woman, but the wife of a Brahmin, no less. But years ago, she had run away with a man from a lower caste. No one knew where she had gone, but this man had just seen her looking for snails in a small pond. Her clothes were torn, she did not have a single piece of jewellery on her; there was a little boy sitting near the edge of the water, possibly the child was hers.

'And she recognised you?' Apu asked, surprised.

'Yes. She started crying when she saw me, then asked after her parents. She told me not to tell them I had seen her. She was happy enough, she said. What was written in her destiny had happened, she had no complaints.... Torn clothes or not, she still looked like a goddess. After all, she was born and bred among Brahmins!' said the man.

Apu said nothing more, but could not stop thinking of this woman: a beautiful lady from a good home, wading through knee-deep water in a pond to look for snails, clad in a dirty, torn saree. The image remained in his mind for years.

⁕

One day, Apu reached his school to find his teachers in a state of great excitement and apprehension. Many of them were rushing about, shouting instructions. The school hall was being decorated with marigold garlands. The maths teacher, for no apparent reason, had filled the blackboard with long and complicated calculations. The compound and the corridors were looking so clean and tidy that any regular visitor to the school would have been amazed. The headmaster was busy going through papers in the school office, the admission book and the ledger in which teachers recorded their time of arrival every morning.

The reason for such excitement soon became clear. An inspector was going to visit the school at one o'clock, Apu was told. The maths teacher began instructing them on how to greet the inspector when he entered the classroom.

A horse-drawn carriage came up and stopped outside the school a little before noon. The headmaster was certainly not expecting the inspector quite so soon; nor had he finished putting his papers in order. However, when he saw the carriage arrive at the gate, he dropped everything and ran to meet its occupant. Apu's maths teacher, who had fallen silent, suddenly came to life and began explaining the difference between solids and liquids, for he also taught science. (Normally, at this time of the day, he enjoyed a quick nap in the class.) In the next room, the geography teacher was having a smoke. The soft gurgles of his hookah ceased abruptly and his voice rose above the general noise in his class: 'You all know what an orange looks like, don't you? Our earth is shaped like an orange. Moti, do be quiet. Our earth, boys, is shaped—Haren, stop that at once!—shaped like an orange, and therefore....'

The headmaster walked back to the school building, followed by the inspector. He was short, fair, probably in his early forties, dressed in a long coat over trousers, a silk scarf round his neck, white canvas shoes on his feet. His voice was very deep. He finished going through the relevant files in the office, and visited the first class. Apu could feel his heart beat faster. His class would be the next to be inspected. His teacher began speaking a shade more loudly.

The inspector entered the room, and glanced at the blackboard. 'Are they doing fractions?' he asked.

'Yes, sir,' the maths teacher said proudly, 'I teach maths, you see. I had already taught them simple fractions before they came to this class.'

The inspector then told each boy to read aloud from a book. When Apu rose to his feet and began reading, at first his voice trembled. But within a few moments he had himself under control and by the time he finished, he knew he had read very well. Even to his own ears, his voice had sounded sweet, clear and steady.

'Good. Well done!' said the inspector. 'What's your name?'

He asked him a few other questions before leaving his class to visit some of the others. Finally, he was taken to the refreshment room for a glass of coconut water and a plate of sweets. Just before he left the school, Apu's teacher handed Apu a piece of paper. 'Go,' he said hurriedly, 'go and stand near the gate. Hand this to the inspector when he comes out. It is an application for a couple of day's holiday. He liked you. I'm sure he'll agree if you tell him.'

The whole school rushed out as soon as the inspector's carriage disappeared. The headmaster stopped Apu briefly to say, 'The inspector was very pleased with you. I want you to sit for the board examinations. You must prepare yourself.'

Apu began walking briskly, his heart full of joy, not so much because he had been chosen to sit for the board exams, but because the inspector had agreed to give them a couple of days off. It was much later than usual. He quickly made his way to a small bridge that he passed every day, and stopped by its side to eat the food Sarbajaya had packed for him: rotis, grated coconut and a piece of jaggery. This was a part of his daily routine. The bridge stood where the road turned. It was not easily visible from either side. A mulberry tree provided both shade and privacy for a quick meal. Under the bridge was a pool. Apu could see a dim reflection in the water if he leant over. He had a vague and baseless belief that the pool was full of fish. So he broke off small pieces of roti and threw them into the water, straining to see if any fish accepted his offering.

Then he climbed down to wash his hands at the pool. Suddenly, his eyes fell on the figure of a man in a field nearby. He was dark, short, but well-built. His hair was thick, long and unruly. Across his back were slung a bow, a quiver of arrows, and a big bundle. Around his neck were green and red beads. He appeared to be gathering dry twigs. Deeply curious, Apu called out to him: 'What are you looking for?' Then he walked across to join the man and got chatting.

It turned out that the man was a Santhal. He came from some place far away, called Dumka. But of late, he had been living in Burdwan, and had come walking all the way from there. His destination was unknown and unspecified. He would walk for as long as he could, taking himself wherever he wanted. He did not have to worry about food, for he ate whatever animal he could kill in the woods he passed. In fact, he had recently killed a bird, and was collecting twigs to build a fire. He had also picked a few aubergines somewhere along the way. He was going to roast both. 'What bird did you kill?' asked Apu. The man took out a large harial dove from his bundle. Apu was very impressed. He had never seen a real bow and arrow, with which it was possible to do real shikar. 'Can I look at one of your arrows?' he asked. The man handed one over to him. Its point was sharp, made of iron. Feathers of wild birds were tied to the other end. A truly fascinating object.

'What else can you kill with this, apart from birds?'

'Anything. Rabbits, foxes, mongooses ... even tigers. But

to kill a tiger, you need the juice from a special creeper. The point of the arrow has to be dipped into it, you see.'

Having gathered enough fuel, the man lit a fire under the mulberry tree. Apu stayed rooted, watching with enchanted eyes how the man plucked the feather off the bird, and set it to roast, throwing in the aubergines afterwards.

By the time he could bring himself to turn homeward again, it was almost dark. The Santhal had finished eating and left with his bundle and weapons. Apu had never in his life met anyone like this before. What a wonderful life it was—go wherever you fancy, whenever you like, collect your own food on the way and, at the end of the day, build a fire to cook it. Oh, with what relish the man had just eaten his simple meal of roasted meat and aubergines, adding nothing but just a sprinkle of salt!

A few months passed. One morning, as Apu got ready to go to school, he discovered to his surprise that his mother had not made his breakfast.

'You cannot go to school today, Apu,' she said. 'The Sarkars want you for a special puja. They sent a message yesterday.'

'What! And you said yes? No, Ma, I cannot go about doing pujas any more. People might want pujas done every day ... surely I cannot be expected to miss school that often? Get me something to eat, please Ma, then I'll be off.'

'Listen to me, Apu,' Sarbajaya pleaded. 'Do you know what they said? It isn't just the Sarkars. All their neighbours are also getting the same puja done. Everyone wants you. If you go, you'll be able to bring back a large basket of rice, not to mention other things. Please, Apu, do this for me, there's a good boy.'

Apu paid no attention. In the end, he left without having breakfast. Sarbajaya could feel her eyes fill with tears as she watched him go. She could never have imagined Apu would pay so little heed to her wishes. This was something he had never done before.

Apu reached his school to find that the headmaster, Phoni Babu, was looking for him. As he stepped into his room, he found Phoni Babu doing his duties as the postmaster, since the local branch of the post office operated from his room, and he had this dual role to play.

'Come in, Apurbo,' he invited, 'your marks arrived this morning from the office of the inspector. Congratulations, my boy. You stood first in the entire district. I am so glad you took the board exams. Now, they say they'll give you a scholarship—five rupees a month—if you go in for further studies. You'll do that, won't you?'

Before Apu could reply, his maths teacher entered the room. 'I've just told him,' said Phoni Babu, 'and I want to know if he will go to high school.'

'Of course he will!' the maths teacher was most emphatic. 'He's such a bright boy, and the whole school is proud of him. If he doesn't go to the high school, who will? You needn't think any more about it, sir, send the application right away. Why did you even bother to ask him? We all want him to go ... heavens, I worked so hard to get him to understand fractions!'

Apu was still finding it hard to take it in. He stared speechlessly at the headmaster. Phoni Babu pulled out an application form, scribbled a few lines on it, and offered it to Apu. 'Sign your name here,' he said, pointing, 'I have told them you are prepared for higher studies. I will send it off immediately.'

That afternoon, Apu was allowed to leave the school

much earlier than usual. As he made his way back through the green fields still full of bright sunshine, Apu thought constantly of his mother. He had left her looking very sad this morning. He knew how much pain he had caused her. Everywhere he looked—in the shadows under the banyan trees, in the call of the invisible dove hidden behind shaal leaves—he could feel her pain. This was another afternoon he never forgot, even when all the other memories of this time scattered in later years like the beads from a torn necklace. This one bead remained, like a priceless pearl.

Sarbajaya had not eaten all day. How could she feed herself when her son had left without eating a morsel? But the Sarkars were kind people. They had sent a lot of prasad. Sarbajaya gave it to Apu when he got back from school. Still feeling restless, Apu ate quickly and went out again for a walk.

The fields that bordered the village were lying empty. Their crops had been removed. Apu stared at their emptiness and began dreaming again. He had won a scholarship! Even now he could hardly believe it. He had spent only a year in the junior school. But his mother did not know yet. The bright red sky, stretching over the fields, for as far as his eyes could see, held such mystery, such promise for the future. Apu shivered with a strange thrill. But what was his mother going to say? Was she still hurt? Still in pain? How was he going to tell her? The empty fields and the golden clouds on the horizon all seemed tinged with sadness. The shadows and the gathering dusk spoke of her sorrow. Apu turned to go back home.

An oil lamp flickered on the verandah as Apu came in. Sarbajaya was waiting for him. 'There's some fruit left,' she said, peeling a banana for him. 'Everyone missed you today, Apu. The Sarkars sent someone to fetch you, but I had to say you'd gone to school. Then they had to get someone else … it was quite late by then … they were really sorry you weren't home. If only you'd....'

'Ma,' Apu said finally, 'I am glad I did not go off to do their puja. Something happened at school today. The headmaster called me as soon as I got there, and said … said I had won a scholarship. I came first in the whole district. If … if I now join a high school, I'll get five rupees a month. But that would mean going away to a boarding school.'

Instantly, Sarbajaya's face went pale. She stared at Apu in silence for several moments. Then she said slowly, 'What did you tell them?'

'Nothing. It's just that if I don't study any further, obviously I don't get the money. If I do, those five rupees will take care of my expenses in the boarding house. I won't have to pay any tuition fees, they'll treat me as a free student.'

Sarbajaya could find nothing to say. What Apu had just told her made perfect sense. If a child won a scholarship and wanted to make good use of it, how could a parent stop him? Nowhere on earth could anyone ever be justified in pulling their child back from the road to success and keeping him home.

The day had begun badly, but who knew it would end like this? It seemed as if she was being punished for some unknown crime. There was no way she could ward off the inevitable. She was too weak, too powerless. All she could do was watch helplessly as all her own dreams and plans for their future rose and disappeared like morning mist.

❧⟨◉⟩☙

About a month later, the news of Apu's scholarship was confirmed by a report in the press. Sarbajaya, now resigned to her fate, began making preparations for her son's departure.

Apu had never lived anywhere on his own, he was totally inexperienced, completely alone. Who would take care of his needs, provide what was needed even before he could ask for it? Sarbajaya began packing everything she thought was necessary: two kanthas, one to spread on his bed, the other to cover himself with; a glass, a bottle of home-made ghee, a bag of coconut sweets, a bottle of coconut oil, a small bronze bowl with a flowery pattern round its rim from which Apu liked drinking his milk, and a dozen other little objects. She put a clean case on his pillow and, while she went about getting more things to pack, she spoke constantly. 'Look, if there are bad boys in the boarding house, or in your class, and they try to cause trouble, you must tell your teachers at once. And don't, for heaven's sake, go to sleep in the evening before you've had your dinner. Remember there won't be anyone there to wake you and make sure you don't go to bed on an empty stomach. If you start feeling sleepy, go to the kitchen and tell them to give you whatever's ready. All right? Are you listening, Apu?' She did not even wait for his reply. As soon as she finished one set of instructions, she remembered something else and started again.

The night before he was to leave, Apu packed one or two things himself. One of them was a notebook in which his father used to write songs. He took it out of an old trunk and added it to his other belongings. Harihar's writing was clear, the letters and the words brought back so many memories. He could almost hear Harihar's voice, singing the same songs, which were so inextricably linked with memories of the quiet evenings when he had returned home tired from playing in the fields, the dark clouds of an autumn afternoon, the mysterious nights back in Nischindipur, lit occasionally by bright moonlight. He even thought of their early days in Kashi, Dashashwamedh Ghat, and the other singers they had met there.

32

Until the last day, Sarbajaya had been secretly hoping against hope that, somehow, Apu would change his mind. But he showed no such sign. He appeared to have no hesitation at all in leaving his old life behind, crushing under his feet what she herself had built up, inch by inch, with such patience and perseverance, to ensure her son had a reasonably secure future. Why did the unknown hold such attraction for him? *Where* was he going to go? Sarbajaya's love for her son blinded her to one simple fact: Apu had heard the call of the outside world. Anyone who answered that call had a heavy price to pay. Never would the safe confines of home be adequate for him. How could Sarbajaya even hope to keep him hidden under her aanchal all his life?

Apu left the next morning. Sarbajaya put a dot of dahi on his forehead just before he stepped out, to pray for his safety and welfare.

'You'll come back home as soon as you can, won't you?' she asked anxiously, 'There's Itu puja coming up. Surely your school will close for that?'

Apu laughed, 'Itu puja? No, Ma. This is a big district school. They won't close for something silly like Itu puja. I won't come before the summer holidays.'

With a superhuman effort, Sarbajaya stopped her eyes from brimming over. Shedding tears at the time of departure might bring bad luck for her son.

Apu touched her feet, slung his heavy bundle over one shoulder and went out.

It was a cool, crisp morning in December. The previous day had been grey. But today, a golden sun glowed through broken clouds, touching the top branches of a mango tree. Its leaves glittered. Wild flowers peeped from green bushes under bamboo groves, signalling on this beautiful morning the colourful dreams of a bright future.

THREE

It had only just started to get light. The occupants of the boarding house at the Diwanpur Government Model Institution had not yet woken up. Only a couple of teachers were walking in the compound. A milkman arrived and was stopped by one of them. 'Show me the milk you've brought today,' he said, 'What you gave us yesterday was little more than plain water!'

The other teacher followed him quickly. 'Don't, Satyen Babu, don't buy any milk from him,' he cautioned. 'You must wait until the other milkmen arrive. I know someone, he's quite reliable and won't cheat us. You're new here, so you don't know … you must not buy milk from just anyone who comes along!'

A boy emerged from a corner room, craning his neck to look at the Coronation Tower clock, which stood at some distance. Satyen Babu's companion spoke to the boy: 'Sameer! Didn't that new boy arrive last night? The one who won the district scholarship?'

'Yes, sir. He's still asleep. Shall I call him?' He moved towards an open window and called: 'Apurbo! Wake up, Apurbo!'

A slim and good-looking boy of about fifteen came out, rubbing his eyes.

'You are Apurbo Kumar Roy?' asked Satyen Babu. 'You won a scholarship, didn't you? Where do you live? ... Very well, I'll see you later in school.'

'Sir,' Sameer added, 'the warden hasn't yet told Apurbo where he's going to stay. Could you please speak to him?'

'Why? There's an empty seat in your room, isn't there? He can share the room with you, surely?'

This was exactly what Sameer wanted to hear. 'Thank you, sir,' he said cheerfully, 'but please tell the warden, sir.'

The two teachers left. 'Who were those men?' asked Apu.

'Teachers. Both will teach us this year.'

Apu felt a little worried. Perhaps they had expected to find him awake and ready for the day? Perhaps all boarders were required to rise long before this? Had he started his stay here by breaking a rule, albeit unknowingly?

Later in the morning, feeling a little more sure of himself, he went to inspect the school building. He had got here quite late last night, so there had been no chance to look at it properly. All he had seen was a white structure in the dark, its details unclear and hazy. But it had filled his heart with joy and a sense of wonder.... He would become a part of this school from tomorrow! He remembered the high school he used to pass when he was still in junior school in the city. How often he had watched the students there, all in uniform, playing football in their massive playground. How badly he had wished he could join them. Only the children of the rich could go to a school like that. But now ... now his cherished dream was going to come true.

The warden of the boarding house, Bidhu Babu, called him just before ten o'clock.

'You can stay in Sameer's room, he's a good boy,' he said. 'He can show you around ... your home is quite far from here, isn't it? Well, just one word of warning: never use anything but the water in the school tank to have a bath. Don't try bathing in ponds. Remember that. You may go now, the bell will ring any minute.'

Classes began at half past ten. Apu entered his classroom clutching his books tightly, his heart beating fast. The room was quite spacious, the blackboard was large, desks and chairs were placed in neat rows, everything was spick and span. The pupils rose to their feet as the first teacher entered the class. This was something new to Apu. In his old school, they had been taught to stand up only when a visiting dignitary—such as an inspector—made an appearance. He was well and truly in a bigger school now, where every little daily practice was different.

He glanced out of a window and caught sight of the teacher in the next class: dressed in trousers and a jacket, glasses perched on his nose; a long salt and pepper beard came down to his chest. He had given the boys in his class a written assignment, and was pacing in the classroom. 'Who is that man?' Apu whispered to the boy sitting next to him.

'That's Mr Dutta, our headmaster. He's a Christian. He knows very good English.'

Apu was disappointed to learn that Mr Dutta would not teach his class. Apparently, he taught only the very senior students.

The school library was right next door. The smell of old books, mixed with the smell of naphthalene, reached Apu where he was sitting. A smaller school would never have had such a well-kept library, he thought.

The bell rang out again to mark the end of their class. How deep it sounded. It was a proper bell. In his old school, there had just been a thin metal sheet, which was struck a few times between classes.

After the last class, the boys from the boarding house ran to the playground and started playing various games. Sameer and another boy called Noni introduced Apu to a few other boys. They wanted to play cricket. Apu had never played it before, but Noni handed him his own bat and began explaining its rules.

Soon it was time to go back. The other boys left. Apu saw an almond tree in one corner of the playing field. He went and sat under it. A little distance away stood the government dispensary. A number of patients were gathered there. The sound of a small girl crying rose above all other noise. Apu grew preoccupied. This was his first day away from home, without his mother, amidst complete strangers. Seen in that light, it was certainly a memorable day in his life. His mind was filled with a medley of thoughts ... so many broken images from his varied past came back to him.

Sameer lit his table lamp when they returned to their room. Feeling quite depressed, Apu lay down. After a while, Sameer looked at him and said, 'Aren't you going to do your homework?'

'Yes, in a minute.'

'All right. But keep your light on, or the warden is going to scold you. He'll come and check on us very soon.'

Apu got up and lit his own lamp. Sameer was right. Bidhu Babu turned up within a few minutes. 'How are you getting on, Apurbo? I hope Sameer has been looking after you? ... Good, good. Have you got all your books? ... All except geometry? Very well, you can buy one from the school store. I'll get it for you, one rupee and five annas.'

Bidhu Babu left. Sameer went back to his studies, but turned his head a moment later to find Apu lying in his bed again. Sameer left his books and came over to join him. He pulled up a chair and asked, 'You are thinking of home, aren't you?' Apu nodded.

'Who is there at home? ... Just your mother? ... No one else? She must miss you!'

'Yes. She ... why, what's that bell for?'

'That's to announce dinner. Let's go and eat.'

After dinner, a few other boys came and joined Apu and Sameer in their room. Bidhu Babu had disappeared into his own room. There was no chance of his emerging again on this cold December night. Each boy in the house made the most of it.

'Come, Nripen, sit on my bed,' Sameer said, closing the door, 'Shishir, you can go and sit over there. Apurbo, can you play cards?'

'Suppose the headmaster ...' began Nripen.

'No, no. He won't come this way, never fear.'

Apu agreed to play, but realised soon enough that his knowledge of cards, limited as it was to the games he had played years ago in Nischindipur with his mother and sister, was wholly inadequate here. The other boys were experts, he had no hope of winning against them. Besides, in the presence of so many new faces, he began to feel shy and ill at ease once more.

'You play, I'll watch,' he said after a while, laying down his cards.

'Oh, come on!' Shishir said impatiently, 'I'll teach you everything in two days. Go on, pick them up.'

There was a sudden noise in the passage outside. Shishir hid his cards instantly and turned into a statue. Apu noted with considerable admiration how perfectly still he held himself. Perhaps even a real statue would have moved more than Shishir did. Everyone else in the room was just as silent. Sameer turned his lamp down. There was no further noise. Finally, Nripen opened the door and took a quick look down the passage. 'Nothing, it was nothing,' he announced, 'come on, let's start again.' He fished out his own cards from under Sameer's mattress.

At around eleven, all the others went back to their own rooms, walking stealthily.

'Do you do this each night?' Apu asked Sameer, 'Doesn't the warden know what's going on? What if he finds out? Tell me, who was that boy who was sitting quietly in that corner?'

He was younger than all the others, possibly no more than fourteen. Apu had liked him. It was clear that although he moved in the same circle, he had no interest in cards.

The next day was a Saturday. Most boys were given permission to go home for the weekend. Apu had only just arrived, apart from which he had no money to pay for another journey so soon. He stayed behind, wishing nevertheless that he could have visited his mother this Saturday.

He returned to his room in the evening and lit his lamp. He was alone, Sameer had gone home. Never before had he stayed alone in a room like this, with such bright white walls. He sat on his bed, looking around happily. His eyes fell on Sameer's table. 'How nice it'll be if I can have a table like that!' he thought, 'I must ask Sameer how much it cost.'

Then he rose and took his books to the table to prepare for Monday's lessons. The first lesson was algebra. If there was one subject that terrified him, it was mathematics.

Just as he had opened his maths book and cast a nervous glance at the relevant chapter, someone walked in through the open door. Apu looked up to find it was the same quiet boy he had seen last night.

'Oh, do come in, sit down,' he invited.

'Why didn't you go home?' the boy asked.

'My home is quite far. Besides, I only came the day before yesterday. How come you are still here? I didn't quite catch your name ...?'

'My name is Devabroto Basu. Everyone calls me Debu. I did so want to go home, Apurbo da! But the warden wouldn't let me. He said, "You went home last weekend, so you can't go again." Isn't that unfair?'

Apu agreed. Debu sat down and began talking of his home and his family. His home was about twelve miles from Diwanpur, he had to go there by train. He missed his family very much, he felt he *had* to go home each Saturday, but the warden ...! It was clear that he was so upset at not being allowed to go home that he was not prepared to talk of anything else.

After a while, even Apu began to feel lonely and depressed. 'If he doesn't let me go next Saturday, I'm going to speak to the headmaster!' Debu muttered. Then, suddenly, he jumped up and said, 'Did you see this? Did Sameer tell you?' He took Apu with him and stood before a large window. Then he showed him how two of its bottom bars could be removed and replaced. When removed, it left a gap large enough for a young boy to pass through. 'Don't tell anyone about it, please,' Debu implored, 'Sameer and Ganesh are the only people who know.'

A little later, dinner was announced and the two boys left together. Before they began eating, Apu took out a piece of paper and showed it to Debu. 'Tell me, do you know what this word means?' he asked. The word 'literature' was printed in large letters on it. 'No, I don't, but we can ask one of the senior boys,' Debu replied. He showed it to Monimohan, who was senior to them by a couple of years.

'It means books and writing ... you know, sahitya,' he

explained. 'It appears to be an advertisement for the Macmillan company. Where did you find it?'

'Just outside the library,' Apu replied. 'Perhaps it had been blown out of the room. Look, it smells of naphthalene. I do like this smell!' He smiled and put the piece of paper carefully away.

Classes resumed from Monday. Apu settled down gradually and lost some of his early apprehension. One day, something interesting happened in his English class. Satyen Babu was their English teacher. He had just given them a few sentences in Bengali for translation into English, when their headmaster walked in.

Apu looked upon Mr Dutta with a great deal of awe. He was reputed to be very stern. Even the teachers treated him with reverence. Apu jumped to his feet with everyone else as he came in. Mr Dutta picked up a book from Satyen Babu's desk and looked briefly at the title page. 'This book has a name on it: Victor Hugo. Who was Hugo? Can anyone tell me? ... You? ... What about you?'

Complete silence greeted this question. No one had heard the name before. Each of them came from an ordinary family in a small town of Bengal. How could they have heard of Victor Hugo?

The name sounded vaguely familiar to Apu, but his turn to answer the question came and went while he stood mutely, his brain whirring frantically to capture pieces of a hazy memory. By the time the penny dropped, the headmaster had moved to the other side of the room. Lines out of the pages of an old magazine rose before Apu ... it must have been one of the old issues of the *Bongobashi* magazine he used to devour in Nischindipur, and it was a column called *Letters from England*. He spoke quickly, 'Hugo is a writer. A famous French writer. His statue stands by a road in Paris.'

41

The headmaster had not really expected a correct answer from anyone in this class. He wheeled around to face Apu, his eyes glinting behind his glasses. Totally overwhelmed by his own response, Apu shrank within himself, lowering his gaze.

'Right!' said Mr Dutta. 'But the statue is actually in a park, not by the roadside. Anyway, you may sit down now. All of you.'

He left the class. Satyen Babu was very pleased with Apu. He took him to his house in the evening. He lived alone in a small house. Apu noted how neat and well kept it was. He made tea for both of them. 'You need to pay more attention to English grammar,' he said to Apu. 'Don't worry, I'll show you which areas to concentrate on.'

By now, Apu had lost some of his shyness. He pointed at a glass case and asked, 'Are all those books yours?'

'Yes.' Satyen Babu opened the case and showed him the books. Most of them were to do with the law. Apu's teacher was preparing for a law exam. He picked out a book and gave it to Apu. 'You may read this one. It's a historical tale.'

Apu wanted to look at a few other books, but in the end, could not bring himself to ask if he might.

In less than three months, Apu made friends with everyone in the boarding house. Shy as he was, he could never have achieved this on his own; but, as it happened, all the other boys wanted to befriend him. In fact, each seemed to vie with the other to show how close he was to Apu. At dinner, one would offer Apu his seat, another would offer to share his food. At first, Apu felt greatly embarrassed by this. But the day a senior student called Ramapati gave him a piece of lemon from his own plate, Apu couldn't help feeling a little proud of himself. Ramapati was a studious young man, known to be very good in English and in the good books of the headmaster. 'He clearly knows I am not like the others,' Apu thought that night. 'Does he ever offer anything to any of them? Never. Why, he doesn't even speak to them!'

Another month passed. Apu grew very fond of a hibiscus bush in the school compound. On quiet Sunday afternoons, he would sit there amongst heaps of dry leaves, his back to the sun, and read. He had finished reading many of the books in the library. A major problem there, he had discovered, was that most of the books were in English. Almost every book that appeared attractive, or had pictures in it, was written in English. Apu still found it difficult to understand the language. All he could follow was the caption under each picture.

A few weeks later, the headmaster called him to his office one day. Apu was immediately filled with a nameless horror, but he made his way to the office and hovered near the door. Another gentleman, clad in trousers and a jacket, was sitting with him. Mr Dutta nodded at Apu. He entered the room.

'What is your name?' asked the gentleman. Apu told him. The gentleman glanced at something scribbled on a piece of paper, then picked up an English book and passed it to Apu.

'Did you borrow this from the library?'

Apu glanced at the proffered book and saw that it was called *The World of Ice*. Yes, he had borrowed it recently, but had not been able to follow it very well.

'Yes,' he faltered.

'Yes, sir!' roared the headmaster.

'S-sorry, sir. Y-es, sir!' Apu's legs began shaking, his mouth felt dry.

'What is a sledge?' asked the visitor.

'A kind of vehicle drawn by dogs,' Apu replied. He thought

43

of adding something about sledges being used on the snow, but failed to find the right words.

'How is a sledge different from other vehicles?'

'A sledge ...' began Apu, then stopped. Was it all right to say 'a sledge'? Or should he have said *the* sledge'? Quickly, he decided to speak in the plural. 'Sledges have no wheels,' he said.

'What is the Aurora Borealis?'

Apu's face brightened. Only the other day he had read about it in one of Satyen Babu's books. He had not understood everything, but had learnt the correct pronunciation (it was now the biggest word in his vocabulary) and its meaning. 'Aurora Borealis,' he now said, 'is a kind of atmospheric electricity.'

'Good. You may go now.'

Apu came away, but could not help overhearing the last few remarks the visitor made to the headmaster. 'Most unusual for a boy of his age. What name did you say? A strikingly handsome boy, too. Good, good.'

He learnt much later that the visitor had been a senior inspector of schools. He was on a surprise visit.

Apu went later that day to Ramapati's room. Ramapati had offered to help him with his maths homework. He obviously came from a well-to-do family. The spotless sheet on his bed, the towel on his pillow, the marble inkwell on his table, the pens and new nibs arranged neatly in a row—all spoke not only of his own tidy habits but also of his affluence. After finishing his homework, when Apu rose to go, Ramapati said suddenly, 'Look, it's nearly time for Saraswati Puja. I want you to lead all the younger boys. You must get them together and go out to collect donations.'

Apu said nothing, but on his way back, told himself firmly that he would have nothing whatever to do with collecting donations. He was far too shy and timid for such a job, and

44

he knew it. 'If only ...' he thought, his mind turning to the things in Ramapati's room, 'if only I could have an inkwell like that!'

He returned to his room to find Debu sitting quietly at Sameer's table, resting his head on it.

'Hey, what are you still doing here, Debu? I thought you'd gone home!' Apu exclaimed.

Debu replied without raising his head, 'It's that stupid warden. He wouldn't let me go. I did not go home last Saturday. You know that, don't you? But he said he couldn't let me go every weekend. He just wouldn't listen to anything I said.'

Apu felt very sorry for Debu. He was younger than any of his other friends. Everyone knew how eagerly he looked forward to going home and seeing his people again. Why was the warden so unnecessarily strict with him? 'Shall I get Ramapati to speak to Bidhu Babu?' Apu offered. This time, Debu looked up and gave him a wan smile. 'Bidhu Babu has gone,' he said, 'yes, he himself has gone home for two days. He sent the bearer to buy fruit and vegetables for his daughter. I saw him. In any case, there are no more trains today that go to my home town.'

Apu decided to create a diversion to cheer him up. 'We could play a game. Look, you could be a thief—or a spy—and I'll be a detective and I'll catch you. See that paper over there? That's an important map, or it could be the design for a new war ship. You'll steal it and disappear, but I'll be hot on your trail ... I read such a novel the other day, it's terrific. It's called *The Nihilist Mystery*. I'll get it for you.'

Debu tried to do as he .was told, but the game did not get very far. He had not read the novel, so did not have a clear idea of what was required of him. Besides, his heart was not in it anyway. He allowed the enemy to steal the precious design for a new war ship with such shocking docility that it became clear that, had Debu ever been appointed a Russian spy, the Czar would never have had to wait until the Bolshevik revolution of 1917 to see his decline.

It was now quite late in the afternoon. Debu suddenly glanced out of the window and said, 'Can you see the clock tower? What time is it, Apurbo da? Please don't tell anyone, but I am going home. Now.'

'Now? But you just said there were no more trains!'

Debu lowered his voice, 'No, but it's only a matter of eleven miles. If it gets dark, there's bound to be a moon. I'll be all right.'

'Have you ever walked eleven miles before? Do you have any idea how late it's going to get by the time you reach home? What if anyone found out?'

Debu agreed that it would not be easy. He accepted that there would be hell to pay if Bidhu Babu learnt about his disappearance. But he did not care. He had to go home, and he would.

'Very well, if you are so determined, let me come with you,' Apu said.

'No, no, you must not do that!' Debu beseeched him. 'You have not left this place even once since you arrived. If you suddenly disappeared, everyone will find it suspicious.'

This was true. So Debu left on his own. Apu felt concerned, but did not speak to anyone about it. However, the next day—which was a Sunday—it transpired that many of the boys who had remained in the boarding house had noted Debu's absence at dinner. When Sameer returned in the evening, Apu told him what had happened. Neither knew what to do about it. How could Debu get back the following morning and pretend he had never gone out?

The next morning, however, Apu saw to his amazement that Debu was sleeping in Sameer's bed. Sameer had gone out to wash his face. He returned soon and explained what had happened. Apparently, Debu had come back after midnight and started to rattle the window in their room that had the loose bars. Afraid that the noise might wake the others, Sameer had removed the bars and smuggled him in.

By this time, Debu was awake. Apu, agog with curiosity, asked him to tell him all about his adventure. When did he reach home on Saturday? Was it very late?

Yes, Debu had reached home safely enough, but they had almost finished dinner by the time he got there. His mother was helping his little brother cross their big courtyard when Debu turned up suddenly. They were perfectly amazed to see him.

With a pang, Apu thought of his own mother. He had not seen her for so many months. If his house was as close as Debu's, he'd have been to visit her several times. But Monshapota was more than a train journey away. He had to go part of the way by boat, and walk the rest. The total fare came to one rupee and eight annas. Where was he going to find all that money? Eight annas was all he had managed to save so far.

Nothing happened on Monday. By Tuesday, however, Debu's disappearance was common knowledge in the school. How it had leaked out was a mystery, but nearly everyone seemed to know that he had gone home on Saturday without the warden's permission, and sneaked into the building on Monday. Sameer turned pale as he thought of the implications. What was the headmaster going to do to him if he discovered that Sameer himself had had a significant role to play?

But he need not have worried. It turned out that when questioned, Debu had made a full confession, saying that he had returned very early on Monday morning. No one had seen him steal into the boarding house. What Sameer had done remained a secret. Much relieved, Sameer tried to save the situation by speaking to Ramapati. 'Why don't you talk to the headmaster, please?' he begged. 'You know how homesick he gets ... Debu's still a child, and it's true that the warden did not let him go home for three weeks.'

Ramapati and a few other senior boys went to the headmaster to plead on Debu's behalf. But their plea was summarily rejected. Mr Dutta had already sent out a circular to each class, announcing Debu's punishment. He was going to be caned in the school hall during the lunch break. Everyone was required to be present.

The boys filed in in absolute silence. Debu was brought next, very much like a sacrificial lamb. His pale and frightened face evoked no pity in Mr Dutta's heart. Picking up the cane, he made another announcement: Debu was only going to be caned because this was his first offense. Had that not been the case, he would have been expelled.

Debu cried out in pain as the second blow fell on him. It was followed by another, then another. The more he cried, the more sternly did the headmaster shout, 'Stop it! Bend this way, bend!'

Apu could not bear to watch it any more. He began sobbing and went out on the verandah. He was reminded of the time when he, too, had been similarly and wrongly punished by Mr Roychowdhuri in Leela's house. When he returned to the hall, Sameer was looking out for him. 'Why are *you* crying so much, Apurbo?' he hissed. 'Stop it at once, or the headmaster will get even more cross. He will scold you, too!' Apu forced himself to wait with the other boys until they were all dismissed.

Soon it was time for Saraswati Puja. Everyone was expected to make a contribution, but when some of the other boys came and told Apu he'd have to pay eight annas, his heart sank. That was all he had. But he had not learnt to say no, so he handed over the required amount without protest.

Sameer watched him in silence. Then, when the others had gone, he said, 'You didn't have to do that, Apurbo! Why do you spend your money when you don't have to? You really ought to be more careful.'

'Oh really? Very well, sir, will you teach me how to be more careful, sir?' Apu laughed.

'I am not joking, Apurbo. I have seen you waste your money pretty frequently. Why do you go out with Noni and Rashbehari and buy them food?'

'So what if I do? They come and ask for a treat, so I take them out. What's wrong with that?'

Sameer looked very annoyed. 'Ask for a treat! Yes, of course they would because you are foolish enough to believe what they tell you. And they know it, too. They make fun of you behind your back. Did you know that? They think you're a fool.'

'Never! What are you talking about?'

'I swear they do. Why would I lie to you? I heard Rashbehari brag about how easily he can make you spend your money on him. Who told you to buy them banana-flavoured sweets?'

Sameer was quite right. This was the first time that Apu was in charge of his own finances. Never in his life had he had the freedom to spend money any way he liked. When his scholarship money reached him at the beginning of every month, he felt like a king. After paying for expenses at the boarding house, he was usually left with two rupees. For someone who had never had twelve paisa to his name, the sight of one hundred and twenty was enough to make his head spin and send him on a spending spree. Most of the time he bought expensive stationery and ate out. Very often, other boys would come and demand to be treated. This request was usually preceded by high praise for Apu's intelligence, his performance in class and his generosity. Flattered and moved, Apu spent his last remaining pennies on them, living in great penury thereafter. Sometimes, a few boys borrowed money from him, then forgot to return it. Shy as he was, Apu could not bring himself to remind them.

Now, when Sameer saw that his warnings were falling on deaf ears, he gave up and went off to play badminton. Apu picked up a book and made his way to his favourite spot under the hibiscus bush. Shadows had gathered there now. He remembered there were fresh green leaves on the bush. Before leaving his room, he opened a small jar and checked how many sweets he had left. Then he popped a couple into his mouth and thought, 'When I get my money next month, I'm going to buy some of those pineapple lozenges. How tasty these are!' He had never had fruit-flavoured sweets before.

He began crossing the school compound and was going past the library when he saw something that made his heart give a sudden lurch. One of the school clerks was speaking to a man, standing near the gate. Almost unconsciously, Apu went forward to take a better look. The other man moved, turned to face him for a moment, made a gesture with his hand, then picked up his umbrella which he had kept propped up against the gate, and departed.

Apu stared after him for a few seconds, then sighed and retraced his steps. That man looked exactly like his father. He had not seen his father for four years. He never would. His eyes started brimming over, but he wiped them impatiently and went to the hibiscus bush. Then he began turning the pages of his book absently until he found the old familiar picture that accompanied a poem. He had read it many times.

Thousands of miles away from home, from family and friends, a young soldier was lying on the sand in the dry, harsh, cruel desert in Algeria. He was very close to death.

There was no one to look after him, except a fellow soldier who was offering him sips of water from a leather container. Looking at the unfamiliar, hazy, uneven sandy terrain, the glowing red evening sky as the sun began to set, date palms and, in the distance, rows of camels, each with its face raised, the dying soldier could only think of the place he had grown up in, by the side of the Rhine. He had left his mother there. Friend, he said, you must tell my mother, do not forget.... *For my home is in distant Bingen, Fair Bingen on the Rhine*!

Apu himself had not seen his mother for five months. He could no longer stand staying in the boarding house. He could not stand going to school every day. He could not bear to live without seeing his mother.

On such lonely afternoons, memories of Nischindipur always came back to him. Today, suddenly, he thought of a particular day when he had accidentally killed a little bird. A lot of birds had been making a great deal of noise outside their house. Little Apu had picked up a stone, and thrown it at them, without thinking even once of the possible consequences. To his amazement, he saw the smallest bird fall to the ground with a broken neck. The others flew off. He had not imagined for a second that the stone he had thrown would actually kill a bird. Greatly excited, he had called his sister, Durga. 'Didi, come here, quick!' Durga had come out and picked up the bird. 'Let me have a look!' she had said, examining it closely. There was blood around the bird's mouth. A little blood got smeared on Durga's fingers. 'Poor little thing. Why did you have to kill it?' she scolded her brother.

Apu had been feeling quite triumphant. His face fell at his sister's words. 'What day is it today? Monday, isn't it?' Durga went on. 'Look, if we cremated it by the river, its spirit will be set free.' Then she found a matchbox and used dry leaves to light a fire under a tamarind tree by the river. The dead bird was partially burnt, then its body thrown into the water. Durga folded her hands and said a prayer. 'You must *never* do that again, all right? Did you see how badly its neck was crushed? Birds just fly around in the woods, they don't do anyone any harm, do they?' Then she cupped her hands and brought water from the river to wash the place where they had built their fire.

When they returned home that evening, who knows if the spirit of the bird, set free for ever, had given them its silent blessings?

'Apurbo da!' called Debu. 'I knew I'd find you here! Why, what's the matter? Why do you look so sad?' With the sound of Debu's voice, all memories of Nischindipur disappeared from Apu's mind.

'No, it's nothing. I'm all right,' Apu forced a smile. 'Come on, let's go and find Rashbehari and the others.'

'No,' Debu said firmly. 'Please don't try to be friendly with them. They are a bad lot. I heard Vinod telling the dhobi you might not pay his bill. They make fun of you, Apurbo da. You must stop being friendly with them.'

This was almost exactly what Sameer had been saying earlier. Apu felt both puzzled and hurt. 'Who says I am not going to pay the dhobi's bill? I'll pay him as soon as I get my allowance next month. I couldn't pay him this week only because I had no money. Why should they ...?'

'I told you, they are all stupid. They laugh about what you write in your notebook, and why you come and sit here by yourself. They think you are mad. And then you go and give them a treat!'

'What have they got to do with what I write in my notebook? I wasn't even going to show it to them. I did only because Noni asked to see. What strange people!'

Now he felt angry and embarrassed. His notebook was more personal than a diary. Sometimes, he felt oddly restless.

52

He was driven to distraction by his longing for his village, its wide open fields, glowing red in the evening sun, small white flowers gleaming on dark water like the diamond stud on a new bride's nose, clusters of colourful flowers on high grounds. Where were the trees that were so much a part of his life? Where was the greenery? Apu felt suffocated in Diwanpur. His only relief came through his imagination. In his notebook Apu described the land his mind felt thirsty for. In it there was a river, deep dark woods, singing birds, a golden sun at dawn and at dusk, and flowers. Innumerable, endless flowers. Even without stepping out of his little room in the boarding house, he could take a walk by the river, or down a green meadow.

'I am never going to show any of the others what I write,' he vowed silently. 'This is the end of my friendship with them. See if I ever help them with their English translation, or anything else!'

FOUR

Winter gave way to spring. Green young leaves appeared on the bare branches of the trees that stood in the school compound. The leaves on the almond tree near the cricket ground had a reddish tinge to them, particularly when they caught the morning sun. They looked beautiful. And it was not cold at all.

Rashbehari and some other boys in the boarding house decided to go to a local fair in a village called Mamjoan. In fact, Mamjoan was famous for this particular fair it held every spring. Bidhu Babu agreed to give them a couple of days off.

Apu forgot his vow and joined Rashbehari's group happily enough. He had not been to a fair ever since he left Nischindipur. Mamjoan was about six miles away. The boys had to make their way through fields and narrow tracks. Apu felt as if he had been released from prison. He watched with utter delight the people in the little villages they passed, the potters busy at their wheels, shopkeepers weighing various objects, a drumstick tree laden with flowers—it was this life that he had missed so much, the life that flowed endlessly day and night, sometimes in joy, sometimes in sorrow, but always free, undeterred by bells, unmindful of holidays and weekends.

At one place Apu saw a group of men stirring date juice in a large pot over a fire. He wanted to stop and watch. 'You really are mad!' Noni said crossly. 'What's there to watch? Come on!' Apu looked a little sheepish, but refused to leave. 'Maybe they'll tell us a few stories? Men like these always have plenty of stories to tell. It'll only take a few minutes,' he pleaded. But the others were not as passionately interested in the lives of men from a small village, so they left Apu behind.

The men, as it happened, were very pleased to see Apu and made him welcome. He forgot his shyness and asked a lot of questions. They offered fresh juice in an earthen mug, although Apu had not stopped in the hope of finding refreshment. He spent almost an hour watching how jaggery was made, and chatting with the men.

It was twelve o'clock by the time he reached the fair. His friends were nowhere in sight. Hundreds of people were milling about. Apu felt both hungry and thirsty after having walked six miles in the sun. But he had very little money on him, so after buying some light snacks at a stall, he drank a lot of water.

He spent the next few hours roaming from one stall to another. Many of them were selling paan, lemonade and cigarettes; others were holding shows. Apu peeped into one and tried to see what was being shown. In this one, it turned out, birds were going to perform tricks. A man at the entrance stopped him. 'How much do I have to pay?' Apu asked. 'I can give you two paisa. Will you let me go in?' But the show had started. The man told him to come back in half an hour.

Magic shows, in particular, were being announced with great fanfare. Several tents had been put up for this purpose. Outside one of these, Apu saw a couple of men, covered from head to foot with coal tar, standing on a raised platform, pulling long, colourful paper chains out of their mouths as a sample of all the extraordinary items that were going to be presented inside. It reminded Apu of an old book he had seen in his father's collection called *Mysteries Galore*. It had contained recipes for such astounding feats as bringing a chopped head on to the stage and making it speak, making things disappear before a large audience, and producing a mango from a tiny sapling. Little Apu had wanted to experiment, but the list of ingredients was so long and so complex that he was forced to desist. Perhaps these men had learnt their tricks from a book like that? Heaven knew how that book got misplaced when they left Nischindipur.

Apu soon lost all track of time. He had not yet found his friends, but in the ever-increasing crowds, all the fun and laughter and the music, he did not feel lonely at all. There was so much to see. A bullock cart went past, with faces of children peeping out of it, avid with curiosity, trying to take in the live advertisement outside the magic show. Then he saw that nearly everyone was smoking. He pushed his way to a cigarette stall and, after waiting for a while, stood up on a wooden crate. 'Give me a cigarette!' he said, stretching an arm over the shoulder of another man. 'Here's a paisa. Look, over here! Give me something of good quality.'

Here was a bookstall. Its owner—an old man with glasses (kept in place by pieces of string tied to the broken frame)—had spread a number of empty sacks on the ground, and displayed the books over them. Apu picked up a copy of *The Arabian Nights*, but put it back again on being told it was for eight annas. If only he had the money! It was a book he had not read before.

He bent down once more to look at the book, but straightened quickly as he caught sight of another boy. The boy was not from his school. But he seemed so familiar ... why, it was Potu, his childhood friend from Nischindipur! Apu strode forward and laid a hand on his shoulder.

The other boy turned, stared at him for a few seconds, then cried, as he recognised him, 'Apu da! I don't believe it. What are you doing here?'

'That's what I was going to ask you!'

'I came to visit my sister. Her house isn't far from here. So I thought I'd come to the fair. But how did *you* get here from Kashi?'

Apu took him away to a relatively quiet spot. There was so much to talk about. He explained briefly about his life in Kashi, his father's death and their new home in Monshapota. Then he asked about everyone in Nischindipur. How were his neighbours? And old friends? Ranudi? Potol, Neelu, Shotuda? The river? How was the Ichhamoti?

Potu could not give him the latest information since he himself had left the village a long time ago. After Apu left and his sister got married, Potu had no one in the village to stay back for. He had travelled for a while, then decided to visit his sister to see if he could stay with her and go to a school. All he could tell Apu was that Ranudi—a girl of about Durga's age—who had been so fond of him, was about to be married when Potu left the village nearly three years ago. By now she, too, must have gone away. Potu kept glancing at Apu as he talked. How handsome he'd grown in these few years! Why, Apu's style of dressing had changed as well!

Apu took him to a food stall and got him something to eat. Then he spent eight paisa on buying two tickets for the magic show, and took Potu in with him. During the show, he said abruptly, 'Er ... after we left, did Ranudi ever talk about me? Mention me at all?' Yes, she certainly did, said Potu. She had often asked him if he had heard from Apu, if he could give her Apu's address in Kashi; but Potu had been unable to help. Others in the village had missed him, too. Apu's eyes filled with tears. How wonderful to know that he had not been forgotten by old friends. If only he could go back! How brilliant those days had been, as fresh as a lotus at dawn. That clear sky, the gentle breeze, the rippling Ichhamoti ... how far removed they seemed, how distant.

He had once read a strange story about a man who had been tricked by a god. He went to bathe in the river and, in the few seconds that it took him to dip his head in the water, he could see his whole life flash before him. The events that were to be spread over sixty years rolled by in less than sixty seconds. He saw himself getting married, saw his children being born, then some of them died, and others were married, and he himself became old. Then he raised his head from the water and saw that nothing had changed. What he had seen was no more than a dream.

Sometimes, Apu wondered if what was happening to him was not just such a dream. Maybe he just fell asleep in the corner room in their house in Nischindipur in the late afternoon on a rainy day. He would wake when the birds returned to roost, and discover that his departure to Kashi, his father's death, his present days in the high school were all part of a dream. He would rub his eyes, find his sister and tell her about it. Why couldn't that happen to him? He'd like nothing more than being able to go back to his old home, find his father again, and be with his sister.

He remembered a poem Satyen Babu had taught them. It was called *Graves of a Household*. When he sat alone and recited the poem to himself, tears came to his eyes. It spoke of siblings, all raised together by the same mother, in the same house. But life took them away to different corners of the world ... some died at sea, some were buried under the sky in unknown lands; others lay in the village, by flowering woods.

Walking alone, such thoughts often rose in Apu's mind. He thought of the poor, and those struck by misfortune. How many afternoons had he spent in Nischindipur, dreaming of people he had read about? The troubled Karna, the exiled Seeta, the poor boy Ashwathhama, the defeated Duryodhan, even the village girl, Joan of Arc. He had not yet learnt to express his thoughts in words. All he had done was build a world peopled with figures from stories and poems. It was the first creation of his own imaginative mind ... the first garland he had strung together with the joys, the sorrows, the hope and despair of his young life. The first star of truth in the glowing evening sky. Who knew what other secret thoughts lay hidden in his mind? Who could understand them?

The magic show was over soon and the two boys went back to the fair. Apu had still not seen any other boy from his boarding house, but that did not matter. He was going to enjoy himself as much as he could. He had not finished looking at everything. 'Potu, you mustn't go back without seeing a jatra. Let's find out when it's going to start.'

'Apu da,' said Potu, 'which class are you in?'

'Why don't you come to our school one day? You'll see what a big place it is, you could stay the night with me.' After a brief pause, he added, 'I've been to so many places, but nothing seems as wonderful as Nischindipur. I don't like it so much anywhere else.'

'Won't you ever go back there? You're sorely missed, you know.' Then he laughed, looking at Apu. 'You've changed, Apu da. Even your clothes look different. You're not a village boy any more.'

Apu felt very pleased. 'This shirt is nice, isn't it?' he said proudly. 'It's new. One of the senior students—Ramapati—has a similar shirt. So I bought this one, it cost me a rupee and eight annas.' What he did not add was that he had bought the shirt on a mad impulse, and had not yet paid for it. He had seen some of the other boys buy clothes and pay for them later. He had tried to follow suit, but despite repeated reminders from the shop, had not been able to find the money.

The evening was nearly over and the light had started to fade. Potu and Apu finally parted company, Potu making his way back to his sister's house. He had had a wonderful time.

Sarbajaya got to her feet as her visitor rose to take her leave. It was the pretty daughter-in-law of the teli woman next door. 'You must come again, Boro Bouma,' Sarbajaya said, standing in her courtyard. 'Sometimes I think of visiting you—I get very lonely, you know—but I'm scared to leave the house empty, ever since I heard about the theft in Goalpara.'

The young woman smiled and left with her three-year-old daughter.

Sarbajaya locked her front door and sighed. She had been all right as long as she had company. But now she was back to battling with loneliness. She thought of Apu all the time. It was five months since he had left. Every Saturday, and every other holiday, she had hoped he would come. She woke in the morning thinking he'd be home by the afternoon. In the afternoon, she told herself he'd arrive in the evening. But weeks slipped into months, yet there was no sign of her son.

She looked at the things Apu had left behind and tried to picture his face. Sometimes she had problems recalling it clearly, and panicked. If she could remember his eyes, she could not always remember the shape of his mouth, or his smile. The more she tried to get a clearer image, the hazier it became. Sarbajaya felt desperate at times. What was happening to her? How could she forget what her own son looked like?

She thought frequently of Apu as a child. She had beaten him one day when he had torn a new shirt. Apu had been shy, but that did not stop him from being very naughty at home. She could never guard her jars of pickles and chutneys closely enough. Apu was sure to steal things. Once she had caught him red-handed. His small frightened face, red with embarrassment, came back to her as vividly as if it had happened yesterday.

She remembered another day. Apu was only three at the time, and he went missing. Even now, Sarbajaya could feel herself shiver when she thought about it. He had been playing under their jackfruit tree, but seemed to have vanished within a few minutes. When no one could find him anywhere, Harihar called a few fishermen to look in the pond behind their house. Sarbajaya watched them dredge the pond, absolutely petrified. Each of those men, including everyone who had gathered to watch, had appeared to be an angel of death. Even her own husband was no different. It was he who had invited those men. Sarbajaya felt as if they had all got together in an evil, cruel conspiracy against her.

When she was virtually senseless with fear, Durga had returned home with Apu. She had found him walking hurriedly down the road that ran by the river, quite unaware of the distance he had travelled alone. He might have tried to return, but it was possible that he had lost his way. That night, after everyone else had gone, Sarbajaya had made a prediction regarding Apu's future. 'This boy,' she had said to her husband, 'will never stay at home and settle down in life like all the others. No three-year-old child would dare leave his home and go off on his own the way Apu did today. You mark my words, our son will never be happy to stay in one place.'

61

Thoughts of Nischindipur came crowding round. She did not like it here, she wanted to go back to her old village. Once, she had been so eager to leave that old place behind, to start life anew. Now, that same place had turned into a land from a fairy tale, totally out of her reach. Lost in her thoughts, Sarbajaya did not notice the fragrant spring evening draw to a close, nor did she see the radiant colours appear slowly, lazily in the evening sky, and then fade into darkness. This happened not just once, but on most afternoons.

Whatever she was given, Sarbajaya tried to save for her son. There was a wedding in the Kundus' house. They sent her a whole pot of sweets. Sarbajaya could not bring herself to eat even one. Every day, she thought Apu might be home soon, he would eat them then. When, eventually, they started to rot, she had to throw the pot away. On festive days, she made preparations to make sweets at home. Who knew, Apu might return. She waited and waited ... where *was* he?

Her son had changed. When was the last time he had hidden behind the door and tried to frighten her? When had he come and given her an unexpected hug? Or peeped from a corner, smiling mischievously? Now he did not speak without thinking, he had certainly become more mature. Sarbajaya did not like it.

She wanted her child back; her sweet, innocent little boy, who was solely dependent on her for every little thing. But her Apu was changing quickly, alarmingly!

Sometimes Sarbajaya felt furious with him. Didn't he know how she longed to see him? Didn't he realise how painful it was for her to spend every single day like this, swinging between hope and disappointment? Very well, she told herself from time to time, if he had stopped thinking of her, so would she. She'd stop caring altogether. But she soon discovered how utterly impossible this was. She lived for Apu. Her life, her very existence would lose its meaning without him.

Today, after her visitor left, she sat down with a heavy heart to finish a few household chores. Suddenly, she happened to glance out of the window and caught sight of a young man walking down the path. His hair was exactly like Apu's—thick, dark and wavy. Her heart leapt, but she told herself not to be silly.

Only a few moments later, someone knocked on the door, softly and gently. Sarbajaya ran and opened it, then stood staring, hardly able to believe her eyes. Apu was standing there, smiling mischievously. She flung her arms around him even before he could bend down to touch her feet.

After meeting Potu at the fair in Mamjoan, Apu had been unable to contain himself. Mamjoan was not all that far from Monshapota, anyway. He had had to borrow the train fare from a friend, but here he was. Shyly, he untied the small bundle in his hand. 'Look, I brought you some needle and thread,' he said, 'and some papad, the kind you used to fry me in Kashi!'

Sarbajaya could not take her eyes off her son. Apu looked different. The shirt he was wearing was new, it suited him very well. 'When did you buy that shirt? It's nice!' Apu was very pleased that his mother had noticed his shirt. 'Everyone says it's a lovely colour. It'll be the same colour as a champa flower, once it's been washed,' he told her.

Sarbajaya began preparations for dinner. Since Apu's departure, she had not bothered to cook in the evening. Apu sat with her in the kitchen, telling her all about his new life. Sarbajaya only half listened, still wondering if she was dreaming. Was this really her Apu? Why, he never used to lean back when he talked. Or thrust his hands in his pockets when he stood up. What she did not realise was that, almost unconsciously, Apu had started imitating certain mannerisms of some of his teachers and fellow students.

His mother interrupted him now and then, asking a number of questions: how many boys stayed in the boarding house? How many others did he have to share his room with? Did he get enough to eat? And did they give him fish both at lunch and dinner? Who washed his clothes? Sarbajaya said nothing about studies or exams, all her questions were related to Apu's physical wellbeing. After a long time, she rediscovered the Apu she knew, in the look in his eyes, the way he shook his head, or lifted his eyebrows. She wanted to stop doing what she was doing and hold him close. Apu went on talking, but his mother simply stared at his face, not listening to a word.

Apu spent the next day at home and left a little before sunset. Just before leaving, he said to his mother, 'Er ... do you think you could give me a rupee, Ma? I borrowed money from a few boys some time ago, I must repay them.'

Sarbajaya seldom had cash at home. Her neighbours sent her foodstuff often enough, but no one gave her money. However, she could not disappoint her son; so she went across to speak to the teli's wife, and returned with a rupee.

FIVE

Two years rolled by. Apu found it increasingly difficult to make ends meet, no matter how hard he tried. He tried to survive only on packets of muri, so that he did not have to pay for food at the boarding house. Then he began washing his own clothes to save on the dhobi's bills. He gave up buying sweets and eating out. Nothing seemed to work.

Each time he went back home—although this was rare—he got a little money from his mother, usually by begging, arguing or throwing a tantrum. Sarbajaya pointed out how difficult it was for her to find ready cash, but always gave in to make her son happy. However, what little she could give him never went very far.

To add to his problems, Potu turned up occasionally. His father had died, and he had left the village for good. His brother-in-law had refused to keep him in his house indefinitely. When he arrived unexpectedly, every two months or so, a dirty bundle under his arm, Apu tried looking after him as best as he could, stretching his own limited means to breaking point. He felt a strong compassion for Potu, but there was really not much that he could do for him.

The one thing Apu could not give up was his passion for books. Fortunately, this did not cost him any money. One day, he read an article on the Milky Way, in a magazine that Ramapati bought regularly. Until then, he had not known very much about stars and constellations. When, only a few weeks later, he actually saw the Milky Way in a clear, cloudless sky, he could hardly believe his eyes. The dark sky seemed to be torn apart by a glowing white mark; he could see neither where it began, nor where it ended. Transfixed, he stared at the sky, his eyes dazzled by the glittering stars.

Things improved a little in the beginning of December. It turned out that the new deputy magistrate required someone to teach his two young sons. He was prepared to provide free board and lodging for the tutor. Apu's headmaster heard about this and recommended Apu's name. Apu had fallen behind with his payments at the boarding house. The warden had reported the matter to the headmaster, but Apu knew nothing about it.

He moved into the deputy magistrate's house a few days later. A portion of their front room had been cleared for Apu to stay. It took him a while to unpack and put everything in order. Then the cook came out to tell him his food was ready. He went in, and found that a single place had been laid for him. This suited him very well for he could not have eaten with a lot of strangers. As he began eating, however, he became aware of a pair of eyes watching him. He looked up quickly and found a lady, possibly the deputy magistrate's wife standing nearby. She came forward and sat near him. What a beautiful woman she was, Apu thought, and much, much younger than his mother.

'Where is your home?' she asked.

'Monshapota,' Apu replied, his eyes once more fixed on his plate, 'It is quite far from here.'

'Who else is there in your family?'

'Only my mother, no one else.'

'Is your father … ? Oh, I am sorry. Don't you have any other brothers and sisters?'

'No. I had a sister, but she died many years ago.'

Apu finished his meal hurriedly, and made his escape.

The next day, after breakfast, Apu returned to his room to find a girl of about thirteen standing there with another much younger boy. Judging by her attractive features, she was the daughter of the lady he had met the day before. Apu did not know what to say to her, so he quietly began getting ready to go to school. The girl and the boy continued to stand, looking at Apu with frank curiosity. Suddenly, for no reason at all, Apu felt he had to do something to impress the girl. He opened his geometry box and spilt its contents on his bed. Then he began to put everything back in the box—his compass, his setsquare, and his protector. Somehow, this simple act made him feel like a man. The girl continued to give him a steady look without saying anything.

He got to know her later, when he returned from school that evening. She reappeared at the door almost as soon as he got back and spoke shyly, 'Ma is calling you inside. Your meal is ready.' Apu went with her and found a laden plate waiting for him. There were hot parathas, two different vegetable dishes and, on a small plate, a few spoons of sugar. Apu felt faintly disappointed. He preferred jaggery. How could anyone enjoy eating hot parathas with a few grains of sugar?

'Shall I tell Ma to bring some more?' the girl asked.

'No, thank you. But tell me, why do you eat sugar?'

The girl turned startled eyes on him, 'Why, don't you like it?'

'No. Sugar is for patients, sick people. There's nothing like a piece of jaggery to go with hot parathas. Why don't you ...' he stopped. The girl's mother had entered the room. The speech he was about to give on the redeeming qualities of jaggery remained undelivered. He did not feel shy at all in front of the young girl, but her mother's presence made him tongue-tied once more.

'Nirmala,' said the lady, 'you must always be present when he eats. From what I can see, he'll never ask for anything and might go back hungry unless we keep an eye on him.'

Apu felt embarrassed by this, but also greatly touched. Perhaps he should call this lady Ma? He wanted to, but felt shy again. He did not know her very well, after all, it might not be proper.

In the next few weeks, Apu realised a few things he had never thought of before. Every member of Nirmala's family was always very neatly dressed. The clothes they wore were not necessarily very expensive, but they spoke of good taste. Even the simple dresses they wore at home were worn with care and a certain style. This was something he had never noticed anywhere else, not even when he lived in the house of the Roychowdhuris in Kashi. There his young eyes had simply been dazzled by their display of wealth, he had not had the chance to think about taste.

Another thought slowly dawned on him. In the atmosphere in which he had been brought up in Nischindipur, in the life they had led there, everything was dictated by one single factor: poverty. All they had been preoccupied with was how to survive, how simply to exist. Beauty and aesthetics in their home and lifestyle had had no role to play. Had Apu not been exposed to the lives of so many other people he had met over the last couple of years, particularly in the deputy magistrate's house, such a thought would never have occurred to him.

Very soon Nirmala became like a younger sister to Apu. She started calling him Dada, and began taking care of his needs without being told. Apu found clean sheets on his bed, his clothes washed and occasionally mended. In return, he told her stories, played word games and kept her and her small brothers entertained. But sometimes, Nirmala felt cross and dissatisfied. Why couldn't Apu tell her of his needs? Why couldn't he order her around? Wasn't that what an older brother was supposed to do?

More than six months passed. Some time in late October, one of Nirmala's uncles turned up for a visit. Nirmala's brother Nontu informed Apu that his uncle had recently returned from England. Amazed, Apu stared at the man. Of medium height, thin and dark and only in his mid-twenties, he did not cut a very impressive figure. *This* man had been to England?

The children called him Amar Mama. He proved to be quite easy to talk to. Apu asked him endless questions. What trees lined the roads in England? Were there any trees there that grew in India? Had he been to Paris? Was it a big city? Had he seen Napoleon's tomb? And the white cliffs of Dover? Had he been to the British Museum? What about Venice? Was it really true that there was something special about the Italian sky?

Amar Mama was much taken aback. How had a boy who had spent half his life in a small village learnt such a lot about England and Europe? He did not, of course, know about the many hours little Apu had spent in Nischindipur, reading the *Letters from England* in the old issues of the *Bongobashi* magazine. Unaware of the lengthening shadows in the evening,

Apu had read on, travelling through a joy-filled path that ran past the Suez Canal and went through the Mediterranean, to glimpse the Corsican vineyards ... and on ... and on. Amar Mama himself had gone to England only to learn how to make soap. To his mind, there was little more to England than grey skies, mist and rain. He had not noticed the trees, nor had he had the time to travel to Italy.

Amar Mama left, and a few more months passed. One day, in the beginning of April, Apu had an accident. It happened while playing football. He hurt his knee, and fell down, crying with pain. His friends picked him up and brought him to Nirmala's house. Nirmala herself was away with her brothers, visiting a relative. Her mother rushed out to the front room and sent for the doctor at once. Apu's handsome face had turned red with pain and discomfort, he could not straighten his right leg. But the doctor arrived shortly and announced it was only a sprain. Nothing was broken.

Nirmala returned in the evening. She came into Apu's room, took one look at him and said, 'Serves you jolly right, Dada! A just punishment for being so restless all the time!' Then she disappeared inside, leaving Apu feeling hurt and dismayed. She came back in half an hour, grinning mischievously. 'I asked for some hot water, and when it's ready I'm going to start with fomentations. That's what the doctor said. Yes, it may hurt, but *I* am not going to care!' Then she sat for nearly an hour, fomenting Apu's injured knee. Her brothers turned up, demanding stories. But Nirmala shooed them away.

The next morning, Apu was left on his own. Nirmala came back in the afternoon, and stayed with him for a long time, chatting and reading aloud to him. Then they played their favourite game. One would throw a line at the other, asking him to make up another line to rhyme with the first. Both were very good at this, so neither would accept defeat. Nirmala's mother looked in on them, and was much amused.

'You might form a poetry society,' she said. Embarrassed, Apu fell silent. Even now, he could not bring himself to call her 'Ma', although Sarbajaya had asked him to, and certainly that would have pleased Nirmala's mother very much.

❧

It took Apu a few weeks to recover. He returned home one rainy evening—more than a month since his accident—soaked to the skin. Nirmala, who was sitting in their drawing room reading, looked up as Apu ran into his room. 'Look at you!' she exclaimed, closing her book, 'Why didn't you take an umbrella?'

For some reason, Apu was in a good mood that day, 'Get me a cup of tea, and something to eat—quick, I give you three minutes!' he said, laughing. Nirmala looked at him with surprise. Apu never spoke like this. She smiled back at him and said, 'Forget it, Dada, I cannot make a cup of tea in three minutes. Why are you in such a hurry, anyway?'

'Well, it won't be for long, will it? Another three months, then I'll be off.'

'What are you talking about?'

'My final exams are only three months away. Then I'll go away, perhaps to Calcutta, to study in a college.'

Nirmala had not considered this possibility. Her face fell.

'You'll go away from here?' she asked foolishly.

'Yes. You'll be relieved, won't you? My staying here meant a lot of extra work for you, didn't it? Hey, what's the matter? Listen, Nirmala, I was jok … '

But Nirmala had left. Unable to stop her eyes from brimming over, she had run back inside without waiting for Apu to finish. Apu felt a little contrite. 'I must stop teasing her,' he thought, 'How can I ever forget her kindness when

71

I had sprained my knee? She might have been my own sister, not once did I feel I was away from home and with people I didn't know!'

A few days later, Potu came to see him again. Unable to go to school, or even find himself a roof over his head, Potu now spent his time visiting all the girls from Nischindipur, who had got married and moved away. They were happy to have him for a few days, going so far as to pack him food when he left, or give him a little money. He had even been to see Ranu, he said, and stayed eight days at her place. Ranu had secretly given him three rupees, and a lot of food.

'Did she mention me?' Apu asked.

'Oh, yes. She said I must take you with me the next time I go to visit her. She even gave me the rail fare. But ... when I came back, I fell ill. I had to go back to my sister's. So all that money went on paying for my medicines, and fruit, and other things. My sister could not afford it, you see,' he said apologetically. 'I have never seen anyone as kind as Ranu di. She is still so fond of you ... she had tears in her eyes when she spoke of you, Apu da!' Potu added.

Suddenly, a lump rose in Apu's throat. He quickly turned his face away, pretending to look at something outside the window. Potu went on chatting, then left after a couple of hours.

The next three months passed quickly enough. Luckily, the matriculation exams were held in Apu's school, so he did not have to travel anywhere else. Mr Dutta, the headmaster, called him to his office after the exams were over. In the last few years, a close relationship had formed between the stern headmaster and Apu, without either of them realising how strong the bonds of affection could be.

'When are you going back home?' Mr Dutta asked.

'Next Wednesday, sir.'

72

'What do you plan to do now? You will study further, won't you?'

'Yes, sir. I certainly wish to go to a college.'

'What if you don't get a scholarship this time?'

Apu did not know what to say. He only smiled.

'Never mind. Have faith in God, everything will work out eventually, you'll see. Wait, let me read to you these few lines from the Bible....'

Mr Dutta was a devout Christian. He often read out from the Bible in class. Apu loved to hear those words of wisdom. In his mind the tragic face of Jesus under his crown of thorns, the love that shone out of his tranquil eyes, had made a permanent place. Apu had had no difficulty at all in accepting Jesus as unquestioningly as he had accepted his own Hindu gods and goddesses, or the quiet, dignified saffron-clad figure of the Buddha, or indeed that of Sree Chaitanya.

'You must go to Calcutta,' Mr Dutta added. 'Some small towns have colleges, too, but they are not very good. They may be cheaper, but if you wish to broaden your horizon, Apurbo, you must go to Calcutta.'

'Yes, sir. I intend going there, sir, nowhere else.'

'Very well. I have got something for you here.' Mr Dutta passed him a copy of *Les Miserables*. 'This is the copy you borrowed so often from the school library. You may keep it. I will buy another. Good luck!'

Apu had never been very good at expressing himself verbally. Rather overwhelmed by the headmaster's kindness, he stood mutely for a few moments, then quickly touched his feet and disappeared.

Mr Dutta watched him go and sighed. He had been a teacher for thirty years. But never before had he come across a student like Apu. Imaginative, idealistic, perhaps just a little foolish and impulsive, but totally innocent, guileless and with an amazing thirst for knowledge. He was going to miss his quiet intelligent eyes, full of wonder and silent questions, that had compelled him to stop and consider anew his own responsibilities as a teacher. In some ways, Apu had been an inspiration to him. He might never find a similar pupil.

It was with a heavy heart that Apu began getting ready to leave Diwanpur. How quickly the last four years had passed! Debu bade him a tearful farewell. 'I think I'll leave school, Apurbo da,' he said sadly. 'With you gone, I'll have no friend left. I may as well go back home.'

Nirmala came to his room later in the day. It was quite warm, although there was a strong wind. Apu had shut his door to keep the wind out, and the dust and dry leaves it inevitably brought with it. Nirmala pushed the door open.

'Come in, Nirmala!' Apu invited, 'Have you just come back from school? You had a function today, didn't you? I saw your chief guest getting out of her car. A very fat lady, wasn't she?'

'Oooh, fat she certainly was!' Nirmala giggled, then seemed to remember something. 'You are leaving today!' she exclaimed.

'Yes, that's right. I have to catch the two o'clock train. I haven't got much time. Can you call Ramdharia? I might need his help.'

'Why, has Ramdharia always done your work? I can help you with your packing.' Nirmala opened his old tin trunk and wrinkled her nose in disgust. 'What filth have you packed your case with? Look, do you really need to keep all this? Shall I just throw it all away?'

'No, no, no!' Apu shrieked, horrified. Every little object in his trunk was filled with memories. Years ago, Durga had found a broken nest for him. He had kept it in his trunk. Then there were pieces of paper with his father's handwriting on them. Each piece of this 'rubbish' was precious to Apu.

74

'What!' Nirmala exclaimed. 'Do you really have only two shirts? No more?'

Apu laughed. 'Where would I find the money to get any more? If I had the money, I would have got one made like the one Sukumar has. That colour would have suited me very well. I would have looked really quite....'

'All right, all right, that's enough. Don't try to show off before me! Look, here's your key, don't lose it. Let me go and see if the cook is getting your meal ready,' said Nirmala busily. 'How long do you have left?'

'A couple of hours. I must see your mother, Nirmala, and say goodbye to her. Heaven knows when I'll see all of you again.'

'You may well *never* see us again. You are not going to come back here, are you?'

Apu tried to protest, but Nirmala stopped him. 'No, don't say anything. I have come to know you pretty well, Dada. You won't ever come back. I know it. You are really quite cruel and heartless.'

'Heartless? That's unfair! How can you ...?'

'I must go. The cook won't do anything unless I tell him to hurry.' Nirmala left quickly.

Nirmala's mother had tears in her eyes when it was time for Apu to go. But Nirmala got busy doing something of such utmost importance that it proved impossible for her to come out to say goodbye. Her mother called her several times, then gave up. Apu left feeling hurt and puzzled.

But he soon got over it, particularly as he climbed into his train. A train journey, even now, made him feel excited possibly because it was still something of a rare event. He sat by a window and thought of the time he had spent in Diwanpur. Most of all he thought of Debu and Nirmala, the two people closest to him there.

When he got off the train and made his way to Monshapota, he forgot even these two friends. There was a faint fragrance in the air—where was it coming from? Loose leaves lying on the ground? Flowers? Some trees were shedding their leaves; he saw new leaves on others. Bright red polash flowers glowed on several branches, like the flames on lamps lit for evening aarati.

A sudden wave of joy and excitement swept over Apu. He forgot Diwanpur. Debu and Nirmala were already a part of his past. He was a young man now, about to take his first step into a new world. The shadowy woods, the distant call of a bird on this lazy evening, the sky that was a shade of peacock blue, the soft scent of bokul, were all mixed with a touch of intoxication. The strange mixture of emotions that rose in his heart—pride, enthusiasm, a breathless anticipation for the unknown—made Apu feel quite lightheaded.

The world was beckoning him once again. How could he not respond? To feel in his heart an invitation from the distant world, a feeling of romance underlying it, was something he had inherited from his father. Like his father, he wanted to break all shackles and run after the unknown, without pausing to think. In the fragrant breeze, and the crimson glow of the setting sun, he could read a message from the future. It was a message of romance.

SIX

Apu discussed the whole situation with his mother at some length. How could he study further if he did not get a scholarship this time? Sarbajaya had never been to Calcutta, nor did she know anything about the special prestige attached to the term 'college student'.

'Haven't you studied enough?' she asked.

'No, Ma,' Apu replied, 'but please don't worry about me. I'll manage somehow, even without a scholarship. So many poor students live in Calcutta. I'll simply be one of them ... something's bound to work out.'

He could not sleep a wink the night before he was to leave. His heart trembled, it felt tight inside his throat. Would he really be in Calcutta in less than twenty-four hours? Calcutta! He had heard so much about it. There was such a lot to see ... strange and wonderful things. There were huge libraries, he had heard, where one could just walk in and spend the whole day in the reading room.

All night, he tossed and turned in his bed. The thick branches of the tamarind tree behind the house made everything look darker. Why was it taking so long for dawn to break? Perhaps ... perhaps he would not get to go to Calcutta. So many people died suddenly, didn't they? Who knew, he might die suddenly, too. Oh God, please God, don't let him die without seeing Calcutta, without studying in a college, at least for a few days ... please, please God!

He did not know anyone in the city, nor was he familiar with its streets. All he had was an address Debu had given him a few months ago. It was the address of one of his uncles. 'All you have to do is mention my name. My uncle will look after you,' Debu had said. And he had a street-map of the city, torn from an old railway timetable. Apu kept both pieces of paper in his pocket before getting into the train.

He had seen a big city before, but even so, Calcutta surprised him. He came out of the Sealdah railway station and stood staring at the flow of traffic on the road outside. What were those vehicles? Trams? And those speeding silently? They must be motor cars. There was something like a wheel attached to the ceiling of the stationmaster's room, spinning with great gusto. An electric fan, he surmised.

Debu's uncle lived in a lane near Amherst Street. It proved very difficult to find his house. With the help of his map, Apu at last managed to find Harrison Road. Luckily, his luggage consisted simply of a bundle and a small bedroll. Carrying the former in his hand, and the latter tucked under his arm, he then found Amherst Street, after which it did not take him long to get to the right house.

Akhil Babu, Debu's uncle, wasn't home, so Apu had to wait until evening for him to turn up. When he did arrive, he received Apu with great kindness. On learning that he had not eaten all day, Akhil Babu ordered a meal for him instantly. After his meal, Apu went up to the roof and stretched out on the floor. It was now quite dark. He felt very tired.

Nothing, however, could take away his excitement. He was finally in the city of his dreams ... would he get to see the famous museum one day? And the Maidan? Then there was the bioscope. He had seen it once in Diwanpur—there was a train in it, a man running and waving his arms and pulling faces to make people laugh. A group of visitors had brought it with them to the school. But here, apparently, what they showed had a proper story with characters in it. He would ask Akhil Babu how far he'd have to travel to see the bioscope.

The house Akhil Babu lived in was not his own. It was, in fact, a mess where many other men lived. Apu began going out from the next day, on the advice of several other members of the mess, to look for the job of a private tutor, or to enquire about cheap accommodation elsewhere, or to see which college would have him as a free student. Presidency College, the best known and the most prestigious, was bound to be the most expensive. Apu did not go anywhere near it. He did not like the look of Metropolitan College, or City College, so he tore up the application forms he had filled. Eventually, he found Ripon College, and thought it was most suitable. The building was tall and large, which impressed Apu. He completed the necessary forms and was admitted. Then he went in with another boy to inspect the class rooms. There were electric fans in each room. The other boy showed him where the switches were. Apu spent a few most enjoyable moments switching them on and off.

He began going to college, but realised soon enough that staying in Akhil Babu's mess was going to be most difficult.

There was nowhere he could study. Three other men shared his room. There was no furniture; everyone slept on mattresses spread on the floor. Their belongings were contained in three steels trunks, there were three pairs of shoes arranged in a corner with brushes and shoe-polish, and three hookahs. Apu's roommates left early, then returned at six in the evening, simply to rest quietly in the room, smoking their hookahs and talking occasionally of what happened in their office. Then they had dinner and went to sleep. Akhil Babu, who worked as a private tutor after work, returned later than the others and seemed to have no energy left for anything except going straight to bed. Going to work, eating and sleeping appeared to be the only aim in life for the members of this mess.

Apu felt most out of place. He had never lived anywhere with so may adults. But what could he do unless something else came up? He had very little money, but he had promised his mother he would send her money as and when he got himself a scholarship. There was no chance of getting a scholarship now. What was he going to tell Sarbajaya? How was she going to manage?

Things changed a little a month later. Akhil Babu found Apu a job. He would have to teach a young boy for fifteen rupees a month. The money wasn't much, but something was better than nothing. About the same time, he learnt that three other boys in his college were sharing a room somewhere. They agreed to take Apu in. Apu moved in with them happily enough. At least he was now going to be with his own friends.

The three boys came from Murshidabad. Among them, Sureshwar was the oldest. He was doing his MA. He also appeared to be the richest. His monthly earnings came to forty rupees. Janaki earned twenty, and Nirmal a little less than that. Their joint expenses, sadly, often exceeded their joint income, but Sureshwar always paid the difference without telling anyone. It took Apu a couple of months to realise this. But Sureshwar laughed it off when Apu mentioned it one day. 'You can do it, too, when you start to earn a little more,' he said.

Nirmal walked in with a packet in his hand, reciting lines from Tagore. He was the same age as Apu, very well-built and muscular. Then he broke off and said, 'Peas, fresh peas!' offering the packet he was carrying. 'Fry them with green chillies ...!' Apu snatched it from him. 'Show me!' he demanded, taking a quick look, 'Yes, that's lovely. Someone light the stove, please, I'm going to get some crisp muri. How much should I get? Four paisa's worth? Would that be all right? One, two, three....'

'Apurbo, don't point at me like that!' Nirmal complained.

'I will, I will. Three ... three ... three ...' Apu laughed and, shaking his finger at Nirmal, ran out before Nirmal could catch him.

'He's quite mad!' Sureshwar said with a laugh. 'You should see the number of books he has brought from the library.'

Often, in the evenings, the other boys asked Apu to sing. Everyone knew he had a good voice. But he had not yet lost his shyness. After much persuasion, he would sing a couple of songs at the most, never more. However, he was perhaps more fond of Tagore's poetry than Nirmal. Whenever he found himself alone, he recited lines from his poems with great enthusiasm.

Among his professors, Apu liked Professor Basu the best. He taught history. Apu did not feel like going to college on the days when there was no lecture on history. Professor Basu always appeared dignified, his bright eyes gleaming behind the pince-nez he wore, from which flowed a black ribbon. Apu became attentive the instant he saw the professor enter his class, and listened carefully to every word of his lecture. Professor Basu was a first class first in MA. A true pundit, in Apu's view. He appeared to have the entire history of mankind on his fingertips, from ancient Egypt, Babylon, Assyria, to the rise and fall of the ancient Indian civilisation.

History was followed by logic. As soon as the roll call was over, the number of students in this class began to diminish. Usually, Apu sat at the back during these lectures, and read novels or poetry borrowed from the library. Logic did not appeal to him at all. One day, he was so deeply immersed in his book that he did not hear the lecturer speak to him. He looked up only when he became aware of a sudden silence. The whole class was looking at him. Hastily, he stood up.

'What were you reading, Apurbo? Anything to do with logic?'

'No, sir. It ... it's *Palgrave's Golden Treasury*, sir.'

'Why? Suppose I mark you absent in my class? Why don't you pay attention?'

The professor resumed speaking. Janaki nudged Apu and whispered, 'Serves you right, Apurbo! We told you to slip out after the roll call, didn't we? Come on, let's get out now.'

In a class of a hundred and fifty students, it was not difficult to slip out if one sat close enough to one of the open doors at the back. They were left open for this specific purpose. Janaki was the first to go. Another boy followed him. Then Apu followed suit. It was something he had never done before, but at least now he was free to go back to the library.

The librarian greeted him warmly. 'Roy moshai, aren't you going to give us something for Puja?' he asked. This pleased Apu no end. Even five months ago, no one knew him in this city. Now, here was someone calling him 'Roy moshai', and expecting a special tip from him for Durga Puja. It made him feel very important. 'Tomorrow, I promise!' he said happily. 'Can you give me a volume of Gibbon today?'

Back at home, he tried reading Gibbon, but did not like it. There were far too many details. He got bored, and changed it the next day for a different book on history.

⚬◈⚬

Apu's newfound happiness did not last long. The room he was sharing with the other boys soon had to be given up, shortly before Puja. It was already difficult to make ends meet; then Sureshwar suddenly lost his job. Nirmal and Janaki made their own arrangements. Sureshwar joined a mess. Apu went with him, but could not afford to take a room. He kept his few belongings with Sureshwar, and had his meals by paying a guest charge. At night, he slept in the corridor. From the fifteen rupees he earned, he had to pay three rupees to his college. The remaining twelve would never have got him very far, but Apu kept telling himself he could manage.

Then, one day, he lost his job, too. His pupil was ill, and had been advised a change of air. His father paid him an extra month's wages, and said goodbye.

Apu put the money in his pocket and returned to Sureshwar's mess, lost in thought. What was he going to do now? He found a letter waiting for him. The writing on the envelope was unfamiliar. He opened it quickly, to find that it was a letter from his mother, but she had had it written by someone else. The reason for this was simple. She had hurt her hand and was in considerable pain. Could Apu send her three rupees?

Sarbajaya had never asked him for money. Apu remembered the number of times he had pestered her for the odd rupee—sometimes more—when he went home from Diwanpur. Sarbajaya had had to borrow or beg from her neighbours, but she had never complained. This time, she must have been desperate, or she would never have got someone else to write to him.

He counted the money he had. After paying his college fees, he would have twenty-seven rupees left, out of which fifteen must go to Sureshwar's mess. He owed them that much for all the meals he had had. Then he'd be left with twelve. 'What if I send Ma ten rupees?' he thought. The more he thought about it, the more he liked the idea. 'When the postman arrives with the money order, Ma will ask him how much it's for, and she'll think it can't be for more than two or three rupees. What will she do when she finds out it's for ten? She'll be ever so surprised ... she'll talk of nothing else when I go home!'

Apu went to the big post office in Boubazaar and sent off a money order. The thought of his mother's face, happy and amazed when the money order reached her, brought him a great deal of comfort. 'I'll manage with two rupees,' he told himself. 'Something will turn up.'

He had made a new friend in college. His name was Pranav Mukherjee. He did not have much money, either, and like Apu, was a regular visitor to the library. It was in the library that they first met. It soon became clear that Pranav had read a lot more than Apu. He mentioned names Apu had never even heard of— Nietzsche, Emerson, Turgenev. But that was not all. Pranav was also a far more disciplined reader. Apu read what his eyes fell on. The library was packed with stuff that aroused his curiosity. *Gases of the Atmosphere* by Sir William Ramsay. Apu had to find out what gases there were. *Extinct Animals* by E.R. Lancaster. What animals were these? *Worlds Around Us* by Proctor. Oh, he *had* to read that one!

Pranav laughed at him. 'You read as if you are playing a game. If you want to be a serious reader, Apurbo, you have to bring order and method in what you read!' Apu tried, but failed, and remained as impulsive as ever. However, encouraged by Pranav, he did read Turgenev, which he greatly enjoyed. He read every book of his that the library could offer, nearly sixteen of them. He felt as if a door to a whole new world had been opened, full of tears and laughter. Then he read Gibbon again, with more perseverance this time; and a translation of *Iliad*. Although Nietzsche proved difficult to grasp, he read two or three of his books, too.

It was Pranav who told him about a house in Shyambajar, where meals were provided for poor students. Apu had never tried to find out about free meals, not so much because it would have hurt his pride, but because he was both shy and ignorant. When Pranav told him of this place, he went willingly enough. He had no choice now.

It was obvious that the house was owned by someone extremely wealthy. A chowkidar stopped him at the gate. On being told why he was there, he took Apu to what seemed to be an office. A man was sitting under a fan.

'Yes?' he asked.

'Er … I've come to enquire about free meals for students,' Apu faltered.

'Did you apply?'

'Apply?'

'Yes. We take fresh applications in June. Our numbers are quite limited, you see. You'll have to come back next year. But by then, we may stop the free meals altogether. Things aren't looking too good.'

Apu came away silently. He had never asked a complete stranger for anything, nor had he had to bear the pain of disappointment. His eyes smarted. He now had less than a rupee left in his pocket. Who could he turn to? Akhil Babu? He was already much beholden to him. Sureshwar? But Sureshwar himself was finding it hard to make ends meet.

A few days passed. Apu had the odd meal either with Sureshwar, or with Janaki. Then, one day, after having spent the whole day on an empty stomach, he was forced to visit Akhil Babu. The older man received him with the same kindness as before, and gave him a meal. Apu stayed to chat afterwards, but failed to tell Akhil Babu of his predicament. If he did, he knew Debu's uncle would insist on his staying with him again, and that would only amount to taking advantage of his kindness. Apu could not do it.

On his way back from Akhil Babu's mess, Apu saw a big house. A car was parked near its gate. Whoever owned the house was surely rich enough to give him all the help he needed. It was simply a matter of finding the owner and talking to him. Should he do that? Suddenly, he remembered Leela. She lived somewhere in this city, in a similar house. She had once suggested that he live in her house to finish his education. He did not have her address. In any case, seven years had passed since he had last seen her. She must have forgotten him. She might even be married. But could he have gone to see her and seek her help, even if he had known where she lived? Never.

What was he going to do if nothing worked out? Return to Monshapota, and never go to a college again? Never see his new friends, or visit a library, read about the stars in the sky, or ancient Rome, the French Revolution, or the extinct dinosaurs?

The next day, Janaki offered a temporary solution to his problem. He knew of a temple where a meal was offered each night after aarati. That was where he himself had his evening meal. As he was going back to his village for some time, he could speak to the priest and arrange to have Apu take his place until he returned. Would that suit Apu?

Suit him? Apu felt as if Janaki had offered him the moon! The arrangement worked out quite well. Apu liked the simple vegetarian meals the temple provided; just occasionally he was even given a small share of the money received from devotees. But it did mean going without food the whole day.

He bought himself muri in the afternoon and drank a lot of water. That kept him going until classes finished, after which sometimes he came out of his college feeling sick with hunger. But there was no point in going early to the temple, for the meal was never served before the aarati was over, and there was no fixed time for it. Sometimes he had to wait until ten o'clock. On other days he could get to eat by eight.

One day, Apu arrived for his history class to be told that none of his friends were going to attend it.

'Why?' he asked, surprised. 'What's CCB done?'

Professor Basu, who taught them history, was generally known as CCB.

'Nothing,' a boy called Murari said. 'It's just that he said he'd ask questions about the history of Rome. You know jolly well how cross he'll get if you can't answer him correctly.'

'Do you know, I haven't even bought the book on Roman history!' cried Gajen.

Manmatha, who had once studied at St Xavier's, raised his arms and pirouetted, like a ballerina. Then be began humming an English song.

'Yes, but we'll lose a day's attendance,' Apu said.

'So what?' asked Pratul. 'A day's attendance should not matter. But even that can be taken care of. I can stay until the roll call is over, then sneak out. Could you do it? From CCB's class?'

Apu was willing to meet the challenge. 'Of course,' he replied, 'I'll slip out after you. Yes, I can do it, provided you give me a treat afterwards.'

'OK. We'll see.'

Apu ran up the stairs. 'Why are you teaching him something like this? It's not right,' said Gajen.

'What do you mean? You think he's some sort of a saint?' Pratul demanded.

'No, Pratul, he really is rather simple and innocent. Why, the other day....' began Murari, but Pratul cut him short. 'I know, I know, he can get away with most things just because he's good looking. If each of us had his looks, we'd have received certificates of merit, too!'

'Don't talk such rubbish, Pratul, You're getting worse every day!'

At this moment, the principal's car was seen arriving at the gate. The boys simply melted away.

As his name was called out, Apu said, 'Present, sir!' then began to look for a suitable opportunity to get out. This did not prove easy. To start with, CCB addressed his first question to him: 'Was Merius justified in his action?' Good God, who was Merius? Apu had not been paying a great deal of attention to CCB's lectures lately. He stood mutely. The professor tried asking a different question: 'What do you think of Sulla's ...?' Apu stared at the ceiling, looking uncomfortable. His friend Monilal stuffed a handkerchief into his mouth, but could not stop laughing. Unfortunately, the professor had seen him. 'You, you there, behind the pillar!' he exclaimed. Monilal gave up trying to hide behind a pillar and stood up. It turned out that his views regarding Merius and Sulla were exactly the same as Apu's. He, too, stood in complete silence. Apu nudged the boy sitting next to him, and said, 'Good, rightly served! Why was he laughing at me?'

'Sh-sh, CCB will look this way again if he hears any noise.'

'Now I am going to....'

Nripen spoke urgently from the row behind. 'He's going to ask me next. Please, please, someone, tell me the date he wants. Quick!'

The same boy replied: 'What date? Who knows anything, anyway? Why don't you just get out of here?'

Apu had been watching the professor like a hawk. He happened to be looking away for the moment. If he turned his gaze back to this part of the hall, it would be impossible to get away. This was his chance. Apu stirred in his seat, looked around briefly, then slipped out. He was followed by Nripen and the other boy. They sprinted down the stairs, without wasting another moment. Apu looked at his companions and laughed, once they were safely back on the ground floor. 'Oh, just a few more seconds, and we'd have been caught!'

'Do you know what happened yesterday?'

'Look, let's go to the common room. I can see the principal's car standing at the gate. He may come down any minute,' Apu said.

A little later, they all left the college. There were no more classes today. Pratul and his group were nowhere to be seen. Puzzled, Apu went to look for them in the library. Yes, they were there earlier, the librarian said, but they had left quite some time ago.

Apu felt a sharp stab of disappointment. He had been so looking forward to having something substantial after just one plate of muri in the morning. Hunger gnawed at his insides.

'What funny people!' he thought sadly, 'Pratul did agree to give me a treat. Why else would I have missed the lecture? Why couldn't they wait for me? If I could eat something now, waiting until eight this evening might not have been so bad. It's Monday, so they're bound to have the aarati by eight. I could have managed. But now … oh God … how hungry I feel!'

SEVEN

Apu had always been poor, but never before had he faced such enormous hardships. His parents had indulged him, and even when things had seemed very difficult indeed after his father's death, he had not had to starve. Sarbajaya had protected him from the harsh realities of life as only a mother can protect her young. Diwanpur had been difficult, but even so, it had been possible to indulge in a few luxuries occasionally. But then, things were that much cheaper then.

Calcutta was a different story. Besides, a war had started in Europe. Clothes had become impossibly expensive. He had only one good shirt—made of tulle—which he had to wash every other day. He could not go out until it was dry. Sometimes he was forced to put it on even before it had dried properly. The effort of washing it in the morning made him doubly hungry.

A plate of muri did nothing to help. There were days when Apu felt strange while attending his classes, an empty stomach made his head feel so light that he could not concentrate.

There was an additional problem of accommodation. Sureshwar had finished his final exams and gone home. His room in the mess had gone to someone else. But before leaving, Sureshwar had spoken to someone he knew in a medicine factory. His acquaintance had agreed to share his room with Apu, at least temporarily. The room was small and directly over the factory. Half of it was crammed with empty cartons and packing boxes. Behind these, endless rubbish had been stashed over a long period of time. There was a faint stench that refused to go away. There were mice, too. Already, Apu had discovered two tiny holes in his only good shirt. Cockroaches abounded, but what Apu found most objectionable was his roommate. He was grateful to him, but the other man seemed to have absolutely no notion of cleanliness. Fond of his hookah, he got up several times during the night and left heaps of used tobacco on the floor. Apu got tired of cleaning up after him.

Walking aimlessly, one day he found himself near a tram stop. A hawker was selling newspapers, shouting out the headlines. There was fresh news about the war. Apu paid no attention. He looked idly at the people standing at the tram stop. Suddenly, his eyes fell on a young man wearing glasses. His face seemed familiar. Where had he seen him before? The young man glanced in Apu's direction and caught his eye. Now Apu could recognise him. It was Suresh. His father used to own the property next to Apu's house in Nischindipur. They had once been neighbours, although Suresh and his family had moved out of Nischindipur long before Apu. Their property had stood abandoned for years. Suresh happened to recognise Apu as he moved forward eagerly. 'Why, Suresh da, it's you!' he said.

'Yes. Apurbo, isn't it? Do you work here?' Suresh spoke lightly. He had clearly become a city lad. There was a certain polish and sophistication in his appearance and speech, which suddenly made Apu feel a little unsure of himself.

'N-no. I am a student. First year, Ripon College,' he replied.

'I see. So where are you off to now?'

Apu did not answer his question. 'Where is Jethima?' he asked instead. He had always called Suresh's mother Jethima. They had not been particularly close to Apu's family, but now he felt as though Suresh and his mother were people he had known all his life. In his own excitement, he failed to notice the very casual tone Suresh was using. It was true that he had recognised Apu, but that had made no great difference. Suresh was not overcome with joy.

'Ma? Ma is in Shyambajar. That's where we live now. We bought a new house there.'

'And your sister? Atashi di? Is she there? Sunil? What's Sunil doing?'

'Sunil's still in school. All right then, I must catch this tram.'

'What are you doing these days, Suresh da?'

'I am a medical student. I'm in my third year.'

'I will go and visit you one day.'

'Very well. Goodbye.'

Suresh jumped into a tram. Apu ran alongside and asked hurriedly, 'Your address? Suresh da, you didn't tell me....'

'24/2C Vishwakosh Lane, Shyambajar,' Suresh shouted. The tram disappeared.

The following Sunday, Apu wore his tulle shirt (having washed it the previous evening) and borrowed some polish for his shoes. He would meet Suresh's mother and sister. He had to dress as well as he could.

It proved fairly easy to find the house. It wasn't very large, but built according to the latest design. A maid opened

92

the door and showed him into the drawing room. Apu noticed electric switches on the wall and felt very pleased. It was nice to think someone he knew lived in this house. But Suresh was not at home. He would have to wait. Apu did not mind. He sat admiring the furniture, the clock on the wall, the calendar, the paintings, the old roll-top desk in a corner. To think he knew the people who owned these lovely things! He felt a little proud.

It was quite late by the time Suresh arrived. Apu rose to his feet and greeted him with a smile. 'Why, it's Apurbo!' exclaimed Suresh, 'When did you get here?'

'A long time ago,' Apu replied, 'What a nice house this is, Suresh da!'

'Yes ... my uncle bought it.... Could you excuse me for a moment?'

Suresh went into the house. 'He's gone to tell his mother I'm here,' Apu said to himself. 'Now he's going to come back and take me in to meet her. Then she'll ask me to stay for lunch.'

Suresh returned an hour later. He sat down, leant back lazily and said, 'So ... what have you been doing with yourself?' Then, without waiting for a reply, he picked up a newspaper and began reading it. Apu noted with some surprise that he was chewing a paan. How could he have a paan before lunch? Or had he eaten already?

Another hour passed. It was now one o'clock. Suresh went on reading his paper, just occasionally throwing a few casual questions at Apu. Then he put the paper aside, rose and said, 'Why don't you read the paper, Apurbo? I must go and lie-down. I say, would you like a daab?'

A daab? Why would he wish to have the water of a green coconut before lunch? Taken aback, Apu stammered, 'Why, n-no, I don't think....'

'Very well,' said Suresh indifferently and went inside again.

Apu continued to wait patiently. It was now half past two. When did these people have their lunch? Or was lunch delayed today because it was a Sunday? Ah, that must be it. But when another thirty minutes passed, it finally dawned upon Apu that there was something wrong somewhere. There had been a mistake, but who had made it? Was it he, or was it they? The pangs of hunger had grown so strong that he could no longer sit still. He half rose to his feet, but at this moment he saw Suresh's younger brother, Sunil, come out of the house; before Apu could call out to him, he picked up a bicycle and went out. This sight of the young boy made him feel both pleased and surprised. Was it really the same Sunil? He remembered going to a dinner with him in Nischindipur. The host had given them packets of food to take back home. For this reason, Sunil's mother had called Apu 'the son of a greedy Brahmin'.

He felt no rancour to think about it. These people belonged to the most cherished part of his life. He had not come here for any selfish gain, but simply to meet old friends. It did not occur to him even once that his sudden arrival might be seen as an imposition, or an attempt to worm his way into their house. It was only his inherent sense of wonder that had brought him here. Who knew that, one day, he would meet here in Calcutta the people who owned the house next to his own, back in Nischindipur? This simple fact was enough to enchant him. It was as if, walking down the long and weary road of life, he had suddenly turned an unexpected corner, and found a green wood full of fragrant flowers.

Not everyone possesses such a sense of wonder. Only a mind that is alive, alert, generous and capable of accepting new thoughts and new images, can experience wonder. Those who have called wonder the 'Mother of Philosophy' have not been able to capture its true meaning. Wonder itself is the 'philosophy', the rest merely defines it.

Suresh re-emerged after three o'clock. 'I had night duty, you see,' he said, yawning, 'I didn't get any sleep last night. So I had to lie down ... I believe there's a hockey match this evening. Would you like to come with me?'

Apu felt a little contrite for having blamed Suresh earlier for going to sleep. If he had not slept the night before, naturally he was tired. But clearly it was time to go.

'No, thank you,' he said, rising, 'I have an exam tomorrow, I must go back and study for it. Only ... er ... can I just see Jethima before I go?'

'Of course. Come with me.'

Apu followed Suresh with hesitant steps into an inner room, where his mother was sitting. 'Ma, Apu here would like a word,' Suresh said. 'Remember Apu? From Nischindipur?'

Apu quickly touched her feet. Now he knew that Suresh had simply kept him sitting outside, he had not found it necessary to tell his mother, or anyone else, about his visit. Jethima said, 'Oh yes, I see. What do you do here, Apu?'

Apu had hardly ever spoken to this lady. Her grave face and arrogant behaviour (which, as a child, he had not been able to grasp fully) used to frighten him. Now, he swallowed and stuttered a little: 'I ... I ... study in Calcutta ... in a college, that is.'

Jethima seemed surprised. 'In a college? When did you finish school? Didn't you go to Kashi?'

Apu explained. 'I see,' said Jethima briefly. Almost immediately, a young woman in her early twenties came in, accompanied by a girl of about sixteen. Apu recognised the older woman. It was Atashi, Suresh's sister. 'Atashi di! I am Apu,' he said. Atashi behaved with greater warmth than her mother. She recognised him, and seemed quite willing to spend a few minutes chatting. Jethima left the room in a few seconds. Apu was not introduced to the other girl, but he caught her staring at him. Then she and Atashi left together.

What was Apu going to do now? Should he simply get up and leave? Wouldn't that be rude? He no longer felt hungry, but strangely dizzy. Slowly, he rose to his feet and stepped out. The young girl was crossing the passage outside. Apu called her, 'I am going now. Will you please tell Jethima? Er ... I have some work, you see....'

The girl stopped and looked at him. 'But you didn't even have a cup of tea!' she exclaimed. 'Wait, let me go and tell my aunt.'

'N-no, no,' Apu said hastily, 'please don't bother. I don't really want any tea.'

'It's no bother.' The girl disappeared, and returned a little later with a cup of tea and a plate of halwa. Apu pounced upon the plate and gobbled what was on it. The hot tea burnt his mouth; then he poured some into a saucer to cool it.

'Are you a cousin or something?' the girl asked. 'No, it's all right, you may leave the plate here. Would you like some more halwa?'

'No, thank you. I ... I am not very hungry. And yes, I am a distant cousin.'

When he returned to his room quite late that night after his dinner at the temple, he discovered that another man had turned up for the night. This was nothing unusual. The workers in the factory downstairs received visitors occasionally, who were offered the same room. Normally, Apu wouldn't mind, but this room was so small and cramped that it became impossible to move with three people in it, let alone sit and read in peace.

Apu had met the new arrival once before. He was in the business of supplying potatoes to wholesale dealers, and was given to talking nonstop. Apu was forced to come out almost as soon as he returned.

'Where are you off to again?' the man called.

'Just outside. It's so hot today.'

A few moments later, the man spoke again: 'Whose bed is this? Sir, is it yours? Look, look, I spilt water near your bed, please remove it ... damn!'

Apu came back and moved his mattress as far as he could from a pool of water in the middle of the floor. What could he say? He had been allowed to stay here only because his roommate had felt sorry for him. How could he protest if things were not to his liking? To tell the truth, today he was too preoccupied to notice or feel anything, even anger. He stood on the little balcony outside, staring at the old wooden railing and its peeling paint, and thought of Suresh's house. What a lovely house he lived in! They had electric lights and fans, such beautiful furniture, their women had so much style. They had tea and snacks on the dot of four ... Lakshmi smiled on them, they lacked nothing.

It was only he and his family that seemed cursed. Why was his mother forced to live alone in a village? Why was he floating around in the city like this, on a half-empty stomach, without a penny in his pocket, wearing an old shirt? What had he done to deserve this?

❦

Three days later, there was a special puja, called Jagaddhatri Puja. Apu had no idea the people of Calcutta celebrated it with such fanfare. He had never seen such a thing in the village. Shehnais were being played in every lane, and garlands of deodar leaves were strung on doorways.

In the next lane, a puja was being held in the house of a rich man. When darkness fell, Apu could see a iarge number of guests going into the house to have dinner. What if ... what if he slipped in with them? It was such a long time since he had been to a big dinner. Could he do it? Who would recognise him, anyway?

Apu stood in his balcony, swinging between temptation and fear.

EIGHT

In the winter session of their college, Pranav read an article at a debate, arranged by their college union. It was called *Our Social Problems*. He had worked hard on it, using strong and difficult English words, to describe a number of problems, such as the remarriage of widows, education of women, demands for dowries and child marriages. Each problem was presented from his own point of view, but what he said went in favour of the traditionalists. He spoke well, with a clear diction, and with appropriate gestures to drive home a point. At times, he curled his right hand into a fist; at others, he raised it and clutched the air, or thumped the table in front of him, to prove the utter futility of educating women and the necessity of marrying people off in their childhood. His friends and supporters provided a deafening applause.

Manmatha—who was at St Xavier's before—rose to offer the opposite viewpoint. Most boys looked upon Manmatha with a certain amount of awe, for he knew Latin. No one dared speak English in his presence, in case he found fault with their pronunciation, and jeered at them. He appeared to know all there was to know about Western etiquette, no one could question his authority. Once, a hapless classmate had gone with him to eat at a restaurant, and had had to suffer endless taunts for a whole week, just because he had held the fork in his right hand. When Manmatha began speaking, he spoke with confidence. His language was even stronger, his accent almost like an Englishman's. However, as things turned out, that was not enough to see him through. To start with, his arrogance and snobbery had made him very unpopular. Then, when he began to criticise age-old traditions, a number of students got angry and started crying: 'Shame! Shame!' and 'Withdraw! Withdraw!' Manmatha's own band of followers, on the other hand, began clapping loudly. As a result, things became so noisy that no one could hear a word of the concluding part of his speech.

Pranav's supporters outnumbered those of his opponent's. They praised Pranav sky high, and called Manmatha a heretic. Some asked how he dared to question Hindu beliefs, when he had not read any of the scriptures. Others were annoyed with him because he said he knew Latin. Some of them now openly expressed their doubt about the truth behind this claim. One of them stood up and said, 'If this speaker's command over Latin is the same as his command over Sanskrit, well....'

At this point, seeing that the attack was getting increasingly personal, the professor of economics, Mr Dey, who was presiding, felt obliged to intervene. 'Come, come,' he said, 'Manmatha has never said that he is a Seneca or Lucretius— have the goodness to come to the point.'

This was the first time Apu had attended a debate. In his old school, despite the headmaster's assurances, debates had never become a part of their activities. Today, Apu found the proceedings childish and laughable. What was the point in talking about subjects so trite and hackneyed? He decided to read a paper at the next meeting of the union. *He* would show everyone how to speak on a totally new subject that no one had ever thought of.

It took him a week to finish writing his paper. He called it *The Call of the New*. All things old and established were going to be changed. In literature, or social behaviour, or one's personal attitude ... one would have to accept what was new and different. Apu based his arguments on what he had felt himself. The joys and sorrows he had experienced every day for nineteen years, his memories of his childhood, the affection in his sister's eyes, his friendship with Ranu, Nirmala, Debu; bright sunny skies, or moonlit nights, days of hope and days of despair; these had all built something special in him, something that was both great and wonderful. Like the silent rays of the sun that travelled millions of miles to nourish a tiny sapling, helped it grow and bear fruit, the eternal truth of life had slowly unfolded itself in his young mind. Sometimes, he felt a strength within himself, an overwhelming emotion, that he knew could not be contained within. It had to be expressed, and once it was, it would wipe out all old and worn out ideas, and the trivialities of life. He would be the first to show the world the power of the *New*.

Having finished writing his paper, Apu went around bragging to his classmates, in his usual manner, about what a marvellous piece he had written. No one could ever have imagined such a subject, such language! The secretary of the union was the young professor of logic. When Apu went to inform him about his intention to speak at the next debate, he said, 'Very well. But what shall I write in my notice? I mean, what's the title of your paper? What is it about?' On hearing the title, he smiled. 'That's a good title. But why not *A Word from the Old*?' he joked. Apu smiled back, but did not say anything.

On the appointed day, the hall was packed. The vice-principal, who was supposed to preside over the meeting, could not come. Mr Basu, the professor of history, was asked to take his place. When Apu rose to speak, at first both his voice and his legs started to tremble. This was the first time he was facing such a large crowd. In a few minutes, however, he could feel himself relax. What he did not realise was that although what he had written was spirited enough, it brimmed with every weakness of youth and inexperience, strong emotions, fiery idealism, proud declarations of having the power to discard the old system, its benefits notwithstanding, and a somewhat reckless criticism of the establishment. A great hubbub broke out when he finished. His opponents hit back with as much vigour, and Apu was severely criticised. It did occur to Apu, however, that those who were speaking against him had really no basis for their strong comments. None of them had enough experience to really understand the subject he had chosen. All they could do was put him in the same bracket as Manmatha, and call him antisocial and a traitor.

Apu felt somewhat taken aback by this response. Had he not been able to make himself clear? Perhaps he ought to have taken a little more trouble over his paper. With the exception of a handful of close friends, everyone in the large gathering had turned against him. Now he had no cause to envy Manmatha for his share of booing and catcalls. Finally, when the president allowed him time to defend himself, Apu tried to explain things more fully. He had noted down a few points when his critics were shouting. Now he tried to address them. However, very soon he began to lose track of his reasoning, which only gave the others another chance to laugh at him.

This made Apu angry. He stopped trying to be reasonable, and became emotional instead. He called everyone narrow-minded, and concluded his speech with a satirical tale. Finally, he recited two lines of Emerson and sat down, striking his table with his fist.

The students left the hall, still talking noisily. Most of them were calling him names, suggesting that his sole intention in presenting the paper had been to show off his knowledge. He had recited these lines from Emerson:

> I am the owner of the sphere
> Of the seven stars and the solar year.

The boys called him arrogant and presumptuous. But Apu had not referred to himself at all when speaking those two lines, although it was true that he *had* wanted to show everyone how different he was from all the others. Besides, he could hardly deny that he had a habit of bragging, perhaps more than anyone else.

His own friends stayed close, offering words of encouragement. Then, when the crowds thinned a little, Apu said goodbye to his friends. As he was about to go out of the main gate, a younger boy, of about seventeen or eighteen, stopped him. 'Just a minute, please!' he said shyly.

Apu had never seen him before. He was slim, good looking, and wearing a thin silk shirt. On his feet were naagras, embroidered with golden thread. 'Er ... do you think you could let me read your paper?' he asked hesitantly.

Suddenly, Apu's hurt pride raised its head once more. He handed over his paper to the boy, and said gravely, 'Kindly make sure you don't lose it. You are ...? Oh, are you doing science? I see.'

The next morning, he found the same boy waiting for him at the gate, just as the first class was about to start. He returned Apu's paper, said 'namaskar' and quickly disappeared. Apu went to his lecture, and was absently turning the pages of his article, when a piece of paper slipped out of it. The whirring electric fan above made it fly, but the boy sitting next to him caught it and handed it back to him. On it was a poem, written in pencil. It was addressed to him. Running to sixteen lines, what it said basically was that Apu had a wonderful vision, and was a worthy son of his motherland.

Much taken aback, Apu read it again. There could be no doubt that it had been written for him. Oh, what joy! In his excitement, Apu forgot that he was sitting in a classroom, and Professor Basu was engrossed in describing the amazing generosity of some Roman emperor. As he tried to show the poem to the boy sitting next to him, Janaki gave him a sharp nudge and whispered, 'CCB is looking straight at you, can't you see? Sit still, for heaven's sake, or he'll yell at you.'

Oh God, how long would CCB continue to jabber? If he couldn't get out and show this poem to everyone soon, he would die. He also had to find that boy again.

After his classes were over, Apu saw the boy standing near the gate. Perhaps he was waiting for him. Flattered and proud though he felt, Apu found himself becoming tongue-tied again, once he came face to face with his admirer. Luckily for him, it turned out that the other boy was even more shy. After hesitating for a while, Apu shook his hand. Then they started talking. Neither mentioned the poem, though both knew that was the only reason why they were meeting. The boy was called Anil, Apu learnt. A few minutes later, he said, 'Let's go out somewhere, I mean out of the city. I feel breathless here—sometimes I can't see even a single stalk of grass anywhere.'

Apu looked at him with surprise. Anil was obviously different from the others. Apu had spent nearly a year in Calcutta, but had not heard any of his friends bemoan the absence of grass in the city.

104

They got into a train, and climbed out after four stations. Apu had never visited the place before. There was open countryside, dotted with flowering bushes. They began walking down a narrow track that ran through a field, and resumed their conversation. They had already become good friends. Sitting under a tree by the field, Anil told Apu about himself.

He had been brought up in Hazaribagh in Bihar. His family owned a mica mine. Hills and forests, rivers and waterfalls were as much a part of his life as woods and streams had been a part of Apu's. Anil grew misty-eyed describing the sunsets he had seen behind bluish hills, the fragrance of shaal flowers in early April, bright red polash in the forests that made every branch look as though lamps had been lit for an evening aarati. After dark, tigers came out of the deep forests to drink water from the mountain springs. Anil had seen their pug marks on the wet sand many times.

Things were going quite well, but suddenly, for some reason, mica stopped being a profitable business. Anil's family sold the mine off and moved to Calcutta. Anil found the city claustrophobic, his fellow students dull and unimaginative. 'Their minds are filled with such small, petty issues that I don't think they could even begin to understand anything profound, even if they tried!' Anil said in conclusion. 'Only you, Apurbo, seem to be different. When I heard you speak the other day, I thought here's someone who does not fall into this category.'

Apu felt both pleased and reassured. When he was in Diwanpur, the boys there had made fun of him for his love of nature. It had not taken him long to realise he was different from most other students, but he had accepted that quietly, without ever feeling superior in any way. His heart was too generous and tolerant to be harshly critical of others. Even so, talking with Anil made him feel he had found a kindred soul, he need not be alone any more.

Later in the evening, on returning to his room, Apu lit his old lantern and read Anil's poem again. Here was a true friend, who would stand by him, help raise his self-esteem, and bring out what talents lay within him, hidden like a precious jewel.

Then he glanced at the second bed in his room. A third person was going to sleep in this room tonight. A relative of his roommate had arrived this evening. About thirty years old, he worked in the railways in a suburb of Calcutta. He had little education, but liked speaking in English, without seeming to care that his knowledge of the language was not what it should be. He also tried to be overfriendly, and talked incessantly of the theatre. Had Apu seen such-and-such actress? She was just brilliant. Had he seen the latest play in which so-and-so had acted? Her acting, and her songs, were just out of this world.

Apu hated such idle chatter. He had no interest in the theatre. Why couldn't he have a little room of his own, he wondered. He would read at his own desk, may be keep a few flowers in a vase. There was no way he could look out and see the sky from this room. And it was so dirty! How long would he go on cleaning up the mess the others created with their used tobacco? Just look at the pillow, the case his mother had made for it was so badly torn. If he could save a little money, he would go out and get a new pillowcase made.

The next day, Apu went to the docks with Anil, to look at the Ganga as well as the ships anchored there. The ships had such funny names. One of them, in particular, caught his eye. It was new, the paint on its body gleamed in the sun. 'It's an American cargo ship,' Anil told him. 'It will go to Japan from here, then return to America.' Apu saw a laskar in blue uniform standing by a railing, peering down into the water. Oh, what a lucky man he was! He had had the chance to travel everywhere in the world.

Perhaps he had come through a typhoon near China, spent lazy afternoons in the palm groves of Penang, leant over the railing as he was doing now, and witnessed the fury of a wind-tossed, turbulent sea. But did any of it matter to him? Did *he* consider himself lucky? Of course he didn't. Had he seen Mount Fujiyama from the far distance and felt enthralled? Had he ever got off his ship to inspect the plants that grew on the coastline of Japan? Would he know if any of the flowers back home also grew on Japanese soil? Had he ever seen the sierras of California, away from the bustle of ports and noise of the cities, and sat alone on a rock, just as the sun began to set, and watched its glory spread across a silent, blue sky?

Never. Yet, it was that other man who would get to travel. Apu, who longed to see the world, would remain stuck in the city, simply to read and to dream. Why couldn't *he* get out? Out and away from the noise and the smoke in Calcutta? This was an unforeseen problem for Apu. He had had no idea that winter in Calcutta could be so difficult. The thick, stubborn haze that enveloped the city soon after dusk both blinded and choked him. He had to get away.

The job of a sailor, certainly at this moment, appeared ideal.

Ship Ahoy! ... Where are you coming from?
From Calcutta, on my way to Port Moresby.
What was that in the distance, standing high in the air?
The Great Barrier Reef ...!

Apu thought of the old sea captain, Tasman, caught in a terrible storm. He lost his mast, his sails were torn, but he continued to float for twelve days until he saw land. Yes, it was there ... once called Van Diemen's Land, now Tasmania ... The blue horizons beckoned him, Apu could almost see the skuas flying over the ocean, and hear the roar of the huge waves crashing against the barrier.

And what about that huge mountain that raised its head way beyond the shore? Perhaps it stood in the middle of an empty, desolate desert, where there was nothing but endless stretches of sand and clumps of cactus ... but perhaps, hidden somewhere in its depths, was a gold mine, or may be there were black opals to be found? Hundreds of men had travelled in the scorching sun to look for gold and gems, but none of them returned ... their skeletons gleamed white in the hot sun.

Anil's voice brought him back to reality. 'Let's go home,' said Anil, 'it's getting late. What good is staring at these ships going to do?'

❦

The next day, the two of them missed college and did a round of the offices of various shipping companies, starting with P&O. It was lunch time by the time they got there. Most of the clerks were either having a cup of tea or smoking. Anil did most of the talking, while Apu simply stood behind him.

'We are looking for a job on a ship,' said Anil, 'do you know of anything?'

A thin, balding man gave them the once-over.

'A job on a ship? What ship?'

'Any ship will do.'

Apu nodded vigorously, his heart pounding in his chest. What was in store for him today?

'I don't think you can get a job like that ... go and speak to the Marine Master upstairs.'

They went, but the Marine Master shooed them out. From P&O, they went to BISN, Nippon-Eusen-Kaisha and Turner-Morrison. No one seemed interested in them. Running up and down various flights of stairs made Apu break into a sweat. Eventually, when he found himself on the third floor of the office of Gladstone & Wylie, he lost his shyness and barged into the room of their Marine Master. He was an Englishman, tall and hefty, with a moustache the size of which Apu had never seen before. He started to speak, but the Englishman simply frowned and rang a bell. One of his Indian officers appeared, gave Apu and Anil a startled glance and said, 'Who let you in here? Come on, come with me.'

He took them to him own room, and heard their plea. Then he gave Anil a steady look.

'Why do you want to work in a ship? I mean, of all things? Are you running away from home, young man? Are you cross with your family for some reason, both of you?'

'No, of course not. Why should we be running away?'

'Well then, I can't think of any reason why anyone in their right mind should want the job of a laskar.' The officer smiled. 'Do you have any idea what it involves? You'll have to sign a contract for a year, and be made to work like a slave. The food you'll get on board will be very different, don't think they'll bother to cook you the kind of meals you eat at home. You may even be asked to work in the boiler room as a stoker. It will be unbearably hot and airless, and you'll have to pick up great heavy coal shovels. You could never do it with those skinny and delicate arms, I can tell you that. If the engineer catches you resting, he'll whip you hard. Think about it.'

Anil and Apu refused to be discouraged.

'Is there a ship about to sail shortly?' Anil asked.

'Yes, there's one called *Golconda*, sailing next Tuesday. It'll take cargo to Colombo, and then on to Durban.'

'Please, sir,' Apu opened his mouth this time, 'we can do it. Can you help us? We can stoke the engine—no, we wouldn't mind the heat—and eat what we're given and ... and ... all the rest of it. All we want to do is just be there. Won't you....'

The officer raised a hand, now more deeply convinced than ever that these two boys were running away from home.

'Give me your names and addresses,' he said. 'Before I put you on a ship, I'd like to meet your families.'

After another five minutes of begging and pleading, Apu and Anil had to admit defeat and go back home, sorely disappointed.

NINE

❧❀❧

Apu returned from college one afternoon and was about to take off his shirt, when his eyes fell on the window of the house opposite. He could not believe what he saw. Written with chalk across the wooden shutters were the words: *Hemlata will marry you*. The words had been written by a woman, there was no doubt about that. Apu stared for a few seconds, then burst out laughing.

The window was only a few yards away from his own, for the alley that separated the two houses was a very narrow one. Now that he thought about it, he remembered having seen a girl of about fifteen standing at the window, clasping its bars. She had thick wavy hair and was pleasant enough to look at, but certainly he hadn't found her beautiful. Occasionally, she had smiled at him, then quickly hidden behind the curtain. Sometimes she closed and opened the shutters unnecessarily, just to attract his attention. She also changed her clothes frequently, three or four times a day, and came and stood at the window on any pretext. 'What a strange girl, quite shameless!' he had once thought, then dismissed her from his mind. What had happened today was entirely unexpected.

He had returned home feeling depressed because the owner of the small restaurant where he had been having lunch lately had caught him today and demanded a settlement of old unpaid bills. Apu had eaten there for several days without making any payment in cash. He had promised to pay the man a lumpsum for every meal eaten in the past, but had not been able to find the money. The owner had run out of patience today.

Now, however, Apu's anxieties dissolved in laughter. Wait till I tell my friends, he thought, grinning to himself.

He did not see the girl that day, though he noticed on returning to his room in the evening that the words had been wiped clean. The next day, he saw the girl before going to college. She had just had a bath, her damp hair hung down her back; wearing a saree with a red border, she was holding the bars on her window again, and looking out. Apu caught a fleeting glimpse of the golden bangle on her rounded, shapely arm.

When he told his friends in college, Pranav, Janaki, Satyen and everyone else was vastly amused. 'Romance on the window!' said Satyen, 'I had only read about it in trashy novels, but this is real life!' The laughter continued, and not all of the remarks made were expressed politely.

A few days passed without any further message from Apu's admirer. Then the same offer of marriage reappeared. It was written in such a way that it was visible only from Apu's room. If only he could show it to Pranav! Then the writing disappeared again, and all was quiet for a couple of days.

The third day began with an overcast sky and a shower. After returning from college, Apu tried to get some sleep; but even when the noise from the loaded lorries abated in the yard downstairs, the men on the afternoon shift in the factory began hammering metal bars on wooden crates. Apu gave up trying to sleep, left his bed, and saw immediately that the girl had reappeared at the window.

This time, Apu decided to take things a step further. He, too, went and stood at his window. When the girl caught his eye and smiled, Apu smiled back and spoke to her. 'Why, Hemlata, are you really prepared to marry me?' he asked lightly.

'Yes!' the girl replied, raising a hand to replace a pin in her hair.

'Oh? But I am a Brahmin!' Apu said gravely.

'So are we,' the girl shot back and smiled again. 'I told you my name,' she added, 'what's yours?'

'Apurbo Kumar Roy. Look, let me tell you something. You must not write things like that. What if someone else saw it? It's not right.'

'Who will see it? No one possibly can, not from my house, anyway.' Hemlata darted a quick look over her shoulder. 'I must go now. I can hear my aunt coming. Are you usually here in the evening?' She moved away without waiting for a reply.

Apu started laughing once more. Then a sudden thought struck him. Was the girl perhaps slightly mad? The more he thought about it, the more likely did it seem. The look in the girl's eyes had not been entirely normal. Yes, that must be it. No sane and normal girl would behave like this, surely?

Suddenly, Apu's heart filled with pity and compassion for the girl. He had occasionally seen her father—or at least a male guardian of some sort—waiting for a bus. He was middle-aged, had a perpetual stubble on his face, and did not appear to be particularly well off. Perhaps he worked as a clerk somewhere. His daughter—or niece—had simply happened to fall in love with Apu. Yes, that was entirely likely. Apu felt like speaking to Hemlata again, to offer her words of sympathy and comfort. But what if anyone found out? Let them!

∼◈∽

Days slipped into weeks. One morning. Apu found a small advertisement in a newspaper asking for a private tutor. A doctor needed someone to teach his child; and Apu needed a job rather badly.

He left immediately, and turned up at the address given to find that at least fifteen others had already beaten him to it. The drawing room on the ground floor was packed with other candidates. The doctor's consulting room was on the first floor. He was busy with his patients. Apu found a chair in one corner and sat down, feeling amazed that so many had noticed the small advertisement. Why, it was barely visible among all the other notices! Oh God, here were some more people arriving. There was hardly room for them all.

No one seemed to know anything about the child that had to be taught. 'Do you know how old he is? I mean, which class is he in?' asked the man sitting next to Apu. No, Apu knew nothing about it. He just sat in silence and watched the others go up a wooden staircase one by one, and come down a few minutes later, looking grim. The doctor had started interviewing the applicants. He was obviously a man hard to please. 'What if I am rejected, too?' thought Apu anxiously. Perhaps he'd have to give up college altogether and return to Monshapota. But how would he manage in the village?

A little later, a servant came and announced that the

doctor would not see anyone else. It was much too late in the day for him. Those who still wished to be considered for the job should write down their names, addresses and qualifications on a piece of paper and leave it with him. They would be recalled, if necessary.

No one paid any attention to these words. Each man in the room was convinced that a personal meeting with the doctor would be enough to make the right impression. The child's father only had to see him to decide he'd make the ideal tutor. The person who seemed to get most perturbed by this sudden announcement was the man sitting next to Apu. It turned out that he had come the day before, and told the doctor how poor he was and what a difference the job would make to him. Having done that, he was more or less sure that he would get it, this business of interviewing all the others was a mere formality. He was the first man to make his way up the stairs, ignoring the horrified and protesting servant. The others followed suit almost instantly.

Apu did not know what to do. If he did get to see the child's father, perhaps he could make a case for himself, although he knew very well he could never tell a complete stranger about the abject penury he lived in, and how desperately he wanted this job. When he had first arrived in Calcutta, he had assumed he would be able to get support from someone rich. After all, there were so many rich people in the city, surely one of them would agree to help him out? But, at the time, he did not know himself all that well. It was not in his nature to tell anyone about his own hardships just to gain their sympathy. He wanted people to think well of him, he had no wish to be pitied. So he went about bragging, telling lies to cover up the truth, and pretending to be what he was not. This was a trait he had inherited from his mother. He would much rather have died than told anyone that he was starving, or that he was penniless.

After hesitating for a while, Apu followed the others up the wooden stairs. A middle-aged man was sitting in a room, still arguing with the same candidate who had seen him the day before. The others had surrounded these two figures and were all trying to get in a word edgeways. From outside the door, Apu heard the doctor say, 'But what am I going to do with someone who hasn't even passed his matric exam?' The argument continued for some time. Eventually, however, everyone was obliged to leave. Apu had been standing outside throughout. Now, slowly, he made his entry. 'Er ... I believe you require a private tutor? I saw your advertisement ...' he broke off. Even to his own ears his words sounded false, even foolish. Anyone would think he had not seen any of the others, and had no idea why there had been such a big crowd in this room even a few minutes ago. He had not meant to sound like that, but the words just slipped out. His experience in approaching a prospective employer was so limited that he had still not learnt to express himself properly, with confidence.

The man's eyes swept over him, from his head to toe. Then he showed him a chair and said, 'Please sit down. How far have you studied? Oh, you're doing IA, are you? And where are you from? ... I see.' The man stared hard at him for several minutes. Then he suddenly said, 'Look, I have a daughter. It's she who needs extra tuition. Obviously I have to be careful about who I choose to teach her. But you ... you seem ...' he broke off, and sent for his daughter.

A young girl of about fifteen entered the room. She was slim and pretty, her eyes large, her fingers long and slender. She was dressed in a silk jacket, a saree with a wide border, a thin gold chain round her neck and plain gold bangles on her arms. Her hair was very thick, arranged in the style of Japanese women.

'This is my daughter, Preetibala,' said the doctor. 'She goes to Bethune School. This is your new tutor, Preeti. He'll

116

start teaching you from tomorrow. Yes, he strikes me as most suitable. You're very young, aren't you? How old are you? Nineteen? But there's a look of distinction about you ... yes, I think you'll do.'

Apu returned to his college, still feeling dazed. It was not simply the joy and relief at having found a job. What pleased him much more was what Preeti's father had said about his appearance. A look of distinction! That was no small matter, surely? He told all his friends, even his roommate, about it. When they asked him about his salary, he gave them a figure that was much larger than what he had been offered. Even his pupil's physical attributes were much exaggerated to impress everyone.

However, when he began teaching her from the next day, he realised that Preetibala was very different from the cheerful and affectionate Nirmala of Diwanpur. She spoke little, but when she did, it was always with a touch of arrogance. Over the next few weeks, she continued to speak to him as if she had the right to order him around—explain this, do that, you must spend extra time today, I have an exam tomorrow ... it just went on. She even demanded an explanation if he failed to turn up one day. Any joy Apu might have felt on getting the job was drowned by anxiety and apprehension. What if Preetibala found some fault with his teaching and told her father? Apu knew he would lose his job instantly.

A month passed. When he got his first salary, he sent some money to his mother. On his way back from the post office, he ran into a friend. 'Why don't you come with me to chor bazaar?' said his friend, 'I found a good pair of opera glasses yesterday. I have to go back and collect them.'

Apu had never heard of chor bazaar. He was amazed by the variety of the objects up for sale—furniture, pictures, clocks, clothes, shoes, toys, books, gramophones, curtains, sheets, even soaps and toiletries. None of it was new, but to Apu, the prices seemed very low. A flowerpot was for six annas, an inkwell for ten. For eleven rupees, one could buy a gramophone *and* a stack of records! In all this time in Calcutta, no one had told him of the existence of chor bazaar.

The next day, a mad impulse made him return to the bazaar with what money he had left. The first thing he bought was a pair of flower vases. His old passion for a good inkwell prompted him to buy the one he had seen the day before. Then he bought a Japanese curtain, four pictures, a few plates, a mirror and a ring with a fake stone. To these he finally added a brass table lamp, simply because he had once seen a similar lamp on Leela's table. When he returned home, a coolie carrying his new possessions, his heart was bursting with joy. Never before in his life had he owned so many things. Still convinced that he had got a terrific bargain, he had no idea how badly he had been cheated.

He spent the rest of the day cleaning his room and setting everything up to his satisfaction. The pictures went on the wall, the curtain hung from the door, the mirror was fixed in one corner, the flower vases were placed by the window (although he had forgotten to buy flowers), and the inkwell was rubbed and polished until it shone. There was an empty packing box lying outside. Apu dusted it, brought it inside and put the table lamp on it. Then he sat down to read, but kept lifting his eyes from his book to glance proudly at all the new objects. Now *his* room had everything that rich people had in theirs. He had never had the money to buy anything pretty. But now ... now he was going to indulge himself. He refused to live any more like a buffalo languishing in the slush by a pool.

The next day, seized by a desire to show off, he invited all his friends to his room: Pranav, Janaki, Sateesh, Anil, and even the snooty Manmatha.

'Hurrah!' exclaimed Manmatha as he arrived, 'Look what our Apurbo has done! Where did he get this cheap old curtain? Hey, who's going to eat all this stuff?'

Apu had borrowed a large iron kettle from the supervisor of the factory downstairs, and an old-fashioned stove. He was going to make tea for his friends. His new plates were heaped with samosas, kachauris, gulab-jamuns, as well as fruit. More than half the food disappeared in just a few minutes. Apu kept talking as he did his duties as the host, and he talked rather a lot. His ancestral home in the village, he told them, was a huge mansion with two storeys. Even today, his family were well known in that region. They had once been zamindars, but his ancestors piled up a lot of debt, so everything had to be sold. If it wasn't for that, why, Apu would not be living in such a small room at all!

Pranav got up and began pouring the tea. He managed to spill some on Janaki's feet, which made everyone laugh. Sateesh went and lay on Apu's bed, saying loudly, 'Tell me, Apurbo, whither lives the heroine of your window-romance? Could it be opposite this window here?'

With the exception of Anil, everyone else burst out laughing and began peering out of the window.

'No, no, don't do that, there's nothing to see. I only told you a pack of lies—there's no girl, really. I made it all up!' Apu said hurriedly. He had only felt pity for Hemlata ever since it had occurred to him that she might be insane. He felt both hurt and annoyed by the behaviour of his friends. 'Look at this curtain, I bought it only the other day,' he said, trying to get the others to move away from the window. Then he remembered the ring he had bought, and took it out. 'Guess how much it cost me?' he asked happily. Manmatha took one look at it and said, 'It's only a piece of glass, and the band is certainly not made of real gold. You shouldn't have had to pay anything at all. Pooh!'

This proved too much for Anil. He had seen Manmatha wrinkle his nose at the curtain, too.

'You are not a professional jeweller, Manmatha,' he said crossly. 'Why do you pretend to know everything about everything?'

'I don't have to be a jeweller to see that this stone's only a fake. It's not a diamond, or a ruby, or an emerald.'

'That's all you know! Diamonds and rubies and emeralds are not the only stones in the world. This is carnelian. Did you know there was any such thing? It's found in mica mines. We owned mica mines in Hazaribagh. I know carnelian very well, I have seen it many times.'

Anil knew the stone on Apu's cheap little ring was not a carnelian at all, but he could not allow Manmatha to put his friend down. For the next few minutes, he spoke nonstop, describing the various qualities of topaz and carnelian, the two types of stone he had seen in Hazaribagh. Everyone, including Manmatha, fell silent before his superior knowledge.

Then Pranav began a song, bringing the argument to an end. After that, everyone relaxed and chatted, and cups were refilled frequently. Then it was time for them to leave. Only Anil remained at Apu's request. When the others had gone, he turned to Apu and frowned. 'Why did you have to do this, Apurbo?' his tone held a mild rebuke. 'Who told you to spend all your money on buying this stuff?'

Apu laughed, 'Why? What's wrong with wanting to live in style? I mean, it's nothing much, but....'

'When you don't have enough money to pay for food, it's honestly quite extravagant ... but never mind that. Just think of the other things you could have bought with your money. A whole set of the works of Gibbon from that second hand bookshop, or a pair of binoculars. I know an English lady who is selling a pair because she needs the money. Very cheap, and in very good condition, too. I could have shared the cost with you.'

120

Apu gave an embarrassed smile. For the first time, it dawned upon him that he should not have spent his limited resources quite so impulsively. He had always wanted a pair of binoculars. Now it would be sold to someone else. But he did want to live well, he did want to have beautiful things in his room. What was he to do?

Anil said nothing more. He was secretly annoyed with Apu for having filled his room so happily with these cheap, second-hand objects. But he had no wish to hurt his feelings further.

'You didn't eat much, Anil,' Apu said to cover his embarrassment, 'shall I fry some more papad?'

Anil declined. 'Let's go out somewhere,' Apu suggested. 'To the Maidan, or the river.' Anil agreed readily. He said, 'Apurbo, have you seen the men who live in little lanes, who do nothing all day but chat about the latest scandal, or the price of fish? Some of them are as young as twenty, others might be fifty or sixty. But they're all the same. How I hate them! Even on such a beautiful evening, none of them would dream of going out anywhere, their minds are incapable of imagining there's a world outside. I cannot stand such rank stupidity. It makes me sick.'

'I know. But the Maidan isn't really all that good, is it? I mean, think of the noise of the traffic, the petrol fumes, the noisy trams ...!'

'I'll take you to visit someone tomorrow. He's a friend of a friend, just returned from South Africa. That's where he was born and brought up. His father has recently brought their entire family to Calcutta. He hates it here. Oh, the stories he tells about his life in Africa! I envy that boy, I really do.'

Intrigued, Apu wanted to go that very instant. 'No, we'll go tomorrow, I promise,' said Anil. Then, after a pause, he added, 'Look, forgive me for all those things I said earlier. Do you know why I got annoyed? Because people like you aren't made for such cheap finery. Let me tell you something.

The men who are leading us at the moment are all getting old. I don't mean just the political leaders, but people in other areas ... poets, for instance, or writers, or scientists and doctors, even patriots. They will all retire one day, or die. Who has to take over the reins from them? Surely it is those who have the gift, the power to give something to others? To show the way, to lead? Should these people waste their time in empty talk or shallow thinking?'

Apu laughed at Anil's words, but was secretly quite pleased. Anil obviously thought Apu had something to give, he held a spark that others lacked.

'Yes, do let's go out,' he said and the two friends went out together.

TEN

❧

T eaching Preetibala proved to be a rather daunting task.
The arrogance and contempt in her behaviour was rare in
such a young girl. Apu could not make her out. He went to
her house because he needed the money, but he had to drag
himself every day. Sundays and the other occasional holidays
brought some respite and great relief.

One day, he used a pencil encased in silver that belonged
to Preetibala, and took it away by mistake. The next day,
when his student asked for it, Apu realised to his horror that
he had lost it. It must have slipped out of his pocket. 'I ...
seem to have misplaced ...' he began hesitantly, 'I can buy
you another. Perhaps tomorrow ...?'

Preeti frowned. 'It was a birthday gift from my
grandfather,' she said shortly. After this, there was no point
in offering to replace the lost object. 'I can't take this much

longer, I'll have to look for something else,' thought Apu gloomily.

A few days later, there was a holiday. Much relieved, Apu stayed at home that day. When he turned up at Preetibala's house the following evening, she greeted him with, 'Why weren't you here yesterday?'

'Because it was a holiday, Preeti.'

'A holiday? Why, our manager, our servants, our driver … everyone else came! Why couldn't you? I could not finish my homework, and so I was detained today until five o'clock.'

Suddenly, Apu lost his patience. Then his anger was replaced by profound sadness. After a short pause, he said quietly, 'Look, Preeti, I am neither your servant nor your driver. I did not come yesterday because it *was* a holiday and all the schools and colleges that I know of were closed. If you think what I did was wrong, I suggest you look for a tutor who will not mind being treated like a servant. Please tell your father I will not come here again.'

When he came out of Preetibala's house, Apu thought of Nirmala in Diwanpur. He had been a tutor to her little brothers, but Nirmala's mother had always treated him like a son; and to Nirmala herself, he had been a brother. Only now did he realise how lucky he had been to get their affection. And Leela? What about Leela? His heart gave a sudden lurch. What was the use of thinking about these people now? They belonged to his past.

The next few days passed somehow, for Apu had managed to save a little. One day, in college, he heard some amazing news. Pranav had left his studies and gone off to help the freedom fighters. Everyone said he had become an anarchist.

A month after Pranav's departure, Apu arrived at the small restaurant where he had been having his meals, to find the owner waiting for him again. His past debts had been settled after he began teaching Preetibala, but in the last few weeks, fresh ones had piled up. The owner was not going to take any more risks. 'I don't let anyone eat here for free,' he said. 'I would have stopped you ages ago, but I thought I should give you a little time ... after all, you go to college and you are a gentleman. But now, Babu, I have had enough. If you cannot pay what you owe me, well, that's my bad luck. But please don't come back here again.'

His words were fully justified. But Apu was not prepared for such harsh words. They almost brought tears to his eyes. He had had no intention of cadging free meals. If he had the money, of course he would have paid all his bills. But how could he, he was practically penniless!

There was more in store. Two days later, he found a notice on the college notice board that nearly made him faint. Students who had not been paying their college fee regularly had been asked to pay up within a week. If they did not, they would not be allowed to take their final exams.

Apu had paid the monthly fee only a couple of times— at the very beginning, and once when he was still teaching Preetibala. He owed the college ten months' fees, which came to sixty rupees. How was he going to find all that money, when he did not have enough to pay for a square meal? Perhaps he'd be barred from taking the exams. When his college reopened after the summer holidays, no one would allow him to sit with the students in the second year. All his hard work, everything he had done simply to stay on in the city, would just go down the drain.

Apu returned home and began preparing his evening meal. He had started to cook his own meals now, having realised that it worked out to be much cheaper than eating out. He did not have to buy fuel. The little pieces of wood that were strewn on the floor of the factory where the carpenters worked were enough to light his stove. Even his limited resources were stretched to obtain a packet of rice and some potatoes. Sometimes he could even get an egg or two. He boiled everything together. A meal like that seldom cost him more than five or six paisas.

'Bahu, bring me the big plate, please, and—oh!—the smaller one, too. I'm nearly finished here!' he called. Bahu was the wife of the chowkidar of the factory, Shambhudatt Tiwari. They lived in the same building. Since Apu had no plates of his own, Bahu let him use theirs. Today, she brought a brass pot of drinking water and a few green chillies.

'Careful, I'm not going to touch your fish curry!' she said with a smile.

'Fish curry? Forget it, this is only a handful of rice and a couple of potatoes. Bahu, could you give me some haldi? I'm tired of eating this colourless stuff every day.'

Bahu was a very kind woman. She did not mind carrying and fetching for Apu, or washing his used plates. Normally, no Brahmin woman from Bihar would have done it. Apu had tried to stop her, but she had said, 'You are like a son to me, Babuji, why should I mind?'

❧◈❧

A few days, later, he received a letter from his mother. She had slipped and hurt her foot. Not only was she in pain, but also in financial distress. Apu could hardly eat that day. How bad was it? Was anyone looking after his mother at all? Perhaps she had not eaten for days. Perhaps she was too ill to even inform the neighbours.... Apu's mind raced ahead, imagining a dozen hardships. Even the few pieces of boiled potatoes he had made for himself proved difficult to swallow.

Something else happened to add to his misery. The manager of the factory had told him three months ago that he wanted to use Apu's room purely as a store-room. Apu should look for somewhere else to stay. However, in the last three months the matter had not been raised. Apu, unable to ask anyone else for accommodation, had assumed the idea had been dropped. But now, the manager called him again and began to put a great deal of pressure on him to leave.

It did not end there. Apu ran out of his meagre savings. There was nothing left for him to do but try to sell the few things he had bought in chor bazaar with such joy and excitement. The plates went first of all. It was not easy to find a buyer, but eventually a shop selling second-hand stuff bought them for less than a rupee. The flower vases went for eight annas, and two of the pictures for ten. But Apu still clung to his curtain.

Buying rice was no longer possible. Apu discovered chhatu: grains crushed to a powder that could be eaten with either a piece of jaggery or salt and spices. When he was a child, Sarbajaya used to make chhatu at home only on special occasions. Now it became his only source of nourishment. Apu had once eaten it with great relish, pestering Sarbajaya to give him extra jaggery. But now he had to make do with salt and green chillies, borrowed from Bahu. He did not like eating it every day, but it was both cheap and filling.

A few more days passed. A brief calculation showed him one morning that what little money he had left would not go beyond ten days. Chhatu might be cheap, but it was not, after all, available for free.

Apu spent a great deal of his time in looking for advertisements for situations vacant, both in the newspapers in his local library as well as notices pasted on lampposts. Most notices asking for a private tutor—which was really what Apu was interested in—were displayed on lampposts. But more often than not, by the time Apu saw them, they had been discovered by many others and the address given was almost always torn off.

Roaming the streets for long hours made his clothes dirty, but he could not wash them. One day, he saw Tiwari Bahu soaking their own clothes in a large pot. Apu went to her hesitantly. 'Bahu,' he said, 'do you think you could give me some soap powder? I'll soak this shirt and my dhoti ... then when I get back from college, I can wash them properly.'

Bahu smiled. 'Give those to me, Babuji. I'll add them to this pot ... no, it's not a problem.'

Gratefully, Apu handed over his clothes to her, thinking, 'What a kind woman she is! If ever I can get some money together, I'll repay her kindness.'

Walking aimlessly, it occurred to him occasionally that he might well have to give up college and go back to Monshapota. But even there survival would not be easy. The teli family and the Kundus had got another Brahmin priest to come and live in the village. They had given him land and, judging by the last letter from his mother, they had become quite indifferent to her. If Sarbajaya was finding it difficult to feed herself, how could he go back and add to her worries? Besides, how could he give up college? His studies? Oh, that was impossible!

He could tell how much he had changed in the last year. He had learnt to look upon the world through new eyes; life had a different meaning now. In fact, a year in Calcutta had taught him to view life and the world in such a way that would not have been possible if he had spent as many as ten years in Monshapota or Diwanpur. It was not just going to college that had made the difference; nor the lectures of all his professors. It was the library, and its endless rows of books, that had made him a new man. He was so grateful to it.

He could forget his troubles—even hunger and thirst— when he was in the library. The hours he spent there were spent in a sort of trance. An insatiable desire to find answers to the questions that rose in his mind made him read whatever he could find on a given subject. Sometimes he wanted to read about stars and planets; or he'd be seized by a desire to acquaint himself intimately with life in ancient Greece or Rome ... to be swiftly followed by the poetry of Keats, or the life of Napoleon. Sometimes his passion for a subject stayed for just a couple of days. At other times, he spent months pursuing it. His imagination always centred round something great, or wonderful—famous paintings, tales of the rise and fall of civilisations, the craters of the moon, the present war, or the life of a great man. The small and the trivial had no place in his mind.

The manager of the factory met him again to remind him of the need to look for another room. Where on earth could he go? A totally empty pocket forced him to take his precious curtain and sell it. The picture on it showed a Japanese scene— a cherry tree laden with blossom, a lake with lilies in it, a pagoda on the other side and, in the distance, the snow-capped peak of Mount Fujiyama. It was this picture that had made him buy it for three rupees and eight annas. Now he sold it for little more than a rupee. He managed on that for a week, going so far as to buy a packet of rice and some spinach on the first day. Then, a week later, he was penniless once more.

He left for college without any breakfast. When he returned in the evening, his head felt funny once again, his legs refused to move. His chief problem was not being able to tell anyone, for thanks to his own foolish habit of boasting and telling lies, most of his classmates thought he was actually from a reasonably wealthy family. The handful of boys who knew the truth—Janaki, for instance—were too poor themselves to help him.

Apu went straight to bed on returning from college. He had had absolutely nothing to eat all day. After eight o'clock, however, he could not bear it any more. He went to Bahu and said, 'Could you give me some daal, please? I'm not very hungry, so I won't bother with cooking. But if I could have just a little daal, I could soak it now and eat it later.'

The next morning, the first thing that dawned on him was that he was totally penniless. How long could he go on starving every day? Yesterday, he had felt as if a thousand wasps were stinging his stomach. Several glasses of water had stopped him from fainting. What was he going to do today?

Apu rose, washed his face, then walked about until ten o'clock, looking for notices on lampposts. Then he went straight to college. Although no one else said anything, Anil asked him two or three times, 'Why do you look so tired? Are you unwell?' Apu shook his head and changed the subject. When he came out of the college a few hours later, still hungry, he suddenly remembered his mother's letter. He had got it twelve days ago. Neither had he sent her any money, nor had he written a reply.

The thought brought fresh waves of anxiety. Was his mother starving like him? If so, she would not tell anyone, either. Apu knew her well.

What on earth was he to do? Should he go to Suresh's mother and tell her everything? If she could lend him some money, at least he could send that to his mother. But then he realised that even if he did go to see Jethima, he would never be able to ask her for money. She frightened him. Should he try Akhil Babu? No. He did not earn a lot of money, it would not be fair to him. Then he suddenly remembered a classmate, who was supposed to be well-off. Apu did not know him well, but in sheer desperation, he decided to give him a try. He lived in Boubazaar. His house clearly belonged to an old and wealthy family. It had three storeys. Large and old-fashioned pillars graced its front, and there was a large area to hold pujas. Pigeons fluttered on the parapets. His classmate appeared, looking for him. 'Who's

130

asking for me? ... Oh, it's you. Roll number twelve, aren't you? Sorry, I don't know your name. Do come in.'

They began chatting. It took Apu only a few minutes to realise that he could not possibly raise the question of money. What could he say, anyway? Listen, could you lend me a few rupees? How awful that would sound! The very thought made him blush. He rose to go. 'You can't go yet!' his friend exclaimed. 'Wait, let me get you a cup of tea.'

The tea arrived, accompanied by a plate of fried snacks, sweets and pieces of papaya. Apu fell upon the plate like a hungry wolf and ate greedily. A few sips of hot tea dispelled the dizziness, and he began to feel normal again. Then it became even more obvious that there was no way he could ask this boy for financial help. When he finally said goodbye and left, he could actually laugh at himself. 'How could I even think of it?' he wondered. 'Thank goodness I didn't blurt out anything. How absurd it would have sounded!'

That night, lying in bed, another thought struck him. The next day was the Bengali new year. His college would be closed. Should he visit Jethima, and pay his respects? It was his duty, after all.

Besides, surely on the first day of the year, she would insist on giving him a meal? She would have done that the last time, if Suresh da had told her about his arrival. But of course he had forgotten ... he'd made a mistake.

The next day, it did not take Apu long to realise who had made a mistake, not once but twice. When he turned up at Suresh's house at nine o'clock, there was no one in sight. It took him a while to find the courage to step inside. Then he found Jethima and touched her feet. Anyone but Apu could have judged from her face that she was not exactly overjoyed to see him; nor did she appear interested in learning about his activities. To cover his own embarrassment, Apu

131

began asking her about her children and got a few careless, indifferent replies. Then she left him abruptly. Apu sat for more than an hour, leafing through a magazine. Suddenly, a wedding card slipped out of it. To his amazement, he saw that it was a card announcing Suresh's wedding. It had taken place a month ago, but no one had informed him. Apu stared at it, both surprised and hurt. They knew where he lived. He was family ... or, at least *he* thought they were his own people! How could they have left him out?

At half past ten, Apu said goodbye to Jethima and left. Once he was out of the house, he felt he could breathe easily once more. Then he suddenly felt like laughing. What would Jethima have done, he wondered, if he had said to her face, 'Look, I'd like to have lunch with you today!'

Before he could reach home, the owner of the restaurant caught him on the way, angry and impatient. He had already paid two visits to his house, but Apu had not been home. A new year was starting today, he said, and he was going to open a new account book. He wanted all old debts settled. Some of it he had written off, yes, but the rest must be paid. 'You did not pay me for all the rice you ate, Babu!' the man shouted. 'But you had puris for nine days. You knew that would cost you seven annas every day. So that comes to three rupees and fifteen annas. For three months, I have been chasing you. I tell you, Babu, I *will* collect that money before I open my new book today.'

It was Apu's fault. Unable to resist temptation, he had had puris without waiting to consider his financial situation. Now, he noticed that the other man's raised voice and strong words were attracting a lot of attention from passersby. Afraid of further humiliation, once again Apu spoke without thinking. 'I will make a full payment by this evening,' he said.

Later that day, Apu found a new advertisement for a teacher in a primary school. It had obviously been pasted only

132

a little while ago. No one had yet had the chance to remove the address.

It turned out to be a private house in a narrow alley. The front room had been hired to run an upper primary school. When Apu arrived in the evening, there were a few old men sitting there playing chess. One of them was the headmaster. They were looking for someone who could teach mathematics for just ten rupees a month. Jobs were hard to come by, they said, so what they were offering should be good enough.

Apu felt his heart sink. The dark and dingy room, the mindless complacence on the faces of these old men, even just being near them seemed to stifle him. It was not because of their age. He had known other old men, and enjoyed their company. It was simply the atmosphere in the room where they were sitting. Life, or joy, or what was most precious to Apu, a spirit of adventure, a quest for knowledge, had no place here. Stagnation was all these men could offer.

Apu left quickly. When he emerged from the lane, daylight had virtually gone. For the first time, he felt afraid. How was he going to pass another night, then face another day? What worried him the most was the thought that he had still not been able to send any help to his mother. She must have spent all these days hoping to hear from him. What had happened to her?

On his way back to his house, Apu saw the house of a Marwari, decorated with colourful electric lights. Although it was not yet completely dark, they had been lit. There was clearly a wedding in this house. A delicious smell of fried puris came wafting from it. Apu saw a few cars arrive at the gate. Suddenly, he stopped. 'Suppose,' he thought, 'I go to them and I say I am a poor student, I haven't eaten all day. Will they not give me something to eat? Of course they will. It's such a big house, and so many people are going to be fed here tonight. What's the harm in asking? No one will recognise me here.'

133

In the end, however, he could not do it. No matter how hungry he was, no matter how much he wanted to go and ask to be fed, his old shyness stopped him, as it had done so many times in the past.

Was it time to admit defeat? Should he simply go back to the village? His entire being rebelled at the idea. His heart told him here in the city was life, light, freedom. Back in the village would be darkness and drudgery. Here, his poverty was only physical. There, he would not be able to stop poverty of mind and intellect.

But did he really have a choice any more? He had tried so hard, but now he had no money to buy himself food, to pay his college fees, or even find himself somewhere to stay. The college authorities might allow him to take the exams, but unless he paid every penny he owed them before the results came out, they would certainly not let him join the second year of his course.

It was dark when he finally reached home. He climbed to the roof and sat under the sky. There were pieces of broken china lying in a corner. Apu picked one up, closed his eyes and threw it on the ground, just as his sister had taught him to do as a child. 'If it falls on its back, I'll go back to Monshapota,' he told himself, 'if it doesn't, I'll stay on here.' Then he opened his eyes, and found the little piece lying flat on its back.

He tried again, with the same result. He did not dare try a third time.

Then he closed his eyes and thought of Vishalakshi. Vishalakshi was the village deity Apu had worshipped unswervingly in Nischindipur. His faith in her, even after all these years, had remained as implicit as ever. He thought of the many tales he had heard about the goddess's kindness, about her power to help those who prayed to her with all their heart.

He was praying now. Would her powers work in the city?

ELEVEN

Apu was allowed to take his exams, although his promotion to the second year of his course still depended on the payment of overdue fees.

A few weeks after the exams were over, Anil told him one day that he had stood first in mathematics and physics. The results were not yet out officially, but he had learnt this from one of his teachers. Apu felt very pleased for his friend. Anil was a truly sincere, broadminded and intelligent young man. The only thing about him that Apu did not like was his irrepressible urge to attack and criticise others, sometimes with unnecessary vehemence. But that was the only weakness in his character. Anil was most definitely above all the pettiness and meanness that most men of his age seemed to suffer from. That was really the main reason why he and Apu had been drawn together. Neither was content with his lot. Both wanted to see the world, both dreamt of great deeds.

Anil admired Apu for something else. Apu wrote very well. He had filled a number of thick, bound notebooks with poems, articles, stories and even a whole novel. His stories were full of youthful emotions, in his poetry he tried to copy Tagore's style, and in his novel there was love, adventure (this included pirates), pathos ... nothing was left out. But all of these had made Apu rise further in Anil's esteem.

They went to visit the Botanical Gardens over the weekend. Anil had another piece of good news. He had saved it for this day, for he wanted to be away from the noise of the city and sitting amidst the thick, long grass by a lake when he told his friend about his future plans. His father had a close friend who was very fond of Anil. Since Anil had done so well, he had offered to pay for him to go to England for further studies. It was simply a matter of waiting another year to finish his ISc, and then he would be in either England or France.

'I'll go to either Cambridge or the Imperial College of Science and Technology ... there's Rutherford, and then there's Thomson, it's a matter of great privilege to be able to see them ... and then when the war stops I might go to Germany as well. After all, it *is* the land of Goethe and Ostwald....' Anil stopped for a second, then went on, 'I'll try to arrange for you to join me. Maybe we could go to America together? I'm sure it could be arranged, it's just a matter of time!'

Unbeknown to him, Anil had been influenced by the innocent childlike qualities in Apu's nature, which helped control the aggressive side to his own character. Apu's words, Apu's enthusiasm took him out of the smoke-filled, smelly, narrow alleys of the city, into a wide open space under a moonlit sky, on the edge of a deep wood from which came the sound of the bird's fluttering wings, beckoning him to explore a new world, and unravel all its mystery.

The two of them spent some time discussing routes and places they wanted to see. Then Apu said, 'Look, let's make a pact. Give me your hand. We shall never work as petty clerks anywhere, will never hanker after money, or tie ourselves down to anything small or trivial, all right? We'll ... we'll do something really great, something truly worthwhile with our lives!'

The two friends shook hands warmly. Anil went on speaking about his dreams. After finishing his studies in England, he'd go to both America and Japan. And when he got back home, he'd spend his entire life doing research. Normally, Anil seldom spoke about himself—and in this respect he was different from Apu—but today, in his excitement, he became quite garrulous.

Apu, in his turn, spoke of his thoughts and feelings that he had not shared with anyone before. 'When I was a child,' he told his friend, 'I had an old, torn book called *Geography*. It spoke of stars that are so distant that their light has not reached the earth, even today. I used to lie in a boat on the river in the evenings, and wonder about it. Then, before my eyes, the evening star would rise over a tall tree. Looking at it, I used to feel ... I can't quiet describe that feeling to you ... it used to give me a sense of upliftment. I was too small then to realise its implications, but even after growing up, whenever I have felt sad or depressed, I have looked at the stars in the sky, and each time, there has been that surge of joy. You know, an almost transcendental feeling ...!'

Much later in the evening, they left the Botanical Gardens and caught a steamer back to Calcutta.

❧❦❧

The next day, they met in their college common room and spent a few more minutes making plans. Then Apu left to attend a lecture.

Anil came out of the college building and, still feeling happy and excited, had a cup of tea at a stall. Then he stood debating whether or not he should go to College Street to buy a book.

There had been a slight pain in his lower abdomen for sometime. Now it seemed to have grown a little worse. Anil decided against walking part of the way and made his way to a tram stop. The first tram that came was too crowded. 'I'll take the next one ... let me first go and post this letter,' he thought. The red postbox was only a few feet away. A Muslim was sitting near it with a huge basket of green bananas. Anil walked up to the postbox, then leant forward, balancing himself on one leg, so that his feet did not knock against the basket of fruit. He had just raised his right hand to drop the letter into the box, when it seemed as if a sharp spear was pushed right through his stomach. Anil clutched his stomach and tried to push the pain away, but his legs gave way at this moment, and he fell, his head catching a corner of the basket. He cried out, and saw dimly the Muslim man quickly rise to his feet, shouting. A large number of people gathered round him. What's the matter? ... Are you unwell? ... Go on, give the man some air ... here, take my handkerchief ... ice, get some ice!

There were only two names Anil could utter: 'Ripon College ... Apurbo Kumar Roy.' His eyes fixed themselves on the signboard of a shop, and his mind registered that it said 'Ganesh Chandra Daan—Industrial Chemicals', before everything went dark.

When he regained partial consciousness, he thought he was lying in a box—or was it a room?—but it was moving constantly, and there were voices. A rather loud car horn blared somewhere ... the pain was killing him. Then everything went hazy once more.

When he opened his eyes again, he found himself in bed, staring at a bright white wall. Sitting by his bed were his father and an uncle, and three other men he could not recognise. Two English women dressed as nurses were walking about briskly. Was this a hospital? Which hospital? What had happened to him? Oh God, why didn't the pain go away? Why did he still feel so faint?

It was not until the next day that Anil learnt what had happened. Someone from the street had found Apu in the college and told him that Anil was lying outside, unconscious. Apu and another boy called Satyen had rushed out and called an ambulance. Then a few other boys had joined them and brought Anil to the Medical College hospital. Anil's parents were informed. The doctors said it was a case of strangulated hernia. They took him to the operating theatre at once.

Apu came to see him in the evening on the second day, and found Anil fully conscious. His pale lips parted in a smile when he saw Apu. He was now feeling much better. The pain had taken a long time to subside, even after the operation. 'Sit down, Apurbo,' he said, clasping Apu's hands. 'There's nothing like good health, is there? The last couple of days were wiped clean from my life!'

'Don't talk so much. How is the pain now?'

Then he saw Anil's mother sitting by her son's bed. Apu touched her feet.

'I've heard how much you did for your friend,' she said. 'What would we have done without you?'

'Do you want to see something funny?' Anil interrupted, 'Look, if I ring this bell, a nurse will come running to me!'

He picked up a small bell and rang it. Almost immediately, a tall nurse turned up. When she left, Anil's mother scolded him, 'What did you do that for? Don't do that again unless you really have a reason to call a nurse!'

But Anil was laughing, and Apu joined him.

After chatting with him for a while, Apu left. Unwilling to go back home, he went for a long walk around the Maidan. It was dark by the time he got home. Almost as soon as he had stepped into his room and switched the light on, Satyen and a cousin of Anil—Apu had met him at the hospital—rushed in, looking distracted. 'We've already been here twice to look for you!' Satyen panted, 'Come at once. Haven't you heard?'

Apu looked enquiringly at Anil's cousin.

'Anil died suddenly at half past six,' he explained briefly.

Apu ran back to the hospital with the others. Anil's body had been taken off the bed and placed on the floor. It was covered with a white sheet. The little private cabin hired for him was full of people. A group of his classmates arrived with a wreath. Then his body was removed to the cremation ground.

It was three o'clock in the morning by the time the funeral was over. Everyone else went to bathe in the river afterwards, but Apu did not join them. He did not feel any attraction— or respect—for the Ganga in Calcutta. He would have a bath when he got back home.

Anil's father, despite his grief, was looking after everybody. Twice, he had come to Apu to ask if he was all right, did he feel sleepy, did he need anything? His concern brought tears to Apu's eyes.

Satyen gave him his wristwatch for safekeeping and went into the water. Apu sat on the ghat, staring at the sky. The night was almost over, but the sky was still glittering with stars. The Great Bear was visible just above the tall chimney of the Jessop's factory. A handful of stars in the eastern sky had only just started to fade before the approaching dawn.

At this moment, Apu's mind felt empty. He could not yet feel any grief. All he could think of was that only three days ago, he and Anil had planned their future together. And he had told Anil of the joy and wonder he had felt as a child on watching the first star rise every evening. Now, his mind filled with the same wonder. Every winking star seemed to be throbbing with some inexplicable emotion. Beyond them lay an eternal mystery. Where had Anil gone?

As time went by, Apu was engulfed by a deep depression and lethargy. Even going to the library seemed an effort. He missed Anil most terribly.

One evening, he found himself in College Square. He spotted a bench and sat down. He still did not have a job, his future was uncertain as ever. How long could he go on like this?

'I might have joined the ambulance service,' he thought. 'So many other boys from my college did. But Ma would never have let me go!'

Perhaps going back to his mother, at least for a while, was the best thing he could do.

Then he noticed the man who was sitting on the same bench beside him. He was a middle-aged man with a long beard. The veins in his arms stood out like cords.

'Do you know when the next swimming competition is starting?' he asked Apu.

Apu could not help him. He knew nothing about swimming competitions, but they got talking about swimming and sports. Gradually, it emerged that the older man had travelled abroad for many years, in Europe and America. Curious, Apu asked him his name. 'My name is Surendranath Basu-Mallik,' the man replied.

The name rang a bell instantly. Apu sat up and looked at him properly. After a few moments' silence, he said, 'I think I know you. Didn't you use to write a column called *Letters from England* in a magazine?'

'Yes, so I did! But that was a long time ago, more than ten years ago. How do *you* know about it? Did you ever read any of it?'

'Read? I used to devour every word, and live for the moment when the magazine arrived. I was only about ten at the time. I cannot tell you how your columns inspired me.'

Mr Basu-Mallik was very pleased to hear this. 'Strange, isn't it,' he remarked, 'how a few words written in one corner of the earth can affect someone thousands of miles away? I used to write those columns from my boarding house in Hempstead, and a little boy in an obscure village in Bengal read them with such eagerness ... good, good! Young man, I am so pleased to hear this!'

They continued to talk. The man no longer seemed a stranger to Apu. It was this man who was responsible for all those joyous moments of his childhood. It was through his columns that he had learnt about foreign lands; it was he who had sown the first seed of wanderlust in his young mind.

Apu returned home with new joy in his heart. Who knew he would meet the writer of those columns at a time when he needed to be pulled out of depression? Life itself was the biggest asset anyone could have. Apu knew now that it did not matter what he did, or where he went. His own will to live, and the flow of life that surrounded him, would hold him together, sustain and nurture him. Somehow, anyhow, he would find a way to live.

❧

It was dusk, but not yet dark. One of the young women from the house of the telis—called Boro Bou—was chatting with Sarbajaya at her front door. She saw Apu coming along the path and said with a smile, 'Guess who's coming to visit you, Ma Thakrun?'

142

Sarbajaya felt her heart flutter. Who was it? Apu? No, no, it couldn't be!

A minute later, she was running down the path to throw her arms round her son. She held him close, his sleeve became wet with her tears. To Apu, she seemed smaller, frailer and much more vulnerable than he remembered her. She had lost weight. Her hair—dry and unkempt—had come undone. But her face was still beautiful, the lines on her forehead still relatively smooth. Apu wanted to hold her, and protect her from all the worries, all the problems and every danger the world night heap upon her. He had never felt like this before.

That night, Sarbajaya made khichuri for Apu. It was one of his favourite dishes. After almost a week, Apu got to eat a full meal.

'Do you eat khichuri in the city?' Sarbajaya asked him.

When Apu was a child, his mother had veiled their poverty and the harsh realities of life through dozens of lies, a hundred little deceptions. Now it was Apu's turn. He replied, 'Yes. They make khichuri quite often.'

'And in the morning? What do you usually have for breakfast?'

Apu promptly gave her details of imaginary breakfasts: he had puris sometimes, he said, and sweets and tea. Food was no problem where he lived, he added.

He had lost his job as Preetibala's tutor months ago, but had not told Sarbajaya about it. Now she asked, 'That girl you teach ... she's quite rich, isn't she? Is she pretty?'

'Yes, she's quite good looking.'

'I wonder if they ... if they'll consider marrying her to you. Wouldn't that be nice?'

'Ma!' Apu laughed, now embarrassed, 'what a thing to say! Why should they even think about it? They're rich, and I ... well, just look at me!'

Sarbajaya remained unperturbed. She was convinced her son was a prize catch for any girl. 'Thank God she doesn't know the truth!' Apu thought silently. He had noticed that not once had his mother mentioned her own problems, or even referred to the fact that he had failed to send her any money when she was in dire need of it. On the contrary, she brought out a new bowl and a glass and said, 'Look, I got these for you in exchange of a few old torn cothes. Do you like them? See how big the bowl is?'

Apu looked at her beaming face and thought how easy it was to impress his mother. This bowl she was showing him was nothing. What would she have said if he could show her those lovely plates he had bought in chor bazaar?

The next few days passed very peacefully. After the grim struggle in Calcutta, Apu enjoyed every moment of this brief holiday. At night, he slept in the same room as his mother and asked her to sing, just as he had done as a child. Sarbajaya laughed and said, 'Don't be silly. I can't sing any more.'

'Of course you can. Come on, we could sing together. What was that song we used to sing back in Nischindipur?'

Sarbajaya remembered how difficult it had been to make Apu sing when he was a little boy. Occasionally, when the women in Nischindipur got together with their children, many of the little ones were asked to sing. Apu had a very sweet voice, but was painfully shy. Yet, there were times when he did want to sing. She could tell, because on such occasions, he came to her invariably and said, 'Don't ask me to sing today, Ma. I am not going to.' In actual fact, it meant just the opposite. So she would then say to him, 'All right, Apu, why don't you sing for us now?' After a few shy denials, Apu would start singing, happily enough.

She looked at her son, and could barely recognise him. Was this young man—so tall, so handsome, so strong—the

144

naughty child she had reared? Apu did not make childish demands any more, he did not hide to frighten her, he did not get cross if he was denied anything. But, in the look in his eyes, in his smile, Sarbajaya could still see her child—full of wonder, innocent, unspoilt. 'In my next life, dear God,' she prayed silently, 'let him come back again as my child. I ask for nothing else!' The joy Apu had given her in his childhood had filled her heart to the brim. It was the nectar of life that had provided her the strength to bear all the pain, all the sorrow of her later years.

Sometimes, Apu asked her to tell him stories. 'You read such a lot, and in English, too. Why don't *you* tell me a story?' Sarbajaya replied.

Apu talked about his college, his friends and his hopes for the future. Sarbajaya had plans, too. She would like to see him married, she said. 'Wait till you finish college. I've heard of a girl ... not far from here ....'

'I forgot to tell you, Ma,' Apu said suddenly, 'I met Jethima and Suresh da ... yes, the same Jethima from Nischindipur.'

'Really? What did she say to you? What did you get to eat at her place?'

Apu launched into a description of a great variety of imaginary food.

'That's good, very good. Tell me something, Apu? Will you take me to Calcutta one day? I've never been there. Couldn't I spend a couple of days at your Jethima's house, and go to Kali Ghaat?'

'Yes, of course. I'll take you after Durga Puja.'

Sarbajaya went on dreaming, 'Remember that mango orchard in Nischindipur, Apu? The one we once owned, and then it went to Bhuvan Mukherjee? I'd so like you to take it back from them. May be one day ...? When you are older, when you've got a job, and when you're married? It would be lovely, wouldn't it?'

It was nothing much to ask for. But to Sarbajaya it meant a great deal. Apu knew it. He could feel her pain. But what he was not sure of was whether she would survive long enough to do what she was planning. He shivered and tried to shake off this sudden feeling of foreboding. But his mother was certainly not getting any better. He tried to comfort her, staying by her when she fell asleep in the afternoon. When she woke, he placed a hand on her forehead and said, 'You're quite warm again, aren't you?' Sarbajaya brushed it off and began chatting again. 'Does your Jethima ever mention me? What *does* she talk about?'

Apu replied as best as he could, but his concern grew deeper. How was he going to live if anything happened to her? He looked out of the window quickly, and saw the setting sun casting its last golden rays on the wild plants that grew outside their fence, and on the small patch of land where Sarbajaya had grown spinach. Would she stay alive long enough to eat it? Would she ever go to Calcutta, or see their mango orchard again?

How lonely the evening was ... there was sadness everywhere ... in the fading daylight, in the noise the mynahs and babblers were making, even in the fragrance of the blossom that hung on the branches of the aata tree. His heart ached. Tears came to his eyes. But he forced a smile, and held his mother close.

Soon it was time to go back. His college was about to reopen. Apu left, but the boat he had to take to get to the railway station arrived late. Apu missed his train.

It was a difficult day for Sarbajaya. She had to keep herself busy, to stop herself from brooding. Late in the afternoon, she collected all the dirty clothes she could find and went to a pond to wash them. Apu arrived a little before dusk, dumped his luggage on the verandah, and ran to the pond. 'Ma!' he called from behind her.

Sarbajaya started, then turned and said with a mixture of disbelief and pleasure, 'You! You didn't go?' Apu grinned. 'No, I couldn't catch the train. Let's go home.'

For years afterwards, Apu remembered the look of pure joy and contentment that he saw on his mother's face that evening, in the shadow of a bamboo grove. He had never seen her look so happy before.

He returned to Calcutta the following day.

His college had reopened that morning. A list was hanging on the notice board, announcing the names of all those who had passed the exam, but had not been promoted to the second year because they had not paid their college fees. Apu scanned it quickly, expecting to find his name on top of the list. To his complete bewilderment, however, he found his name missing. How could this be? Why, he had not paid any fees for ten months!

A couple of days later, he went to the college office. There were other boys demanding to be told why they had not been promoted. 'You know very well, young man, why are you wasting my time?' said a clerk irritably, pointing at a register. 'Look, it's written here in black and white!'

Apu bent over the register with all the others. It was a complete list of all the students who had passed. Some had 'D' written in red ink against their names. It stood for 'Defaulter'. It was these students who had been denied promotion. But there was nothing against his own name, not even a tiny red speck.

It was obviously a mistake. Perhaps the same clerk had made a mistake, and that was all there was to it. But Apu came out, still in a daze. This little incident made a very deep impression on his mind.

A particular memory from his childhood came back to him. After the death of his sister, he had often sat by the river on winter evenings and wondered: had she gone to hell? He had read a description of hell in the Mahabharat. What was his sister doing there, surrounded by huge, terrifying birds, and the messengers of death, who were even worse? The very thought made a lump rise in his throat, and tears sprang to his eyes. All the kash by the riverside, and the silk cotton trees, appeared blurred. No, no, no, cried his heart. His lively, vivacious sister could never have gone to hell. It was not the right place for her.

Then, when a dull red, mysterious light filled the sky, his little childish mind begged the invisible power behind it: please, please, don't let any harm come to my sister. She has suffered enough. She doesn't deserve any more.

Many years had passed since that day. But Apu had not lost that simple, childish faith. Even a few days before returning to Calcutta, he had thought: why shouldn't things work out? I am going back to do something good. People pray for so many different things. I am praying for knowledge. Surely God will help me, grant me my prayer, in some way? His faith in God had, in fact, been strengthened by Mr Dutta, his principal in Diwanpur. He had often talked to him about God and religion, and taught him to believe. Perhaps he had known that, one day, his words would bear fruit in Apu's young mind.

❧◉❧

Classes started again, and so did the rains. It was August now. It drizzled continually, everywhere one looked the roads were muddy and full of puddles. Apu felt depressed and lonely once

148

more. A year ago, he had arrived here looking for opportunities. He did not know a soul. Now he knew a few people, it was true, but there had been no change in his own situation.

His room over the factory was gone. He was floating from one mess to another, depending on the kindness of some of his friends who agreed to share their room with him for a few days. His attempts at finding the job of a private tutor had failed, and the question of accommodation was causing him much anxiety. The friend he was currently with appeared to be quickly losing his patience. He knew Apu's situation, but did not hesitate to ask him one day why he was taking so long to find his own place. This hurt Apu very much.

Then it occurred to him that selling newspapers might be a good idea. Investigations revealed that each copy had to be bought for three paisa, straight from the office of a newspaper. Then it could be sold for four paisa, leaving a net profit of one. But where was his capital going to come from? Suddenly, he thought of Tiwari Bahu. She and her husband still lived in the factory. Bahu heard his plan, then lent him two rupees. 'I don't want any interest from you, Babuji,' she said, 'but we are going to our village for a visit in two month's time. Do you think you could return the money by then?'

Apu nodded vigorously. Tiwari Bahu was no less than a goddess. Apu felt deeply grateful to her.

He ran to the office of the *Amrita Bazar Patrika* the next day. But dozens of other people had already arrived there. Apu failed to fight his way through. By the time he could get his share of the papers, it was quite late. Then there was another unexpected problem. Apu discovered, to his dismay, that he was no good at all in calling out to people and hawking his papers. He felt shy and self-conscious if anyone so much as looked at him. But a lot of people did, if only because it was unusual to find a good-looking young man, clearly educated and from a good family, doing this job. 'Why are they all staring at me like that? Am I a clown, or what?' he thought crossly. Then he made himself go up to a man and say politely, without looking directly at him, 'Would you like a paper, sir? *Amrita Bazar*?'

On his first day, he could only sell eighteen. Things improved from the next day, however, as he felt a little more sure of himself. He managed to sell quite a few on trams.

Towards the end of the month, Apu acquired a partner. It happened in a rather dramatic manner. He arrived in his college one morning to find a commotion raging in front of the library. A lot of people were talking at once. Many voices were raised in anger.

It turned out that a boy from a different college had been to the library, and was trying to leave with a book tucked under his shirt. But he had been caught. The principal, who had been informed, seemed to be in favour of handing the boy over to the police. However, one of the senior lecturers intervened, and he was allowed to leave.

Apu recognised the boy when he saw him. He had met him last year when he used to have his evening meal at a temple. The boy was called Haren. He was a student of Metropolitan College. One evening, when it had suddenly started to rain heavily, Apu and Haren had both run to seek shelter under someone's portico. That was when they had got talking. Like Apu, Haren was a poor student. He, too, had to walk many miles just to have a free meal.

Instead of going to his class, Apu followed him out. Haren was walking as fast as he could, without really looking where he was going. When Apu caught up with him, he gave him a distraught look, then recognised him. Now he could not contain himself any more, and began crying openly. His situation, it turned out, was worse than Apu's. There was no one to help him in the city. The free meals had stopped, he owed a lot of money to various people, and was really at his wits' end.

Apu took him to Mirzapur Park, which happened to be close by, and made him sit on a bench. Then he looked properly at Haren. He was dark, his face pock-marked, his hair dry and dishevelled, the sleeve of his shirt ripped from the wrist up to his elbow. Apu felt his own eyes smart. 'Look,' he said, 'there *is* something you can do. Why don't you start selling newspapers? That's what I do. Come on, let's have something to eat. There's a man selling peanuts. Would you like some?'

Haren joined Apu the next day. They managed reasonably well until October, then things began to look grim again. Apu had very little money left after returning what he had borrowed from Bahu. Where was fresh capital going to come from?

In the meantime, the preliminary tests were over. Now he had to find a great deal of money once more to pay both the tuition fees for the second year, as well as the exam fees. This time, he would definitely not be allowed to take the exam without paying what was required. What was he going to do? Stand aside and watch all his other classmates walk into the examination hall? Who could he tell? Who would listen to him, anyway?

Help came most unexpectedly. Apu ran into Manmatha one day. With Anil and Pranav both gone, he had virtually no close friend left. Apu suddenly found himself confiding in Manmatha. Manmatha stared at him for a few seconds. Then he simply said, 'Why didn't you tell me before?'

To Apu's amazement, within a few days, Manmatha raised enough money to pay most of his outstanding tuition fees, chiefly by collecting contributions from both students and teachers. This was a big relief, but how was he going to pay his exam fees? Manmatha and another boy—the same boy Apu had once visited but had been unable to ask for help—

went to appeal to the principal. Couldn't a portion of Apu's tuition fees be waived? Then he could pay the exam fees with the money left over. Luckily, the principal agreed.

The question of the fees settled, Apu began to look for accommodation again. He went back to the manager of the factory. If he could get to stay in his old room for even three months, he would have a place where he could study. The manager was not available, but some of the other workers, who knew and liked Apu, gave him some useful advice. 'Go to Mr Lahiri,' they said. 'Mr Lahiri is one of the directors of this company. If you can bring a letter from him, our manager will let you have the room at once.'

Apu took Mr Lahiri's address and went to see him in Bhowanipore. But he was a busy man, his room was always full of people. Apu went three or four times, but could not get beyond the portico of his house. He just sat on a bench for hours, hoping to catch Mr Lahiri as he came out, but each time he had to return disappointed.

Then he went back on a Sunday, quite determined to have a meeting. Mr Lahiri was not at home, he was told, but was expected shortly. Apu sat on the same bench, and prepared himself for a long wait. To his astonishment, a maid emerged from the house a little later and said to him, 'Could you please come with me? Didimoni is calling you.'

Didimoni? A young woman? Why should a young woman from this house call him? Surely there was some mistake?

The maid shook her head. He had been spotted by her mistress, and she wanted to speak to him. Somewhat taken aback, Apu rose and followed her in. She took him down a narrow passage, past a large room filled with book cases, a huge felt-topped table and leather furniture, across a small courtyard with a chequered marble floor, and stopped before a smaller room. Through its open door, Apu could see a woman, eighteen or nineteen years old, sitting at a table, bent

152

over some papers and writing busily. Dressed in a simple saree with a red border, a light gold chain around her neck and gold bangles on her arms, her hair tied in a loose knot, she looked beautiful. The maid motioned him to go in. Apu stepped in rather uncertainly.

The woman glanced up and smiled, rising to her feet.

Was this a dream? Apu's jaw fell open, he could hardly believe his eyes. Almost involuntarily, he gasped, 'Leela!'

TWELVE

❧⟨◉⟩❧

Leela continued to look at him, a smile still playing on her lips. 'So you've recognised me? I could hardly recognise *you*!' she said. 'How long is it since we last saw each other? Eight years?'

Apu finally found his tongue. This beautiful young woman certainly was Leela, yes, but it was someone totally unknown to him. It was only the way she smiled and moved her hand that seemed familiar.

'Ye-es, at least eight years ... you look so different!' he exclaimed.

'I saw you twice before, on my way to college. I was getting into the car the other day, when I saw someone sitting under the portico, and I thought, where have I seen him before? Then, this morning, I happened to look out of the window of our drawing room, and saw you again ... and this time I knew who it was. I told my mother ... she's coming ... what are you doing here in Calcutta? Oh, Ripon College? How long ...? Two years, and you did not visit us in all that time!'

The warmth and affection in Leela's voice brought back memories of childhood. This was how she had always spoken to him. But a gap of eight years made Apu feel a little self-conscious.

'How could I have come? I didn't know where you lived,' he replied.

'Oh. So how come you are here today?'

Apu opened his mouth to speak, then shut it again. How could he tell Leela he was here to get himself a roof over his head? Fortunately, Leela went on speaking. 'How is Ma? Is she well? Good ... you are in your second year, aren't you? I am in my first year. Arts.'

An older lady entered the room. Apu felt surprised to see her. She was Leela's mother, he knew her as Mejo Bourani. Now she was dressed as a widow. Although she had not lost all her former beauty, it was difficult to recognise her at once. Apu touched her feet.

'Please sit down, Apurbo,' she said, 'Leela told me yesterday she had seen someone who looked like you ... then when she said this morning she was positive it was you, I told the maid to go and bring you inside.'

Leela's mother was no less affectionate towards him. As she asked after his mother, and about his studies, Apu could not help thinking fleetingly of Jethima and Suresh. Neither had ever shown half as much interest in his affairs as Mejo Bourani, and he had thought of *them* as his own people!

Mejo Bourani left after a while to get him something to eat.

'Er ... when did your father pass away?' Apu asked Leela when her mother had gone.

'Three years ago. We live here with my mother's family.'

'Oh, I see. How are you related to Mr Lahiri?'

'He's my grandfather. He's a barrister, but is now retired. My uncle has taken over now, he practises at the High Court. He returned from England last year.'

Tea and snacks were brought in. Apu ate what he could, then decided to take his leave. Leela invited him to a party just before he left.

'You must come to our house next Wednesday in the evening. It's my little cousin's birthday, you see. You *have* to come, Apurbo Babu, promise me you won't forget?'

Suddenly, Apu felt a little hurt. Apurbo Babu? Why did Leela have to turn all stiff and formal? If she thought of him as a friend—and her behaviour certainly indicated that she did—why add 'Babu' after his name?

Even when he got back home, he could not stop thinking of Leela. She held a special place in his heart, that no one else could take. But the woman he had rediscovered today was not the same whose memories he had cherished all these years. The Leela he had once known had faded into a distant dream. Would he ever be able to see her again? Was he pleased to have met her today, or had the meeting caused him pain? Apu was not altogether sure.

The following Wednesday, Apu washed his tulle shirt. 'I'll wear what I've got, there's no need to try and borrow anything from someone else,' he told himself. But he knew the tulle shirt was hardly the kind of garment one wore to a party. 'Why couldn't I meet Leela when I had a little money?' he thought wistfully, 'Why did it have to be now, when I have absolutely nothing?'

He was received by Mr Lahiri himself. A friendly man, he chatted with Apu for a while and made him feel quite at ease. Leela arrived in a few minutes, but could not stay for long. Other guests had started to pour in—men and women—

all fashionably dressed, exuding wealth and charm. Apu felt very proud to be sitting among them. How many young men got the chance to get invited to such a party? He couldn't wait to see his mother. Here was something worth talking about. How pleased she'd be, how proud!

The men sat with him in the drawing room, talking about subjects Apu knew nothing about. Many of them were either barristers or doctors, and some had studied in England. At first, two men were discussing local politics, then a debate began on whether or not a man with a university degree could turn to agriculture and make a success of it. A middle-aged man with salt-and-pepper hair, wearing golden-frame glasses, began speaking. He spoke with a drawl, and paused every now and then to inhale from his cheroot. 'Look, Mr Sen,' he said, 'you and I could not rush into agriculture. It must be bred in the bone. It isn't enough to simply buy farm equipment to make a go of it.'

His opponent was a man in his mid-thirties, dressed in western clothes, strong and well-built. He leant forward impatiently. 'Excuse me, Ramesh Babu, I think your argument is quite baseless. Do you mean to say things like education, organisation, capital—none of these have a role to play in agriculture?'

'It has, but only a secondary one.'

'Really? So you think no one but the child of a farmer can ever go into agriculture? Because it is not bred in his bone? That's absurd. Let me tell you something. When I was in Cambridge, an Irish boy used to study with me. He was good-looking, had long hair, and his temperament was really that of a poet. He could stay awake all night, having a good time with his friends; then he'd suddenly start playing his violin, or he'd write, or just sit quietly and think. Do you know what he did once he'd got his degree? He went to Canada and got himself a plot of wild, uncultivated land. He spent the next three or four years in that unbearable cold, living in a small wooden cottage. The law said one had to live on the land for five years before one could own it fully, so he just stayed on. He cleared it himself, working alone—two hundred acres of land, can you imagine? Just think how long....'

In a different part of the room, another lively discussion was underway. Someone was saying, 'This morality you are talking about ... well, all that is now old fashioned. Surely you'd agree that it was once created under special circumstances, just to protect a society, or an individual? So ...'

'Is that what you think? Then I must say you are all opportunists. Isn't there any such thing left as normative values? What if ...?'

At first, Apu was perfectly happy just to listen, and look around. How beautiful that electric lamp was with its marble shade! And those attractive chintz covers on the settee, all the expensive furniture, large mirrors on the wall, huge roses in brass vases from Moradabad. Could anyone ever have imagined that he would one day be included in a gathering like this? He, who was only a boy from a poor family in a small village, who had had to walk for miles to go to a school? Apu's heart brimmed with joy. Wasn't this what he had always dreamt of? To be a part of the educated and sophisticated class? He wanted to savour every moment of it.

A man wearing a pince-nez was sitting next to Apu. He was still deeply engrossed in an argument with an older man sitting opposite. Young, fit, smart and well-dressed, the man was a barrister and spoke well. His name was Heerak Sen. It suddenly occurred to Apu that he should make a contribution to the conversation, instead of letting it simply wash over him. He might never get the chance to come to such a party again. If he could say something now, later he could think about it, recapture the moment ... wouldn't that make his happiness complete?

The subject of the debate had changed from agriculture to something quite different.

' ... I don't know, Bimal Babu,' the man with the pince-nez was saying. '*I* think the human body is like an engine. An engine would run as long as there's steam inside it. If it runs out of steam, well ... that's the end of everything, surely?'

Apu thought this was his moment. Yes, this was something he could comment on. He had to make an effort to overcome his shyness, but he did succeed eventually and blurted out, a little desperately, 'Sorry, sir, I'm afraid I cannot agree with you. It's all right to compare the human body with an engine, but if you're trying to say that it's the body that's all important....' His voice trailed away. Everyone in the room had stopped talking and was staring at him, some with open surprise, others with a mixture of curiosity and amusement. Apu realised this, became even more self-conscious and tried very hard to conceal it. He began speaking again, but someone interrupted him and said, 'May I ask you, sir, what you do for a living?'

'I ... I am a student. I will take my IA finals this year.'

The man with the pince-nez turned to Apu. 'Would it not be better, sir, if you tried offering your views *after* spending a few more years at the university?' he said. His voice was so quiet and he uttered the words with such solemnity that everyone burst out laughing. Apu's face turned as red as a pomegranate.

If he had not already convinced himself that he was inferior to every man present in the room, that he did not really deserve to be a part of such a smart crowd, that it was a matter of great honour for him to be here, Apu might have felt anger. But he simply could not think of himself as an equal. Even to get angry called for a certain amount of confidence and courage. Apu could not find it. His face hot with embarrassment, he blundered on. 'What has studying at a university got to do with anything? I know for sure that no student in the final year of graduation could beat me in any subject, be it history, or poetry or general knowledge!'

He had no idea how childish his words sounded. Everyone started laughing again. Then they proceeded to ignore him completely, and went back to chatting among themselves. Apu sat there for another half an hour, but he had become invisible to the others. When they left, they shook hands with one another, without so much as a glance at Apu.

He sat mutely, stupefied by the open rudeness of these other people. 'Never mind,' he told himself fiercely. 'How does it matter if they aren't interested in me, or what I know? Only one person knew me well, and that was Anil.' Then he tried to slip away, but Leela caught him and took him inside the house. She knew nothing of what had happened in the drawing room … dear God, she must never find out!

'Look, Ma, I found Apurbo Babu trying to leave without having had his meal!' she said. Then she pointed at a boy of about nine, and said: 'Do you know who this is? He's my little brother. I had invited you to come to his annaprashan, years ago. Remember?'

Some of her classmates were present in the room. 'He can sing very well,' Leela declared, having introduced him. 'But heaven knows if he'll agree to sing here. I have known him since we were both children, and I've never seen anyone so shy. Will you *please* sing tonight?'

Leela's friends turned out to be a persuasive lot. Apu had to give in in the end. The evening ended far better than he'd expected after the fiasco in the drawing room.

But, as he finally made his departure after a very good meal, he told himself firmly, 'I'll never go back to that house. What have I to do with the rich and the wealthy? Never again!'

The turmoil in his heart took a long time to subside.

Apu received a letter from home five days before his exams were to begin. It had been written by Boro Bou from the house of the telis, to let him know that Sarbajaya was ill.

He reached Monshapota the same day, but not before it was dark. Sarbajaya was lying in bed, wrapped in a kantha. She sat up quickly as she saw him arrive. She had been ailing for quite some time, but had not told Apu for fear of disturbing him before his exams. Seeing that she was not getting any better, her neighbour had taken it upon herself to inform Apu. The strange thing was that it did not appear to be serious; or, at least, it did not keep her confined to bed all the time. She felt unwell in the evenings, and her nights were full of discomfort, but she felt better during the day and went about her household chores. However, Apu did not fail to notice that she was looking weak and frail.

'Don't get up, Ma! Have you got a temperature? Let me see?' he asked anxiously.

'No, no, don't be silly. It's nothing. This is normal, I mean I've had it before at this time of the year ... I'll be better by April. Sit down and tell me about yourself. How's that young girl you teach?'

She was still referring to Preetibala. The smile on her wan face now brought tears to his eyes. He quickly untied the bundle he was carrying and took out a few oranges, apples and a pomegranate. Knowing how pleased Sarbajaya always felt if one could buy things cheap, he pointed at the oranges and said, 'Do you know how much I paid for these in the city? Only ten paisa!'

The truth was that they had cost him thirty.

Sarbajaya leant forward eagerly, 'Really? Let me have a look. These ... these would be at least fifty paisa here. Our market is full of bandits!'

'And look at this bundle of paan. I bought it for just two paisa.' He had actually paid four.

Sarbajaya looked at him and thought: he's growing up. He's learnt to manage his money so much better.

Apu toyed with the idea of telling her about his meeting with Leela, then decided against it. He knew the impossible dreams his mother cherished in her heart. She might well get excited and say, 'Couldn't you and Leela get married one day?' What was the point in raising her hopes? She had suffered enough.

Apu took care not to talk of anything that he felt she would not understand. In the three days that he spent with her, he described his world only in terms that he knew would suit her limited understanding.

Every day, Sarbajaya went to bed soon after lunch. Apu sat by her, talking constantly. Gradually, the afternoon sun moved to the west, falling first on the roof of the kitchen, then climbing on to the top of the madaar tree by the fence, before reaching the bamboo grove. The shadows lengthened, making Apu feel alone and solitary, just as he had felt during the summer holidays.

Sometimes, Sarbajaya would smile and say, 'I'll have you married as soon as you finish college. I've spoken to someone, you know. It was the girl's grandmother. A very nice woman. She visited me here....'

Apu's eyes would fall on the shelves on the wall. Sarbajaya kept special foodstuff on these: a jar of pickle, or a pot of mango-cake. An old habit made him get up and walk stealthily across for something to eat, hoping his mother wouldn't see him. This was not difficult since Sarbajaya lay with her eyes closed.

On his last day, however, she opened her eyes unexpectedly and caught him in the act.

'What do you think you are doing?' she scolded. 'That pickle's not yet ready to eat. I have to put it out in the sun, it'll take a few days ... *don't* touch it with your dirty hands.

162

Must you stand so close to that shelf? No, no, that's my new gamchha and you've happily spread it on your shoulder ... honestly, Apu, you're not a child any more, but you do behave like one!'

A sudden thought pierced his heart. Here she was, talking of getting up and placing jars of pickle in the sun, but would she? Apu shivered. Suppose she never got up again? Suppose she ...? Why, didn't he see her face only yesterday, when he was stealing a piece of mango-cake? She had looked so pathetic, so helpless, burning with a high fever, her eyes tightly shut. The hands that had held the reins of her house and his life for twenty-one years were losing their grip. Would they ever be able to regain their strength and their lost control?

Apu left on the fourth day. He had to, for his exams started the following day. He promised to return as soon as they were over. To his amazement, when he woke at dawn that day, he found his mother already up and bustling about in the kitchen, simply so she could fry him hot parathas, and pack his lunch before he left.

This had never happened to Sarbajaya before. When Apu left, it seemed as if the world had come to an end. In the evening, particularly, her heart felt heavy with a strange loneliness she had never experienced before. It seemed as if everyone she had ever known had left her to face life alone. She felt completely helpless. Memories came crowding round, little events she had long forgotten, some happy, some that still brought tears to her eyes.

This had been happening to her for over a month. Every time she found herself alone, unable to keep busy with her work, scenes from the past would fill her mind. She remembered her childhood. They had a cow called Budhi ... and there was Himi, her best friend. Sarbajaya and Himi had planted marigold, which they watered religiously. Once, when their village was flooded, they had gone for a swim, clutching their pitchers, and nearly got drowned ...!

Her wedding ... it had rained heavily during the day. Her little brother—he was then alive—had smuggled in a sweet and thrust it into her hand, although as the bride, she was not supposed to eat anything until after the wedding.

Apu ... little baby Apu, like a doll ... when he learnt to talk, the first word he said, for some obscure reason, was 'wet'. She had given him a sweet, to keep him quiet for a while ... did you like it, Apu, how was it? ... Little Apu sucked the sweet in his toothless mouth, then raised his beautiful face and said, 'wet'. Thinking about it brought a smile to her lips, even today.

She developed a sharp, piercing pain in her chest that afternoon. Boro Bou dropped in to see her a couple of times, then massaged her chest with hot oil. But she had to go back home in the evening, and Sarbajaya was alone once more, in her empty little house. She could feel her temperature rising.

Soon, it was dark. The moon rose, large and nearly full ... it would be a full moon in just two days. For the first time in her life, Sarbajaya felt afraid to be alone. As the night grew darker, she began to feel breathless, as if she had dropped to the bottom of a lake and couldn't get out again. Choking and perspiring profusely, she tried to sit up, forcing herself to take a few deep breaths. Now she felt absolutely terrified. What was happening to her? Was she going to die? Was this how death came?

Who could she turn to at this time of night? She made a supreme effort to pull herself together. *Why* was she so

164

frightened? Why was she thinking of death? Surely death did not come like this? This was nothing ... it would pass ... she was just being foolish.

She had done so many things in her life that were wrong, even sinful ... how many times had she stolen, just to feed her children? A bunch of bananas from somebody's private land, or a cucumber from their kitchen garden, hiding it under her bed, pushing it out of sight. Once she had borrowed ten spoonfuls of oil from a neighbour, but returned only five—and that, too, to the neighbour's sister-in-law, who hadn't been present the first time. 'I only took five, honestly!' she had said. How many lies had she told, how many times had she been insulted in her life? All her life? But why was she thinking of all this today? Why couldn't she stop?

The room was totally dark. What was that noise under her bed? Mice! It was time to get a mousetrap, or nothing would be left of the grains she had stored away in sacks.... But was it really just mice? Or was it something else? That irrepressible terror returned, crawling up from her toes, rising higher, spreading a cold numbness as it rose. No, it wasn't her toes. The numbness was creeping up from the tips of her fingers ... why couldn't she believe the noise was being caused simply by scurrying mice? What else could it be? She had never had such strange thoughts before, such absurd doubts.... Suddenly, another thought flashed through her mind: it was not fear that was tickling first her feet with icy fingers, then her hands, and then her whole body. It was death. Death? Petrified, she tried to clamber to her feet, she tried to scream ... for some time she thought she had succeeded ... she'd screamed herself hoarse with all the power left in her lungs; she was exhausted now, she couldn't go on screaming ... but no one heard her, no one came. With a start, she realised she hadn't moved an inch, she was still lying in bed; nor had she uttered a single sound. It was all in her mind.

That creepy, crawly feeling had frozen her body, as if a huge black spider had caught her in its web, paralysing her with its poison ... she couldn't move even a muscle.

The earth glowed in the moonlight. There was only one person she could think of ... Apu ... Apu ... how could she leave him? It was impossible! Now, to her astonishment, she realised she had been crying all this while without knowing it. Why, her pillow was wet with tears!

How glorious the moonlight was ... her terror seemed to ebb away ... now there was joy, and so much love! The sky ... the old, familiar sky, seemed to melt with the love that surged through her heart ... melt into the moonlight and pour down on earth ... drip, drip, drip, drip ... until the last drop was finished.

Tears welled up in her eyes again ... who was standing at her window, silhouetted against the moonlight, smiling at her? Sarbajaya's eyes fixed themselves on the window, her thin, pale face lit up with wonder and pleasure. Apu! It was Apu. But not the Apu who had left her ... this was the little child she had held in her arms in her home in Nischindipur. She had seen this face so many times during the dark nights in March, just like this night, when the moonlight had come through the thick bamboo groves, seeped in through her broken windows and played on her child's face—a face as sweet and as pure as a flowering bud.

Little Apu ... his eyes had held such innocent wonder ... his hair was a mass of curls ... simple, shy, quiet and dreamy, he had known nothing of the ways of the world ... where had he gone? soaring high in the sky ... higher and higher ... beyond the dark blue clouds ... beyond the stars ... higher and still higher ... until he slipped between wisps of clouds and she could see him no more.

Death had come to fetch her. Death was standing at her door, but it had come in the guise of her child, to embrace

her with love, to lift her with infinite tenderness ... what a
sweet smile it had ... death was so utterly beautiful!

❧

When Boro Bou arrived in the morning, she found the front
door unlocked.

'The poor lady must be very sick indeed, she couldn't even
get up to lock her door,' she said to herself as she stepped in.

Sarbajaya lay in her bed, apparently in deep slumber. Her
neighbour hesitated before trying to wake her. She had never
seen her sleep so peacefully. But she had to be woken, if only
to say what she wanted done for her. Boro Bou called her
a couple of times, but got no reply. Sarbajaya did not move.
Boro Bou tried once more, then—suddenly suspicious—came
forward for a closer look.

In an instant, she realised what had happened.

❧

The news of Sarbajaya's death aroused a rather strange feeling
in Apu's heart. It was partly joy ... incredible as it might seem,
the truth was that when he received a telegram from the telis
in Monshapota telling him that his mother had died, his
immediate reaction was to feel a sudden surge of relief, as
if he had just broken away from a shackle. It did not last for
more than a few seconds, however, and was quickly replaced
by fear and shame. What was he thinking of? How could he
feel relief at his mother's death? Hadn't he seen her spend
every moment of her life working to make him happy? And
did he think of her as a shackle, a stumbling block on his
way? How could he be so cruel, so completely heartless?

But no amount of self-reproach could wipe away the
truth. He *had* felt an odd mixture of joy and relief, just for

a second, there was no denying that. He, who had loved his mother with all his heart!

Confused and upset, Apu left for his village. He got off the train at Ula, and decided to walk the rest of the way. This was going to be his first visit home, knowing that there was no one there to greet him with a smile. As he passed the river—a thin, narrow strip at this time of the year, he could walk across if he wanted to—he realised his mother must have been cremated by its bank the day before.

He reached home in the evening to find that the front door was locked. Who would have the key? The telis next door, perhaps. Apu sat on the step that led to the front verandah. Then his eyes fell on a bunch of burnt straw lying in the courtyard. He gave an involuntary shudder. He knew the rituals that had to be observed after a cremation. Those who had taken his mother must have returned here to warm their hands over a freshly-lit fire, and chew a few neem leaves to purify themselves.

His mother had gone for ever ... she was no more ... and he'd never be able to see her again. A part of his mind had still not taken it in, but the sight of those charred bits of straw came as a merciless reminder of the bitter truth. The silent earth and the red-gold sky only echoed the pain in his heart. He was now totally alone in the world. Apu stared at the pile of straw with empty, unseeing eyes.

Then he noticed something else. The kantha Sarbajaya had been using of late was hanging from a rack in the open courtyard. It was one she had stitched herself years ago, with paisley motifs in red thread. What was it doing here? Surely it should have been destroyed, when they destroyed the body?

Apu could not tell how long he had been sitting outside when the teli's son, Nadu, turned up and said, 'When did you get here, Dadathakur? How long have you been sitting

168

here like this? Why didn't you come straight to our house? Come with me now, and we'll ...'

'No,' Apu interrupted him. 'Could you just get me the key, please, if you have it? I'd like to go in and see what's to be done with my mother's things.'

Nadu brought the key. 'I'll be back soon, Dadathakur,' he said, 'you go and have a look inside.'

Apu stepped in. His mother's bed was lying empty. The sheet, the pillow, even the mattress had been removed. There was a bowl under the bed with something soaking in it. He picked it up. There were some herbs ... his mother's only treatment for her illness.

Footsteps sounded outside. A voice said, 'Who's inside?' Apu replaced the bowl where he had found it and came out. It was Nirupama, the same woman who had been a witness to his various mistakes as a young priest. He had grown very fond of her over the years.

'You!' Nirupama sounded very surprised. 'No one told me you were here. When did you arrive?'

'I don't know ... half an hour ago, may be.'

'Oh. I came only to put that kantha back. I washed it this morning.'

'Why? Wasn't ... wasn't Ma still using it?'

'No. She told Boro Bou to remove it the day before she passed away. It was something she thought you might use, so she did not want it spoilt. What she had on when ... when she was found was an old blanket. But even so, I thought I'd wash the kantha and put it back. Look, Apu, you must come back with me to our house. No, you really must. You haven't eaten all day, have you?'

Apu followed her like a robot. How did Nirupama guess he had not eaten? Why, Nadu saw him, too. *He* didn't say anything.

Nirupama's family treated him with great kindness. The old Mr Sarkar offered him a lot of comfort. Then Nirupama brought him fruit on a small plate. Apu was now supposed to be on a special diet until all the rituals following Sarbajaya's death were over. Bearing this in mind, Nirupama herself had soaked moong daal, and crushed and mixed it with banana and jaggery. Apu had never eaten anything mashed by someone else. At first, he felt faintly sick to raise it to his mouth; but realised after the first mouthful that it tasted no different from what he himself might have produced.

Later, Nirupama helped him light a stove and cook his own meal.

Apu returned to Calcutta after the final ritual was over. He took his mother's nutcracker, her nailcutter and a couple of money-order receipts bearing her signature. Just before he stepped out, his eyes fell on the shelf on which the jars of pickles and chutneys were still standing. These and a few other belongings were still there, to be touched and used and consumed by anyone who happened to come along. There was no one to stop or scold. Apu could feel a lump rising in his throat. He did not want this. No, he did not wish to be free, he did not want total independence.... Come back, Ma, scold me again, stop me from touching these objects, beat me, if you like ... just come back. Just be here again.

Apu came back to Calcutta, but discovered that he could no longer take an interest in anything. His exams were over. He felt lonely and depressed all the time ... all he wanted to do was get away somehow, away from the city. But where could he go to? Who could he go to? Now he was truly alone in the whole world.

170

Unable to stay indoors, he often rushed out of the little lane he lived in, and watched the people on the main road, travelling by car, or stopping for a minute to go into a park. How happy they seemed! Big families came together sometimes, the parents had their children, the children had their siblings, or cousins and aunts and uncles. Why was he so totally alone? Even visits to the library did not help for he could not concentrate on anything at all. He went in, only to feel restless and charge out again. If only he could get away ... to the Himalayas, to Kedar Badri, Haridwar, walk in dark pine woods, meet holy men, visit temples ... he had read so much about these things. Surely setting off on his own should not be a problem?

But he had no money. Even the puja after his mother's death had had to be arranged with money given by others. The telis had given him twenty rupees, Boro Bou had given an additional ten, and Nirupama had given him fifteen. He had not kept any of it for himself.

Three months passed. In his later years, Apu did not like looking back on these months. In fact, if he happened to be passing the little lane, he would perhaps glance at it from the main road, but he never stepped in to look at his old house.

Towards the end of June, he saw an advertisement. Men were needed because of the war. An office in Park Street was handling appointments. He went there that afternoon. The recruiting officer was sitting behind a table littered with printed forms. Apu picked one up and asked, 'Where would you send your men?'

'Mesopotamia. We need people to work in the railway and transport departments. Have you any experience with the telegraph, or perhaps you can work as a motor mechanic?'

'No. I have no such experience, but I could handle clerical work.'

'Sorry. We are looking only for those who might have technical knowledge of some kind ... you know, drivers, or men to operate signals, even station masters.'

Apu came away and went back to roaming the streets. It was while walking aimlessly one day that he met Leela again. He was waiting to cross a road in Dalhousie Square, when he heard someone call his name from a yellow Minerva car that was caught in the traffic. He turned to find that it was Leela, together with a few other women he could not recognise. Her brother was sitting next to the driver.

'What a strange man you are, Apurbo Babu!' Leela exclaimed, 'Why didn't you come to our house again in these three months? You just disappeared after that night. Why, my mother ...' she broke off, suddenly noticing his changed appearance. 'Why, what's the matter?' she asked. 'Have you been ill? Why is your hair so short? What's happened?'

Apu smiled, 'Nothing. Nothing happened. I am fine.'

'How is your mother?'

'Ma? Ma is no more. She's gone, she died last April.'

Apu laughed—loudly, a little madly.

Leela stared at him. Perhaps the passage of long years had dimmed the affection she had once felt for Apu, perhaps the wealth she had inherited had started to change slowly the sweet and unspoilt outlook with which she had viewed him as a child; but now, the look in his eyes and his senseless laughter, pierced Leela's heart like a sharp knife. In a flash, she grasped the whole situation. Apu was motherless, friendless, penniless, simply roaming around like a vagabond ... who was going to take care of him?

For a few seconds, she could not speak. Then she found her voice and said, ' You must come to our house tomorrow. You should have told us before ... at least you could have met my mother ... promise me you will come tomorrow morning? Oh, by the way, give me your address. Don't forget, please, I'll wait for you!'

The car left. Apu went back home, deep in thought. He had not missed the look of instant sympathy that had sprung in Leela's eyes. For months, his heart had ached for sympathy and comfort. Leela and Mejo Bourani would certainly be able to give him that ... but, no he could not bring himself to visit them again. Not now. Not like this.

Three days later, he received a letter. This was surprising, for no one except Sarbajaya had ever written to him. Who could have sent him a letter now? He opened it quickly.

'Dear Apurbo Babu,' it said, 'you were supposed to come to our house on Monday. It is now Friday, but we are still waiting to see you. My mother, particularly, would very much like to see you. I hope you will be able to visit us at five o'clock this evening. We shall be expecting you.' It was signed 'Leela'.

Apu spent a long time thinking things over. Should he go, or shouldn't he? What good would it do if he did? They were rich people; in what way could he think of himself as an equal? What gave him the right to visit them whenever he felt like it? It was good of Mejo Bourani to have thought of him. She was a kind lady. But how could she ever take the place of his own mother? Mejo Bourani was a rich man's daughter and a rich man's wife. The place in Apu's heart that was reserved for his mother could only be occupied by Sarbajaya. She had earned it, through her love, her pain, her sorrow, her failings and the thousand insults she had suffered in her life. Another woman, who travelled in a huge Minerva car, could never gain the right of entry into his heart and replace his mother, no matter how kind or affectionate she might be.

173

Towards the end of the month, Apu's final results came out. He had passed with distinction, and had obtained the highest marks in Bengali. He would be given a gold medal for that, he learnt. But he could think of no one he might share this news with. The few friends he had left had all gone home for the summer holidays.

Should he go to Suresh's house and tell his mother? After all, they were family. But he decided against it. Jethima might not like it if he turned up unexpectedly. Why invite trouble?

THIRTEEN

All the colleges reopened by the middle of July, but Apu made no attempt to get himself admitted anywhere. Professor Basu called him to his office one day and tried to persuade him to do an honours course in history. But Apu declined. He saw no point in doing a BA course. He could read enough at the Imperial Library that would teach him more than the course syllabus. Besides, he did not have the money to pay the required admission and tuition fees.

He had to find a job, though. The little money he had saved during the time when he was selling newspapers had dwindled ages ago. Now, after his mother's death, he could not find the energy to start again. All he had was the job of a private tutor. His pupil was a small boy. But the money he earned could barely pay for simple meals. For days on end,

175

all he had been able to cook for himself had been just boiled rice, potatoes and some daal. He did need more money to pay his rent, buy new clothes and other necessities. Besides, he had learnt through bitter experience that the job of a private tutor was as transient as a drop of water on a lotus leaf. It might be here today, but who could guarantee that it would be there tomorrow?

After many days of scanning every newspaper, Apu first went to a chemist called Pioneer Drugs. Their factory and shop both were in the same premises. When Apu presented himself, there were very few people around. He came face to face with a fat, middle-aged man.

'Are you looking for someone?' he asked.

Apu smiled shyly, 'I came ... I'm here because I saw your advertisement.'

'I see. And did you pass your matric exam?'

'Oh yes. I finished IA ...'

The fat man lost interest immediately. 'No, you wouldn't do,' he said, leaning back on his pillow. 'We're not looking for someone who's been to college. All we want is a man who can help with labelling and bottling our stuff. It's gruelling hard work, too, and we cannot pay more than fifteen rupees to start with. No, it isn't something a young college student like you would like doing.'

Apu left. A few days later, he went to a hardware shop on Clive Street. The man who met him here was very fashionably dressed, but his face was hard, the look in his eyes both cold and lewd. Apu associated such a look with men who drank and had questionable morals.

'What do *you* want here?' the man asked, with undisguised contempt.

Apu swallowed, feeling small. This man looked like the spoilt son of a rich man. Apu had seen similar men while living in Burdwan, in Leela's house. He knew the type.

'I believe you need workers here? I passed my IA ...' he began, but was cut short immediately.

'What can you do? Do you know typewriting? No? Well then, get out of here. We're not interested in degrees ... get lost!'

Apu happened to mention this incident to an uncle of his pupil. He sympathised. 'These hardware shops are all the same!' he exclaimed. 'Just because they're making a lot of money right now—because of the war, you know—they think they own the earth. Even the small-time agents are making quick money now.'

'Really?' Apu asked eagerly. 'Couldn't *I* become an agent?'

'Why not? Look, my father-in-law is an agent in the big market in Clive Street. I'll take you there. An educated young man like you should be able to do well.'

Apu began visiting Clive Street from the next day, but discovered soon that no one was even prepared to speak to him. After making a round of all the shops, someone finally asked him, 'Can you get us screws? Five-by-five jaws?' Apu had no idea what this meant. But he noted it down in his book; at least it was something to look for. However, when he got nowhere with his queries, he realised that he had been asked to get such a thing only because the shop knew it would not be easy for him to find it.

One day, he learnt that the United Machinery Company were looking for lead pipes. Apu got the details and agreed to procure and deliver it, without really realising what he was letting himself in for. As things turned out, neither the buyer nor the supplier agreed to pay for delivery. Apu got the material loaded on a bullock cart at his own risk, telling himself that he would pay its driver from his own commission. After all, this was his first job; surely it was the experience that counted, more than the money?

When he demanded his commission, however, he drew a blank. The buyer refused to believe that he had not included it in the price he had quoted. Apparently, every agent did that, and that was the normal practice. Apu had been totally unaware of this, but he failed to convince anyone. Bewildered, he looked around, but the driver of the cart blocked his way. 'Who's going to pay *me*?' he asked.

An old Muslim had been standing in a corner and watching the whole spectacle. When Apu was finally free, he approached him. 'Babu, how long have you been doing this work? You don't know much, do you?'

Apu was obliged to admit his lack of experience. 'Well,' said the man, 'you appear to be educated. Why don't you join me? I deal with big machinery—engines, boilers, things like that. You could make more than five hundred rupees at one go. My only problem is that I don't know any English. If you could join me ...?'

Apu felt himself going over the moon. Even the money he had just had to part with simply to pay the driver of the cart did not seem to matter any more. He spoke at length with the Muslim, whose name was Abdul. Apu gave him his address, and agreed to meet him in Clive Street the next day at ten.

That night, Apu thought: perhaps this will finally take me somewhere. I'll get to earn a little money.

A whole month passed. Nothing happened. Abdul said to him one day, 'How do you expect to get any work if you keep disappearing every day after two o'clock? Where do you go, anyway?'

'The Imperial Library. I read there until seven every evening. If you come there one day, I can show you what a big library it is.'

The library attracted him like a magnet, particularly the section on history. But he had read enough about wars and revolutions. Where could he find the true story of man? Not

178

kings and queens who had dazzled historians with their political moves, or their glamorous costumes, but the poor, common man. What happened to him when he ran out of food on a long journey? Or, when a young son could gather enough money to buy a new horse, who knew with what joy he had filled his mother's heart? The library was packed with the history of the last six thousand years, but no one had made a record of these tiny details. There were volumes on the policies of emperors in India, or other rulers in China, or England, or Greece or Rome. But Apu wanted to read about the lives that had been lived every day by the corn fields, or olive groves, or the vineyards, or the shadows under myrtle bushes in these countries. How had they spent their lives? What were their joys and sorrows? What gave them hope? What caused them despair? He wanted to know about it all, feel every heartbeat.

Something else struck him. It was the continuous march of time. He was not particularly concerned with whether one historian had recorded past events with more accuracy than another. What intrigued him was simply the passage of time, and what it did to man. Thousands of years ago, there had been all those kings, queens, emperors, ministers, slaves, greedy noblemen, young men and women. Many of them had betrayed close friends for money and power, and thrown them, without any hesitation, before the executioner's axe. Where had they gone? In the eternal ocean of time, they had all disappeared like frothy bubbles. How had their efforts been rewarded? Even when their greed was satisfied, what had they achieved?

❧

Apu continued to run around in the hardware market, but nothing seemed to work. He had no wish to make a great deal of money, but making even a little proved impossible. The atmosphere in Clive Street choked him. Everywhere he looked. there were people talking of profits and losses, trying to get a good bargain, always moving with caution. Their constant talk of money struck Apu as both obscene and frightening. Every day, he ran away to the library to gain a few moments of peace and quiet.

One day, Abdul asked to borrow two rupees. He was in dire need, he said. He would return it the following week. Perhaps he had a family. Apu knew only too well what it meant to be penniless. He brought a rupee from home the next day and gave it to Abdul. His own regular source of income still came from that small job as a tutor.

About a week later, Apu was woken by the sound of someone knocking on his door. He opened it to find Abdul standing outside, a smile on his face.

'Oh, it's you, Abdul! Come in, come in. What brings you here?'

'Adaab, Babu. Let's talk inside. It's a nice room. Do you live here alone?'

'No, sit down. Would you like a cup of tea?'

After finishing his tea, Abdul revealed the reason for his arrival. He had heard that a big boiler was available for sale somewhere in Barrackpore. More importantly, he had also found a buyer for that boiler. If they could sell it, they would make a neat profit of at least three hundred rupees. The only problem was that one of them had to go to Barrackpore immediately to see the boiler, and pay them an advance. Abdul himself had no money. What were they going to do?

'But won't the buyer himself wish to inspect the boiler?' Apu asked.

'Yes, of course. But we have to see it first, before showing it to the buyer. I know the buyer well. Even if we get only one and a half per cent, we still make four hundred and fifty.

Don't worry about the buyer, Babu. What I need to know is how to find the money straightaway.'

Apu had received his salary only the day before. 'How much do you need?' he asked.

Abdul made a rough calculation. It was decided finally that eight rupees would tide them over for the moment. Abdul would go to Barrackpore at once and report to Apu in the evening. Apu took out eight rupees and gave it to Abdul.

In the evening, he went back to Clive Street and waited eagerly for Abdul. Abdul did not turn up—not that day, nor the next. More than a week passed, but there was no sign of him. Apu looked everywhere, asked everyone he knew. One of the shops said, 'Abdul? He's a big crook. How much did he take from you? You'll never get it back, rest assured. Why did you give it to him at all?'

At first, Apu did not believe this. Abdul was a good man. Besides, why should Abdul try to cheat him, of all people?

Gradually, however, he was forced to face the truth. It turned out that Abdul had gone back to his village. Before his departure, he had collected all his payments, seven or eight days ago. Old Mr Biswas, who sold screws and nails, said, 'How come you saw him regularly for months, and still didn't realise what kind of a man he was? A number one fraud, that's Abdul. You should have made enquiries about him, you know. Everyone knows him here. That's why he's had to leave the hardware market, and is trying to get into big machinery. But thank goodness you lost only eight rupees. It might have been worse.'

It might, indeed. But eight rupees was all Apu had had with him. To Mr Biswas, it might have appeared a small amount. To Apu, it was everything. He had handed over his entire salary to Abdul. How was he going to manage now? Feeling totally distraught, Apu walked past the noisy share

181

market in Clive Street, and went on walking, until he passed the house of the Viceroy and found himself in the Maidan. Then he went to the south of the fort, and finding a quiet corner, sat down under an almond tree.

Only this morning, his landlord had reminded him about his overdue rent. He owed his roommate some money, too, who was getting increasingly impatient. Apu badly needed a new shirt, and had decided to get one made this month, even if it proved difficult to find the money. Where was a single penny going to come from? How could Abdul cheat him like this? Why, he had thought of him as a friend, and trusted him so much as someone who had stood by him in his hour of need!

He sat alone for a long time in the blazing sun. It was about half past one. The sky was clear, with only a few kites flying like tiny black dots, rising further and further away. A grasscutter was cutting the grass which had grown long and thick in the recent rains. In the distance, a tram was going to Kidderpore. On the river, he could see the tall mast of a ship; on the fort, too, there were radio masts ... one, two, three, four ... how blue the sky looked! Suddenly, Apu realised something. Here was the open beauty of nature everywhere ... in the trembling heat of an August afternoon, and the boundless blue sky above. It made him think of a different world. The sun ... the stars ... memories of his mother, his sister, Anil ... the world beyond death, where in the eternal dark night, comets flew, swishing their fiery tails; the earth and the moon and all the other planets whirled around like spinning tops. *He* was a part of the same glorious creation, he had a share in it. Seen in this light, the loss of eight rupees, all at once, seemed laughably trivial.

It was now five o'clock. Apu had not realised that a game of football had started nearby. He came out of his reverie only when the ball bounced up and landed before him. He stood

182

up, got hold of the ball, and kicked it straight back to the linesman, who had already started running.

⋘◉⋙

A few months later, quite unexpectedly, Apu ran into Pranav. Pranav had been arrested and put in prison by the British government because of his political activities. On being released, he had looked for Apu everywhere, but no one knew where he had gone after leaving college, although someone mentioned he had found a job.

'I spent nearly a year as a guest of the government,' Pranav laughed, 'I looked everywhere for you ... anyway, tell me how you are. I believe you are working now? How much do you get?'

'Yes, I work for a newspaper. They pay me seventy rupees a month,' Apu smiled proudly.

This was not altogether true. Yes, he had finally managed to get a job. It was also true that he did work for a newspaper, but he was paid only forty rupees. After the necessary deductions, what he was usually left with was little more than thirty-three.

'It's an important job,' he went on, 'I have to translate into Bengali all the reports that are sent by Reuter. Read the article called *Art and Religion* next Wednesday. I wrote it.'

Pranav started laughing. 'You wrote an article on religion? What do you know about it, Apu?'

Apu looked cross. 'I know plenty. By religion I do not mean organised and collective religion. I've spoken of the religion every human being must follow, in his own personal life, in his own personal way. All of us ...'

Pranav interrupted him. 'Not here. If you must give a lecture, let's go to Gol Deeghi.'

On reaching Gol Deeghi, Pranav found a quiet corner and got Apu to stand on a bench. 'I hope this doesn't attract a crowd. If it does, I won't say a word, Pranav,' Apu declared. Then he spoke for nearly half an hour, expressing his views, freely and sincerely. When Apu had finished, Pranav thought, 'He has obviously thought a lot about this subject. He's slightly mad, but that's why I like him so much!'

Apu climbed down from the bench and asked, 'How was it?'

'Good, very good. You're clearly very sincere, though somewhat touched in the head.'

'Don't be daft!' said Apu with an embarrassed laugh.

'Apurbo, you should not have left college, although I know—and I said this to Vinay the other day—that what you'll manage to learn even without going to college will be far more than what they'll ever achieve. It's because you have a real desire to learn.'

Apu felt very pleased, almost like a child, by these words of praise. His face lit up. 'Let me get you something to eat,' he said. 'You cannot imagine how long it's been since I saw a single friend, or had any fun. Not since Ma died.'

'Your mother? She died, too?' Pranav asked, surprised.

'Oh yes, nearly a year ago. Didn't I tell you?'

There was a restaurant in front of them. Apu caught Pranav's hand and dragged him there. Pranav liked the easy affection with which Apu caught his hand. 'Everyone has friends,' he thought to himself, 'but how many show such warmth and sincerity? Apu's a jewel.'

Apu filled him in while Pranav ate. 'But how did you get a job? It could not have been easy,' Pranav remarked.

'No, sir. You can say that again.' Apu laughed and told him about his experiences at the hardware market, and the final fiasco with Abdul.

'Then,' he went on, 'after many days, I happened to hear

184

that the BNR were taking new staff to replace some of their workers who were on strike. Anyone who knew a little English could get a job.'

'And did you?' Pranav sipped his tea.

'Yes. All they did was look at the certificate from our college principal. Then they gave me an appointment letter—on a printed form, no less—and said I'd have to go to Ganjam district. It's quite far from here, but that suited me very well. Forty rupees a month, they said. At first, I was so happy that I went into a tea shop and had four cups of tea! Which reminds me, would you like something else? No, don't say no, come on! Waiter, another omelette ...'

'Stop it, Apurbo. You haven't changed, have you? Must you spend all your money just because you happen to have some?'

'Shut up and listen. I went back home, still feeling happy. But then ... later at night, I suddenly thought it would not be fair. I mean, after all, I would be taking the job of someone who was on a strike. I'd be depriving him of his livelihood. It *was* very tempting, I must admit, to hang on to that appointment letter and get away from here, but in the end, I couldn't do it. I took the letter back to them and said I could not accept their offer.'

Pranav looked straight at him. 'I knew it, Apu. From the moment I saw you in the college library, I knew what an idealistic young man you were. What you did does not surprise me at all. But what about this job that you're actually doing? When do you have to go?'

'Not till nine o'clock in the evening. Then I have to stay awake till three in the morning. That's what I still have not got used to. Until midnight, I can manage, but after that I cannot keep my eyes open. I keep nodding off at my desk ... then I have to get up, splash my face with water, and get back to work. My eyes turn red and swollen each night, working by electric light hurts my eyes, and it's so infernally

185

hot in the room where I have to sit. Still, I guess I must not complain. It is a job, and I am lucky to have it. The good thing is that I can sleep till ten or eleven in the morning. Then I am free to spend the whole day in the library.'

Pranav had finished eating. As he reached for a glass of water, Apu stopped him. 'No, no, don't drink any water,' he said, 'let's go to College Square. I know a place where they sell lemon squash. Have you ever had it? Most refreshing ... come on, let's go.'

The rest of the evening passed most pleasantly. Anil and Pranav were the only people in college that Apu had ever felt really close to. Having now found Pranav again, he could not stop talking. 'Why don't we,' he said, 'get out of here on a Sunday and go to a village? I haven't been out in an open field for years, or walked in a wood, or heard birds chirping in trees. I have almost forgotten what it feels like. We could build a fire ourselves, and cook and have a picnic. ... a lot of flowers should be out at this time of the year. I'll tell you what they are called. I know a lot about wild flowers, you'll never see them in the city.' Then he added, 'What about tonight, though? Let's go and see a play!'

Apu bought two tickets to sit in the gallery. When the play was over quite late at night, he said, 'What's the point in going to bed now? We could sit somewhere and chat all night.'

When they came to Cornwallis Square, Apu leapt over a fence and landed in the middle of the square. Pranav followed suit. 'Here's a bench. We could sit here. I'll be an actor ... look at me, Pranav. I could speak the lines from a play, exactly like an actor.'

Pranav laughed. 'Don't shout too much, there are policemen about. You'll have us arrested,' he said. In a few minutes, however, he found himself joining his friend, laughing and rolling on the bench. Apu started reciting poetry in a theatrical fashion and was getting quite carried away, when

Pranav looked up and gave a horrified gasp. A constable was standing on the pavement. Apu stood up on the bench. 'Hail, Holy Light! Heaven's First Born!' he shouted. Then the two friends promptly ran in the opposite direction, leapt over the fence once more, and disappeared.

Dawn was about to break. They found themselves in Amherst Street. Apu sat down on the front step of a red building and said, 'Where can we go now? Let's just sit here until it gets light.' Then he started laughing again. 'Did you hear what I said to that constable? Hail, Holy Light ... didn't I sound like an actor? Ha ha ha!'

'I had no idea you were so completely crazy. You didn't let me sleep a wink tonight, Apu. Anyway, you could sing a song now.'

'A song? Whoever lives in this house will come charging out.'

'Not if you sing softly. Come on, Apu. For heaven's sake, do stop laughing!'

❧❦❧

A couple of weeks later, Pranav met Apu again. 'Do you still want to get out of here?' he asked. 'I've come to fetch you, Apu. A cousin of mine is getting married next Monday. She lives in a village in Khulna. We could go there on Friday, and get back after the wedding is over. We'll have to go by steamer ... you'll love it. What do you say?'

Luckily, it did not prove difficult to get a few days' leave. Apu got on the train with Pranav with a light heart, quite excited at the prospect of a holiday. He had never been to Khulna before. When the steamer dropped them at a ghat from where they had to take another boat to get to Pranav's uncle's house, Apu looked around in wonder. The river was lined on both sides with endless supari and coconut trees, and bamboo groves. There were little houses with tin roofs. These tiny villages had strange names—Swarupkati, Joshaikati.

Two rivers met near the village where Pranav's uncle lived. One came from the southeast, and the other from the west, each curving like the crescent moon. The water was greenish where the two rivers joined. Pranav's uncle lived within half a mile, in a village called Ganganandankati. He appeared to be the only man there with a large house, that could boast of past grandeur.

Apu had often imagined a house like the one he now saw. Far from the bustle of a city, standing by the side of a big river in a small unknown village, the house he had pictured had several rooms, wide verandahs, a huge compound with separate buildings to act as a temple, a room for the priest, and a large hall where scores of people could stand and watch a puja being held. It had all these features, but everything bore signs of decay. The walls were cracked, the courtyard unkempt, declaring openly that the owners had once seen better days, but were now left with little except the need to show that their dignity and old values remained untarnished. This house that Pranav had brought him to matched almost every detail of the imaginary one.

Rows of coconut trees ran straight from the ghat to the front gate of the old mansion. To the left was a wide verandah, and to the right was a garden, and a gate by which stood two yellow pitchers. There was a temple and a hall, but their days of glory were clearly over. Some of the parapets over the windows were broken. What was left did not look very sound, either. A number of pigeons were looking for food in the big open courtyard, some occasionally fluttering off to the roof. A huge old and unused palki stood in a corner. Its handles were shaped like a shark's head. In its time, it must have been lifted and carried by as many as sixteen men.

They were greeted by joyous cries: 'Here's Pulu!' 'Good to see you, Pulu!' 'Who's this with him?' 'Your friend? Good, good. Welcome, young man ... I'll get someone to carry your luggage inside.'

Pranav took Apu inside to meet his aunt. 'I've seen you before ...' she said, half to herself, staring at Apu, 'your face is so familiar.'

'No, Mamima,' Pranav laughed. 'You could not have seen him before. He's never visited these parts.'

'I know that. I may not have met him, but his face ... it's handsome like the face of a young god, like Krishna. I have seen it in temples.'

Apu quickly bent down to touch her feet. 'May you live long,' she blessed him, 'Where is your home, son?'

The hot, oppressive day gave way to a pleasantly cool evening, once the sun had set. The evening aarati started in the temple. Apu sat on the roof, the sound of bells and conch shells reaching his ears. Pranav, after an afternoon nap, had gone somewhere. Apu did not mind being left on his own. This was a new experience for him, a new world altogether, so far removed from the busy life in the city he had grown accustomed to. The moon had just risen in the sky, and was now visible through the branches of a coconut tree. Apu shivered with a sudden thrill. What had caused it? The sounds from the temple? The moon? Apu could not tell. His thoughts began to grow confused. A lot of distant memories came crowding in his mind.

Pranav's voice brought him back to reality. 'You wanted to see trees and greenery, didn't you?' Pranav said, 'Are you happy now?'

Apu began to speak, but there were footsteps on the stairs. 'Is that you, Meni?' Pranav called, 'come here for a minute.'

A girl of about thirteen came up the stairs and looked at them in silence, smiling a little. 'Who else is with you?' Pranav asked. Several other women had followed Meni. She glanced over her shoulder and said, 'Noni di, Mej di, Shorola ... they're all here. We're going to play cards up in the attic.'

Apu stole a glance at the others and thought they were all pretty.

'Meni is my uncle's youngest daughter,' Pranav told him. 'It is her sister who is going to get married on Monday. Isn't Aparna with you? Go, Meni, call Aparna. She's the prettiest of the lot.'

Meni rejoined the group near the stairs and said something Apu could not hear. It had the effect of making them break into giggles. A few moments later, a very attractive girl of sixteen or seventeen came up and stood at a distance, her eyes lowered demurely.

'Apu is my friend, Aparna,' Pranav remarked, 'you may look upon him as another cousin. There is no need to feel shy.'

Aparna smiled, but did not stay long. Obviously a quiet young woman, she moved away almost at once. Apu could not help admiring her thick, long hair which swung as she turned. A line from an English novel he had read recently kept coming back to him: Do they breed goddesses at Slocum Magna? Do ... they ... breed ... goddesses ... at ... Slocum Magna?

Apu never forgot that night.

❧

The next day, Pranav showed him round the whole property his uncle and his family owned. It was huge and sprawling. The other side of it was occupied by various cousins and other relatives, although some of them had gone away to live in Kashi. Their rooms were lying empty.

In the evening, Apu heard a strange tale from an old gentleman. Apparently, about two weeks ago, a weaver's young son had disappeared from a neighbouring village. Only recently, he had been found lying unconscious by the river. When he was revived and brought home, he declared that he had been taken away by a fairy. In order to prove this, he produced cloves, cinnamon and nutmegs from his pocket. They were all gifts from the fairy, he said. None of those objects grew anywhere near the village where he lived.

What pleased Apu the most was the lunch Pranav's aunt herself served him. For a long, long time, no one had fed him with so much love and affection; nor had he had the chance to eat so many good things, cooked with the best ingredients. In his mother's humble household, none but the very basic spices were ever used.

FOURTEEN

On the day of the wedding, Apu began lending a hand with the preparations, working as if he was one of the family. He was told to decorate the place where the groom and his party would come and sit. He spent all day spreading carpets and durries, and covering them with spotless sheets. Glass shades and lanterns were hung on the walls, garlands made of deodar leaves swung from doorways. Then he wrote little poems for the bridal couple, wishing them luck, and copied them out on several pieces of paper for distribution among the guests. It was past three o'clock in the afternoon by the time he finished.

The bridegroom's father was a wealthy man. Their village was several miles away. The groom and his party were expected to arrive by boat in the evening. The priest had identified two different hours, both equally auspicious. If, for some reason, the groom's arrival was delayed, the marriage could still take place at ten o'clock that night.

Apu found his friend, and said, 'From what I can see, we'll have to stay up all night. Let me go and get some sleep now. Call me when the guests arrive.'

Pranav took him up to the attic. 'It's not all that noisy here. I think you'll be able to sleep far better here than anywhere else. I'll come back and wake you in a couple of hours,' he said.

The room was small, but airy. Tired after the day's work, Apu fell asleep almost immediately.

He had no idea how long he had slept, but was woken by the sound of someone calling his name.

He sat up quickly, rubbing his eyes. 'Is the bridegroom here already? It's quite late, isn't it?' he began, then stopped as he saw the look on Pranav's face. Something had happened. Something awful. 'Why, Pranav, what's the matter?' he asked anxiously. 'What's wrong?'

Instead of giving him a reply, Pranav sat down and held his hands. There were tears in his eyes. 'Apu,' he begged, 'save us. Please help us. It is a matter of our family honour. You must marry Aparna tonight, there isn't much time left. If you don't, we'll never be able to show our faces ... Aparna's life will be ruined.'

Apu would have felt less surprised if he had been suddenly struck by lightning. What was Pranav saying? Had he gone completely mad? Or was this a bad dream?

At this moment, two gentlemen from the village entered the room. One of them said: 'We don't know you, but Pulu here has told us about you. Look, these people are in trouble—very serious trouble—and we are all counting on you. If you don't help them....' his voice trailed away. Apu, still speechless but now a little less sleepy, looked from one

193

to the other, his eyes asking a thousand questions. What exactly had gone wrong?

Plenty, as it turned out. What had happened was this: an hour after sunset, the boat carrying the groom's party had arrived at the ghat. The place was crowded, since people from all the neighbouring villages had come to watch the festivities. The groom was received warmly and put in a large old fashioned palki. As he was being brought to the bride's house, amidst great fanfare, to sit where Apu had worked all day, something completely unforeseen had happened. The groom had jumped out as the palki was being lowered in the courtyard, and begun barking like a jackal.

Apparently, he had made this noise so loudly and for such a length of time that it could not possibly leave any doubt in anyone's mind. The man chosen to marry Aparna was totally insane. At first, his father and some of the older men had rushed forward to calm him down, but he had just ignored them. Together with scores of neighbours, friends, relatives and many others, Pranav and his family had watched this spectacle helplessly, shocked and embarrassed beyond belief. People had exchanged glances, some of the women had started to cry. Who could ever have imagined something like this would happen at the wedding of a girl from the Banerjee family, who were well-known and respected everywhere?

The men in the other party did their best to play it down. Some said it was nothing, the poor boy was probably feeling unwell … after all, he hadn't had anything to eat all day, and then he'd travelled for miles in sweltering heat. Others said that they had heard he was slightly eccentric, but it was not to be taken seriously. Perhaps the whole thing was just a reaction to the heat, all the excitement, the music, the band and everything else.

In a few minutes, things began to settle down. The groom fell silent, the other men offered soothing and apparently rational explanations, and—for a moment—it looked as if all was going to be well. Even Aparna's father seemed prepared to overlook and ignore what had just occurred. In any case, he had little choice in the matter.

The wedding might have taken place as planned, but for Aparna's mother. It was she who had put her foot down. She had taken Aparna to her room the minute she heard what had happened, and locked the door from inside. Neither mother nor daughter had emerged from the room, despite hours of pleading by her husband and various others. All her mother had said over and over was that she would never allow her sweet and innocent daughter to be married off to a lunatic. She did not care what people said, or whether their family honour was at stake. If necessary, she would chop her daughter in two, then kill herself. People who knew her could tell this was not an empty threat. They also knew that if her mother did indeed find a knife and struck her, Aparna would not utter a single word in protest. She would accept her mother's decision calmly and in silence. In view of this, no one had dared break open the door.

'Now,' said the other gentleman, 'do you understand why we have come to you? If you don't step in and marry Aparna, either there will be a murder in this house, or that poor girl will never get married. Do you think it will ever be possible to find her another man? She'll be seen as cursed, no one will want to have anything to do with her. She does not deserve that ... she's beautiful like a goddess, so pure, so totally innocent ... who knew such a terrible scandal was waiting to happen at *her* wedding? Please, please say yes. We couldn't possibly find another suitable boy before sunrise.'

Apu's brain ceased to function. He felt as if a thousand drums were beating inside his ears, his head throbbed and ached ...` what an awful dilemma his fate had thrown him into! He had always been terrified of ties. His mother's death last year had released him from the final bond that had held him to another person. Now, when he was free at last, how could he commit himself to something as binding as marriage?

Suddenly he remembered Aparna's face. He had seen her downstairs, only this morning. She hadn't spoken, but he had seen her beautiful face, and watched her move with a serene grace. Yes, she was certainly like a goddess ... a goddess likely to be killed by a sharp knife. Either that, or he must give up his freedom. What on earth was he to do?

But where was the time to think? Pranav was still speaking, the other two men were clutching Apu's hands, begging him yet again. He might have brushed them off, but it seemed as if Aparna herself was standing before him, waiting patiently for his decision, looking quietly at him with her large, dark eyes. He could not ignore the silent plea in them.

'Very well,' he said, 'just tell me what I have to do.'

When Apu came down, there was no one in sight. The music had stopped, the guests had left. The crazy groom and his family had been offered shelter for the night by a distant cousin. The entire household had retired behind closed doors. Only a handful of people were gathered in the courtyard, whispering among themselves, and—strangely enough—the priest was still seated where the main ceremony was to take place. He had taken his seat soon after sunset, and had not left it, despite all the hue and cry.

Pranav and the others took Apu to him.

What followed remained hazy in Apu's mind, like printed photographs in newspapers. Totally dazed, he had neither time nor inclination to observe what was going on. Yet, somehow, a few trivial details automatically sank in. Someone was breaking open a green coconut in a corner under the shamiana. The coconut was round and had a dark, reddish shell. The implement being used had a handle made of bamboo. For many years, these minor details remained firmly embedded in his memory.

The bride, clad in a silk saree and loaded with jewellery, was brought to join him. Suddenly, the whole house came to life again. Someone began blowing a conch shell, women started to ululate, dozens of people surrounded the bridal couple. Apu followed the priest's instructions mechanically, donning a silk scarf, wearing a new sacred thread, repeating mantras like a parrot. Various other rituals followed, which he went through in the same manner, barely taking anything in. Something tingled up his neck, past his ear ... no, it was actually creeping *down* his neck, he thought.

Aparna's mother was crying. But it was she who wiped his face with one end of her own saree, when he started to sweat. An elderly lady said, 'Didn't your daughter worship Shiva most devoutly? Now she's been justly rewarded. What a handsome man she's marrying!'

Apu glanced up only when it was time to take the first look at his bride. A sheet was hung over their heads, and the bride and groom were told to look at each other. Shy as she was, Aparna kept her gaze firmly lowered to the ground. Apu looked at her curiously, for as long as he could. Her features were well defined but soft, the line of her jaw blending smoothly with her little chin. There were tiny beads of perspiration on her forehead, a few strands of hair had escaped and were hanging loosely around her ears; her golden earrings glinted in the lamplight. Anyone who described her as a goddess was absolutely right.

After the wedding, Apu found himself in a room packed with women. Everyone who had left had returned hurriedly to see this new bridegroom. A few hours ago, none of them was aware of his existence. Never before in this village had there been such excitement, particularly in the middle of the night. However, what they all agreed on was that this complete stranger, picked up from nowhere to fill an empty slot, seemed in every way suitable for and worthy of a girl like Aparna.

Had Aparna's mother not been such a spirited woman, none of this would have happened. Aparna would certainly have been married to the other man. Her mother had remained unmoved even when her husband—known for his grave and stern demeanour—had said to her, 'What do you think you're doing? Open the door, Boro Bou, think of my prestige, our honour!'

Now, Apu heard her saying, 'The minute I saw this boy with Pulu, I felt so drawn to him, as if he was my very own. Pulu has brought so many of his friends to this house, but I've never felt this way about anyone else. Just imagine, there I was thinking I'd never be able to show my face to anyone on this earth, and now ... what would we have done if he hadn't come with Pulu?'

The same elderly lady said, 'He had to come. Don't you see? You and I might have tried to find another man for Aparna, but God has made him for her. It had to happen.'

'We need your good wishes ...' Aparna's mother choked. None of the ladies present had dry eyes. Apu himself had to struggle to fight back tears. His mind filled with a deep respect for Aparna's mother. He had never felt this for anyone except Sarbajaya, and Leela's mother.

Pranav, to Apu's great embarrassment, turned traitor. He appeared amidst all the women and announced that the new groom was a good singer. This created a major stir. Aparna's mother left at once in order to put him at ease, but Apu began to sweat and go red in the face. However, the other women showed him no mercy. In the end, he sang a Tagore song, and then, pressed even further, sang another. This prompted an old lady to jab Aparna's arm and say, 'Hey, what are you waiting for? Your husband thinks he's the only one with a good voice. Go on, why don't you sing, too? Then we'll know who's got real talent!'

Apu gave a start. Husband? He was a husband? Who was

198

this good-looking young woman sitting demurely beside him, resplendent in all her finery? Was it his wife? His own wife?

What remained of the night passed quickly. The women went home as the sun rose. A little later, members of the previous wedding party turned up, threatening to take Aparna's father to court. After a long exchange of heated words, abuse and curses from both sides, they finally left. Pranav said to his uncle, 'Apu may not be rich, but he is a far better human being than the retarded child of a wealthy man. I have seen him struggle for the last three years, without support from anywhere ... I admire him immensely. He is a real man.'

Apu did not have a proper home to take his bride to. A day later, Aparna's family had to make arrangements for their first night together. Apu entered his room quite late at night, to find flowers and garlands everywhere. Aparna's friends had spread champa flowers on the bed. Apu could smell their faint, sweet scent from where he stood.

Aparna had not yet arrived. Apu waited eagerly for her, his heart tembling with anticipation. He hadn't had the chance to see her or speak to her after the wedding. What could he say to her now? What would she say to *him*?

Aparna came into the room much later. Another wave of disbelief and a feeling of unreality swept over Apu. Who was this woman? His *wife*? What could it mean?

She was standing uncertainly near the door. Apu forced himself to speak: 'Wh-why are you standing there? C-come and s-sit here with me!'

Laughter rang out at once—not inside the room, but from the group of young women who were standing just outside the closed door, trying to eavesdrop. Apu naturally had no idea they were there. But his bride smiled and came and sat down on the bed, as far from him as she could get. She was still very shy. At this moment, Apu heard an older woman scolding the young girls outside. To his relief, they were made to retreat and the sound of suppressed giggles subsided.

Now a little more sure of himself, he glanced at his wife and asked, 'What is your name?'

She replied softly, without raising her eyes, 'Sreemati Aparna Devi.' She smiled as she spoke. Her smile was as sweet as her face. Apu stared at her smooth cheeks, her graceful neck, her perfect chin, and felt mesmerised.

Both were silent for the next few minutes. Apu's throat felt parched. He poured himself a glass of water from a jug and drank it thirstily. Then, unable to think of anything to say, he blurted out:

'Tell me, are you very unhappy to find yourself married to me? You must be!'

His bride smiled again, but said nothing.

'I knew it. You have every right to be unhappy. But I ...'

'Don't be silly!'

Her first words, addressed to him. Apu felt as if he had received an electric shock. This was amazing. After all, it wasn't as if no woman had spoken to him before. But he had never felt like this.

A soft breeze wafted in through an open window. The smell of the champa flowers seemed to fill the room.

'It's nearly two o'clock,' Apu said after a while, 'Don't you want to sleep? Er ... you'll sleep here, won't you?'

He had never slept in the same room with any woman save his mother and his sister. How could he now lie on the same bed, next to a woman he didn't know, with whom he had no ties of blood? He began to feel rather uneasy. Then a sudden movement accidentally made his hand brush against the bride's. Apu could feel his whole body shiver again, with

200

an inexplicable thrill. In the light of the lamp, his handsome face looked unnaturally bright.

Hesitantly, he raised his hand once more and placed it on Aparna's shoulder. 'When you saw me the other day ... the day I arrived ... what did you think?' he asked.

She smiled again, gently removing his hand.

'Tell me what *you* thought,' she murmured. Then she held up her arm and moved closer to the lamp. 'Look, look!' she exclaimed, 'I have got goosepimples. Why should that have happened? Do you know why?' A slight smile was still playing around her lips.

No one had ever spoken to him like this. Was this romance? Was this what he had read about, heard about, thought about all these years? Why, it was nothing like what he had imagined it to be! What utter nonsense had he imagined, anyway? How could he have known without an intimate contact with the world, the real world of flesh and blood ... with life ...?

Apu began to feel strangely lightheaded, as if he was drunk. The air in the room felt heavy ... he had to get out in the fresh air. 'It's so hot in here!' he said to his wife, 'I'm going out on the terrace for a minute. I'll be back soon.'

There was no one on the moonlit terrace. A cool breeze came from the river. Apu stood there, trying to grasp everything that had happened to him in the last two days. None of it had made any sense until this moment. Now he realised its full implications. Two days ago, he had nothing and no one to call his own. He had no family, friends, not even a roof over his head that he could say was his. But now, two days later, it was a different story. Out of nowhere, a young woman had appeared by his side. He did not know her, but she seemed very close, like a true friend who he knew would stand by him through all eternity.

Suddenly he thought of his mother. Where was she now? She had spent years dreaming of seeing him married. In her little house in their village, she had made such plans, voiced such desires. With her body consigned to the flames, every dream, every hope, every aspiration had been burnt, charred, reduced to only a handful of dust. Never in his life had he celebrated a happy event without his mother ... he could not even think of not sharing his happiness with her. But now....

His eyes smarted. His vision got blurred. Still he continued to stand silently, the moonlight washing over him, as though it was the blessing his poor dead mother was sending him from the heavens above, to soothe and calm his troubled heart.

FIFTEEN

❧❀❧

Apu returned to Calcutta the next day. Back in his old busy, noisy life, he looked back on the last few days and often wondered if it had all been a dream. Could it really be true that, only last Friday, he was with a woman in an unknown village by a river in a land far away, and, as the full moon began to set that night, he had said to her, 'What if I don't come back later this year, Aparna? I mean, not even once?'

At first, Aparna had merely smiled and lowered her eyes without saying anything. 'That won't do,' Apu had insisted, 'I want an answer from you, Aparna. I'll come back only if you say you'd like me to, not otherwise.'

Aparna had blushed and protested, 'That's not fair. Who am *I* to say anything? You must ask my parents.'

'Very well. I won't come back then. If you don't want me to ...'

'Did I say that? All I said was that it's not up to me, is it? If *you* want to come, of course you must.'

The conversation had not got very far after this. Apu might have felt hurt at his wife's reluctance to give him a straight answer, but at that moment, curiosity overcame every other emotion. He had not yet started to look upon her with love. Had he done so, no doubt her words would have caused him great disappointment.

One evening, back in Calcutta, he found a man selling champa flowers near Gol Deeghi. Apu strode forward eagerly and bought some. Their smell brought him joy, but this time his joy was mixed with pain ... a feeling of emptiness ... an awareness of having found something and lost it again.

He sat down on the grass absentmindedly and tried to recall his first night with Aparna. What did she look like? Just in a few days, her face had become a little hazy. The harder he tried to remember all the details, the more quickly they seemed to fade. All that kept coming back were her dark eyes, and her thick lashes as she lowered her gaze. How shy she was! Shyness seemed to engulf her whole being ... from her forehead down to her beautiful eyes, then to her soft cheeks ... just for a second, her whole face came back to Apu, then disappeared again. But he could remember her smile. Never before had he seen a woman smile with such unspoilt innocence.

Pranav visited Calcutta six weeks later, with tales of how proud Aparna's mother was with her new, handsome son-in-law, and how she could not stop talking about him. She had tears in her eyes when she heard that Apu had no one in the world. This pleased Apu very much.

'Is she really so pleased with me? Just think, Pranav, she hasn't even seen me in good clothes. Did I tell you I had once starved myself to have a silk shirt made? Why couldn't you have come then, and taken me to meet your aunt? You had to come when that shirt was old and torn and gone forever. Hey, how do you suppose I would have looked if I'd worn it?'

'Like Apollo Belvedere, no less. I've seen other men full of vanity, Apu, but none like you!'

But Apu was far more interested in Pranav's cousin than his aunt. What had Aparna said about him? Was she happy about their marriage? Or did she regret not being able to marry the other man, the rich man's son?

The rich man's son, Pranav told him, had gone totally insane. He had to be kept in a locked room. Apparently, he had regained enough sense the day after the wedding to realise that he had failed to acquire the bride he had chosen himself. Even now, he kept asking everyone, 'Didn't I get married? Why didn't I?'

This piece of news saddened Apu. Pranav had started to laugh, but Apu stopped him. 'Don't laugh, Pulu,' he said. 'Is it his fault that he's mad? How can he be blamed for the way he is? Poor man!'

Pranav continued to chat, giving him all the other news, omitting only what Aparna's father had said to him. Unlike her mother, he was not pleased to find his daughter married to a man who had no money and limited prospects. Apu's good looks—which had made such an impression on his wife—had left him quite unmoved. It was his belief that Pranav had conspired with his aunt to get his friend married to Aparna. Angry and disappointed, he had refused to give Apu even a quarter of the dowry that had been promised to the original bridegroom.

Apu tried to visit his wife during the time of Durga Puja, but failed. Not only was it difficult to buy himself new clothes, but it also turned out that his father-in-law was not particularly keen to have him back. His letter to him, unlike that of his wife, offered no warm invitation. All it said was that Apu should devote his time in looking for a good job. This was the time for hard work, this was the time to look for opportunities. If he wasted his time away in idleness, that was hardly proper ... and words in that vein.

❧❦❧

By the time Apu could get enough leave and make adequate preparations to visit his bride again, a year had passed since his wedding. Not a single day had gone by during this time when he did not think of Aparna. When he went to the library, he found himself looking for romantic novels more than anything else. In so doing, he discovered that the dramatic fashion in which he had got married was not, after all, all that rare in novels. There were numerous instances.

The night before he left was spent in absolute agony. Apu could not sleep, getting up at least ten times to see if his new haircut suited him, or whether he looked better in a new tussore jacket rather than a white kurta.

When he finally reached Aparna's house, it was raining heavily. Her mother, on receiving the news of his arrival, rushed out in the open courtyard, despite the pouring rain, to welcome him. The whole household seemed to ring with joy.

After dinner, Apu was shown to the same room where he had spent the first night together with Aparna. She came quite late at night.

Apu could not take his eyes off her. What a difference a year had made to her! When he had left her, she was beautiful, yes, but little more than an adolescent girl. Now she seemed to be a totally new woman. She was not dazzlingly beautiful like Leela, but what she had was something very rare. Truly, she looked like a goddess. It was as if nature had made her with the softness of green leaves, and the sweet innocence of all the wild

206

flowers that grew by the river in the deep woodland. This was not the face he had tried to remember all these months. He could not have imagined such beauty.

Apu was the first to break the silence. 'I am not going to talk to you,' he said, 'why didn't you write to me even once?'

Aparna smiled shyly, looked away, then raised her dark eyes to meet his.

'And what about me?' she asked softly. 'Why shouldn't I feel cross with *you*?'

'Cross with me? Why? Oh, I see. Is it because I didn't come before? You mean you thought of me? You wanted me to come? Liar!'

Aparna's face grew serious. 'No, no, don't say that. We expected you to be here for Durga Puja. Ma waited for you every day. And I ...' she stopped.

'Go on. What about you?'

'I don't know.'

'Don't know? I see. You mean you're sorry to have got me as your husband? You'd much rather be married to that other ...'

'Sh-sh. Why do you keep harping on that? You mustn't. You *know* I never think like that. Oh, by the way ...' Aparna suddenly seemed to have remembered something, '... Pulu da said you were thinking of going off to the war. Is that true?'

'Yes. I'll join the army, as soon as I get back to the city.'

Something in Apu's tone made Aparna laugh. 'All right, that's enough. Please stop being cross with me,' she said.

Apu smiled in return. 'Tell me, Aparna, do you know who are involved in the war?'

'Of course. The English are fighting the Germans. I do read the newspaper, you know.'

A recent shower had brought the temperature down. Now the sky was clear. Moonlight fell on the wet earth and a light breeze brought its gentle scent into the room.

'Do you think you could get champa flowers somewhere?' Apu asked suddenly, 'Could you ask someone to get them for us? To spread on our bed at night?'

'There is a plant in our garden. Getting the flowers should not be a problem, but *I* couldn't ask anyone. You must do that. You could perhaps tell my sister tomorrow morning.'

'Very well. But do you know why I asked for champa specially?'

Aparna smiled, dimpling sweetly. She had caught his meaning without having to be told anything explicit. What an intelligent woman, Apu thought.

'There's something else I'd like to tell you, Aparna. I want you to come with me when I leave in a few days. I couldn't take you to Calcutta, but will you be happy to live in my home in the village?'

'You'll have to tell my parents.'

'Yes, of course. But what do *you* think, Aparna? How do you feel about it? It won't be easy. You'll have to do everything there, without any help from a servant. It's a small house, just two rooms with a thatched roof.'

'I wouldn't mind at all. Look, I know everything about you, and your situation. Pulu da has told us. Stop worrying about it. I will go wherever you take me.'

The night wore on. Neither could sleep that night.

Apu left with his wife, as planned. His father-in-law raised a few objections at first, advising Apu once again to find a better job before thinking of starting a new life with Aparna, but his wife stopped him. 'I know our daughter very well,' she said. 'She won't be happy here on her own. Let her go with her husband. Surely it's her happiness that's most important?'

208

Apu could hardly believe his luck. Imagine being alone with his wife, all day, every day, without worrying about who might see or hear them!

On the steamer, however, Aparna stayed in the section reserved for women. Three hours passed in separation. Then they alighted at the ghat from where they had to catch a train.

The train was not expected for several hours. Apu found a small room not far from the river which could be hired for these few hours. Many other passengers did the same.

'Look, you don't have to buy any food,' Aparna said. 'There's a kitchen here. I can quite easily cook us a meal.'

This amused Apu very much. The thought of setting up house, actually cooking and eating a meal in this little room, had not occurred to him. He went off to buy groceries, and returned to find that his wife had had a bath, changed into a saree with a zari border, and was busy making preparations in the kitchen. Her damp hair hung down her back. On her forehead was a little dot of vermilion. She looked up with a smile.

'I met the landlady. Do you know what she said?' Aparna's eyes danced. 'She asked me if you were my brother! Then, when I started laughing, she got all flustered and said, 'your husband? I see, I see!' And then ...' Aparna broke off, now too shy to go on and repeat the whole conversation.

Apu stared at her, enchanted. Back in Aparna's house, he had always seen her at night. He knew she was beautiful, but now little details caught his eye—how shapely her arms were, there was such magic in her movements! And this woman was his ... the only person in this world he could call his own!

It proved quite difficult to light the stove. When Aparna could not get it going, Apu tried himself, but the pieces of wood stubbornly refused to light up. His eyes turned red and started to water. The landlady saw them struggling and took pity on them. 'Tell your husband to get out of the kitchen,' she said to Aparna. 'I'll do it for you.'

It was now time for Apu to have his bath. Aparna told him to hurry. He returned from the river to see that she had got the landlady to buy sweets from the local market. These were placed on a plate, together with pieces of fresh papaya. Aparna had even made sherbet in a glass. 'A regular housewife!' Apu laughed. 'Very well, we'll see how good you are, madam, when it comes to adding salt to everything. Let's see if you can get that right.'

Aparna accepted the challenge. 'All right, we'll see,' she replied. The she nodded happily like a child and said, 'And what will you give me if I do?'

'I could give it to you right now, if you like. Do you want it?'

'No! Stop being naughty.'

Aparna began cooking. Apu stole into the kitchen and stood right behind her. Even now, he was finding it hard to believe that this attractive young woman was actually with him, now a part of his life.

Aparna had tied her hair into a loose knot. Apu bent down quietly and pulled it. She gave a start, turned around and pretended to be cross. 'What did you do that for? Didn't you realise it might hurt? Do that once more, and I won't cook you any lunch.'

It suddenly occurred to Apu that his mother used to speak to him like this, with the same affection in her eyes. Durga, Ranu, Leela, and now Aparna ... it seemed to him that each of these women, who were all so close to him, spoke at times like his mother, as if Sarbajaya herself was trying to spread her love through all of them.

When it was time to catch their train, Apu suddenly recognised a man he had earlier seen pacing on the platform. It was Satyen Babu, one of his teachers in Diwanpur. He had finished studying law and left Diwanpur before Apu's own departure. He appeared very pleased to find an old student.

He asked after all the others he had taught. He was now practising at the high court in Patna. Judging by his appearance, he was doing quite well. Even so, he said, 'I miss those days in Diwanpur. Those were such happy times.'

On reaching Calcutta, Apu hired a phaeton to show Aparna around the city. He noticed that although this was her first visit there, she did not display a vulgar curiosity about anything. At all times, she appeared calm and collected. Perhaps she had inherited this poise and dignity from her mother.

It was dark by the time their bullock cart drew up before Sarbajaya's little house in Manshapota. For the first time, it dawned upon Apu that he had indeed acted in haste. At least the neighbours should have been informed. But Apu had not told anyone because he felt that, in the absence of his mother, no one else should be allowed to greet his wife in her home.... Only Sarbajaya had that right. Who else could take her place?

The house—bearing visible signs of damage—stood in darkness. There was not a single soul to light a lamp and welcome them. Aparna stood mutely under a guava tree, while Apu struggled with a tin trunk and other pieces of their luggage. Then she stepped forward to lend him a hand, moving all their luggage inside, aided only by the occasional matchstick Apu managed to light.

To tell the truth, Aparna was quite bereft of speech. She knew her husband was not a rich man, but nothing had prepared her for such stark poverty. The house—if it could be called that—had lost a part of its thatched roof. The fence that protected the front verandah was broken, presumably by cows or goats that had wandered in. Wild plants had grown everywhere. Some strange insects were making a droning noise. There were fireflies in the bushes. Was this where she was to start her new life? A lump rose in her throat. She thought of her mother ... her aunts ... her little brother ...

how long must she spend here before she could see them all again? Oh God, she'd die if she had to spend all her life in this house!

Apu, in the meantime, had found a lantern and lit it. In its dim light, Aparna saw that rats had dug up the floor, there were heaps of earth strewn about. Apu dusted a corner of the bed—there was no mattress or sheet on it—and told her to sit down. Then he picked up the lantern and went out to bring in the last piece of their luggage. Sitting alone in the dark, Aparna felt her flesh creep, and tears prick at her eyes. Apu returned a second later, saying apologetically, 'Sorry, I should not have left you in the dark. Look, I'll leave the lantern near the door, all right?'

Half an hour of dusting and cleaning made the room habitable for one night. Having done that, it occurred to Apu that there was no way they could cook dinner. Not only was the kitchen in a state of disrepair, but they did not have anything to cook, anyway. Aparna came to the rescue. She opened a small bundle and said, 'Look, there are some sweets here. Ma had packed these this morning ... and I forgot all about them. There's plenty for both of us.'

Apu felt considerably embarrassed. Used to dealing only with his own needs and always acting on impulse, he had not stopped to consider Aparna's comfort. 'I should have realised ...' he began, 'we could have got something at Ranaghat. Even now, I *could* go and get some milk and rice from somewhere, but that will mean leaving you alone here. Should I go?'

Aparna shook her head in silence.

The house next door was locked. They had all gone to Calcutta, or someone would have turned up to make enquiries.

But the news spread quickly enough the next morning, which brought Nirupama to their door.

'What is this, Niru di?' Apu laughed. 'In my mother's absence, you ought to have been here yesterday to welcome the new bride. But you decided to take your time to get here, didn't you? Well, the bride is already installed!'

'You,' Nirupama complained, 'are as mad as you were at fourteen. How could you do this to your wife? How could you expect her to spend even one night in this dirty, broken old house? Why didn't you tell me you were coming? Only you could do this, Apu!'

She gave Aparna a gold coin as a gift. Then she threatened to take her away to her own house. 'No, no, please don't do that,' Apu said hurriedly. 'Help her settle down here in this house, Niru di. This is my mother's house, after all. You can take her away every evening for her to sleep at yours, I wouldn't mind that.'

Nirupama heaved a sigh of relief. She had grown very fond of Apu ever since the day when, years ago, he had turned up at her house to act as a priest. It had caused her a great deal of distress to see him leave the village after his mother's death, knowing that he had no one in the world to take care of him. Her natural feminine instincts had wanted him to stop wandering and settle down. It brought her a lot of comfort to see that he had.

Apu returned to Calcutta the next day, but went back to the village the following Saturday. An amazing sight greeted his eyes as he stepped in. Aparna had worked wonders, even in these few days. The wild plants that had turned the courtyard into a veritable jungle had been removed, the floor cleaned and levelled, the walls painted. There were even new shelves on the wall in their bedroom. The whole house was spick and span. The only help Aparna had had was from an old maid who worked next door. Apu did not have to be told how hard his wife had to work. And to think that this was the first time she had lived in a mud hut! Her father's house might be decaying in most parts, but it *was* a huge mansion and Aparna had always been spared the necessity of doing any of the heavy housework herself.

Over the next few weeks, Apu travelled back to the village every Saturday; but soon discovered that was working out to be far too expensive. So he stopped, and decided to wait until the next break he was likely to get for Janamashtami, though that was a couple of months away. His days were now spent in waiting for the postman. Who knew the figure of a man, clad in a khaki uniform, could arouse such huge waves of hope and excitement in one's heart? Who knew that an employee of the Amherst Street Post Office could have the power to take him either to the heights of elation, or plunge him down to the depths of despair? He remembered his college days. Only his mother used to write to him in those days. After her death, no one had written to him for a whole year. He used to envy the friend who had the room next to his in his mess. 'Half the letters that come to this building are always for you!' he had said to him one day. His friend had laughed. 'Those who have a family, or know a lot of people, would naturally get a lot of letters,' he had said. 'You don't know a soul, do you? Who's going to write to you?'

Apu had felt hurt, because unpleasant though it was, what his friend had said was true. But today, it was a different story. He finally had someone to write to him.

Apu left his office at three o'clock the day before Janamashtami. He had not told Aparna he was coming. The thought of her surprised face caused him much amusement.

214

It was not yet dark when Apu got home. The house was empty. His wife was either at the ghat, or had gone to visit Nirupama. Apu found a soap, washed his face, then found a mirror and combed his hair with extra care. After that, he hid his bag and removed every sign of his arrival. Having done that, he left the house and went for a long walk.

He returned half an hour later to find that Aparna was back in the house. She had lit an oil lamp, and was reading by its light. Apu walked up to her stealthily and stood behind her. This was an old trick he had often played on his mother. A slight noise made his wife turn her head. Seeing the figure of a man, silhoutted against the door, she dropped her book and scrambled to her feet. Apu burst out laughing.

'You!' Aparna exclaimed, somewhat embarrassed, 'when did you get here? Why, I had no idea ...!'

Apu went on laughing, 'I fooled you completely, didn't I? Do you always get scared so easily?'

'Scared? I could have died! How could you frighten me like that? You didn't say a word about coming. In fact, I didn't hear from you for a whole week.'

Apu retrieved his bags. 'How have you been, Aparna? Have you heard from your mother?'

Aparna did not answer him. 'You seem to have lost a little weight. Have you been ill?' she asked. But Apu was taking things out of his bag.

'Look,' he said, 'I got you some writing paper. It's the same as mine. It's quite good, isn't it? There are twenty-five sheets here. And I've brought you some new books.... What's for dinner, Aparna?'

'What would you like? I've got ghee ... let me make something with potatoes ... and there's some milk....'

❦

Apu rose the next morning and found, to his surprise, that Aparna had created a kitchen garden behind the house. Little patches had been cleared and fenced in to grow spinach and aubergines. Tiny saplings of marigold had been planted along the front verandah. Creepers went up to the roof of the repaired kitchen. In time, they would bear gourds and pumpkin. Apu was staring at these with frank amazement, when Aparna joined him and said, 'There is something else. You haven't seen it, have you? Come with me.'

She took him to a corner of their courtyard and showed him a tiny plant. A thrill ran down his spine. Quite uncannily, his wife had guessed his dearest wish, and had planted a champa tree.

'It will grow here, won't it?' Aparna asked anxiously.

'Of course. But tell me, Aparna, why did you think of champa? Why not some other flower?'

Aparna gave him another shy smile and looked away. 'I don't know. Anyway, I'm not going to tell you!'

Apu had not told her how or why this particular flower had come to mean so much to him. But she did not need to be told, and for that Apu felt truly grateful to her.

'Can you put a fence over here?' Aparna said. 'There are far too many goats in your village, I have to say. I spend every afternoon sitting on this verandah with a cane in my hand, to make sure my plants don't get eaten up. Sometimes, Niru di and other women come and chat with me. Niru di is such a good woman.'

It rained the whole day, and did not stop even when darkness fell. Perhaps it would go on all night. 'Why don't you come and sit in the kitchen?' Aparna asked, 'I could make you hot rotis.'

'No,' Apu said, 'tonight, let's eat together, from the same plate.'

Aparna demurred at first, but had to give in when Apu

insisted. 'Sit next to me,' Apu said, 'like this ... yes, come closer ... more....' Then he put his arm around her and said, 'Now let's eat!'

His wife laughed at him. 'You look so simple, my dear,' she said, 'who would say your head's full of such naughty ideas?'

The upshot was that Aparna failed to get a full meal that night. Apu kept chatting throughout, not realising that he was quickly demolishing the stack of rotis Aparna had placed on their plate. Afraid that her husband might not get enough, she could not bring herself to eat more than three.

After dinner, she said, 'Didn't you say you had brought me new books? Where are they?'

In some ways, she was very much like Apu. Both were young, full of wonder and enthusiasm, eager to talk endlessly all night. Apu took out a book of poetry and said to her, 'Come on, read us a poem!'

Aparna turned up the lamp with her long and slender fingers, and pulled it closer to their bed. After hesitating for a few seconds, she began to read. Apu had no idea she could read poetry so well. But, when he praised her, she stopped instantly and put the book away.

'It's your turn now,' she said, 'why don't you sing a song?'

Apu sang as many as three songs. Then they went back to chatting, making little plans for their future. 'If only my mother was here today, Aparna!' Apu said after a while. 'I keep thinking of her. She had wanted me to get married. She would have been so pleased to see you.'

'I know. But I am sure she can see us from wherever she is,' Aparna replied quietly. Then, after a brief pause, she added, looking straight at her husband, 'I have seen her.'

'What!' Apu gave her a startled glance.

'Let me explain what happened. Some time ago—I can't tell you the date—one afternoon, I got a letter from you. It

217

was quite late, I had been working in the garden all morning. Anyway, I had a late lunch, and then fell asleep on the back verandah. And then ... I had a dream. I saw a lady—a beautiful lady, she looked a little like you, and she was wearing sindoor in her hair, and a red-bordered saree. She stroked my hair very affectionately and said, 'Don't go to sleep now, silly girl, it'll soon be dark. You might make yourself ill if you sleep outside like this.' Then she took out a little box of sindoor and put some of it in my parting ... and I woke as she touched me. It seemed so real that I actually put up a hand to feel my hair, but there was nothing, no trace of fresh sindoor. I sat up at once, my heart was beating so fast ... but I realised who she was. It was Ma, it could not have been anyone else. She had come to welcome me into the family. I never spoke about it to anyone. You're the only one who knows.'

Apu said nothing. The rain still beat down on the roof, insects had started their drone, an occasional gust of damp wind made the lamp flicker. He could smell the fragrance that rose from Aparna's hair. Slowly, his eyes filled with tears. This was a strange moment. Apu realised this was a night he would remember all his life. But still he could not say anything.

Eventually, Aparna said, 'Sing another song.'

'No, you read more poetry.'

The momentary heaviness in his heart lifted, and the two of them began chatting once again. 'It won't be long before dawn breaks,' said Aparna after a while.

'Why, do you feel sleepy?'

'No. Tell you what, why don't you stay an extra day?'

'And miss office tomorrow? No, I can't do that.'

Aparna was right. The sun rose soon and the night came to an end. She started to rise, but discovered that her husband had tied one corner of her saree to his own kurta. She was obliged to sit down again.

'You're mad!' she laughed, 'How could you even think of doing this? Untie the knot at once, before our maid turns up. She'll be here any minute. If I am not out and about, what will the old woman think? To stay in the bedroom when it's so late ... how embarrassing!'

Apu turned away, making no attempt to release her. 'Oh my God, don't do this to me, I beg you! Look, I can hear her coming. Please ...' Aparna continued to plead.

Apu remained unmoved. Finally, the old woman began banging on their front door.

'Wake up, Bouma!' she called, 'you need to give me your dirty dishes. Don't you want them washed?'

This time, Apu relented. With a laugh, he untied the knot and allowed Aparna to go.

Then he changed his mind about going to office and spent an extra day with her.

SIXTEEN

❧❦❧

There was a health exhibition on at the University Institute. Apu was a member, and had been made in-charge of the section on food and children's health. He spent quite a lot of time at the institute. Some of his old friends turned up at times. One day, in the common room, he had an argument with Manmatha, who was training to be an attorney. It was Apu's belief that India would gain independence soon after the war. Why, hadn't Lloyd George said in England: 'Indians must not remain as hewers of wood and drawers of water'?

It was in the institute library that he learnt one day that Joan of Arc had been canonised. This surprised and pleased him very much. He had always admired Joan, even as a child in Nischindipur. She was a part of those dreamy days, spent by the river, in the shadows of trees. Later, he had seen a film on the annual memorial service held for her in France. Seeing the mile-long procession in which there were people from all over the world, army officers dressed in their uniform, all gathered in the tiny village of Domremy, Apu had felt very moved, very proud.

Her canonisation simply proved what he had always believed in. Religious fundamentalism and its resultant cruelty could not last for ever. It was inevitable that the star of truth would rise one day, and wipe out the darkness of ignorance that might have lingered for centuries.

These thoughts filled his mind and made him somewhat preoccupied, as he started to climb down a flight of stairs to go into the exhibition hall. Suddenly, he heard someone call his name. He stopped and turned to find a young woman, but could not recognise her immediately. After a few moments, he exclaimed, 'Preeti! Isn't it Preetibala? How are you? Did you come to see the exhibition?'

Preeti had grown up. Judging by her appearance, she was married. She nodded, smiled and turned to the elderly lady she was with. 'Ma, this is my teacher, Apurbo Babu,' she said, 'do you remember him?' Apu bent down and touched the lady's feet. Preeti went on speaking, 'Why did you leave so suddenly, Master Moshai? I was young then, I often spoke without thinking. We had no idea you'd take my words to heart. After you left, we tried to get in touch with you, but no one could give us your address. What are you doing these days?'

'I'm still working as a private tutor, but I also have a job with a newspaper.'

'I see. Master Moshai ... if I ... if we asked you to visit us again, won't you come to our house?'

Apu looked at his erstwhile pupil. He felt no rancour now, only a certain amount of affection. She had been too young to realise the implications of her words, it was he who had acted in haste. 'Of course I'll come and visit you!' He laughed. 'You don't have to sound so apologetic, Preeti. You're quite right, I should not have lost my temper so easily. You were young. I ought to have known better.'

Reassured, Preeti and her mother left after exchanging addresses.

Time ... thought Apu ... the changes time could bring to a person! What right had anyone to judge others?

❧❦❧

The next two months passed somehow. Apu went back to Monshapota on the first day of Durga Puja. He found Aparna chatting with a number of other women. It turned out that she had invited them over for a meal to celebrate the beginning of Puja. She got up as she saw Apu arrive, pulled her saree to cover her head, and joined him inside.

'I am so glad you are here!' she said, 'I made banana fritters today.'

'Really? Where are they? Give me some.'

'I will, when you've washed your hands and made yourself more respectable. You are such a glutton. Why can't you wait just a couple of minutes?'

The others left. Aparna placed a laden plate before Apu. 'M-m-m,' Apu said, munching happily. 'These are delicious. You've become quite an expert cook, I must say.' Then his eyes fell on beautiful white patterns drawn on the walls. 'Hey, who drew those?'

'Who do you think?' Aparna laughed, 'I did a Lakshmi Puja last month. That's when I drew those designs of alpana. I even fed a few Brahmins. If you were here, why, you would have been fed, too!' Apu grinned at her words. 'My mother was very fond of feeding people. She would have loved all this. I remember once ... we had just moved here ... an old man turned up and said to me, 'I am very hungry. Can you get me some muri, please?' I went and told my mother, 'Ma, there's a man at the door. He wants muri, but I think he'll be very pleased if you could make him some rotis. Will you please do that, Ma?' Do you know what my mother did?'

'She made rotis for him?'

'No, she did better than that. She used to make ghee for me sometimes. So she used that ghee and fried this man nearly ten parathas—just to please me. Oh, you should have seen that man's face when she served him a meal on that verandah!'

Later that night, Aparna said rather unexpectedly, 'I have recently heard from my mother. She's going to send my cousin to fetch me after Puja. I haven't been to visit her since I came here. Will you go with me?'

Suddenly, Apu felt hurt. Here he was, so looking forward to spending a few days with his wife. But what was she thinking of? Going back to her family! Very well then, let her go, if seeing her mother was more important to her.

'You can go whenever you like,' he said indifferently, 'I couldn't get any leave, so there's no question of my going with you.' So saying, he turned away and began reading. When he made no reply to her next remarks, Aparna assumed he was tired and possibly sleepy. So she went to sleep herself.

Aparna's cousin, Murari, arrived the day after Puja ended. Aparna's mother had instructed him to persuade Apu to come back with him. Murari began to put some pressure on Apu to change his mind. 'Are you mad?' said Apu, 'I've already used up all my leave. If I don't go back to work tomorrow, I'll lose my job. I am not a zamindar like you, Murari, I cannot afford to lose it.'

Aparna realised her husband was hurt and angry, but there was nothing she could do. 'I can hardly send my brother packing,' she said, 'I've got to go with him, can't you see that? Surely you'll get some time off for Kali Puja? Why don't you come and visit us then?'

Apu did not reply. Aparna left in a couple of days. Apu began to feel incredibly lonely as soon as she had gone. He would probably have returned to Calcutta himself, but was forced to spend the night in Monshapota since Aparna and Murari went by the evening train. Aparna had left his dinner for him. Although serving puris at dinner was an expensive business, she had somehow managed to do that while her cousin was here, simply to save her husband any embarrassment. Apu ate his meal, and felt more depressed than ever. There was a bright moon in the sky. A bird kept calling from a tree in his courtyard. It almost brought tears to his eyes. 'How could she leave me alone in an empty house like this?' thought Apu. In his moment of hurt and pain, it did not occur to him that it was the same empty house in which his wife had spent day after day, waiting for a brief visit by him.

A month passed. Apu did not write to Aparna even once. 'What have I done to you?' she wrote to him. 'Can't you see I did not want to leave you? Why are you punishing me like this? I haven't heard from you for over a month. Please, please write to me!' This pleased Apu no end. Serves you right, he thought. Go and visit your people, why should I care? Then a sudden thought dawned upon him. Was he really so important to a beautiful young woman? Everywhere he went—on the tram, in his office, or at home—he couldn't help thinking there was someone in this world who was thinking of him all the time, pining for him, whose life was without meaning because he had not written to her. This was a totally new experience. Waves of joy and excitement swept over him. For the first time in his life, he felt a sense of power. All right then, he thought gleefully, he would make her suffer. Make her more anxious, give her sleepless nights.

Aparna's plea fell on deaf ears. Apu did not reply to her letter.

In his personal life, Apu had found happiness. In his office, however, things began to look grim. The owner of the paper called a few members of the staff to discuss what could be done. It was clear that the paper did not have long to live.

Tired and dispirited, Apu made his way one day to Leela's house. He had not visited her for two years. When he turned up unexpectedly, she exclaimed, 'You! Why, did you lose your way, and found our house by accident?'

Her tone held both joy and surprise. Suddenly, Apu felt very guilty, even a little ashamed. He could only smile a little foolishly in reply. 'You must be very busy this year,' Leela went on. 'It is your final year, isn't it? But surely you could have visited us before?'

'Final year? Oh no. I left college two years ago. I am working now,' Apu replied.

Leela stared at him for a few moments, as if she could not believe her ears. Then she said a little sadly, 'Why? What did you do that for? *You* left college?'

The look in her eyes caused Apu a certain amount of pain—it told him how much she cared. Still, he decided to speak lightly. 'There just didn't seem any point any more,' he said, 'so I gave it up.' Such levity in his tone hurt Leela a little. Was Apurbo really the same person she had known? Or was he perhaps ...?

'You are still in college, aren't you?' Apu went on.

'Yes. I finished my IA this year. Now I am in my third year. Are you still at the old address, or have you moved?'

They were joined by Leela's mother, who received Apu with the same affection as she always had. Then Leela showed him some of her latest drawings. After a few pleasant moments with them, Apu rose to go. Leela came to the front door to see him off. Apu stopped suddenly and said, 'When we were both children ... in your house in Burdwan, you had recited a poem at a wedding. A very funny poem. Do you remember it?'

'Good heavens, I had totally forgotten about it. Fancy you remembering. That was ages ago.'

'And then ...' Apu added, almost to himself, 'one day you made me drink half the milk in your glass, you wouldn't listen to my protests ... remember?'

He smiled as he said this and looked at Leela, but she said nothing. Apu began to walk away, then looked back, to find that Leela had turned her face away and appeared to be looking at something else.

On his way back to his house, Apu kept thinking of Leela and Aparna. Aparna was undoubtedly most beautiful; but the kind of beauty Leela possessed could not possibly be compared with that of another woman. There was something divine about her looks, her voice, even the rhythm in her movements. She did not seem to belong to this world at all.

He realised that he loved Leela, loved her deeply, but in a totally different way. The nature of his love was serene and tranquil. It brought fulfillment, but it did not set his pulses racing, or arouse any great passion in his heart. Leela was his childhood companion; he felt a tender affection for her, compassion and a strong bond of friendship, almost as if she was his sister.

226

A few days later, Mr Lahiri's chowkidar brought him a short note from Leela. She had some special news, she said. Could he go to her house again, either the same day or the next?

This time Apu saw no reason to ignore her request. When he arrived at eight the following morning, Leela met him in the same room where he had found her the first time. She was dressed very simply, but looked lovely as always. Everything she wore seemed to suit her so well. But her beautiful eyes still looked a little sleepy, her hair was slightly dishevelled. A few loose strands hung around her face, sweet as a lotus at dawn.

'Have you only just woken up?' Apu teased her. 'Why, do you think you no longer need to rise early just because you are in your third year at college? Do you realise it's eight o'clock? Look, are your sure you're fully awake?'

Leela laughed. She loved the way Apu could bring good cheer each time he met her. Even when things had looked bleak, she had always seen him laugh and make light of the situation. Why, he had given her the news of his mother's death with a laugh! But she had not failed to see the pain behind it.

'I had a late night last night,' she explained. 'I'd gone to the cinema with my aunt, to the late show. It was past one o'clock by the time I could go to bed. No, I have not become inordinately lazy, I assure you. Wait, let me bring tea.'

She left briefly, and returned with tea on a tray. The entire tea service was made of Japanese lac, Apu noted. With the tea came toast, boiled eggs in their shells, boiled and halved potatoes, and some green leaves Apu could not recognise. Everything was hot and steaming.

'Whose idea is it to have such a Westernised meal? Your grandfather's? Eggs in their shells! What are those leaves?' Apu asked.

'Oh, that's lettuce,' Leela said with a smile. 'Let me get

the shell off your egg. What's that mark on your chin? Did you cut yourself while shaving?'

'No, it's nothing. Why don't you sit down, aren't you going to have tea with me?'

Leela's younger brother, Bimalendu, entered the room and greeted Apu with a smile. He was ten or eleven years old, a handsome young boy. Leela poured him a cup of tea. Then the three of them spent a few very pleasant moments, just chatting. Leela showed Apu some of her own paintings, and spoke of her hopes and dreams for the future. She would either do MA, or if she didn't do that, she would try to go to Europe straight after her graduation. Getting her grandfather's agreement shouldn't be a problem, she thought. She would visit all the art galleries in Europe, and go to Ajanta only when she came back. Then she got up and showed him some books on art that she had bought. 'Look at these pictures ... I love this one of St Anthony,' she said. 'He seems lost in meditation, doesn't he? I pay for these in instalments. Would you be interested, by any chance? I could tell the canvasser who comes to our house.'

'How much do you have to pay every month? May be this one ...?'

'No, no, you don't have to buy any of the books I've already got. You can easily borrow them from me. Wait, let me show you another picture.'

Apu glanced at the picture, and then at Leela's face. Yes Boticelli's Princess Dest was certainly a beautiful woman. If only there was someone with the talent of Boticelli or Da Vinci, who could draw Leela's lovely face, capture on canvas her blooming youthful body! He couldn't help mentioning it. 'Do you know what I've been thinking, Leela?' he said. 'If I could draw, I would have used you as a model.' Leela made no reply. 'Oh, by the way,' she said suddenly, 'Tell me, Apurbo Babu, if I could find a job for you, would you do it?'

'Why not? What kind of a job would that be?'

'You could do it easily enough. My grandfather is the attorney of a big estate. Those people need a secretary. They'll pay a hundred and fifty rupees, so I heard. Grandfather has a lot of influence, if he mentions your name, you'll definitely get the job. I called you here really to tell you about it.'

Now Apu remembered having casually mentioned the other day about his newspaper folding up. Leela had sensed his anxiety, and was doing what she could to help. His heart filled with gratitude.

'I heard about this job the same night when you were here last. So I sent you a message the next day. If you are prepared to take it, one letter from Grandfather will get you the job. Come on, let's go and see him. Oh, by the way, you must not go without having lunch with us today.'

As things turned out, however, Apu did not get the job. Leela had failed to tell her grandfather about Apu before sending him that message. The post had been filled two days ago. Looking at her embarrassed and disappointed face, Apu felt more sorry for her than for himself. She obviously had no experience in this matter. How was she to know how many applicants began to eye a post the minute it fell vacant? Poor Leela! Brought up as she was in a wealthy household, how could she be expected to know about such realities of life?

'Why don't you do one thing?' she said finally. 'Look, you have got to do this, you must stop being stubborn. You could still do your BA as a private student, couldn't you? Promise me you'll do it?'

'All right.'

Leela's face lit up instantly. 'Honour bright?' she asked.

'Honour bright.'

Apu left soon afterwards. Leela's kindness brought tears to his eyes. He would do anything to repay her. If *she* ever needed his help, he would be there for her, no matter what.

It was only after he had started walking away that he realised he had not told her about his marriage. He had meant to, but something had stopped him. He could not find a rational explanation for it—there was really no reason to have kept this information from Leela.

SEVENTEEN

A year passed. Durga Puja was just round the corner once again.

It was a Saturday. Some offices were closing for a week from today. Others would close on Tuesday. All the shops were crowded. Handbills were being distributed everywhere— enough to fill a whole basket in just an hour, if one kept them all. There were advertisements of various products, including one of a swadeshi match factory, which was displayed prominently at almost every street corner.

The famous rich businessman, Nakuleshwar Seel, had his office on the ground floor of his palatial house in Aamratola. It was a big office. Several rooms and two large halls were full of his employees. The rooms did not get adequate natural light. Electric lights had had to be switched on, though it was not yet four o'clock in the evening.

The young typist, Nripen, cautiously lifted the curtain that hung before the manager's door and took a quick peep. The manager was Mr Seel's son-in-law, well-known for his despotic behaviour. Few men could have matched his expertise in snatching jobs away with a single stroke of his pen.

Nripen offered him a few papers for his signature. Then he fidgeted for a few moments, wiped his forehead, and blurted out with a red face, 'I ... sir, I ... would like to go home today. I mean, to my village. There's a train at four, you see. If I don't leave soon....'

'You went home last week, Nripen. I allowed you to go early last Tuesday, remember? How do you suppose we'll run a business if everyone begins leaving early every day? You haven't typed a single letter today, have you?'

The concept of holidays and leave was virtually unknown in this office. Everyone was expected to work from eleven in the morning until seven in the evening, Monday to Saturday. If it did not suit anyone, they could find themselves another job. Knowing how difficult that would be, each employee complied with instructions without protest, grateful simply to have a job to come to.

Nripen opened his mouth to speak, but the manager stopped him. 'Did you type the mortgage papers sent by Mallik and Chowdhury?'

'No sir,' Nripen said tearfully, 'they didn't send it.'

'So why couldn't you have phoned them? I have been telling you to do it for a week. You are not a little child, are you? Why does nothing ever get done here unless I do it myself?'

Nripen had to return to his seat, the question of his early departure forgotten. A little before dusk, people from the cash and English departments left. The likes of poor Nripen and other unfortunates had to wait another hour. They had been hired at such low salaries that no one ever thought about

232

them, not even the chowkidars at the front gate, who got to their feet if they saw a senior officer approaching, to give him a military salute. To Nripen and the junior clerks, they paid not the slightest attention.

When he finally found himself outside, Nripen cried piteously, 'Did you see that, Apurbo Babu? Why couldn't the manager let me go at four? So many offices closed at two this afternoon. All those people are home already, having a cup of tea. And look at us! This is pure torture.'

Prabodh Muhuri, one of the older clerks, said, 'Well, if you think so, you needn't come from tomorrow. No one has asked you to put up with it. My God, I feel so hungry I could eat a man! This happens to me every day ... I shall simply starve to death, I think.'

Apu laughed. 'Well, right now *I* am walking next to you, Prabodh da. If you must eat a man, do you think you could find someone else? I mean, spare me, please? I didn't come prepared to die.'

Prabodh was not amused. 'You may joke,' he said, 'you seem to find everything funny. One shouldn't speak to youngsters at all. Do you think you could speak to the manager and get him to increase our salaries? Wouldn't *that* be fun? But no ... you couldn't do that, could you?'

Apu said no more. He concentrated on walking, for he had to walk quite a distance. He had moved to a small room on the ground floor of a house that had several other flats. His room had a tiny kitchen attached to it, but that was all. He had to pay a monthly rent of thirteen rupees for this room. Unable to manage two establishments on a small salary, Apu had brought Aparna to Calcutta and had been living here for a year. He was lucky to have found this job after he lost the one at the newspaper.

Perhaps this is how most dreams—dreamt in one's youth—are crushed. He who dreams of becoming a wealthy industrialist ends up as a quack in a village; others who want to become famous lawyers or globetrotters (and be a second Columbus), finish up as sellers of coal, or school teachers, earning the princely sum of forty rupees a month. What happens to ninety-nine out of a hundred men had also happened to Apu: marriage, a rented room, the job of a clerk, baby food, and other baby paraphernalia. All except the last two items, perhaps, but the general picture was the same.

Aparna was chopping vegetables when Apu got home. 'You are early today!' she exclaimed on seeing him, moving the boti and the basket of vegetables to one side.

'Not all that early, it's seven o'clock,' Apu replied, 'but yes, I suppose I am earlier than usual. Did the oil man come again?'

'Yes, he did, but I told him to come after Wednesday, when you get paid.'

Apu went out on the verandah to wash his hands. Aparna always stored water for him there, since at this time in the evening, the women from the other flats liked using the bathroom.

'Why is this tuberose not standing straight? Could you tie it up with a string, please?' Apu said from the verandah, splashing his face.

Aparna made tea for him. As he sat down with his cup, an argument broke out near the bathroom. ' ... in that case, I suggest you go and find somewhere else to live. Yes, pay a hundred rupees, and move to a posh area, why don't you?' said a loud, rough voice. 'One day you have a headache, the next day your child has a cold ... whenever it's your turn, there's always something wrong. Why don't you simply take the entire top floor—that's just sixty-five rupees—and get us to leave?'

'Another fight with Mrs Ganguli?' Apu asked.

'Yes, who else? It's nothing new, is it? Mrs Ganguli always says just whatever she likes ... Mrs Haldar in the other flat has a small child, and no help at all, so she doesn't get the time. Sometimes, I go and help her out.'

For a whole year, Apu had witnessed these petty squabbles between the other tenants over whose turn it was to wash the staircase and the front verandah. It happened nearly every day. No one appeared to consider how much their words could hurt others. It was this total disregard for other people's feelings, this blinding narrowness of their mind, that distressed Apu more than anything else.

The room he lived in was quite airless. Sitting out on the verandah was perhaps more comfortable, but only a little distance away was a drain which collected all the rubbish from every household—vegetable peelings, fish-scales, stale rice and other food rotted in it. On rainy days, dirty and half-dirty clothes hung all over the house; here was an old and dented tin trunk, there was a bucket of coal. The children looked unclean, clad usually in unwashed clothes. Apu's own room was tidy in comparison, he had even grown tuberoses and other plants in pots; but even so, he could not help thinking that the atmosphere in the whole house was so full of poison that its fumes would choke any attempt to bring beauty and tenderness into it. None of the occupants of the other flats seemed to have any notion of aesthetics, they were happy simply to eat like pigs and wade in the mud. Apu felt suffocated within this constricting belt of ugliness.

Yet, there was nowhere he could escape to. He could not afford to keep a house running in Monshapota. In the city, thirteen rupees a month could not fetch him a better flat in a better locality. It was only Aparna who tried to keep everything neat and tidy. She had made lace covers for their trunks and suitcases, and hung a printed curtain on the window. Their sheets and pillowcases, even their mosquito-net, were always spotless. She swept the floor twice or thrice a day.

The Gangulis lived in the flat above Apu's. One of their relatives had been visiting them for some time, together with his wife and children. The man was ill, and had come to Calcutta for treatment. Clearly a poor relation, he seemed most embarrassed and guilty to be a burden on his hosts, and spent his days simply lying in a corner. His wife, a meek and mild woman, helped as much as she could with all the household chores. If she got a free moment, she came and sat by her husband, casting anxious glances at his face. Mrs Ganguli, however, pounced on her whenever she could, never bothering to mince her words, if she found any lapses in her duties. They were very poor indeed. Apu had occasionally visited the sick man and given him grapes, oranges and pomegranates. He had even bought their oldest boy a new shirt.

This did not, of course, mean that things were any better for him. To tell the truth, he was finding it virtually impossible to manage on his small salary. Aparna was a good and efficient housewife in many ways, but she did not quite understand the business of managing money. Invariably, both of them went into a spending spree during the first few days of the month, struggling hard to make ends meet as the month drew to a close.

All this distressed Apu, but what he resented most was the drudgery at work. From eleven o'clock in the morning to seven in the evening, all he was expected to do was stay seated at his desk, pushing a pen. Only once, in the last eighteen months, had he had the chance to visit the house his employer owned in the country. Having seen it, and the plants and the trees that surrounded it, Apu often dreamt of a house that he would have liked to build for himself. Whenever he got the chance, he drew designs and plans of his imaginary house. Actually, the house itself was not so important, it was the plants that concerned him much more. There had to be great variety in them, he decided. By the front gate he would plant stems of Chinese bamboo. The driveway—a stretch of red gravel—would be bordered with tuberoses and lavender. Above them would rise bokul and flame-of-the-forest, casting a gentle shade.

Sometimes he returned home, and began discussing his plans with his wife over a cup of tea: 'Where do you think we should plant a champa tree?'

Aparna had come to know her husband quite well in the last year and a half. She joined him in talking about his dream with a great deal of enthusiasm. 'Why just champa, surely we're going to have many more plants? How about creepers? Shall we have one going up our window?'

But every dream was shattered each morning when Apu had to return to his office, picking his way through an extremely dirty alley. He wondered seriously if any other place on earth could ever be as filthy. There were nearly fifteen warehouses for dried prawns. On hot, sunny days, things were just about bearable. On wet days, however, crossing this lane became well nigh impossible. There were always a number of cows and bullocks obstructing the way; and mud, cowdung and rotten apples lay plastered on the ground.

Over the last eighteen months, Apu had had to make this journey twice a day. In his office, his older colleagues were quite used to their jobs, they did not seem to mind either the hours or the conditions. Only Apu and the typist Nripen were unhappy.

Nripen kept looking at his watch. 'It's only six o'clock, Apurbo Babu. We can't leave until seven,' he complained.

'I know. Don't remind me. The evening outside is so beautiful, but we must rot here under electric lights!' Apu replied. He felt as if his employers had bought every single evening of his life.

Sometimes, looking thirstily at the evening sky through a window, Apu wondered about his childhood days. How did they get lost in the turmoil of his youth? Where were those blue skies, the open fields, the moonlit nights, heavy with the scent of mango blossom? Birds did not sing any more, flowers did not bloom, the sky no longer plunged down to meet the edge of a field, the air no longer turned heavy with the pungent smell of fresh ghetu flowers. Where were his dreams of romance, those that had seen him through the days of his bitterest struggle? His life had become like a picture drawn in only one colour, starting with files and papers and accounts in the office, and ending with his return to an unclean, untidy house that was little more than a pigeonhole, before rushing off to his evening job as a private tutor.

The only source of joy in his stale, claustrophobic life was Aparna. When she greeted him with a smile as he got home, brought him a cup of tea and something to eat, Apu often stared at her and wondered what he would have done if she had not come into his life. If the little cubbyhole he lived in seemed like home, it was only because she had made it so, with her smile, with her love and care, even by the way she wore a special saree and moved in the room. It was her own magic.

Occasionally, whenever he could find a few minutes, Apu read travelogues at his desk, or pamphlets published by rail and steamer companies, enticing one and all to visit all the remote and exotic corners of the earth. Come to Hawaii, said some. Life was not worth living if one did not see its palm groves, or hear the music of the waves on the sandy beach of Waikiki, when they sang to the stars on a moonlit night.

Haven't you seen El Paso? Come to southern California. Try sleeping on quiet nights under the starlit sky, amidst limestone mountains. When winter comes to an end, you may get to see the first flowers of spring, peeping from behind stalks of dried grass, on a rocky surface. Or come and see the thick forests of tall pine and douglas fir; and look at the shivering reflection of the snowcapped volcano, Mount Mazama, in the clear, ice-cold, shimmering waters of a lake. Or go to the northern states of America, and witness the ever-changing scenery in its silent forests, its harsh, mountainous landscape; hear the deep gurgles of waterfalls; watch herds of reindeer roam by frothy mountain rivers; bears, mountain goats and sheep; hot springs, glaciers, colourful clusters of violets and wild valerian amongst cedar and maple trees. Have you never seen these? Come, we will show you.

Tahiti! Tahiti! Thousands of miles away, who knew under which dark, mysterious ocean, glittering in the bright moonlight, a pearl was born? Coral spread out in the caves under the sea. Apu could hear its call, like distant music. Sitting at his desk, he got lost in his dreams. He would find a quiet corner somewhere in the world, in some beautiful place all those leaflets described, and build himself a tiny hut in a palm grove. From its open window, he would look at a blue ocean and little emerald-green islands, and watch a bevy of unknown birds. At night, huge open spaces in this wonderland, lit by the myriad stars in a strange, unfamiliar sky, would bring him great tales of mystery. Around his hut would be hundreds of wild flowers. There would be no one there, not a single soul—except he and Aparna.

The rich and the affluent he saw everywhere had money, but where was their will to see the world, to see life? Locked in their mansions, surrounded by expensive furniture, cars, and everything else money could buy, they were not merely indulgent; they were prisoners in their own homes. Every window through which they might have caught a glimpse of life was barred.... If only *he* had money! Not a great deal, just a little more. Those who did, knew only about profit and loss. Nothing else mattered to them, nothing else held any interest. Yet, it was their chests and trunks that were stacked with money.

The truth was that Apu was not willing to accept meekly the suffocation imposed by those that he worked for; nor was he going to give up his fight against the meanness and insularity he found everywhere. A love of life and all that it had to offer ran through his veins like a sparkling, bubbling, intoxicating drink. Moments of doubt he might have, but his spirit would not be easily crushed, nor his hopes and dreams torn apart.

Apu's office finally closed for the Puja holidays. Much relieved, he went home straight from work, eager to be with his wife. But today was no exception. Every day, as the afternoon wore on, Apu began casting frequent glances at the clock. After five o'clock, he started to feel as if, trying to swim in this endless ocean of time, he had finally caught sight of the shore. Two more hours to go. Six o'clock ... just one more! His home might only be a cubbyhole, but the presence of his wife made up for everything. Aparna made him forget all his woes.

When he got home, she brought him a cup of tea as she did every day. She tried to spend as much time as she could with her husband in the evening, for she knew that, very soon, he would rush off again to his second job. These moments were very special. Apu always found her neatly dressed when she opened the door, her hair tied back, a red dot on her forehead, the perfect incarnation of a grihalakshmi. She chatted with him while he drank his tea, asking him about his day, and telling him about hers. When he left, sometimes she reminded him about the novels they were reading together. 'When you come back tonight, let's finish reading that story about Maharani Jhindan and Dalip Singh,' she would say.

Apu had taken her a couple of times to the cinema. Aparna could not understand how the pictures moved, nor follow the main story, staring with wonder at the screen. Apu had had to explain the details to her on reaching home.

'Your father wrote to me,' said Apu, sipping his tea, 'asking me to take you there personally. But you know I can't get any time off ... why don't you get Ram to come and take you back? I shall go next month, if I can manage it. If you must go, it's best that you leave as early as possible. I have thought it over, you know ... at a time like this, a woman ought to be with her parents.'

Aparna blushed. 'No,' she said, 'Ram is too young, how could he take me? Besides, Ma wants to see you. She hasn't seen you for so long.'

'Very well. I will go with you. You're right, Ram isn't old enough to take care of you. I mean, you're going to have to move with extra care, aren't you? All right, give me that umbrella, it's time I went. We could leave tomorrow, couldn't we? Oh, give me a cigarette, please.'

'Another one? You've had eight already. Sorry, no more for you, not now. Maybe one more when you get back, but....'

'Please, please, just one. I won't ask for another tonight, I promise!'

Aparna frowned, then smiled. 'As if I'm going to believe you!' she said. 'You'll never go without, I know you.'

Apu did smoke rather a lot. It was his own decision to leave his tin of cigarettes with Aparna. She tried to be strict with him and limit the number he smoked, but she did not always win. Apu pestered her so much that she had to allow him extra ones. However, Apu seldom went out and bought more if he was denied one at home, for he did not wish to cheat his wife. It was only on holidays that he occasionally bought extra cigarettes, but this was rare.

Apu returned later that evening, to find that the little girl called Pintu from the flat upstairs was sitting in one corner of his room, looking pale and frightened. She was the daughter of the ailing man. The whole house was in an uproar. Aparna told him what had happened. 'Pintu here had gone to Gol Deeghi with Mrs Ganguli's little girl, Khuki,' she said. 'Pintu had some peanuts, then went to drink water, leaving Khuki alone for a few moments. When she came back, Khuki was gone. Pintu could not find her anywhere. I've seen Pintu's mother ... she's scared of Mrs Ganguli anyway, and now she's absolutely terrified. I decided to bring Pintu back with me and hide her here, or her mother would have killed her, I think. As for Mrs Ganguli, well ... you know what she is like. Why don't you go up and see what can be done?'

Mrs Ganguli was wailing loudly. Apu could hear every word: 'Vipers! That's what I'd been harbouring ... vipers to my bosom! They *wanted* to do this to me. That's why they wouldn't go, not move an inch. Are they happy now? Dear God, what am I going to do?'

Apu left hurriedly. 'Has Pintu had anything to eat?' he asked before going.

'Eat? She hardly knows what she is doing. Mrs Ganguli has not stopped cursing her. It wasn't Pintu's fault, really. She didn't want to take Khuki with her in the first place, but Khuki insisted. Pintu isn't old enough to take care of another child, is she?'

Eventually, Khuki was found in the Kolutola police station. She had lost her way, and had been unable to tell anyone her name, or where she lived. Luckily, a constable had found her and taken her to the station.

When they returned home with her, Aparna said, 'Thank heavens for that. But Pintu and her family have been told to leave. Mrs Ganguli told them to clear out tomorrow. You wouldn't believe the kind of things she said ... I had no idea one human being could say such things to another!'

'They don't have to leave,' said Apu, 'we are going away tomorrow, aren't we? You're not coming back for months, and I won't be back for another four or five days. Tell Pintu's mother they can stay here in our flat. Where will they go when her father isn't well? In fact, even when I get back, there shouldn't be a problem. I can always go to that mess round the corner, and sleep there at night. You see, I can understand their problem. When I was small, my mother had to face a similar situation, in Kashi. My father fell ill, and then he died … we didn't have a penny. I've never told you about those days, have I? We had to manage on what money others gave us. There were times when my mother and I could get nothing but a packet of daal. That was all we had for dinner, plain arhar daal, soaked in water. I was only ten. I know what it is to be poor. Tell them to move into our flat tomorrow.'

Pintu's mother started crying when it was time for Apu and Aparna to leave. Aparna had done a lot for her in the last few months. If she did not get the time to bathe and feed her children, Aparna had brought them to her room and given them the attention they needed. Pintu, in particular, was utterly devoted to her. She simply couldn't stop sobbing. Her mother was considerably older than Aparna. 'You must write to me,' she said, her eyes still full of tears, 'I will go to the temple and do a special puja when I hear you've had your baby, and all is well.'

They left, leaving the key to their flat with Pintu's mother.

❧❀❧

After a long time, Apu and Aparna found themselves travelling by rail and steamer. Both heaved a sigh of relief. Like Apu, Aparna came from a village; life in the city held no attraction for her. She had never lived in a tiny room like the one that was now her home. When all the other tenants in their building lit their stoves early in the morning, and then again in the evening, the smoke often choked her and made her

243

eyes burn painfully. Brought up in a large open mansion by the side of a river, she had never had to endure such discomfort—sometimes it brought tears to her eyes. Even so, in the last two years, Aparna had seldom thought of her own comfort or convenience. All her thoughts were for her husband. She had developed a peculiar affection for him, almost like that of a mother for her child. Apu's cheerful spirit, his fun-loving nature, the childlike qualities in his behaviour, and his general lack of experience about the complexities of life, all aroused her maternal instincts in a strange way. She had heard of his tragic life and his grim struggle with poverty as a student, although it was Pranav who had told her about it, not Apu. Apu, if anything, had bragged about all the wealth his family were supposed to have possessed, going so far as to mention the huge two-storey mansion that stood by the river in Nischindipur, which he said was his ancestral property. He even told her that he had stayed in a college hostel when he was a student.

An intelligent woman, Aparna could see easily enough how grossly exaggerated these tales were, but she never let on. On the contrary, she encouraged him to go back to Nischindipur. 'Didn't you say you wanted to visit your old village?' she had said to Apu more than once. 'I think you should. Surely that beautiful house of yours needs looking after, and Pulu da told me you own quite a lot of land over there. How will it remain yours if you never go back?'

'Ye-es, I have been meaning to do just that,' Apu had replied hesitantly, 'but that area is so badly infested with malaria, you see. Why do you think we had to move out? If it wasn't for malaria, why we'd still be....'

On unguarded moments, however, Apu often said things that contradicted whatever he had said before about his glorious past. Aparna pretended not to notice. Her mind was fully taken up by thoughts of giving Apu a better life. Raised in a wealthy household, poverty and hunger had been unknown concepts for her. Now, she resolved, she would do everything possible to make her husband happy.

This, in fact, became something of an obsession. She discovered, quickly enough, what Apu liked to eat. Then she learnt to make his favourite dishes, some from Nirupama in Monshapota. Apu found her, on many a wet evening, frying a savoury snack as he returned home from work, soaked to the skin. 'Where are you, Aparna?' he would ask. 'In the kitchen? What are you doing in the kitchen so early in the evening?' Then he would take a quick peep and exclaim, 'Are you frying my favourite snacks? How did you guess ...? Who told you?'

Aparna would rise, offer him dry clothes, and say, 'Why don't you change and sit here in the kitchen? I could serve these piping hot!' Apu's heart missed a beat when he heard Aparna speak like that. His mother had used the same tone. Aparna was as loving, as caring and as aware of his unspoken needs as his mother had been. It seemed as if Sarbajaya had simply transferred her charge from her own old and workworn hands to the younger and firmer hands of his wife. Apu had learnt to look upon women with new eyes. Every woman, he knew, was a mother, or a wife, or a sister. He himself had known three women in these different roles; every second of his twenty-six years had been blessed with the tender loving care he had received from them. He had come to know women very well indeed.

They left the steamer and got into a boat. Murari had come to meet them at the steamer ghat. He got into the same boat, chatting all the while. Aparna pulled her saree over her head and moved to one side. Long, soft shadows of an autumn afternoon played on the water, the left bank was lined with tiny villages, a boat loaded with earthen pots was moored at the ghat in Joshaikati.

Apu felt as if he had been released from prison—the terrors of Mr Seel's office had already faded away. His fun-loving heart danced with joy. After all, he had ties of blood with the green expanse that now met his eyes, the scent that rose from the water.

He grinned at Aparna and said, 'Come on, little bride, remove your veil and take a look around. It's your own homeland, don't be shy!'

Murari smiled and looked away. Aparna, embarrassed, tried to move even further away. A little later, Murari said, 'I have to get off here. I've been told to buy fresh fish from the local market. You two carry on. I'll walk back when I finish.'

He climbed out at the next ghat.

'How could you!' Aparna scolded her husband when Murari had gone, 'what must Dada have thought? Why must you always behave like a naughty boy? I will never go anywhere with you again ... never! You must learn to live alone in your flat.'

'As if I'd care. Did I beg you to come and live with me? I'll be just fine ... I'll cook delicious meals, all for myself.'

'Oh? Delicious meals, eh? As if I don't know what a good cook you are. What will you make? Boiled potatoes, boiled aubergines, everything thrown in together with rice, right?'

'Speak for yourself. Have you forgotten what you cooked the first time we were on our own, at the steamer ghat in Khulna? All that tasteless stuff?'

'Tasteless? Oh my God, what a liar you are! What am I going to do with you? Tasteless, he says, after all the ...'

'Yes, madam. Every mouthful.'

Aparna had started to look cross, but now she couldn't help laughing at Apu's tone. 'Have you ever had bhangon fish?' she asked, changing the subject. 'It's a salt-water fish, but tastes sweet. I'll get Ma to cook you some.'

'Really? And what will you tell your mother? Ma, here's my bel...'

Aparna placed a hand quickly over his mouth and said, 'Sh-sh.'

Their boat pulled in at Aparna's ghat just as dusk was falling. Both hearts were filled with a strange excitement. It was not caused by the fragrance that rose from the bushes on this heady autumn evening; nor was it due to the green rows of trees that stood by the river in dark clusters. The reason for this surge of feeling was simply their own youth— eager, joyous and exuberant.

Apu was back in the same room where he had spent the first night with Aparna after their wedding. Every night since their arrival, he had sat on the same bed and read by the light of a lamp, waiting for her to come. Tonight was going to be his last night. He had to return to the city in the morning.

Outside, moonlight fell on the branches of a coconut tree, white as the plumage of a crane. Staring out at the night, Apu's mind filled with distant memories of similar moonlit nights, spent long, long ago. The story of his life might well have been something out of the *Arabian Nights*. Where was he—living in a tiny cottage in a small village, not even able to get himself a square meal every day? And now he was the son-in-law of a wealthy zamindar. The funny thing was that it was only the present that seemed real. Memories of his past were indistinct, enveloped in a smoky haze.

It was a November night, and quite cool. The breeze bore an unfamiliar scent. 'It is the smell of mist,' thought Apu. Aparna arrived much later. 'What took you so long? I've been waiting for hours!' exclaimed her husband.

Aparna laughed. 'My uncle's bedroom is just by the stairs. If I came up any earlier, he would have heard my footsteps. So I had to wait until he closed his own door. I felt shy coming up before he'd retired.'

At these words, Apu pulled the shutters of the window with a loud clatter. Aparna gave an embarrassed smile and said, 'Are you going to be naughty again? Please don't ... Uncle's still awake, I think.'

Apu opened the shutters again just as loudly and, raising his voice a little, said, 'You forgot to bring me a glass of water, Aparna. Aparna? O Aparna!'

Words failed his wife. She buried her face in her pillow.

They spent what remained of the night talking. When dawn broke, they were still chatting.

'What time does your steamer leave?' Aparna asked, 'you did not sleep a wink, did you? And you didn't let me sleep, either. Look, why don't you try and get a little rest now? I'll send someone to wake you later. You must write as soon as you get home. Oh, remember to send the window curtains to the dhobi. Who's going to wash them until I get back?' Then she stroked her husband's arm lovingly and added, 'How thin you've become! I wish I could keep you here with me. A few days in our village would have improved your health, I'm sure. Calcutta's an awful place, one can't even get enough milk. But I've told Pintu's mother to make you mohanbhog every day. You must have some when you get back from office. At least you won't have to worry so much about expenses now that I'm here. Don't take extra tuitions, please.... Shall I go now?'

'No, no, why are you in such a hurry? It's still quite dark, your uncle's not going to stir for hours.'

'Oh, I've just remembered something else. Do go back to Monshapota and get the roof thatched again. Or else we'll have to spend a lot of money on that house once the rains start. We must start living there again. After all, that's our real home, not the flat in Calcutta. In any case, a straw roof wouldn't last for ever, unless someone actually lived in the house. Look, I must go now. Uncle will get up soon ... let me go, please?'

Aparna left. Apu began to wish immediately he had asked her to stay with him a little longer. No one in the house was awake yet. Why did he let her go? She would never have left him without his permission.

An hour later, Aparna returned to ask him if he would like a cup of tea, only to find him fast asleep. Sunlight streamed through an open window and fell on his face. Aparna closed the window quietly. Her heart brimmed with affection as she looked at her sleeping husband. 'Ma is right,' she thought, while going down the stairs, 'he does look like a god ... one of those faces painted for worship!'

There was no chance for them to meet again before Apu left later in the day. Apu certainly wanted to, but the house was packed with uncles and aunts and cousins. Shy as he was, he could not bring himself to ask someone to fetch Aparna. As soon as he had got into his boat, Murari's younger brother, Bishu, happened to ask, 'Why didn't you say goodbye to Didi, Jamaibabu? I saw her crying in the little room on the landing when you were leaving!'

But the tide was going out with such force that the boat had already been dragged half way to the curve near Joshaikati. Apu could not go back.

❧❀❧

After his return to Calcutta, one day Apu ran into Debu, his childhood friend from Diwanpur. Debu was going to America.

He had done his BSc from Calcutta University, but had never met Apu before since he did not know where he lived. Apu found the news of his departure surprising. He was pleased for his old friend, but could not help feeling a little envious. It was the same Debu, who could not live without going back to see his family every Saturday. Yet here he was, about to set sail for America!

The next three months passed with great difficulty. For over a year now, he had got into the habit of returning home from work, to be greeted by his smiling wife. Now the thought of going back to an empty house was so depressing that he started to go straight from his office to the house of the child he taught in the evenings.

He tried seeing Leela, but her whole family was out of town. They had all gone to Burdwan, Apu was told, to settle some dispute over their property.

One Sunday, he visited the monastery in Belur and wrote a long letter to Aparna on his return, telling her how much he had enjoyed seeing the place. When she came back, they would certainly make another visit together. Usually, Aparna's replies to his letters were prompt. But, this time, there was no reply. A couple of days passed; then four, then that stretched to a week. Apu began to feel quite distracted with anxiety. What could have happened? Had Aparna died? Yes, perhaps that was it. He had troubled dreams that night—he saw Aparna looking at him with tears brimming in her eyes. 'Didn't I tell you I wouldn't live long?' she was asking. 'I told you one night in Monshapota, remember? Somehow ... I had this feeling ... as if someone whispered it to me. I am going now. Perhaps I'll see you again in another life?'

Apu woke with a start, and decided immediately he would not go to his office that day. The next day was a Saturday. He would leave for Aparna's village as soon as possible, and spend the weekend with her. Never mind about his job. He packed a suitcase hurriedly, and was about to leave, when a letter arrived from someone in her family. They were all well, thank God. Oh, what a relief! Apu felt faintly hurt by Aparna's silence. Why hadn't she written?

❦

He returned from work on Saturday, to find Murari sitting in a chair on the verandah outside his flat. Pleased to see him again, Apu exclaimed, 'Good heavens, I have a visiting dignitary here! It's my lucky day today.'

Murari said nothing. He merely took out a sealed envelope from his pocket and offered it to Apu, in absolute silence. Apu stretched a hand to take it, then looked properly at Murari's face. The expression on it suggested Murari was trying very hard to fight tears.

Apu's blood ran cold. Almost unknowingly, a few words escaped from his lips. 'Is Aparna no more?' he asked.

Murari broke down. 'What happened?' Apu went on.

'Yesterday morning, she delivered a baby boy at about eight-thirty. Then ... an hour later....'

'Was she conscious?'

'Yes, throughout. She had even asked her mother to send you a telegram about the birth of the baby. She was fine then. But around nine o'clock, you see....'

Much later in his life, there were times when Apu wondered with amazement how he had managed to stay so calm and ask so many questions. Murari, for his part, went back home and told everyone, 'I had spent all my time during the journey wondering how on earth I was going to break such a news to Apurbo. But I didn't have to say anything at all. *He* dragged it out of me.'

When Murari had gone, it occurred to Apu that he had failed to enquire about his newborn child. Was he alive or not? Murari didn't say. Who knew, perhaps the baby had died, too.

The news spread gradually through the whole building. When Apu returned from work a day later, one of the tenants on the first floor— a Mr Sen—appeared suddenly on the small verandah. 'Please come in, Mr Sen!' invited Apu.

Mr Sen stepped in, dragged up a stool and sat down, clicking his tongue sadly.

'Tragic, utterly tragic! Beautiful as Saraswati, and gifted as Lakshmi, wasn't she? I saw her only the other day, you know, washing your clothes in the bathroom. I wanted to have an early bath that morning, but seeing her I thought, never mind, let her finish what she's doing. Then ... another day, you know, she had made a special fish curry, and sent up a bowlful for us. She was so gentle, so soft-spoken ... what can you do, Aprubo Babu? It's all God's will.'

Mr Sen left, only to be replaced by Mrs Ganguli. Although she was an elderly lady, she had never spoken directly with Apu. Her head partially covered by her saree, she stood outside the door and began: 'There she was, so lively and cheerful, we saw her every day, didn't we? Who could have imagined this would happen? Last night, Nabeen—my eldest, you see—said, "did you hear, Ma, Apurbo Babu's wife has died, he's just been told". I didn't believe him, frankly. But this morning, my nephew, Batul, said the same thing. So I thought let me go and find out. But it took me all day to find just five minutes. The mornings are just madness—breakfast for the two men, and Batul has to go all the way to Dum Dum. It's a new job in a factory, only a little over two rupees a week right now, but his sahib says he'll raise that to four from April. Batul was the only child of his mother ... she died when he was a baby, and he's been with me ever since ... you're not the only one with sorrows, you see, son, we all must learn to live with grief. But you are a man, and still so young, what have you to worry about? You could marry again, couldn't you, not once but ten times, if you so wished?'

Apu heard her in silence, thinking all the while, 'They mean well, all these people who are coming to see me now are good people. But why can't they leave me alone? I'd much rather be alone in my room. Would they understand if I explained?'

It grew dark. A couple of mosquitoes began humming near the potted plants in a corner. Usually, this was the time when Apu would get up, light his stove, and make himself a cup of tea and perhaps a plate of halwa. Today, he continued to sit on the dark verandah, lost in thought.

The sound of a match being struck in his room startled him. Just for a second, his heart beat faster, it seemed as if Aparna was back. Had she been here, she would have lit the stove by now and shone a lamp under a tulsi plant as a part of her evening rituals.

'Who is it?' Apu called.

Pintu emerged from his room. 'Kakababu,' she said, 'Ma wants to know where you keep your bottle of kerosene.'

Apu turned to her in surprise. 'Who's in my room? Your mother? Oh ... it's you, Boudi!' He rose quickly, and found Pintu's mother sitting on the floor, cleaning his stove.

'You didn't have to bother, Boudi, I could have ... I would have ... done something later....'

But Pintu's mother had taken charge. Apu gave her the bottle of kerosene and returned to his chair on the verandah. She made him tea and something to eat, and got Pintu to take it out to him. At nine o'clock, she cooked him dinner in her own kitchen and brought it herself, quietly leaving the plate in his room, covering it with a lid.

Pintu's father was better, though still quite weak. Occasionally, he was seen going out for a walk, clutching a stick. A room on the ground floor had been vacated, so Pintu and her family had somewhere to stay. The doctors were hopeful that they would be able to return home in another month.

The next morning, Pintu's mother made him breakfast. When he returned from work and sat on his verandah again, without even bothering to change his clothes, she reappeared once more to light his stove. Apu went over to speak to her. 'You don't have to do this every day,' he told her, 'I can quite easily get myself a cup of tea from a stall near Gol Deeghi.'

'You don't have to feel bad about this, Thakurpo,' she replied. 'It's no trouble for me, honestly. Why don't you get that stool and sit here? Let me make you a cup of tea.'

This was the first time Pintu's mother had spoken to him directly. She appeared to be around thirty.

She was slim, dark, neither pretty nor plain. Apu sat on the stool near the door. Pintu, who had accompanied her mother, said, 'Kakababu, will you take me to the park? I could get a sapling, and then plant it here in a pot.'

The kettle had boiled. Pintu's mother lifted it from the stove and said, 'Tell you what, why don't I get some flour and fry you some puris? That way you could have your dinner right now. You must be hungry, though I know you're not much of an eater.'

The lady's free and easy tone made Apu lose some of his own self-consciousness.

'Very well. You're most kind, Boudi. I really shouldn't expect....'

'Please stop saying that, Thakurpo. Have you forgotten how much you did for us? Even close relatives would not have done so much. Who would allow strangers to stay in their house? But ... I didn't even get the chance to thank her properly. She was so kind, so thoughtful. Do you know what she used to do? Every day, as soon as you left in the morning, she would go and call Pintu and give her a meal, in case I was busy with nursing my husband and couldn't find the time.

There were times when ...' she broke off abruptly. Suddenly, Apu thought: *She'd* understand. He could talk about Aparna with this lady. She seemed to have the perception everyone else lacked.

The whole day, Apu tried to keep busy, thrusting aside all memories of Aparna, burying them under a pile of work. In the past, he did sometimes steal a few moments to think and daydream, or write poems on scraps of paper instead of doing his office work. But now, he began to work like a maniac, pestering everyone else with reminders about work undone, finishing in a couple of hours what he would normally have taken the whole day to do. Nripen, the typist, got tired of typing his letters for him.

On full-moon nights, Apu missed Aparna more than ever. Why, only last year she had done the Kojagari Lakshmi Puja on such a night. She had looked majestic like the goddess herself; how expressive her eyes were, how beautiful her features! There was something regal about the way she moved her neck, it aroused reverence.

Snatches of conversation kept coming back to him. Back in her father's place, she had said to him one day, 'I wish I could make breakfast for you here, but I feel so shy. My sister can't fry puris, and my mother and aunt are both busy ... you don't get to eat what you really like, do you?'

He tried to write, but found himself throwing it all to one side, thinking, 'What is the use of all this? Why bother?' A huge aching emptiness engulfed his whole being ... his loss seemed quite irreparable. Nothing, no one could fill the void Aparna's death had created. There was nothing before him, no trees, no creepers, no flowers or fruit ... only an endless expanse of dry, hazy, sandy desert.

A month later, it was time for Pintu and her family to return to their village. Her mother said, 'I never had a brother, Thakurpo. You have been like a brother to me, but there was nothing that I could do for you. If you can come and visit your sister sometimes, I shall truly appreciate it.'

Apu gave her most of his household goods, particularly items from his kitchen. Pintu's mother refused to take them at first, but Apu insisted. 'What do I want these for, Boudi? I would only have thrown them away, or given them to someone else. If you took them, that would make me very happy.'

⋘◈⋙

What happened after death? Apu asked a few people, but no one seemed to know; nor were they interested. One day, he happened to be reading the story of Paul and Virginia. It mentioned the dead Virginia returning to visit her lover, Paul. Apu's despondent heart felt eager to clutch at this straw: in a world of darkness, it was a faint glimmer of light. But could the dead really come back? He asked everyone he knew, in his building, his office, in the neighbouring mess. But the people he spoke to were all from the ordinary, mundane world of the living. They had no answer for him. Some laughed behind his back, or winked knowingly at each other, or smiled pityingly, which Apu found most unbearable.

Then he heard about a sadhu, and went to visit him one evening in a small alley in Dormahata. A large crowd was waiting to see him; some simply wanted to look at him, other wanted cures for ailments. Apu had to wait a long time before he was called. This sadhu, as it turned out, was not wearing saffron clothes as most of them did. He was clad in a white dhoti, and a sleeveless vest, and was sitting crosslegged on a low table.

He heard Apu's question and replied gravely, 'How long ago did your wife die? About two months? She has been reborn.'

Apu stared at him. 'How do you know? I mean ...' he began.

'Rebirth takes place soon after death,' the sadhu cut him short firmly. 'No soul, upon leaving a body, lingers for very long. You must believe my words, mister. I know these days young men like you, who have learnt a bit of English, scoff at such ideas. But it is the truth.'

Apu could not believe a word of it. Aparna ... *his* Aparna ... was going to be reborn as a little girl in another eight or nine months in the house of a perfect stranger? In some distant, unknown land, with absolutely no recollection of her life with him? All that love, tenderness, caring and sharing, was no more than an illusion? A pack of lies? Impossible! But he could not sleep at night. Just for a fleeting second, he would wonder if the sadhu was right. Then his entire being would rebel at the idea. What he had heard simply could not be true ... it was just a string of lies, lies, lies! Yes, that's what it was, and he refused to believe any of it. In spite of his grief, suddenly he wanted to laugh. How could the man be so sure Aparna had been reborn? Had he received a telegram to that effect? What humbug!

He continued to pass his days in utter loneliness. After the departure of Pintu's family, his flat seemed emptier. Every little thing brought back memories of Aparna, so much so that he began to find it impossible to spend any time in it. Added to this was the problem of frequent visits by Mrs Ganguli, who suddenly seemed very keen to have him married to her niece. She would barge in the minute she found him sitting alone, and start talking about the transitory quality of life, the beauty and many talents of the said niece, and suggest openly that Apu should pay her a visit in January.

Even cooking just for himself proved to be a problem, although he had done it before. Now he felt strangely angry and hurt. Why should he be left on his own again? The silent nights seemed to choke him, his heart heavy with the dead weight of his loneliness. But things were no better during the day. At home, at work, or out in the streets, there was no one he could call his own.

Most of his friends had disappeared, including Pranav. He was not particularly close to anyone else. The few who greeted him every now and then were not all that understanding or sympathetic. Sundays and other holidays dragged endlessly. Apu thought with wonder of the time when he used to count the days until Saturday. Why, he used to do that even a year ago, his heart full of eager anticipation. And now? Now his heart filled with dread as each Saturday got closer.

The only friend he went to visit occasionally was one he had known in college. He ran a small chemist's shop, specialising in herbal medicines. Apu went there one Sunday, in the hope of being able to forget the painful memories of his life with Aparna, at least for a few hours. His friend, it turned out, was not doing particularly well.

'Oh, it's you!' he greeted Apu. 'I thought you were a creditor. They keep hounding me all day. So I tend to get nervous the minute someone appears at the door. Do come in, sit down.'

'Have you paid back that Kabuliwallah?'

'No, I just couldn't. So either I hide when he comes, or tell him as many lies as I can. I had put in an advertisement in a newspaper, but couldn't pay for it, either. So they went to court, and a bailiff came and sealed everything. I needn't hide anything from you, brother; to tell the truth, I haven't got enough money to buy the groceries today. But that isn't all. Do you know what the real problem is? It's my wife. She's a good woman, very good ... too good for my liking.'

Apu had to laugh. 'What do you mean? You have a good wife, and you don't like it?'

'No. If one is so meek, so docile, so obedient, things get … bland, don't you see? I'd like her to be just a little naughty, just a bit pert, show more spirit. But no. What have I got? Someone who's never learnt to protest. She puts up with every hardship, without complaining at all. She may have to starve, she may not have any decent clothes, but there's not a word from her. If I tell her to turn right, she'll promptly do so. If I say go to the left, she'll turn left. It's all quite useless, there's no spice left in my life. My neighbour's wife, the other day, flew into a rage after a row with her husband, and broke several glasses and some of their furniture. I felt great pangs of envy, I don't mind telling you, and cursed my luck. I cannot stand such a boring old life any more, believe me. I say, do you know of a naughty little girl one might approach?'

'Why? Would you like a second wife? Didn't you just say you couldn't feed the one you've got?'

'That's true, but … you see, I am convinced we are not really suited to each other. If we were, surely we'd have fought, at least once in a while? … Who is it? Tepi? Here's my eldest daughter. Tepi, go and get two paisas from your mother and buy us some savouries. And tell her to make us some tea.'

'Tell me,' Apu asked, 'where do you think people go after death?'

'Don't know. Never thought about it. *You* tell me something. How can I get rid of my creditors? That Kabuliwallah is going to turn up any moment now. I borrowed eighteen rupees from him. He charges four annas per rupee … I haven't paid him any interest for two weeks. What am I going to tell him today? That scoundrel's just about to arrive. Could you … could you give me two rupees?'

'I haven't got two at this moment. Here's one, I'll come back tomorrow and give you the other, all right? Here, Tepi, take these savouries inside, they look delicious … no, no, I

259

don't want any, you eat them … all right, I'll take just one. Go on, Tepi.'

❧

Apu left his friend and spent some time roaming aimlessly. Was Leela back in town? Should he go and check? She had been living with her mother in Burdwan for a year. Her grandfather in Calcutta had helped fight their case and regain some of their lost property. Leela had joined a college to finish her graduation, but had left it after only a year.

He reached Mr Lahiri's house in Bhowanipore just before it got dark. A bearer called Ramlagan recognised Apu and took him in to their drawing room. Mr Lahiri had gone to Ranchi, he said. Leela didimoni? Why, didn't Apurbo Babu know anything about her? Leela didimoni had got married last April. Her husband was a big engineer in Nagpur, and he'd been to England. He looked and behaved exactly like a sahib, you just couldn't tell the difference. He came from a very wealthy family, they were as wealthy as these people. Why, hadn't Apurbo Babu received an invitation to the wedding?

Apu's face fell. 'N-no, I don't think … actually … I mean, yes, but … never mind, I'll get going now, Ramlagan, I'll come back another day.'

On stepping out of Leela's house, the world seemed emptier, lonelier, and far more colourless than ever before. But why should he feel like that? If Leela had got married, wasn't that good news? Why shouldn't she? After all, it was perfectly natural that she should—and that, too, to a wealthy and qualified man, suitable in every way. He ought to be rejoicing.

Apu left the main road and began wandering in the park in front of the Victoria Memorial. In the gathering dusk, he walked restlessly, his mind unable to think of anything else.

Leela was now married. It was something to feel happy about. Good. Very good.

EIGHTEEN

❦

Apu could no longer continue to live in Calcutta.
Everything about it, every aspect of his life—the stifling
routine he had to follow every day, the boring monotony of
his work—became totally intolerable. Besides, a baseless and
unreasonable belief was slowly taking firm root in his mind.
It seemed to him that everything would be all right if only
he could get out of Calcutta. Outside the city, he could find
peace and happiness again.

He left his job at the office of Mr Seel, and eventually
found a job as a school teacher in a village called Chapdani.
The place was actually neither a village nor a town. There
were jute mills, slums where the workers lived, a few shops
with tin roofs, roads littered with coal dust, and the air was
filled with a dark haze. It had neither the neat compactness

261

of a town, nor the clean, green beauty of the countryside.

Pranav arrived from Dhaka during the Christmas break and paid him a visit. He knew about Apu's departure from Calcutta. He reached Chapdani just before dusk. It took him a while to find the place where Apu lived. It was only a small room tucked away in a corner of the market. Half of it was used as a consulting chamber by the local quack in the morning and in the evening. The other half had a bed, covered by a not very clean sheet, a few books, and some clothes on a bamboo rack. Apu's tin trunk was pushed under the bed.

'Do come in,' Apu greeted him, 'how did you get my new address?'

'Never mind that. What made you leave Calcutta and come here? God, how can a decent human being live in a place like this?'

'Why? What's so awful about it? I couldn't stand living in Calcutta any more ... I was prepared to leave and go just about anywhere, when I found this job in the village school, so I came here. Wait a second, let me go and order a cup of tea for you.'

Next to Apu's room was a stall that sold parathas and other fried snacks. It was run by a Brahmin from Bankura. Pranav was amazed to see this man, later in the evening, bringing Apu his dinner—a pile of barely edible stuff—on a dirty and dented brass plate. It turned out that this was what Apu ate every day, it was the only food that was keeping him alive. Apu's tastes had always been simple, he had never been interested in trimmings, but at least those simple tastes had been refined. What had happened to him? Pranav could not remember him looking so unclean, either.

But what hurt and distressed him the most was Apu's visit the following evening to the shop of a jeweller called Bishu, where a number of low-class men had gathered to play cards. Pranav was shocked to see his friend join them happily and spend hour after hour in their company, amidst loud laughter and exchange of lewd jokes.

On their return to Apu's room, Pranav said, 'Come with me, Apu. Let's get out of here. You don't have to stay another day.'

'What makes you say that?' Apu sounded very surprised. 'Why shouldn't I stay here? The people are all so friendly, it's a very nice place. That jeweller you just met is quite an affluent man in these parts. Didn't you see his house? What a lot of granaries he's got! He'd invited me to his daughter's wedding, looked after me very well.' After a pause, he added happily, 'He—and his family—want me to stay here permanently. I mean, not here in Chapdani, but in Begumpur, not far from here. He owns that whole area, so he's offered to give me a bit of his land where he grows rice, and even build a house for me. It won't be anything fancy, of course, a mud hut with a thatched roof, but still ... I could take you there tomorrow, you'll like the place.'

Pranav refused to be swayed. He continued to try to persuade Apu to return, and Apu continued to produce reasons why he should remain where he was. At first, he argued reasonably, trying to establish that he was an important man in Chapdani. Then he ended up getting cross with Pranav and showing it. This had never happened before. Apu had never been known to get angry. Pranav had to give up, and go back to the city the following evening—alone.

Apu was no longer the person he had once known, Pranav thought on his way back. The young man who used to brim with the sheer joy of living, now seemed tired and lifeless. Why, it had never been in Apu's nature to be so easily satisfied if only his basic needs were met; or to cling, like a beggar, to the prospect of support and shelter. Yes, Apu had changed. There was no doubt about that.

Every evening, when he returned from his school, Apu found a chair with a broken arm and sat on the little verandah attached to his room. This was the time when he felt absolutely lonely. The need for company, to be with people, became so urgent that Apu was forced to look for someone to talk to; but most of the inhabitants of Chapdani were either workers of the jute mills, or owners of shops in the market. He did not know many of them. He was glad to have found the group that got together every evening at the jeweller's shop. At least until nine or ten o'clock at night, Apu's time passed reasonably happily.

Facing Apu's verandah was a small railway track, owned by the Martin company. Across it was a pond, whose water was as dirty as it was tasteless. Labourers from the jute mills lived in a slum on the other side. It was at this pond that they washed all their dirty clothes every day. On sunny days, Apu could see from his verandah several brown sarees stretched on the grass by the pond to dry. All the women in the slum wore similar sarees.

Behind the slum were a few almond trees, a pile of bricks, a small rice field, and a jute mill. Sometimes, at night, red and purple lights flickered through gaps in the bricks piled high, going out occasionally, then reappearing again. Apu watched these intently. At ten o'clock, a train arrived from Howrah, went past Apu's verandah and stopped at the station close by. Apu could see its passengers with all their trunks and cases and bundles. A few minutes later, the Brahmin from Bankura brought him his dinner of parathas and vegetables. By the time he finished eating and went to bed, it was usually past eleven. This was his daily routine. It did not vary. Nothing ever changed.

His perpetual need for company and the necessity of finding something to do also took him somewhere else. It was the branch post office, which was not far. Apu visited it every evening and inspected, with great eagerness, the mail that arrived there. At five o'clock, a peon from the suboffice arrived with a sealed bag slung across his shoulder, filled with letters and other documents,. The seal was then broken, and the bag opened with a pair of scissors. At times, Apu said to the postmaster, 'Shall I open the bag, Charan Babu?'

'Yes, yes, go ahead,' Charan Babu would reply, 'let me check my stock of stamps, and do the accounts. Here are the scissors.'

There were postcards, envelopes, newspapers, parcels, money orders.

'How many money orders? Seven? What am I going to do, Apurbo Babu? I haven't got any money here!' Charan Babu wailed from time to time. 'Could you tell me the total amount, please? Fifty-seven rupees and nine annas? Forget it, I just can't do anything about it now. I mean, I cannot be expected to pawn my wife's jewellery to pay for these, can I? I am supposed to account for every penny, you know. No spare cash is ever allowed....'

Visiting the post office became the most enjoyable part of his day. Soon after he finished school, Apu's feet turned automatically towards the post office. What attracted him the most were the envelopes. The mail bag revealed different kinds of envelopes each evening—some of them were white, others pink or green. Since receiving a letter had always been something of a rare event in his life, all letters, but these envelopes in particular, fascinated him. Only Aparna had been able to quench his thirst, but that had been just for a couple of years. At times, the writing on some of the envelopes seemed identical to hers, almost as if Aparna herself had written the address. Apu had received many an envelope like this, back in his little flat in Calcutta. Now, he knew, none of the letters that poured out of the mailbag could be his, there was no chance of anyone writing to him; yet, the attraction those sealed envelopes held was irresistible.

One day, a postcard reached Chapdani from the dead-letter office, having roamed from village to village, adorned with several postmarks, a bit like a devout Vaishnav wrapped in his scarf with the name of his Lord printed all over. The addressee was nowhere to be found. According to the postman, there was no one by that name in the whole region. The postcard lay in one corner of the office, unattended, for a few days. Then, someone swept it out together with other useless pieces of paper. Apu found it among other rubbish reposing on the grass just outside the post office. Curious, he picked it up and read it:

Respected Mejo dada,

You have not written to us for a very long time. Since we do not know where you are, or what your present address is, we have not been able to write to you, either. I am sending this letter at your old address, I hope you will not forget to reply. I cannot understand why you stopped writing to us. Perhaps you have forgotten us completely, or you would have written at least one letter, even if you could not visit us again. How can I let you see in a letter just how concerned we have felt by your silence? Do you think your relationship with us has ended totally? Anyway, I suppose one must accept what is written in one's destiny. I should not blame you for anything. I hope you will not mind my writing like this. If I have said anything wrong, please forgive me as you would forgive a younger sister. How have you been keeping? Please accept my respectful good wishes. I do hope I will get a reply.

Looking forward to hearing from you.

Your sister,
Kusumlata Basu

266

The letter had been written by an unformed feminine hand. It was full of spelling mistakes. Although the writer called herself a sister, she could not be the real sister of the addressee, for he was a Jeevankrishna Chakravarty. How sad that such a letter, brimming with so much emotion and anxiety, should end up in a rubbish heap! The girl either did not know the correct address at all, or had made a mistake in writing it. But the sincerity of her feelings was evident in every word, every letter written by that unsteady hand. Such sincerity deserved to be treated with respect. Apu took the letter away to his room and kept it with his own papers. He could picture Kusumlata Basu quite easily: fifteen or sixteen years old, slim and graceful; thick, wavy, dark hair running down her shoulders; large expressive eyes.... Where was she now, still waiting for a reply from her Mejo dada? Did she realise how futile the whole exercise had been? Why did so much love, such eager anticipation, such warmth from the heart of an innocent, unspoilt young girl have to meet with such a fate? Why did no one even try to appreciate its true worth?

The playing of cards at Bishu's shop that evening continued until quite late. Each time someone suggested calling it a day, Apu made them stay back, refusing to allow the game to be ended. When, at last, it did, and Apu began to walk back to his room, he ran into one of his colleagues from his school. It was Ashu Babu, known as the Third Pundit. He was walking down the road with a stick in his hand, tapping it from time to time. On seeing Apu, he said, 'Why, Apurbo Babu, where are you off to at this time of night?'

'Nowhere. I was at Bishu's, playing cards....'

Ashu Babu suddenly looked around, lowered his voice and said, 'Apurbo Babu, let me tell you something. You do not come from these parts, do you? How did you manage to get trapped by Purno Deeghri?'

This made no sense to Apu. 'How do you mean, trapped? I don't understand!' he exclaimed.

Ashu Babu lowered his voice even further and said, 'Do you think it's nice to be seen going to his house so frequently? And giving them money? You are, after all, a school teacher. People are talking about you. Did you know that?'

'No. What is being said?'

'Surely I don't have to tell you?' Ashu Babu paused for a second and added, 'Leave it. Take my advice, and keep your distance. You are not the first one. There was someone else before you came. Another young man like you. He used to work in a shop. They milked him dry. That's how they make a living. There's been some talk of cutting them out altogether … you know, total ostracisation.' The Pundit stopped again, gave Apu a meaningful smile and went on, 'Besides, what's that girl got to offer, anyway? If you went to the city, you could get much more….'

So far, Apu had been unable to follow a single word, or guess why he was being offered such advice. The last remark, however, made him exclaim in great surprise, 'Which girl? Pateshwari?'

'Ha ha ha ha, who else? Sh-sh, not so loud!'

'What is she supposed to have done? What did you just say?'

'Look, I did not say anything. I only repeated what others have been saying for a long time, there's nothing new in it. Don't get involved with the Deeghris. You are an outsider here, and a school teacher. You come from a decent family, too, so you must think of your character and reputation, mustn't you?'

The Third Pundit finished his speech and went on his way. Apu stared after him, still feeling profoundly puzzled, but by the time he got back home, the whole thing had become clear.

His association with the Deeghri family had begun thus: Soon after his arrival here, Apu got together a few of his students and formed a group of workers to look after the sick and the ailing. One day, on his way back from school, he was stopped by a middle-aged man he had never met before. The man grabbed his hands and almost burst into tears. 'My son has got typhoid,' he said, 'he's been ailing for two weeks. I cannot get time off from my job—I work in a jute mill—so if you don't help me, my son is sure to die. Please, if you could send a couple of your volunteers to my house during the day ... and do you think you could go yourself ... I mean, just a few times?'

The patient took thirty-three days to recover. Apu was present by his bedside virtually every day, working together with the other volunteers. If he had to be given medicine at three in the morning, Apu stayed awake for him, allowing the others to sleep. He sat outside, reading on the front verandah, in case sitting more comfortably made him fall asleep.

One afternoon, the patient suddenly took a turn for the worse. Mr Deeghri, the father of the patient, was away at work, the two volunteers had been sent home to have their lunch, and Apu was alone. It fell to him to reassure Mr Deeghri's wife, get her two daughters to fill hot water bottles and press them to the patient's icy hands and feet until life returned to them.

One day, after his son was fully restored to health, Mr Deeghri said to Apu, 'How can I ever thank you enough for what you did for me? My wife tells me you have no one to cook for you. Well, in the past month, Master Moshai, we have come to look upon you as one of the family. Why don't you have your meals with us? It would certainly be no trouble for us, and should suit you, too. What do you say?'

Apu agreed, and from that day he had been having his main meal with the Deeghris every day.

He had not known them a long time, but they had all been thrown together at a moment of crisis, so it was easy enough to feel close to them, as if he really was one of the family. He began calling Mrs Deeghri 'mashima'. Not only that, he also started handing over his salary to her at the beginning of each month. Mashima did explain where the money had gone when the month came to an end, but did not fail to add a few extra rupees to the list of expenses, making sure those rupees were taken off Apu's salary the minute it was handed to her. Bishu, the jeweller, had once said to Apu, 'Don't let the Deeghris lay their hands on your money. They are not well-off, they need money all the time. Besides, that old Deeghri woman is very clever, she has quite a few tricks up her sleeve, I can tell you. You are an outsider, where's the need for you to mix with them?'

But Apu did mix with them, even with the two girls. The older was called Pateshwari. She was about fifteen, and reasonably fair, but she had never struck Apu as being good-looking. What he had noticed was that it was Pateshwari who paid more attention to his needs than anyone else. Had it not been for her, Apu would probably have had to leave for school every day on an empty stomach. She asked him to give her his used handkerchiefs and washed them for him. During the lunch break, she sent her younger brother to his school with a hot meal. When he sat down to eat at home, Pateshwari quickly stuffed a few paan leaves with masala and left them for him, wrapped in his handkerchief. He was grateful to her for taking care of him, but would not have thought, even in his wildest dream, that other people could misconstrue each action, every little gesture. Apu's mind was quite incapable of such unclean, unholy thoughts.

His initial amazement gave way to anger. Then, thinking things over carefully, he decided to stop going to Mr Deeghri's house from the next day. If nothing else, at least that should save Pateshwari's reputation from further damage, he thought.

Getting a square meal became an even bigger problem, for the Brahmin from Bankura had disappeared with apparently nothing but his cooking implements, leaving behind him a sea of debts.

But life continued. One day, glancing idly through a newspaper, Apu suddenly came across an article on the subject of education. The writer was his old classmate in college, Janaki. Under his name, in brackets, were the words 'on deputation to England'. Apu knew that Janaki had successfully finished doing his MA and BT, and was teaching in a government school. But no one had told him about his visit to England. Who could have told him, anyway? Apu felt quite intrigued by the discovery. Janaki in England? Why, that was brilliant!

He read the article with great interest. Janaki had written about the teaching methods and the daily lives of the students in a well-known school in England. Apu laid the paper aside, and went out for a walk. Janaki—the same old Janaki—was actually in England! Memories of his college days came flooding back. He remembered the temple, where he had gone so often with Janaki, two poor students looking for a free meal. Like him, Janaki had had to struggle a lot as a student. Apu felt very pleased for his friend.

The roads were extremely dusty, mixed with powdered coal. Walking here was not at all pleasant. Slums lined the road. Most men were sitting on dirty string beds, smoking hookahs and chatting, Not for the first time, Apu glanced at the dark and dingy rooms and wondered what made people live in those voluntarily. What tempted them? They did not know, those poor souls had no idea, that every second, the stale, unclean air, the awful atmosphere where they lived, was destroying their minds, all finer feelings, good taste, their characters, even all thoughts of God. Had they never seen the sun, or basked in its light? Had they never spent any time in the green dark woods and seen creepers going up trees? Had none of them witnessed the beauty of this earth under the open sky? Did they not love any of it?

There were no fields near here, the nearest one was in Begumpur, several miles away. Sunday was the only day in the week he could go there. Today, he returned home after only a short walk.

He had spent many days roaming in Chapdani and its neighbouring villages, looking at their local flora, and recording a detailed description in a large notebook. Perhaps, one day, he might write a book on it. When he tried showing it to a couple of colleagues, they laughed the whole thing off. Write a book on such absurd stuff? Was he mad?

This evening, he did not feel like going to Bishu's shop. He could only think of Janaki. In England now ... good, very good. How long had he already spent there? He must have visited the British Museum already. What else had he seen? Old Norman castles, juniper woods stretching by their sides, soft, undulating meadows in the distance, bordered with chalk cliffs, behind which lay the colossal expanse of the Atlantic, hazy in the evening dusk, its waters reflecting the colourful display in the sky when the sun began to set? What trees were there, what flowers grew by the woods in the country? English wild flowers were said to be very pretty— poppy, fox-glove, daisy.

Someone turned up from Bishu's shop to ask him why he had not gone there. All the other players had arrived and were waiting. None of them wanted to start without him. Apu refused to go. No, today he had a headache, he'd go nowhere.

The night grew longer; across the pond in the slums where the labourers lived, the lights went out one by one, the air grew cooler; at ten-thirty the 'up' train chugged slowly past his verandah, the pointsman came to remove the light of the signal.

'Master Babu?' he asked, 'you are still sitting here?'

'Who is it? Bhajua? Yes, I am still sitting here.'

His mind was restless. It hankered after something ... some inexplicable, unfulfilled desire.

Earlier in the day, he had been leafing through a book on astronomy. It was a very good book, one he had bought during the time he used to work for Mr Seel. He had often used it to show Aparna photographs of different planets and explain the whole system of the galaxy. Today, while turning its pages, he had noticed a tiny white insect scurrying across a page. It was so small that unless one had really good eyesight, it would have been impossible to notice it. Looking at the creature, it had occurred to Apu that it, too, was an inhabitant of this world, a part of the galaxy, millions of visible and invisible planets, meteorites, clusters of stars ... here it was, gliding across a page in a book, with all the joy its tiny life had given it. How much life did it have? How much joy?

But what about man? How was man related to the bigger world of stars and other planets? Wasn't he just as insignificant? Of late, sudden doubts had been raising their heads in Apu's mind, as if pessimism and scepticism were determined to cast their shadow. During the monsoon, he had noticed rows of mould grow on wet shoes. Sometimes it seemed to him that mankind, too, had found itself on this earth, only because the warm air and other gases had created a favourable atmosphere for his creation and survival. Man could not possibly have anything to do with the rest of the universe— he was tied tightly to this earth, coming into existence in vast numbers, no different from mould or toadstools after heavy rain, and then vanishing from the face of the earth one day. He found a thousand reasons for happiness, for joy or pride

273

through trivial and meaningless events, just to hide his own weakness and insignificance.

How long did it take for the whole thing to come to an end? Forty years? Just as the life of that little insect had come to an end. It was no different.

How could such foolish creatures possibly bear any relation to that huge world that lay outside this earth? That endless expanse where there were all those other planets, comets, stars and meteorites? To dream of ever seeing a distant land was foolish, as was even to think that there could be eternal life. How could those beings, who grew like mould on wet shoes or toadstool on damp bales of straw, ever aspire to be a part of such infinity?

There could be nothing when death came. His mother had gone, Aparna had gone, Anil had gone—it was as if a great big full stop had been placed. The end. There was nothing else.

Something else occurred to Apu. Could it not be possible that there were beings elsewhere, in a different world, who had evolved independently to form a better and stronger race than the human one? Just as the little white insect in the book would find it impossible to imagine the existence of the galaxy, perhaps for these superior beings, it was just as inconceivable to imagine the world inhabited by man. To them, it would seem as small, as unworthy and without significance of any kind as the world of that almost microscopic insect, which spent its life scuttling through the pages of a book.

Could this be true? Who could tell him?

Where did one go after death? Where did the mould disappear when wet shoes were put out in the warm sun?

NINETEEN

❧◉❧

It was time for Durga Puja once again. In Chapdani, it was held at the house of the local rice merchant, Ramtaran Gui, who was also the school secretary. The teachers whose homes were outside Chapdani all stayed back to do whatever needed to be done for the Puja. They were lucky to have found a job at a time when jobs were scarce. Now they had to keep their jobs, simply by keeping their secretary happy. So they worked all day, for five days, to make sure all the guests were fed and looked after and every arrangement went smoothly. Apu found himself in charge of supplies to the kitchen. He had to remain on duty until eleven o'clock every night. Finally, on the day of Vijaya Dashami, he was free to leave. Apu returned to Calcutta for a visit.

After almost a year in what was little more than a village, Apu felt pleased to be back in the lively city. Vijaya Dashami was always a happy occasion. Apu could recall many joyous and festive moments this day had brought him in the past. It seemed as if the same fun-filled moments would recognise him as an old friend the minute he returned to the city, and would rise and lock him in an eager embrace, their warm laughter ringing in his ears.

Walking through the streets, Apu's thoughts turned to his child. He had not seen him yet. Who did he look like? Aparna, or himself? Apu had always felt strangely displeased with his son, possibly because he had unconsciously blamed him for Aparna's death. He had thought of visiting him during the Puja holidays, but when the time came, he could not gather enough enthusiasm to do so. Only his sense of decency made him send five rupees by money order to buy the child new clothes, thus fulfilling his parental duties.

Having returned to Calcutta on a day like this, Apu felt like meeting old friends and relatives. But none of his friends were in the city, each had moved from his old address. Apu stood at the corner of Grey Street, looking at an idol of the goddess, and thought: where can I go?

Then he began walking aimlessly. Here was a narrow alley, so narrow that two people could not have walked side by side here. It was lined on both sides by small, damp rooms with low ceilings where families of limited means lived. A married woman in her late twenties was frying puris in a kitchen, assisted by two little girls. Perhaps the happy day for eating puris had come again, for them, after a whole year. On a raised verandah, several men were embracing one another; a little girl dressed in a pink silk frock, her face framed by dark curly hair, stared at him through a parted curtain.

Another scene caused him much distress. A middle-aged woman was sitting at a stall, selling muri. A much younger girl, a poor prostitute from a lower caste, was saying to her, 'Let me touch your feet, Didi, please!' then she did quickly touch the older woman's feet, and went on pleading, 'Won't you get me a glass of sherbet, Didi? Bhang sherbet? Listen, Didi, please ...?' The muriwali was not paying her the slightest attention. She was busy chatting with another woman, possibly a maid, who was wearing heavy golden bracelets. The younger woman, however, continued her efforts at drawing attention to herself and hopefully evoking pity in the muriwali's heart. She touched her feet yet again, and repeated her request, 'A little dust from your feet, that's all I want.' Then, after a moment's pause, she added with a little laugh, 'What about a glass of sherbet, O Didi?'

Perhaps this hapless woman, blessed with neither wealth nor beauty, was totally alone, like him. But today, she had emerged from the dark depths of her little tiled hut, draped in her best saree. She was begging to be noticed by the muriwali, simply so that she could become a part of the festivities. In her eyes, that older woman selling muri was probably someone affluent and important.

Roaming the streets, Apu finally went to the house of the friend who sold herbal medicines. He was in his shop, and received Apu warmly. 'Do come in!' he invited, 'where had you been all these days?' he asked.

Apu stepped in. It turned out that his friend was in a situation much worse than before. He had had to leave his former house, and rent a tiled room in a nearby lane, for a little more than three rupees.

'I've no idea how long I'll be able to manage ... my wife and I make pickles and chutneys at home, and make packets of tea, and try to sell them ... it's a grim struggle, I can tell you. Anyway, come to my house,' said his friend.

Apu was taken to another damp room. There was no one at home. His friend's wife and children had gone with some neighbours to watch the Puja near the main road. 'I couldn't get them new clothes this time,' Apu's friend told him. 'I just told them to have the old ones washed by the dhobi. Then I saw tears in my wife's eyes, so got a striped saree for the youngest girl. That's all. Sit down, have a cup of tea. Of course you must, on a day like this. Wait, let me go and call her.'

Apu left as soon as his friend disappeared to look for his wife. By the time he returned, having spent eight annas at the local sweet shop, his friend and his wife were both back.

'Where did *you* go to? What's that packet in your hand? Food? Who told you to?'

Apu cut him short, 'Look, I did not get any of this for you. It's for Khuki, Khoka, and Manu ... and what's your name? Romola? Heavens, your father's fond of fashionable names, isn't he? Here, Boudi, hold this.'

His friend's wife pulled her saree half way down her head, and took the packet from him, looking pleased. Then she made tea and served the contents of the packet to everyone.

Half an hour later, Apu took his leave. 'I must go now, I have to return to Chapdani. I had a very pleasant time, thank you. And I am so glad you haven't given up your struggle; you have real courage, my friend. But, Boudi, I'd like to tell you something. Please don't be so good all the time, or so meek and mild. Your husband doesn't like it. It's good to have the occasional row, preferably an armed combat with ladles and rolling pins. Adds spice to life, see? Mind you, that's not how *I* feel, but that is the considered opinion of my friend. Anyway, good bye!'

His friend followed him out, grinning broadly. 'A word before you go. Your Boudi wants to know whether you'll roam around like a sanyasi all your life, or will you get married again? Go on, answer her.'

Apu laughed, 'No, having seen all that I have, I have no wish to get married again. Tell her.'

Outside on the street, he thought, 'Thank God I found

them. Where else could I have gone, and had such a good time? I wish I could help them more, but where would I find the money?'

He walked on, then seeing a tram bound for Bhowanipore, got into it to go to Leela's house. It was nearly half past eight by the time he got there. There were people talking in Leela's grandfather's library, two cars were parked under the portico. The electric bulbs had silk shades around them to keep away insects. Apu began going up the marble staircase. A familiar smell greeted him as he reached the landing before the hall. He couldn't tell where it came from; perhaps it came from the expensive furniture, or Leela's grandfather's cheroot, but it was there whenever he visited this house.

Leela ... perhaps, in just a few moments, Leela would ... his heart began beating faster.

Leela's brother, Bimalendu, saw him and came running. Apu liked this young boy very much. They had met only a couple of times before, but had grown fond of each other.

'Apurbo Babu, how come you are here today after such a long time?' Bimlendu asked, sounding both happy and surprised. 'Please come in. Wait, let me touch your feet.'

'Never mind that. Where's your mother?'

'Ma has gone to Bagbazar, she'll be back soon. Please sit down.'

'Er ... is your sister here? No? ... Oh!'

In an instant, the entire festival of Vijaya Dashami, and all that he had done the whole day, lost its meaning. But it was not just this one day. Ever since Durga Puja started, Apu had thought of visiting Leela in Calcutta. He had felt sure she would come home, and he would be able to see her on Vijaya Dashami. Today, when the siren at the local jute mill in Chapdani had woken him at five o'clock, he had lain in bed, thinking delightedly, 'I'll be seeing Leela this evening after two whole years!' And Leela was not here.

Bimalendu did not let him leave immediately. He got him a cup of tea and a lot of things to eat. 'I won't let you go,' he told Apu. 'We've got a new ice cream machine, you see. My uncle's friends are making special ice cream with bhang in it. Would you like some? I told them to send up a plate for you, anyway. It's got rose-essence in it.... Why don't you sing a song? I haven't heard you sing for years. Come on, please!'

'Is Leela still in Nagpur? Isn't she going to come back here?'

'No, not right now. She is no longer free to do what she wants. Grandfather did write to her husband, but he said she couldn't go now, may be later.'

Then Bimalendu went on to tell Apu a lot of things that Apu could not have imagined. Jamaibabu (Leela's husband), he said, was not a good man. He was short-tempered and did not treat his wife well, although Leela was strong and assertive enough to deal with him. 'I hear he also drinks a lot,' Bimalendu lowered his voice. 'Didi did not tell us everything, but our cousin Sujata di's son went to visit Didi in the summer holidays. He told us. Do you remember Sujata di? She's here, shall I call her?'

Apu could remember Sujata. He had seen her in their house in Burdwan, on an evening when there was a party. Apu was still only a boy, and Sujata a young and attractive woman. Apu had stared, fascinated, with the innocent and inexperienced eyes of a child, at this figure of a youthful woman, oozing feminine charm as she moved and talked. Twelve years had passed since that day, but Apu remembered it vividly.

Sujata arrived in a few minutes, and after being reminded by Bimalendu, did manage to recognise Apu. She had never met him officially; after all, how many women could be bothered to talk to a cook's son? Not everyone was like Leela. But Sujata

280

did remember a shy and timid young boy roaming on their verandah. She greeted Apu warmly enough. She herself looked much older, having crossed thirty. She had put on a lot of weight, and her hairline had started to recede. She was now a mother. Motherhood had changed her glamorous youthful looks to something much softer and gentler.

'Please sit down,' she said, 'what are you doing nowadays? Where's your mother?'

'I lost her many years ago.'

'Oh. You are married, aren't you?'

Apu explained briefly about his marriage.

'So why don't you get married again?' Sujata asked. 'Look, I am sorry about your wife, but these things happen. That's no reason why you should spend the rest of your life alone. Isn't there a suitable girl in your wife's family?'

What would Leela have said? To start with, she would never have referred to Sarbajaya as 'your mother'. She would have simply called her 'Ma'. How many women could be kind like Leela, who had ignored his poverty and all the other shortcomings in his life, and offered her hand in friendship, in total sympathy, and compassion, and trust? Apu grew preoccupied with these thoughts as he began to make a reply to Sujata's question.

When she had left, it occurred to Apu that motherhood had brought not just softness to her looks. Years of running a household and managing children had taught her something about the hard practicalities of life. He rose to his feet. 'I must go now, Bimal,' he said. 'I have to catch a train at ten-thirty.'

Bimalendu came to see him off, and walked with him a long way from the house. 'Didi came last year in March, and spent a couple of weeks here. Don't tell anyone, but she sent me to your old office to look for you. Everyone there said you'd gone, no one could tell me where. I am going to write to Didi about you … why don't you give me your address? Wait, let me write it down.'

❧

Three months passed. It was Maghi purnima, the full moon night in January. It had been a holiday, and Apu had spent all day on foot, walking through the neighbouring villages. He returned home quite late in the evening, and fell asleep almost immediately.

Much later at night—he could not tell the time—he was woken by the sound of someone knocking gently on his window. It was closed because the night was cold. Apu sat up on his bed and opened it. Someone was standing on the moonlit verandah.

'Who's there?' he asked. There was no reply. Apu quickly opened his door and came out. To his amazement, he saw a woman leaning against the wall behind his window, looking utterly dejected.

'Who is it?' he asked curiously. Then he exclaimed, 'Pateshwari! What are you doing here so late at night? Weren't you at your husband's house? So why …?'

Pateshwari was crying silently. She did not reply. Apu saw a bundle lying at her feet. 'Don't cry, please, tell me what's happened,' Apu went on. 'You can't keep standing here. Where did you come from?'

'I walked all the way from Rishra,' Pateshwari sobbed, 'I left quite late at night … I don't want to go back there!'

'All right, all right, let me take you to your parents. What a silly girl you are! Why did you leave on such a cold night? You are not even wearing anything warm … chhee!'

'I beg you, Master Moshai, please talk to Baba. Tell him I must not be sent back there. I'll die if I have to go back, I'll just die … please, Master Moshai!'

As they got closer to her house, she said again, 'I am so scared to go back home. Will you please speak to my father? Please explain to him why I ...?'

A little drama took place in the middle of the night. Luckily, it was so late that there was no one out in the streets. Apu woke Mr Deeghri and told him what had happened. Mr Deeghri came out, to find his daughter sitting under a mango tree, her head between her knees, still sobbing, and trembling violently in the cold. She was not even wearing a shawl.

Then she went inside, saw her mother and rushed into her arms, a fresh surge of tears streaming down her cheeks. A little later, Mr Deeghri called Apu in and showed him black and blue bruises on Pateshwari's arms, back and neck. Some of them were still oozing blood. Pateshwari had shown these marks to no one but her mother. Her mother had called Mr Deeghri and asked him to take a look. They learnt gradually that Pateshwari had arrived in the village hours ago, but had not found the courage to come straight home. She had sat by the pond for two hours, wondering what to do. Then, still unable to muster enough courage, and with her teeth chattering, she had tapped on Apu's window.

It was clear that she could not be sent back to her husband. Mr Deeghri asked Apu if he knew a lawyer. He had to seek legal advice, to see if he could lodge a case against his son-in-law and claim maintenance for his daughter. Apu returned home and, for the next few days, kept wondering what to do.

When he heard five days later that Pateshwari's husband had arrived and taken her back with him, he naturally felt extremely surprised. But something far more amazing was in store. One day, as he was leaving after his school got over, one of the school peons handed him an envelope. It contained a letter from the school secretary, informing him that his services were no longer required, he was being given a month's notice to find another job.

Thoroughly perplexed, Apu went straight to the headmaster. What was the meaning of such a letter? The headmaster did not like Apu, as it happened. There were several reasons for this. To start with, it was Apu who had formed the group that took care of the ailing, and he acted as their leader. All the boys were devoted to him, they would have done anything he asked them to do. The headmaster could not stand this. He had been looking for a suitable opportunity for quite some time to attack Apu. Now was his chance. Had he found it before, surely it would not have taken him long to teach a lesson to a young man like Apu, who knew so little about life.

The headmaster made it plain that he had had nothing to do with the letter, it was what the secretary wanted. The secretary was more specific. There had been all kinds of rumours, he said, involving Apu and the young Deeghri girl. These rumours had reached his ears a long time ago, but he had not paid any attention until some of the guardians of the students began asking him why a man of such dubious character was being employed to teach in his school. Apu started to protest, but the secretary refused to listen.

'Look, what you are saying is a different issue altogether,' he said. 'We have to look at the whole thing from the point of view of the guardians, and consider the school and the students. Surely you can see that? We cannot employ anyone about whom tongues are wagging, rightly or wrongly.'

Apu's face turned red at these unfair remarks. 'Is this justice?' he cried. 'You are fully prepared to sack someone at a time when you know how hard it is to find a job, and you're not willing at all to find out if what you have heard is true or not? You call this justice?'

The secretary refused to discuss the matter further. Apu came out of his room, anger and frustration bringing tears to his eyes. He could see that the whole thing was the headmaster's doing, but decided not to see him again to plead his case. If he was going to lose his job, so be it. 'But I just don't understand their attitude,' he thought sadly. 'Even someone accused of murder is allowed to defend himself. These people won't allow me even that one chance?'

Over the next few days, only one thought filled his mind. What was he going to do after a month? One of his new colleagues in the school had once published a short story in a magazine and had been paid ten rupees for it. He had mentioned this many times. What if, thought Apu, he did something similar? He had started to write a novel after his arrival in Chapdani. 'I've finished writing ten or twelve chapters already. If I can finish it, won't anyone pay me and publish it? I wonder how it reads. Perhaps I should show it to someone.'

Only a few days before his notice-period came to an end, Apu was in the post office, going through the mail as usual. Suddenly, he found a large, square, thick, green envelope with his own name on it. Much surprised, he wondered who could have sent him something so fancy. It was not Pranav, or anyone else he knew. The writing on it was totally unfamiliar. But opening it now meant unravelling the mystery at once. Apu decided to take it home to read it. That gave him a few extra minutes to savour the excitement, the thrill of the unknown.

The train had arrived at ten o'clock. Shutters were being pulled down at every shop in the market by the time he finished his dinner. It was only then that he opened the envelope. There were two letters—one was short, running to only four or five lines. The other was much longer, written on thick white notepaper. A second later, all the blood in his body seemed to rush to his head. Good heavens, *whose* letter was this? He could hardly believe his eyes. Leela had written to him! The shorter letter was from her brother, Bimalendu. Bimal had written to say that his sister had enclosed her letter to Apu with a letter to him, with instructions to forward it.

Leela's letter ran to nine pages, each page covered with her neat, small writing. He read the first few lines, then went and sat outside in the open. His mind was still in turmoil, his heart bursting with inexplicable emotions. Leela's letter began like this:

Dear Apurbo,

I have had no news of you for years. I have wanted to find out where you were, or what you were doing, but who could have told me? The last time I visited Calcutta, I sent Binu one day to your old address. He met the new tenant who now lives in your flat, but no one there could tell him of your whereabouts. Didn't Binu tell you about this?

I am very unhappy here. I never ever thought that I would end up like this. If we ever meet again, I shall tell you everything. Sometimes, when I am in pain, I think of you and I wonder if you are in as much distress, roaming around on your own, with no one to look after you. This makes me feel even worse. Then, one day, Binu told me that you had gone to our house on Vijaya Dashami. He also sent your address.

Do you remember our house in Burdwan? I have such happy memories of that place, but now it's become impossible to stay there. My uncle died, and his son, Ramen da, began a spree of self-indulgence, crossing all limits. I am sure you have neither seen nor heard of the things he is doing nowadays. He has sunk so low, to depths that I can only call inhuman, and the kind of things he is doing ... if I were to give you

286

all the details, it would amount to writing a book. Apparently, he had gone to a Marwari and mortgaged his share in our property. Now he has filed a partition suit, on the same Marwari's advice, to cheat Binu out of his own share. Could you ever have dreamt of doing such a thing?

***

The night grew longer, but Apu could not sleep. There was so much affection in Leela's letter, such gentle sympathy and compassion, that the loneliness he had suffered for two years seemed to vanish in a flash. Here he was thinking he had no one in this world. Leela's letter changed the whole world into a different place. There was such immense difference between Leela's situation and his, not to mention the physical distance between them ... yet, the warmth of her affection touched Apu's heart like a soothing balm, spreading through his body and mind. Such love and understanding could come only from a woman's heart. Apu forgot his anxiety over the loss of his job, as well as the dead weight of his loneliness. Leela ... there was Leela, thinking of him, always, and worrying about him. What else did he want in life? It did not matter if he never met her again. Only, let this warmth stay in his heart, for ever.

Apu's last day at work arrived about twelve days after he received Leela's letter. His students had been collecting money to hold a farewell party for him, but the headmaster raised violent objections. At first, he called the boys who were acting as leaders and threatened them with dire consequences at their forthcoming exams, if they went ahead with their plans. Then he refused to let them use the school hall to hold a meeting. He said to them, 'If you wish to bid him goodbye, that's well and good. But you must realise that there's need for iron discipline in these matters. A man who has lost his character does not deserve to be treated with respect. I don't want any of you to do so; at least, I cannot allow you to use the school hall for this purpose.'

The boys did not argue. But—despite heavy rain—more than thirty of them gathered in a cottage outside the school premises, read out a citation that had been written without the headmaster's knowledge, and put a marigold garland round Apu's neck. This was followed by refreshments, after which they returned with him to his little room, helped pack his few belongings, and went to see him off at the station.

◈

Apu went back to Calcutta. He had decided to travel—wherever his fancy took him—now that he was truly free. He would be doubly careful this time not to get involved anywhere, with anyone, and keep his freedom.

He went to the Imperial Library and spent a few days poring over maps of India and the atlas, noting down details of Daniel's *Oriental Scenery,* and the travel accounts of Pinkerton. Then he made enquiries at the Bengal–Nagpur and East Indian Rail to get an idea of fares. He had seventy rupees with him. What was there to worry about?

However, before he left, was it perhaps not necessary to go and see his son? Apu left the same day for his father-in-law's house. Aparna's mother, on seeing him, said nothing about his long absence; nor did she chide him for not having visited his son even once. On the contrary, she began to shower such lavish attention on him that Apu ended up feeling extremely guilty. While he was talking to some of the other relatives, Aparna's aunt walked into the room with a little boy in her arms. Apu looked at the child and thought: What a sweet child, whose is it? Aparna's aunt said, 'Go, Khoka, go to him. He's your very own father. Honestly, I've never seen anyone so totally heartless as this man. Go on, Khoka!'

Apu's son had turned three. His skin was fair, his mouth and his chin were like his mother's, his eyes were large and expressive like his father's. On the whole, however, he resembled Aparna more. At first, he refused to go anywhere near Apu. Each time Apu smiled and stretched his arms towards him, the little boy hid his face in his grandmother's shoulder, clinging to her with his small hands. Apu felt hurt by this; but by evening, Khoka had lost his shyness and seemed prepared to become friends. He even called him 'Baba' a couple of times. Then he saw a bird and cried, 'Birdh, birdh, wanth birdh, Baba!'

He had not yet learnt to speak properly. He pronounced each word in his own way, laying stress on the wrong syllable. But he spoke a lot, and every time he opened his mouth, his father felt a strange thrill—as if, ever since the beginning of creation, no other child had ever learnt to say 'Baba', or 'water', or any other simple word. What his son had achieved was remarkable, it was a miracle!

He went out with his son, the latter chattering nonstop. Apu could not understand most of what he was saying, so he simply nodded absentmindedly from time to time and said, 'Really? And then what happened?'

They came across a small bridge. 'Go down, Baba, see other sidhe?' said Khoka, pointing at a slope. 'Very well,' said Apu, 'go down very slowly, and when you get to the bottom, say "cooee!" All right?'

Khoka went down the slope happily, and found himself looking at a lot of trees on the other side of the water. 'A garden here, Baba!' he called.

'Say "cooee!" ' Apu reminded him.

'Cooee!' Khoka responded promptly, his thin, childish voice ringing out like a flute. Then he added, 'You dhoo ith thoo, Baba?'

'Cooee!' Apu shouted, laughing.

On their way back, Khoka told him many other things. The moon here, he declared, was big and round. He had once visited his aunt. The moon there had been very small. Why did they have such a small moon, Baba? Then Apu discovered that his son wasn't just sweet; he was also very naughty. On their return to the house, Apu set him down and took his money out of his pocket to see how much he had left. Khoka began shouting, 'So much money ... come and see, come and see!' Then he picked up a rupee coin and said, 'I won't give this back. I'll buy a marbel!' He laughed merrily, and shaking his head, curled his tiny fist around the coin. Apu felt a little bad to force it out of his grasp, but he had to. What would Khoka have done with a rupee? It would simply have gone to waste.

Before he set off on his return journey to Calcutta, Aparna's mother said, 'Look, I have lost my daughter, I have accepted that. But you ... I feel so much worse looking at you. You have always struck me as someone very special. When I think of you, going through life all alone, my heart just breaks in two. If your own mother was alive today, she would have asked you to marry again, wouldn't she? Besides, think of your child. He needs a mother. Do think about it, son. Do get married.'

Apu's boat reached Peerpur ghat. The salty water of the river glinted in the hot sun. A mercantile vessel was visible in mid-river, with its sails up; in the far distance, near the mouth of the river, was the hazy, smoky outline of the Sunderbans. How strange it all felt! He had come the same way with Aparna before, but now she seemed to have receded so far back into the past—like the indistinct bank across the wide river, the barely visible edge of the forest on the other side of its endless waters.

Apu's boat made its way down the southern bank of the river, its waves splashing against the boat; the bank was quite high in places; in others, it had broken and slipped into the water, exposing the roots of the kash grass. It suddenly dawned upon Apu that he could recognise the place. There was a small canal, a hijol tree standing on its bank. It was here that he had said to Aparna, years ago, while coming down from Calcutta, 'Lift your veil, little bride, look at your homeland!'

It was soon time to catch a steamer and arrive at Khulna. Apu looked at the left side of the ghat. There it was—the little hut with a roof thatched with straw, where he and Aparna had found their first home. Could he ever have imagined during those joyous moments that, one day, he would stare vacantly at the same little hut from a distance, wondering if the whole thing had been a dream?

He continued to stare unblinkingly, his eyes full of wonder, his heart longing with an irrepressible desire to go and look at the little room where Aparna had cooked.... Perhaps that stove she had used was still lying there? Or where he had sat and had his first meal cooked by his wife ... where she had taken out a mirror and a comb for him from her trunk....

He caught the train to Calcutta and sat by the window. They passed station after station, but Apu could only think of the river bank, the woods, the water splashing away with the ebbing tide ... the innocent laughter of a young and helpless child ... and Aparna, emerging form the black waves of the river in the dark night, smiling mischievously as she used to do when they were in Monshapota, and saying, 'I will never go anywhere with you. You mark my words. Never, never, never!'

It was early March. Apu woke on the verandah of the boarding house where he was staying, to find that a sweet southern breeze was blowing and there was a slight nip in the air. It was still quite early in the morning. Lying quietly in his bed, it occurred to him that there was no school to go to this morning, not even a private lesson, there was no need to get ready by ten and gobble down his breakfast. The whole day was his own, to do exactly as he wanted. He was now free … free … free! He had finally broken through every shackle. The thought made his whole body shiver. After a long, long time, he could taste freedom again. He was now simply a traveller in life, about to disappear into the unknown, like that fading star in the morning sky.

He rose with a light heart, called a barber and had a shave. Then he changed into crisp, freshly-washed clothes. Of late, his old passion for the good things in life had returned, which had made him go to a tailor to get a silk kurta made. Today, he went and collected it. Then he went back to the Imperial Library. 'Let me make the most of it,' he thought, 'who knows when I am going to be back again in Calcutta?' In the evening, he went to a lecture on mosquitoes and malaria, arranged by the Rockefeller Trust. It was an illustrated lecture. One particular picture startled Apu. It was the picture of a larva, before it grew wings and flew away. The picture showed the lifeless form of the larva sinking into the water, just as a newborn mosquito spread its wings and rose above the surface.

This could happen to man. Why, the other larvae, still swimming in the water, would consider their fellow being dead, wouldn't they, if they saw its inert body drowning fast? They knew nothing of the insect that had gained new life, and had gone into a different world. They had not yet earned the right to step into that world, the right that must be earned only through death, or what they thought of as death. All right, a mosquito was probably the lowliest of lowly creatures. But surely what was scientifically true of this creature could be true of man?

He returned home, thinking of nothing but this new idea.

The next day, he went to visit his friend, the herbalist, to say goodbye before setting out. He was not available at his shop. Apu found an Oriya servant working there, and sent word through him before arriving at his friend's house. He was still living in the same house. On one side of a small, narrow courtyard were two hand-grinders made of sandstone. His friend was busy grinding something. Next to him was a sheet from a newspaper, on which was resting a small mound of light brown powder. Almost everywhere else in the courtyard, roots and herbs had been set out to dry in the sun.

His friend greeted him with a smile. 'Come in, Apurbo, where were you all these days? Do forgive me, my hands are covered with this tooth powder I'm making. Here, look, here's the printed label. It's called Chandramukhi Tooth Powder, made by the Ladies' Home Industrial Syndicate. These days, it's very difficult to get any sympathy from the public unless ladies are mentioned. That's why I used the word 'ladies'. Do sit down ... where have *you* gone now?' he said to his wife. 'It's only Apurbo. You can come out and make him some tea.'

'Syndicate?' Apu laughed. 'Consisting of just two members? I see. But you and your wife are both very active members, that much is obvious.'

His friend's wife emerged from inside the house, smiling. One look at her told Apu that, like her husband, she had been engaged in grinding herbs on the second grinder. His arrival had made her run inside. Now, although she had clearly washed her hands and tried to make herself presentable, her slightly dishevelled hair and beads of perspiration on the sides of her forehead gave her away.

'What can I say?' his friend went on, 'I am still going through a bad time. My creditors are still coming here every day to harass and insult me. The court issued an order to seal the cash box in my shop. I need to earn at least a rupee every day to manage somehow. Some days I don't, so that day we don't eat.'

'Never mind all that,' his wife interrupted him, 'he's only just arrived. Let him rest for a while, and have a cup of tea. Why did you have to start your tale of woe?'

'Apurbo is an old classmate. I don't go around talking to the neighbours, do I? It's a relief being able to talk to someone I've known a long time. Anyway, why don't you open a packet of tea, and ... er ... is there any atta at home? Perhaps you could make him a few rotis ...?'

'Yes, yes, you don't have to worry about all that,' replied his wife. Then she turned to Apu and added with a smile, 'Why didn't you come back even once after you left us on the day of Vijaya Dashami?'

Over a cup of tea and hot parathas, Apu told them about his plans to travel, and that he would be leaving soon. 'Really?' said his friend, 'well, you can do that because you are alone. But you can see, can't you, how difficult it is for me? God only knows how I've managed to survive the last five years, in a place like Calcutta, with a wife and children. We both work so hard, but all our money seems to go on buying packets and containers, and labels, and paying a commission to the shop that sells this stuff for us. And yet, I have to keep my prices low, or else I'd never be able to compete with the others!'

Then he disappeared inside, returned and said, 'Look, your Bou Thakrun says you owe us a treat. Why don't you settle your debt today? We could call it a farewell feast, except that *we* should have held it for you?'

Apu felt quite grateful to his friend's wife. He had seen how they looked, and their children—thin and each wearing old and dirty clothes—made him want to do something for them. Give them a good meal, if nothing else. But if he had proposed it himself, it might have seemed like charity. His friend might have been offended, who knew? Since the suggestion had come from the other side, it saved him a lot of embarrassment.

He went with his friend and spent six or seven rupees on shopping for their feast. They bought koi fish, lobsters, eggs, potatoes, paneer, yoghurt and sweets. Perhaps it did not run to anything too elaborate, but the gentle and affectionate behaviour of his friend's wife turned the meal into a big event. At one point, Apu began to think that perhaps she had raised the question of a treat simply to get the chance to feed him. She sat and fanned him throughout while he ate, and when he finally lifted his hand from his plate to indicate that he had finished, she protested, 'What? Finished already? No, I'm not going to allow that. You must have some more. Go on, finish the paneer, and who do you think is going to eat those cutlets you've left on your plate?'

At this moment, a young boy of about sixteen arrived and stood in the courtyard. 'Kunjo? Come, come, join us!' invited Apu's friend. 'This is my sister-in-law's son, you see. He lost his father last August. He used to work in a factory on the other side of a railway line. He walked around it every day, but one day he thought he'd save himself the bother, and tried to cross the line by climbing under a freight train that was standing there. The train started just as he went under it. The wheels crushed him instantly ... no one could save him. He left behind two daughters, this boy here, and his wife. They are managing now on what help they can get from others. What else can they do? So my wife told me to send word to them ... we were going to have a good meal, we could share it at least with Kunjo. Go on, son, get a banana leaf if you can't find a plate, and sit down. But go and wash your hands first—what made you get so late?'

There was not much left of the afternoon. Apu continued to chat with his friend after lunch. It was dark by the time he decided to leave. 'I must go now,' he said, finally getting to his feet. ' I had a lovely time today. I hadn't enjoyed myself so much for a very long time.'

His friend called out to his wife, 'Could you please take the lamp and go with Apurbo into the lane? I can't get up now.'

His wife brought out a small kerosene lamp and accompanied Apu into the dark alley outside. After a few moments, Apu said, 'It's all right, Bou Thakrun, there's no need to come any further. It's not all that dark here, I'll manage.'

'When will you come again?'

'I don't know. I expect I'll be away for quite some time.'

'Why? Why don't you get married? It's not a good thing, is it, to roam around like a sanyasi? You don't even have a mother, do you? Anyway, when are you leaving? Won't you come and see us before you go?'

'No, I don't think that will be possible, Bou Thakrun. Maybe when I come back ...? Goodbye then, namaskar.'

The woman stood at the mouth of the alley, still holding the lamp.

The next day, it dawned upon Apu that what money he had with him was quickly disappearing. If he left it any longer, he might not be able to leave at all. But where could he go? He spent a long time thinking, without being able to arrive at a decision. Finally, he made up his mind to go to the station and get into the first train he could find. He packed his belongings and reached Howrah. A passenger train to Gaya was going to leave in fifteen minutes from platform number four. He bought himself a ticket to travel by third class, and found a seat by a window. He spread his bedroll on it and sat down.

Did Apu know where this journey was going to take him? Later in life, he thought many times of the moment when he had bought a ticket from an Anglo-Indian girl at the ticket window meant for third-class passengers, to travel by the Gaya passenger train at half past four, giving her a ten rupee note, and getting five rupees and eight annas in return. He had not consulted the almanac before setting out, yet that particular moment turned out to be so supremely auspicious. If only man could look into his future!

At this moment, however, Apu was not thinking any of this. He had never travelled on the Grand Cord Line. In fact, except for twice during his childhood, he had not travelled by the East Indian Rail, either. Now, like a child, he felt excited at the thought of a long train journey.

For a long time, he had wanted to sit by a window in a train to watch how the scenery changed. He watched eagerly until the train reached Burdwan, after which it quickly became dark and he could see nothing outside.

TWENTY

❦

The next evening, on reaching Gaya, Apu went to the Vishnupad temple to offer special prayers for his dead ancestors. He knew about the Hindu belief that such prayers, offered at Gaya, helped a soul to attain eternal peace. 'What does it matter whether I believe in it or not?' he thought. 'After all, how much do I know? If it does do them some good, so be it.' His prayers included his father's sister, Indir. He could not remember her, but his own sister, Durga, had often talked about this aunt. Then he remembered the old woman in Nischindipur, who, as a child, he had always thought of as a witch. He offered prayers for her, too.

Later in the evening, he went to visit Bodh Gaya. If he truly revered anyone, it was this great sage, the one to attain enlightenment. That was the reason why Apu had decided to call his own son Amitabh.

The smooth, paved road ran by a river, which fell on his left: a thin, narrow strip, looking as if it had stretched its tired body on a bed of pale yellow sand. Across it stood the hills on the border of Hazaribagh. The road was lined with trees, providing shade everywhere, and there were birds—it was really no different from his homeland. Apu sat in his ekka, totally mesmerised. A motor car passed him, coming from the opposite direction, making a return journey from Bodh Gaya. Apu caught a brief glimpse of a fashionable young lady, and a young man, possibly her husband. Who were these people, Apu wondered, who had been so eager to visit this ancient holy land, thousands of years after Buddha's enlightenment? He thought of the night when Buddha had left home ... the sweet face of his newborn child ... and then those austere, severe days of meditation. How could that be linked with the motor car? The day that had dawned today had emerged through the dense forest of time, marching through centuries, destroying all things old and ancient, to pave a way for a new world. Raja Shuddodhan's Kapilavastu had been swept away like froth on this surging ocean of time. But the invisible throne his son had established in many a new Kapilavastu everywhere in the world—who could deny its greatness, who would fail to bow before it, even today, two thousand five hundred years later?

The next day, he left Gaya for Delhi by the Delhi Express. A Bengali couple were travelling in the same compartment, who began speaking to Apu, delighted at having found someone else from their own community. But Apu was not really in a mood to talk. How could anyone want to chat at a time like this? There was so much to see. He peered out of the window, watching eagerly all his eyes could take in— every tree by the track, each little pebble on the ground. When the sun began to set behind a range of hills, the sky glowing red, he could sit still no more. Excited like a child, he opened the door of the carriage and leant out, holding its handle.

'Don't, don't!' shouted his fellow passenger. 'What if your foot slips off the footboard? Close the door, please.'

Apu laughed, 'It feels wonderful, as if I'm flying!'

Trees, canals, rivers, the rocky terrain, the entire district of Shahbad, was slipping away, right under his feet. Apu shut the door and returned to his seat. The moon came out a little later. The train was approaching the river Sone, its wide sandy banks looking strange in the moonlight. What did it remind him of? The Nile? Yes, that was it! Apu's imagination took hold of his mind again. There it was, the river Nile. If he could cross it and go a little further, perhaps seven or eight miles, on a donkey, he would find the granite temple built by the Pharaoh Ramases, dedicated to some unknown god or goddess, still standing there, forgotten by the world, forgotten even by time.

It grew darker. After a while, the other Bengali gentleman said, 'The food on this line isn't very good. We have plenty, please join us.' His wife spread banana leaves and served them puri, halwa and sweets. 'Please take a few extra puris,' offered the husband. 'We'll be breaking our journey at Mogulsarai. You're going straight to Delhi, aren't you?'

This was a new experience for Apu. How was it possible to befriend a total stranger so easily when one was out travelling? Why, living in the same lane in a city year after year could not bring the same result! The gentleman introduced himself. He worked in a government reserve forest near Nagpur. He gave Apu his address, and asked him to visit them. There were no Bengalis where they lived, Apu would be very welcome. The train reached Mogulsarai. Apu helped them with their luggage then bade them goodbye. 'I might just take your offer seriously, and turn up!' he laughed.

The train reached Delhi at half past eleven that night. Apu had been leaning out of the window all the way from Ghaziabad. He could see that the Delhi his train was going to was not the Delhi of S Kapoor, or the members of the legislative assembly, or the agents of Asiatic Petroleum. His Delhi was entirely different—it belonged to the men and women of the past, going back to the days of the Mahabharat. Every brick here was made with all that he had read in stories, novels, poetry, and books on history; every grain of dust had fallen from the feet of all those heroes and heroines he had worshipped, from Bhishma to Sadashiv Rao; from Gandhari to Jahanara. *Dilli hanauj door ast* ... his Delhi was a long way away, several centuries away; no one had seen it.

But it was dark outside. There was nothing immediately visible except signals, and a cabin in the yard with a board saying, 'Delhi Junction East' and a gasolene tank. Then he saw the platform, bright and well-lit, and big. There were all the familiar advertisements of Pears soap, Keating's powder, Halls distemper and Lipton tea.

Apu got off the train, carrying his little canvas suitcase and bed roll. He knew no one in the city, and it was quite late at night. He decided it would be safer to spend the night in the waiting room, which turned out to be on the first floor.

In the morning, he put his belongings in the left-luggage room, and stepped out. Would he perhaps find a procession, stretching half a mile, to accompany a beautiful shahzadi, who might be out in the city, riding a decorated elephant with a golden howdah? And would there be noblemen and others lining the road, with folded hands, to catch a glimpse, or to beg a favour?

No. The modern city of Delhi was no different from Calcutta. Apu noticed even the same advertisement of a jeweller's shop he had seen in Calcutta. Then he met two other men, also from his city. They were going to see the

Qutab Minar. One of them offered to take Apu with them in their tonga to share the cost. On the way to the Qutab, he said, 'I have visited Delhi before and been to the Qutab. They make such heavenly cutlets there ... you've never had any, have you? Aah, we'll order two dozen cutlets before we climb the tower!'

As a child, when he was still studying in Diwanpur, any mention of old Delhi used to make him think of the pile of bricks that stood next to the school. Today, he realised old Delhi was not the pile of bricks he had imagined it to be. He had no idea the Qutab was so far from the main town. What surprised him most was the barren land that lay on both sides of the road like a desert, dotted with cactus and prickly pear. There were broken houses here and there in the sunburnt desolate plain, and disused mosques and minarets, graves, arches and walls. The silent skeletons of seven dead kingdoms were buried under this uneven ground, amidst all the cacti and clumps of bushes, hiding their lost glory—the kingdom of Prithviraj Pithaura, the Slave dynasty, the Tughlaqs, Alauddin Khilji, Siri, Jahanpanah and, finally, the Mughals. Never before had he seen anything like this, nor could he have imagined it. He was so overwhelmed that he fell totally silent, forgetting to turn the pages of his guide book, cr check his map. All he could do was watch in silence this march of time, each scene flitting by like a scene in a film. He nearly forgot himself.

Perhaps the reason for this was simply that his mind was still fresh, his imagination still lively. He had spent most of his adult life in narrow lanes, amidst filth and squalor; yet, his mind was so thirsty to see the world that it now seemed as if he was looking at everything with something more than his normal vision; as if he had a third eye with a deep insight. If he did not open it, what he could see ordinarily would have remained incomplete, meaningless.

After seeing the Qutab, he travelled much further to see Ghias-ud-din Tughlaq's unfinished city, Tughlaqabad. By the time he got there, everything was red-hot in the afternoon sun. From a distance, Tughlaqabad appeared to be a huge fort, built by a demon. Against the grassless barren land, the leafless acacia and the thorny cactus, this demon was standing still, looking down from the high stone wall of his fort, frowning at the entire Aryavarta. No attempt had been made to carve fine patterns on its walls. It was barren, it was harsh, but it had the beauty that comes from valour and from great colossal spaces. Even in its almost barbaric appearance, it was beautiful. Its strange attraction clasped one's heart in a vice-like grip.

It did, however, lack one vital force: life. Everything around it had been reduced to rubble. Huge boulders lay everywhere, blocking all the ways to climb higher. The demon was still frowning, yes, but it was a frown on a dead face.

He recalled Nizamuddin Aulia's curse: *Yahan basey Gujjar, yahan rahey Gujjar.*

Standing on the terrace of Prithviraj's fort, quite unexpectedly, his mind went back to Nischindipur again. When, as a child, he had first read the story of Prithviraj, he had been sitting by a pond, and had imagined his fort to be standing majestically on the other side. Even now, he could see that pond, snails crawling by its side, a bamboo grove nearby. It made Apu laugh.

In a few minutes, the hazy shadows lengthened in this deserted wasteland. The sun finished writing, in fiery letters, the story of the rise and fall of several kingdoms, right across the sky, and sank on the western horizon. Apu had seldom seen such a spectacular sunset. It was a very special moment in his life, almost a spiritual experience. He felt as if he was standing very close to an unseen presence; as if the gods themselves were whispering into his ears. A mixture of fear and amazement brought goosepimples. He had had no idea, until this moment, how confined and constricted his own life had been.

Over the next couple of days Apu saw other historical sights in Delhi. When he saw the simple, grass-covered grave of Jahanara in one corner of the mosque of Nizamuddin Aulia, his eyes filled with tears. He had always admired Jahanara for her love of simplicity—austerity, even—although she was a princess, raised amidst great luxury, surrounded by opulence, power, arrogance. He could hardly believe, even as he stood there, spreading the petals of the roses he had bought at the gate, that he was looking at her grave. Then he called an elderly Muslim from the mosque and asked him to read out the famous Persian couplet engraved on the headstone, and wrote it down. After that, he went to the grave of the poet, Amir Khusro, and spread flowers over it, too.

The next evening, he went to see Shah Jahan's Red Fort, and spent a long time sitting on a stone bench on the open terrace next to the Diwan-e-Khas, in the pale shadows of the late afternoon. No one had ever been able to write a correct account of the lives that had been lived here, he thought. Everything he had read in novels and plays, and stories and poetry, had been a work of fiction, far removed from reality. The Zebunnisa, the Udipuri Begum, the Mumtaz and the Jahanara he had known all his life, were all figments of someone's imagination. What had they to do with the real people? Who knew the mysterious history of this place, exactly as it had happened? The silent Yamuna might be a witness, each and every foundation stone might be a witness, but when had stones ever spoken? When had a river told a story?

❦

Three days later, Apu got off a train at a small station one evening. He had not had a proper bath for days, his hair was dishevelled, his lips dry in the brisk, westerly wind. He did not have a lot of money left, either.

The train left. The station was tiny, facing a small hill. There were no shops in the vicinity, or any other building. Apu came out, and spread out his bedroll on the paved terrace outside the station. He had no idea where he might go next, or where he might sleep. But that did not worry him. His mind was filled with an eager anticipation.

He sat down on a durrie, opened his notebook and wrote for a while. Then he lit a cigarette, and sat quietly, leaning against his suitcase. A few minutes later, he saw a young man—a gond—coming towards him, casting curious glances. He was wearing a toka on his head, and smoking a pipe made out of a shaal leaf.

'How far is Umeria from here?' Apu asked. He had asked the question in Hindi, but at first the man did not understand it. Apu had to repeat it again before he got a reply in broken Hindi. '*Tees meel*,' the man said.

Thirty miles! How was he going to get there? Further questions revealed that the way to Umeria was through forests and mountains. This excited Apu very much. Forests? What kind of forests? Were they very deep? Full of wild animals, even tigers? Oh, good. But how was he to travel? The gond offered to let Apu hire his horse for three rupees. Apu agreed, and told him to bring the horse, which seemed to surprise the gond. It was soon going to get dark, this was no time to set out to travel through forests. But Apu was adamant. How could he miss this opportunity to ride through a forest on a moonlit night? He might never get another chance.

The gond then told him that he was prepared to carry Apu's luggage for him, if he could be paid an extra rupee. Apu left on horseback just before dusk fell, followed by the other man, carrying his suitcase and bedroll on his head.

The night was cool. Apu rode past a small collection of houses at a little distance from the station, and crossed a nullah. Then the path curved, and he entered a shaal forest. The night was amazingly quiet, there were fireflies everywhere and the moonlight seeped in through the leaves, spreading a dappled net on the ground, dotted with light and darkness.

Apu borrowed a shaal-leaf pipe from his companion and some local tobacco, but almost as soon as he had inhaled, he began to feel giddy, so he threw it away.

The forest was truly dense. The path through it was tortuous; there were little streams every now and then, and a small river; fern bushes grew on its rocky bank, the air was heavy with the fragrance of wild flowers. Nocturnal birds called out at times, but apart from that, there was complete silence.

Apu broke into a canter from time to time. He had ridden horses before. As a child in his village, he had caught horses let loose in a field and ridden them. In Chapdani, the local doctor had had a horse. Apu had ridden it occasionally.

Apu and his companion travelled all night, reaching Umeria in the morning, at half past seven. It was a small village. There was a post office, a small market and a few warehouses that stored lac. It was here that Apu's fellow passenger lived, the one he had met on the train to Delhi. He was called Abanimohan Basu. He worked as a forest ranger. Surprised though he was to see Apu, he greeted him warmly. 'Come in, come in! You did not write, so we were not expecting you. We thought you'd probably come much later. You rode all night? My God, you're a dangerous man!'

Apu had stopped at a small river on the way to have a wash, and brush his hair. He was looking far more presentable now. Arrangements were made immediately for a cup of tea and snacks. He took out his wallet, and emptied its contents to pay the gond. Four rupees was about all he had left.

At lunch, Mr Basu's wife served the meal herself. 'I have come to bother you, Bou Thakrun!' Apu laughed.

'It's no bother, believe me. If you did not come, we'd have been very disappointed,' she smiled. 'But somehow I knew you'd come. We were talking about you only yesterday. I said the sahib's bungalow should be cleaned for you to stay in. It's lying empty at the moment.'

'Aren't there other Bengalis, or any other educated people near here?'

'A friend of mine—a Mr Roychowdhuri—is prospecting in the Khuria Hills, looking for copper. He is a geologist, he was in England for many years. He's camping out in the hills, but he comes here sometimes.'

In just a few days, Apu became very close to the Basus. Perhaps such closeness could form only in a place like this, away from the pressures of a city, from the artificial barriers placed by society that preclude natural friendship between people.

One day, scribbling in his notebook, Apu suddenly found himself writing a ballad. It was the kind of thing his father used to write and sing on the ghats of Kashi. When Mrs Basu brought him a cup of tea that morning, Apu said to her, 'Didi, you will hear something new from me tonight.' He had started to call her didi.

'What is it?' she asked eagerly. 'A song? I had a feeling you could sing. I even told my husband.'

'I will sing songs, too, if you like. But I've written a ballad. I will sing it for you.'

Mrs Basu's face lit up. 'Didn't I tell you?' she said to Mr Basu. 'I said, anyone who has such a lovely voice must be able to sing. See, I was right!'

That night, Apu and his hosts sat on their front verandah, which was awash with moonlight. Apu sang his ballad, unconsciously following his father's style of singing. The story he told was a sad one, about the great sacrifices made by King Bharat in the Ramayan. The shaal leaves murmured in sympathy; the night birds cried, as if sharing his pain. No one spoke when Apu finished. He broke the silence himself, by saying with a laugh, 'Did you like it?'

Mr Basu had heard ballads before, but none of it could possibly compare with what he had just heard from Apu. He felt deeply moved. His wife appeared totally overwhelmed. Tears glistened in the moonlight in her eyes and on her cheeks. She could not speak. Living so far from home, this childless couple had felt lonely for years. No one had given them so much joy, for a very long time.

Two days later, Mr Roychowdhuri himself appeared. He turned out to be a most amiable man, nearly forty years old, grey hair around his ears, tall, well-built and handsome. But he seemed to drink rather a lot. He described, at some length, with what difficulty he had managed to get some whisky from Jabalpur. Apu was somewhat surprised to find that Abani Basu drank, too.

'I have heard all about you, Apurbo Babu,' Mr Roychowdhuri said. 'My friends here have told me how talented you are, although I could see that for myself. Anyone who sees your eyes will know you are an imaginative thinker. The rest of us have all become so matter-of-fact! You'll have to sing your ballad again tonight.'

They spent almost the whole night simply chatting and laughing. Three days after Mr Roychowhduri left, a peon from his office brought a letter for Apu. Mr Roychowdhuri needed an overseer for the area where they had started to drill. Would Apu be willing to accept the job? They would pay him fifty rupees a month, and give him accommodation. This was something totally unexpected. It made Apu think. The money he had left amounted to about ten annas. The Basus were undoubtedly extremely hospitable, but obviously he could not spend the rest of his life with them. How strange, why hadn't he thought of the future until now?

Mr Roychowdhuri's bungalow was twenty miles away. Three days later, he sent a horse and one of his men to fetch Apu. Abani Basu and his wife were very sorry to see him go.

The way to Mr Roychowdhuri's bungalow was also through a forest and travelling was not easy. The track disappeared into a thick forest only three miles from Umeria, going northwest. Again, Apu came across little rivers, bushes of fern and streams. He washed his face at one, and realised that the water smelt of sulphur. Wild oleander bloomed in places, and the air was cool. In fact, although it was early April, there was still a nip in the air.

He reached his destination before it got dark. The mine had not yet started to function, its feasibility was still being assessed. There were four or five large, wide rooms with straw roofs. Then there were two big tents, huts for the labourers and an office. The whole area was surrounded by a dense and impenetrable forest, and a range of hills.

'I knew you were a brave man,' said Mr Roychowdhuri, 'when I heard that you had ridden all night to get to Umeria. Even the locals would not dare to travel that way after dark.'

TWENTY ONE

❧

Apu began a new life from that day. It was the kind of life he had often dreamt of, but never thought that it would one day come within his grasp.

The drilling area he was supposed to oversee was about eighteen miles away. Mr Roychowdhuri lent him one of his own horses, and sent him to his place of work the very next day. Apu felt startled when he got there. He loved forests, but had never seen one like this. A dense expanse of trees stretched to a high grassland. There was a thatched house, a well and small huts where the coolies lived. Behind him, and to the south, rose a range of hills. The forest spread in that direction as well; for mile after mile, there was nothing but trees and hills, one after the other, seemingly endless, with not a soul in sight. Just behind the drilling tent, however, there was an open area. A steep, stark column of granite reared into the air, turning red, or grey, or black with a slight coppery tinge, as the evening sun played on it. Apu had never imagined a forest could be so silent, so sombre.

The job, as he soon discovered, involved a lot of hard work. All he seemed to have time for in the morning was a bath and a quick breakfast, immediately after which he had to get on his horse. Work, which needed his supervision, was being carried out four miles away. Twice a week, after work, he had to travel to Mr Roychowdhuri's office, sixteen miles away, to make his report. By the time he got back, it was always dark, sometimes quite late at night.

The total area under his jurisdiction stretched to twenty-five miles. Some of it was plain, at times he had to ride down slopes, or pick his way carefully through rocks and boulders. The slopes were also covered by trees, but the undergrowth was not as thick as elsewhere. But only a quarter of his way ran through this open forest, after which Apu found himself totally cut off from human habitation, and sank deep into the complete isolation of the forest. It seemed as if no one had ever entered its depths, as if Apu was the first man to ride through its dried riverbeds, pushing through the dense growth of bamboo, which had been disturbed only by wild boars and sambars that had carved their own tracks. He did not know what the trees were called, or the creepers, or the many colourful fowers he saw. Sometimes he saw wild orchids; at other times, his eyes were greeted by yellow splashes made by azaleas, the morning air heavy with their scent. He felt as if he was absolutely alone in the world—nothing else existed, except his horse and this lonely forest. How wonderful this seclusion was! It was not the artificial seclusion he might have felt behind the closed door of his little room in Calcutta. It was something he had never known before—something infinitely bigger, that he could not possibly have foreseen. It simply had to be experienced.

He fell in love with the place. Who would ever have thought he would get to live his dream one day? He made his horse break into a gallop whenever he came into open space, ignoring the rocks and heaps of pyrites that dotted the way, avoiding low-hanging branches, shooting past wavering creepers, and flying through the air, simply tasting the exuberance of his youth.

Sometimes, unexpectedly, thoughts of his life in the city came back to him. The small, closed, dark, claustrophobic life he had lived for three long years as a clerk in Mr Seel's office. If he closed his eyes, he could still see it: the typist Nripen making a racket with his typewriter, Ramdhan Babu—the cashier—poring over a fat ledger. Some of the plaster on the wall behind him had worn away, to create a funny shape that looked like a priest sitting down to do a puja. Almost every day, he had teased the cashier, and said, 'Ramdhan Babu, didn't your priest offer you flowers in blessing today?' Oh, how suffocated he had felt in that office! Now, when he looked back, those few years seemed like a long nightmare.

On reaching his bungalow, he usually had a bath, using the cold water from the well. Then he made himself a drink with sugar and wild lemons that grew in the forest. Nothing could be cooler and more refreshing. Ramcharit Mishra, his cook, brought dinner for him: roti, arhar daal, and either pumpkin or bhindi. There was a village twelve miles from his bungalow. The coolies brought weekly supplies from there. No one could get hold of any fish, but Apu went and killed birds occasionally. One day, he chanced upon a deer, well within shooting range. This surprised him very much. Sambar and barasinga were normally extremely cautious, they vanished the instant they caught sight of man. How, then, was this creature standing only twelve yards from his horse? Pleased and excited, he raised his rifle and took aim, but then he saw something that made him stop. The deer was peering out of a bush, staring at him with frank curiosity. Only its face was visible. Perhaps it had never seen a man on horseback. Perhaps it had simply stopped to wonder what kind of a creature he was. Apu's eyes met the deer's, and his heart gave a sudden lurch. The animal's eyes were exactly like Kajal's: large, clear, expressive and brimming with innocent wonder. Quickly, he lowered his arms and unloaded the gun. He gave up shikar from that day.

It did not take him long to finish his dinner, after which he usually took seat outside behind his thatched house, wrapped in the amazing silence of his surroundings. The column of granite towered majestically over everything else, dark and mysterious in the hazy moonlight. A breeze often brought the fragrance of shaal flowers; above his head glittered millions of stars. Apu had not a single companion here, no one could make demands on his time or his thought; there was no excitement, no anxiety. All he had was himself, the strange beauty of this wide, open, rough and rocky place, and the star-spangled sky.

The sky at night had always attracted him, even as child. But how different it looked here! The coolies, tired after a hard day's work, went to sleep soon after dinner. Ramcharit uttered words of caution at times: 'Babuji, don't sit outside at night, there are jackals here.' Even in the summer, Ramcharit gathered twigs to make a fire and sat by it, until he could not keep his eyes open any more. Slowly, when the fire went out, Ramcharit retired to his hut but Apu continued to sit, staring at the silent night, the black sky, the dark earth. Sometimes he caught sight of distant stars through the leafy branches of ebony. They flickered like heartbeats on the magical sky—a sky that seemed full of unfathomable mysteries. Jupiter grew brighter as the night wore on, the Milky Way became visible above the hills in the northeast; meteorites fell, tearing the night apart with fiery nails. Bewitched, Apu

313

watched the progress of the stars night after night ... now the stars seemed to lower themselves through the ebony leaves, now the Milky Way moved above his head, casting itself diagonally across the sky, and Jupiter sank in the western corner. Gradually, it dawned upon Apu how well this place had concealed, behind its serene silence, the tremendous speed with which the galaxy moved. Here was eternity, a picture of continuity and endurance. He had never felt so close to the cosmos before, nor had he studied the world of stars and planets so minutely. Why, had he even dreamt that one day he might?

The hills that stretched behind Apu's bungalow were only half a mile away. To the south they were a little further away, at a distance of about two miles. The wide, open area in front of the bungalow was uneven; young shaal and poplar grew on it. Most of it was covered by half-dried grass. In the west, far in the distance, he could see the faint blue line of the Vindhya hills that enveloped the horizon, and the Chhindwara and Mahadeo ranges. They looked beautiful on clear days, when the westerly wind did not cover the sky with dust. About eleven miles away flowed the Narmada, through a lonely forest. If Apu rose really early in the morning and took his horse, he could bathe in the river and come back by nine o'clock.

The forest to the south looked dense, lonely, rough and remote. When the sun set in the evening, its last rays fell on the bare granite wall, first turning it yellow, then an earthy red, which faded into russet, and then got paler until it suddenly turned grey before finally going black. On the other side, rose the evening star, like the decorative dot on a woman's forehead. The wilderness all around him was engulfed by darkness, as a soft murmur rose in the branches of shaal and other trees. Ramcharit and Jahuri Singh lit their fire to ward off jackals; foxes and wild cockerels began calling, and in the sky above, the stars and planets slowly appeared. The surroundings filled with an air of mystery; sometimes, close to his bungalow, a wild boar raced through the tall grass, making it swing, a hyena laughed crazily in the distance. Late into the night, the crescent moon appeared behind the mountains, slowly climbing higher. It was truly the kind of life he had only read about.

Occasionally, in the evenings, he went for a ride on his horse. All that stretched before him was that half-dried grassland, scattered with rocks of various sizes, dotted with shaal or almond trees. There was another tree that Apu could not recognise. It was large, its branches spreading in different directions to form a wonderful pattern. The hot sun of early April had made it shed its leaves. Its bare branches were silhouetted against the blue sky, as if it had been painted. Three miles from Apu's house was a little mountain river that wound and curved its way down. Apu had named it Bakratoa. It dried up completely in the summer. By its side stood a shaal tree. Sometimes, Apu dismounted here and went to sit on a boulder under the tree, tethering his horse to a branch. To him, the setting looked like a landscape painting.

Bakratoa narrowed into a pool, only a few feet wide, and eventually disappeared into the gleaming yellow sand, its traces hidden under rocks. Stones and pebbles covered both banks; a number of hard, grainy quartzites and pale yellow boulders were scattered on the sand. Perhaps in the ice age, they had ridden on the last wave of a river of ice and been stranded here. The yellow sand might well have grains of gold in it, or else how could it glisten so in the crimson glow of the setting sun? Somewhere in the vicinity was a fragrant creeper, laden with pods. The harsh April sun had made them burst, spreading a musky scent with the evening breeze. At a little distance from the Bakratoa, deeper in the jungle, a spring appeared from the hillside, its waters sounding like an overflowing tank. Down below, there was a pool that retained its water even in the summer. Apu heard that herds of deer went there to drink from it in the middle of the night. He rode out, more than once, in the dead of night to see them, but was disappointed every time.

The summer gave way to the rains. Then the rains stopped, leaving white shefali flowers blooming everywhere in the forest. The mountain spring continued to gurgle. On a moonlit night, Apu returned to the same spot with Jahuri Singh. It was only four days from the full moon; moonlight was playing on the leaves and branches of almond trees, a fresh breeze carried the sweet smell of shefali. The forest, the silent night and the damp night air, all seemed to talk— perhaps they were telling him a story of days gone by, events from a previous life.

The deer did not appear.

Disappointed though he was, Apu realised one thing. Being alone in these isolated places brought a change in his own state of mind. In the city, one's mind might be wholly preoccupied with thoughts of self, desire or ambition. Here, under the colossal expanse of the star-studded sky, these things seemed both irrelevant and insignificant. The mind could expand here, learn to be more generous, tolerant and observant. One's whole angle of vision could change. Even books that had once seemed fascinating, or important in his busy life in the city, now appeared trivial, dull, unnecessary in his present seclusion. What he wanted to read now was what might endure through all eternity. His book on astronomy, for instance, had acquired a new meaning here. It bore a relation to the world of infinity; it taught him to think, and opened a new door to his perception.

In early March the following year, a forest surveyor appeared and put up his tent ten miles away. Apu made friends with him. He was a well-educated gentleman from Madras. Apu began to spend most of his evenings with him, sipping tea and chatting. Occasionally, his new friend used his theodolite to point out planets and stars to him. At times, he even invited Apu to lunch, and made him rice cakes. Apu left early in the morning on these days, and rode back on his horse in the evening.

Usually, on his way back, Apu saw masses of lohia and bijani flowers, spread thickly over slopes. They were in full bloom, now that winter was over. Apu stopped his horse to look at them, forgetting himself, or the fact that it was time to go back home. It would be impossible to describe the beauty of such a scene to anyone who has not seen it: vast numbers of these purple, orange or pale yellow flowers were everywhere, on grasslands and slopes, under the open sky, in the scorching sun, in the shadows under hard basalt or barren granite walls, and in a forest that ran for mile after never-ending mile, without a soul in sight, or the smallest sign of habitation. For hundreds of years, these flowers had bloomed every spring and withered, with no one to witness their glory. Only the honey bees and bumble bees held their own celebration.

એ⊚ઙ

One day, Apu asked Mr Roychowdhuri to give him a few days' leave. He wanted to visit Amarkantak. For some days now, he had been feeling anxious and restless, though he could not work out why. Going away for a few days seemed like a good idea.

'How will you go?' asked Mr Roychowdhuri. 'It's about eighty miles from here, sixty of which are through dense, virgin forest, full of tigers, bears and wolves. If you still want to go, please don't forget to take your rifle with you. And take your horse and a syce, and always try to find somewhere to stay before it gets dark. The tigers here in central India will swallow you like a rasgulla if they find you. That's why I've told you so often, even here, not to sit outside your bungalow at night, or ride in the forest in the dark. But you've never listened to me, have you? You *are* rather reckless.'

Apu refused to be daunted. Brimming with enthusiasm, he left on foot, without taking his horse. On the second day, however, as the day drew to a close, he realised his mistake. Hard, sharp pebbles had cut through his shoes. A huge blister had appeared on his foot, as he was no longer used to walking for miles. Ramcharit had accompanied him, carrying his belongings, all tied in a bundle. He walked behind Apu, without speaking a word. As the evening drew closer, he pointed at a mountain in the far distance and said that they would have to find a path that ran by its side. The mountain was so far that Apu could only see a bluish haze, it was impossible to tell whether it was a mountain or just clouds. How many days would it take them, to reach it, travelling on foot?

He had spent many months in a forest, but the density of the forest where he lived was nothing—absolutely nothing—compared to the untamed wilderness he was now passing through. The stretch of forest that had started early in the afternoon showed no sign of ending, and it would soon get dark.

They came to a slope that rose higher to the top of a hill. Apu and Ramcharit climbed up, only to find, to their horror, that a similar high hill stood behind it. By this time, dusk had started to gather. Apu's foot throbbed painfully, and he felt incredibly thirsty. They had run out of water many miles before, and had not been able to find any more. Apu had managed somehow by sucking the bitter-sweet fruit he had found strewn under ebony trees, but now he had to have a drink of water.

In the far distance, to the west and the north, the bluish range of hills continued. The dense forest on the valley below looked hazy in the twilight. A narrow track slowly wound its way down through the forest. Fortunately, within a mile after crossing the second hill, they found a dak bungalow owned by the forest department. Surrounded by a thick shaal forest, it was a small structure with a thatched roof. People from the forest and mining departments stopped here occasionally to spend the night.

The night that followed offered Apu a strange and moving experience. There was an old man in the bungalow, who had bolted the door and was reading inside. He opened the door on hearing Apu and Ramcharit call. It turned out that he was a Maithili Brahmin. His name was Ajablal Jha, and he appeared to be in his sixties. Although by now it was quite late, he brought out from his little store enough flour and ghee to fry them delicious puris, despite Apu's protests. After dinner, he sat in his room and began reading aloud from the Ramayan. He had a good voice, and soon Apu realised that Jha had considerable knowledge of Sanskrit. He had clearly read ancient poetry fairly thoroughly. With much enthusiasm, he began to recite from memory Sanskrit slokas, and dohas in Hindi from Tulsidas.

Then, slowly, he told Apu his own story. He came from Darbhanga, he said. Having spent his childhood there, he acquired the sacred thread of a Brahmin at the age of thirteen. After this, a small businessman in Kashi offered him a job, and he moved there. That was where he received his education, then opened a small school to teach Sanskrit. It did not work. For many years, he simply roamed like a vagabond, trying his hand at many things, but succeeding at nothing. Eventually, he ended up here, and had been staying in this little bungalow for the last seven or eight years. He lived on his own for most of the time—only once in a blue moon did anyone else arrive here—and survived on what food he could beg from a colony thirteen miles away. He was perfectly happy to live like this. All he needed were his books of poetry, which included a couple of handwritten manuscripts, *Meghdoot,* and a few chapters of Bhatti.

Apu was deeply moved by this simple, if somewhat peculiar, man and his profound love of poetry. Even in exile, his contentment was unmistakable. His only fault appeared to be a tendency to talk too much, as if to show off his knowledge. But he did it so completely without guile that Apu could not hold it against him.

'How are you allowed to live here, Punditji? Doesn't anyone ever say anything?' he asked.

'No, Babuji. There is an engineer called Nageshwarprasad, who knows me, and respects me a lot; so I'm allowed to stay, there's never been any problem.'

After chatting with him for a while, Apu asked, 'Tell me, Punditji, is the forest as dense all the way to Amarkantak?'

'Babuji, this is the famous Vindyaranya, the Vindhya Forest. It continues beyond Amarkantak, for many miles; and yes, it is just as thick. To the west are Chitrakut and Dandakaranya. Do you know the story of Damayanti? She got separated from her husband, Nal, when he lost his kingdom. It was here in this forest that she lost her way. The Ramayan also describes this forest. Listen to this.'

Clearly, this man knew nothing of, and was totally unconcerned with, the modern world. He could speak of nothing without dragging the scriptures or stories from mythology into it. Apu found the man most intriguing. It was not often that one could find someone like him—virtually cut off from civilisation, but totally content to live simply with his favourite books.

Jha began reading again, in his melodious voice. How perfectly the description matched the surroundings! Faint moonlight seeped in through the thick shaal leaves; the leaves of some other trees looked jet black; somewhere, deep in the forest, jackals called.

Apu soon found himself transferred to the world of an ancient civilisation. Trains, motor cars, aeroplanes, trade unions—all things modern just melted away. He could see a hermitage set by the bank of a river, not far from tall mountain peaks. A holy fire had been lit, smoke rising under the evening sky. On deer skin and reed mats sat the sages, some wearing loincloths and others covered in dark deer skin, reading from the Vedas. The mountains stood quietly. There came the fragrance from wild flowers—by the bank of the Godavari, in the woods, there were pretty young girls from the ashram; and, with them, slim, graceful women from a royal household were picking flowers. The water glistened in the pale moonlight, a peacock cried from the cane plants.

Encouraged by his attention, Jha opened a bundle and showed its contents to Apu. It was full of poetry in Sanskrit that he had written himself. 'Babuji,' he said proudly, 'I have been good at writing poetry ever since my childhood. Once, my guru took me to the court of the Maharaja of Kashi. I was given a pair of expensive shawls after I read some of my works. I still have them. It happened thirty or thirty-five years ago.' Then he proceeded to read many of his own poems, explaining the use of different metres, and the merits of his slokas. In the last thirty years, he had written regularly, and still continued to do so. He had kept each poem safely, not one was lost.

Apu's heart filled with a strange feeling of dejection. His father used to write songs and little poems. Where had they gone? People like Jha would never realise that times had changed. Who would ever read all that he had written with such dedication? Who would appreciate its worth? Would any of his hopes ever be fulfilled? What sincerity, and

321

enthusiasm, and joy had gone into his creation! Yet, it would remain unseen and unrecognised, like that postcard he had found in the post office in Chapdani, sent by a young girl to the wrong address.

The next morning, he gave Jha ten rupees as a mark of respect, and a bound notebook to write in. He did not have a lot of money with him, or he would have given him some more. This was one of his weaknesses—if someone touched his heart, he would generously give them what he had, without thinking of the consequences, or his own needs.

About a mile from the dak bungalow, the path rose higher still, running over a plateau, through a jungle of shaal, bamboo and ebony. On his left and right, stood hills of varying heights. The morning breeze, enriched by the sweet scent of shaal blossoms, was so invigorating that it seemed to give him new life. On the fourth day he came upon an extraordinarily beautiful sight in the evening. The path began to slope down. Between the hills on both sides, stretched a valley for about a quarter of a mile. There were flowers everywhere—the red polash glowing like fire. Beyond a low rocky bank, was the young river, Sone, lying in its bed of rocks and orange–yellow sand, its sparkling waters laughing, gurgling and spreading gaiety every step of the way. A peacock flew out from behind a rock and perched on a low branch. Apu was so mesmerised with the surroundings that he could not bring himself to walk away. It was as if someone had, once again, turned into reality the heaven he had dreamt of as a child, and spread it out before his bemused and enraptured eyes.

Never before had he seen a horizon so distant, nor had he ever imagined the depth of the seclusion he could now feel. He looked at the western sky. Far, far away, in the sky over the indistinct, long blue line of the mountains, there was a veritable ocean of colours.

A great surge of joy flooded his heart. Where did it come from? How could he ever describe to anyone the heavenly joy the sight of these wide green expanses held for him? Who gave him such special vision? Who lined his eyes with a magic kohl, and brought him the enchantment of early dawn and dusk, and of sunsets in the green forest?

Looking straight at the encircling curve of the far horizon, he could see most of the forest's greenness fade into oblivion under the evening sky; only in parts was it still faintly visible, smoky and hazy in the distance. The wings of white cranes were outlined against the blue sky, taking them to distant lands. There was nothing here to obstruct either his vision or his mind. It could soar above this familiar world and fly to another, unknown and further away.

It was true, his heart said; it was true that in these silent and peaceful forests, amid the fragrant flowers and light and shadow under the sprawling branches, a new world was born every day, spreading as wide as the distant Milky Way. It marked neither the beginning nor the end; it could neither be seen nor touched; yet, in special and silent moments, it was perfectly possible to feel in one's heart its mysterious presence, extending beyond the boundaries of infinity. In fact, in the past year, he *had*, at times, felt such a magical presence, sometimes in the intoxicating fragrance of shaal blossoms, or in an indistinct range of hills at dusk; or, sometimes, in the solitary, sombre, moonlit forest filled with the cry of wolves; and under the myriad stars etched in the boundless emptiness above him.

Whenever he tethered his horse after a ride in the evening, and sat by Bakratoa, Aparna's face came back to him, occasionally followed by the long-forgotten face of his sister, or memories of warm afternoons in his childhood, and his mother's voice, reading from the Mahabharat. At such moments, it occurred to him that the life and the world we saw every day and knew intimately were not really what mattered. Behind our busy, shallow, mundane existence lay hidden another life, a different world—beautiful, fulfilling, joyous and tranquil. Its flow was eternal, like the river Mandakini, filled with an inexplicable mystery, speeding from one age to another. In its journey towards immortality, it had chosen grief as its companion; tears were the fount from which sprang its everlasting force.

Today, Apu could see that his past, particularly the job he had in the office of Mr Seel, had, in fact, strengthened his vision. How he had yearned for a little open space, couped up as he was in a small, dingy room, from eleven in the morning to seven in the evening! Travelling between his two evening tuitions, he had stared at the sky behind the spire of the big church near the Maidan with such intense longing! Yet, it was this closed, claustrophobic life that had whetted his appetite for a better, freer existence. It had helped him gather and store his strength, not waste it away. Now, even the headmaster in Chapdani seemed like a friend, a great friend. And that innocent, oppressed young girl from a poor family, Pateshwari? She had simply served as a pawn in a huge, divine plan, but had it not been for her role, Apu would not have been forced to leave Chapdani. Had the headmaster and the others not had him removed from his job and his life in the slum among the labourers, he would probably have continued to live there. On an evening such as this one, he would have made his way to Bishu's shop and quite happily passed a few hours, playing cards.

How many people had learnt to recognise life, and understand its true meaning? What one saw was so often affected by the way one was conditioned from birth. It blocked one's vision. The true purpose of life was neither seen, nor appreciated. Besides, how many people bothered to try to understand it, anyway?

324

Amarkantak was still some distance away. 'Ramcharit!' Apu called. 'Get some dry leaves and twigs, and light a fire. I am going to make some tea.' Ramcharit raised strong objections. 'Huzoor, there are wild bears in these parts. We must get to the dak bungalow in Amarkantak before it gets dark,' he warned.

'Never mind. It won't take long,' said Apu and filled a big pot with water. Then he placed it over three large stones, and lit a fire under it. 'Sing a bhajan, Ramcharit,' he said with a smile. 'We've got a good fire going, no bear will dare come near. There's no need to worry, sing all you like.'

The moon rose. Traces of Ajablal's poetry and the portions he had read out from the Ramayan were still lingering in Apu's mind. Sitting by the fire, it seemed to him as if a beautiful woman of royal birth had indeed lost her way in this lonely, desolate forest. She was graceful as a young creeper covered with fresh blossom; her eyes were large and expressive. But her distraught husband had deserted her in her sleep. Now she was roaming all alone. Who was going to show her the way that would take her to her destination?

TWENTY TWO

❧

Three years had passed since the heady days of the Noncooperation Movement. It was at this time that Pranav was released from the prison in Rajshahi.

His days in prison had done nothing to damage his health, but something had happened to his eyes. There was a constant irritation in them, and they watered frequently. The prison doctor had told him to have glasses made, and had given him a letter addressed to an ophthalmologist in Calcutta.

Pranav made his way first to Dhaka, and then to his village. There was no one left in his family except an old aunt. When he reached home a little before it got dark, his aunt was sitting on their broken verandah with her prayer beads. She burst into tears on seeing him. She had a son of her own, who did very little except smoke ganja. She loved Pranav and had looked after him since he was a small child. What was she to do, she sobbed, what could anyone do if Pranav himself went about looking for trouble, despite his education, against all her advice? How long was she supposed to go on living alone, how could she take care of all their property—couldn't Pranav see that someone had torn off a branch from the jackfruit tree, how could she keep an eye on everything, all the time? They should send her off to Kashi, so she could end her days in peace.

It took Pranav four days to soothe and calm her. Then he left for Calcutta, using the letter from the doctor as an excuse. His aunt told him to drop by and visit one of her childhood friends on his way to the city. Apparently, this friend was very keen to meet him. Pranav smiled to himself. About four years ago, when the elder daughter of this friend had reached a marriageable age, his aunt had given him similar instructions, but Pranav had not found the time. Then came the Noncooperation Movement, and his whole life changed. By now, that girl was bound to have got married. Perhaps it was now the turn of her younger sister.

On reaching Calcutta, he looked for Apu. But he was nowhere to be found, not even at the Imperial Library, which was a place Apu was sure to visit if he was in the city. Pranav knew he had left Chapdani, a year before he himself went to jail.

One day, he went to visit Manmatha, one of the few college friends left in Calcutta. Manmatha was now an attorney, doing quite well, although he had only just started to practice. Pranav found him going through some papers in his office. A little later, he realised the reason for Manmatha's good income and that Manmatha was clearly going to prosper further in his business.

At around seven o'clock, Manmatha began to fidget a little, as if he was waiting for someone's arrival. A few minutes later, a large motor car stopped at the front door and a man in his mid-thirties entered the room, helped by two other men. Pranav could tell at once that the man was drunk. One of his companions had something wrong with one eye. The other man was quite good-looking. Manmatha received them with a smile. 'Oh, do come in Mr Mallik ... is this Mr Sharma? Please sit down. Gopal Babu, you can sit over there. Now, have you told him all the conditions?'

Mr Mallik was clearly an experienced man. He glanced at Pranav before saying anything. Pranav began to rise, but Manmatha said quickly, 'Don't mind him. He's an old friend. You may speak freely before him.' Thus reassured, Mr Mallik opened a bundle and took out a few papers from it. This was followed by a short exchange with Manmatha, conducted in low tones. The man with the damaged eye whispered something into the young man's ear, who then signed his name on a piece of paper. Manmatha examined the signature carefully, put the paper in an envelope, and placed it on his table. Then he took out a large bundle of notes and counted them out to Mr Mallik.

Pranav was not foolish like Apu. He could understand well enough what was going on. The young man was called Ajitlal Sen Sharma. He was the son of a zamindar. For whatever reason, he had just signed a handnote for two thousand rupees, and been paid only fifteen hundred. Mr Mallik was obviously his agent, for he returned after seeing the others to their car. After casting another irritated glance in Pranav's direction, he began an argument with Manmatha, once again speaking softly, but maintaining that he had not gone to such a lot of trouble for just seven and a half per cent. Pranav got up and left at this point.

He happened to meet Manmatha the next day. Manmatha laughed on seeing him. 'Do you know what happened last night? That man called Sharma returned at about three in the morning. He wanted another thousand, so I made a neat profit of thirty-five per cent. That man—Mallik—is a crook.

But why should I care? If the son of a rich man wants to give me an IOU for fifteen hundred when he gets only a thousand, that's not *my* problem, is it? I have to make a living. After all, this does not happen each night. Why shouldn't I make the most of it?'

Pranav did not feel greatly surprised. He knew something about people like Manmatha and how they functioned. They thought nothing of cheating a drunk young man to make quick money, and then speak about it openly and proudly. He felt sorry for the young man, who probably had no idea what he had signed, and how much money had actually changed hands.

Pranav left Calcutta after this, and went to visit Aparna's family. Aparna's mother, who had been like a mother to him, was no more. She had died the previous year. Pranav had received the news of her death when he was in jail. His eyes filled with tears as his boat reached the ghat near Aparna's house.

On reaching the house, Pranav had a bath and a meal. Then he decided to go upstairs and rest for a while since he had had no sleep on the train. He walked into a room, to find a boy of about five or six lying quietly in a bed. It seemed as if someone had spread a heap of rose petals on the bed, petals that had now gone dry and stale. He went closer and discovered that he was right. The child was burning with fever, his face was flushed, his lips trembled, and he looked utterly helpless. On a small plate lying near his pillow were two half-eaten rotis and a handful of sugar.

'You're Kajal, aren't you?' Pranav asked. The little boy gave a start, and stared at him with a mixture of fear and curiosity. Pranav's heart filled with sadness. Was there no one to take care of this child? How could the others have left him alone here to fight his illness? And what had they given him to eat? Only rotis and sugar. The poor, ailing boy had eaten whatever he could, but that was hardly the right thing for him to have.

'Why didn't anyone give you saboo?' he asked.

'There's none left.'

'Who told you that?'

'M-m-mamima. Said there was no s-saboo.'

His high temperature was making him breathless. Pranav brought some cold water and began to bathe his head with it, fanning him at the same time. A few minutes later, his temperature seemed to subside a little, and the child appeared less confused and out of breath.

'Do you know who I am?' Pranav asked.

'N-no.'

'I am your uncle, your mama. What about your father? Did he come to visit you? I mean, recently?'

Kajal shook his head. 'N-n-no. Baba hasn't been here … for so long!'

'Why do you stammer so much, Kajal?' Pranav teased him. The last time he had seen him, Kajal had been little more than a baby. Now, looking at his young face, Pranav thought he looked very much like Aparna. The only things he had got from Apu were the tender curve of his mouth and his fair complexion.

Kajal did not answer Pranav immediately. He seemed to be thinking. After a few seconds, he said, 'Is my father never going to come again?'

'Of course he will!'

'Wh-when?'

'Soon. Do you miss him?'

Kajal said nothing. Pranav suddenly felt very angry with Apu. What a heartless wretch he was! How could he leave a motherless little child here, and disappear without a trace?

Who was going to take care of his child? Didn't Apu have even a shred of mercy in him?

Later, when he met Aparna's father, he himself got an earful. 'You did all you could to get my daughter married to your friend, didn't you?' his uncle asked. 'Did you know that, in these five years, he hasn't been to see his own son even once? God knows where he is. How much is he making, anyway? Thirty rupees? Forty a month? When is he going to settle down with a good job? And his son, let me tell you, is just as bad. He's both naughty and stubborn, not to mention foolish. Not just a little naughty like other children, either. Do you know what he did the other day? He got into a bullock cart and went all the way to the bazaar in Peerpur, with a group of drivers. We were at our wits' end, looking everywhere for him. Then, finally, he was spotted by Makhan Muhuri, and he brought him back. It's true what they say— no matter how well you try to look after a daughter's child, he can never be your own.'

Kajal was shy and quiet like his father. Pranav had seldom seen such a beautiful child. There was grace in every movement he made; but he often smiled in a rather pathetic way. He looked so innocent, so vulnerable when he smiled like that that it nearly broke Pranav's heart. Only a few days in this house had told him that after the death of Aparna's mother, there was no one left to take care of her child. Not a single person kept an eye on him, or worried about where he went, when he ate, or what he did. His grandfather clearly could not stand him. Convinced that, like his father, he would turn into a vagabond unless he was raised with strictness, Kajal's grandfather was so stern with him at all times that the poor boy was terrified of him and avoided him like the plague, quite unable to understand why the older man treated him in such a fashion.

Pranav could see all this, but he was in no position to stay on in Kajal's house indefinitely and rectify matters. So, after a brief visit, he, too, had to leave him and return to Calcutta.

❧

During the day, Kajal was fine. But, as soon as it got dark, he began to find it very difficult to cope. As soon as dinner was over, his mamima would say, 'Go upstairs now, and go to bed.' These words invariably made Kajal cower and stand in one corner of their verandah, shivering in the cold. There was no one upstairs. To get there, he knew he had to negotiate a dark staircase. And then there were all those quilts and blankets heaped on a rack in the room next to his. They looked so weird, they took on such strange shapes in the dark ...! In the past, his didima used to take him upstairs and stay with him until he fell asleep. Didima was no more; his aunts thought their duty was complete once he had been fed. One day, he had tried asking one of them to go up with him. This had resulted in another bout of scolding: 'Go up with you and put you to bed?' the aunt had ranted. 'You think I haven't got anything better to do? Just look at you—scared to climb a few stairs! Why, you weren't scared to leave home alone and go all the way to Peerpur, were you?'

There was little he could do. So he gathered his courage and managed to climb the stairs. However, he had to stop again at the door of his room. There was a clotheshorse in that corner—decorated with cowrie shells—under which a number of old hookahs and pipes were kept. The flickering oil lamp cast more shadows than light from its corner—those hookahs looked peculiar when the dim light from the lamp played on them. There was no one on this floor ... none of his aunts, great aunts, or even cousins ... he was alone, left in this dark world full of nameless horrors. A young aunt and

332

a maid did sleep in the same room, but it would be hours before they came up. How long could he go on standing at the door? He was just about frozen to death already. Kajal shut his eyes, as he did every night before entering his room, and rushed in. Then he found his bed, climbed into it, and covered himself from head to foot with his little quilt. But he could not stay like that for very long. Was the room really empty? What if there was something lurking in a dark corner? He lifted his quilt briefly and took a quick, frightened peep before hiding himself under it again. Every detail of all the ghost stories he had ever heard came flooding back. Why did that happen, exactly at this time, every night?

Things were different when his didima was alive. She never left him until he was fast asleep. The first thing Kajal used to do, on coming into this room with her, was to fling himself on the great heap of quilts on his bed, shouting, 'Look, Didima, I've thrown myself into the water ... hee hee ... I'm swimming in a pond ... hee hee!'

When his grandmother succeeded in capturing him and laying him down, he would throw his arms around her neck and say, 'Now tell me a sto-o-r-e-e!' He had to bring his thin, red lips close together to get the last word out. His grandmother laughed at this and said, 'Do you know why you stammer? It's because you eat so much jaggery. Very well, I'll tell you a story, but you'll have to lie quietly. Promise?'

Kajal would nod, and bend his head low, until his chin touched his chest. Then he would glance up quickly and look at his grandmother in silence, his eyes dancing with mischief. 'Stop being naughty,' didima would say. 'I have heaps to do downstairs. Your grandfather's going to return any minute from his game of chess. I have to give him his dinner.' Kajal would laugh at this, and say, 'Dadu can get his dinner from M-m-mamima, you don't have to go. A story, please, Didima?'

Didima would begin a story, but Kajal would still refuse to lie still, until she said, 'I'll leave you the minute your Dadu gets home. Either go to sleep now, or I shall call him here.' This usually worked. The very thought of his grandfather being called to the scene made him stop his pranks and do as he was told.

Where had didima gone? Something had happened one night, something curious and really most peculiar. It was more than a year ago, when he was only four and a half. When he got up one morning, his cousin, Aru, whispered to him: 'Grandma died last night. Did you know that, Kajal?'

'What? What does that mean?'

'It means they have taken her away. She's gone. Late last night, when you were sleeping.'

'Wh-when will she be b-back?'

Aru sounded as if he knew everything. 'She's not coming back. No, never. You're such an idiot, Kajal. They took her away to burn her ... over there.' He pointed at the river.

Kajal did not believe a word of this. Aru was older only by a year, but he always pretended he knew all the answers, and was a big show-off. It was for this reason that Kajal did not like him at all. But he could not help feeling profoundly puzzled. What made Aru think didima would never come back? How strange! Why shouldn't she?

But Aru was right. From that day, didima did indeed vanish without a trace. He often cried secretly, and wondered where she could have disappeared to, in a matter of hours, but he had not found an explanation.

No one sat with him any more while he ate, or stayed with him until he was safely in his bed. No one told him stories, either. Every night, he had to make himself face the dark staircase, get into his room and put himself to bed, all alone.

Kajal had many problems. But this one, he had to admit, was the worst of them all.

TWENTY THREE

❦

Another year passed. It was nearly mid-April.

Apu was returning home after a very long time. One of his fellow passengers, a Muslim, was describing the virtues of melons found in Lucknow, and many others were listening to him attentively. But Apu was staring out of the window, lost in thought. When would they enter Bengal? To him, it was a land from fairly tales, across seven seas and thirteen rivers! For five long years he had not seen its gentle, soft beauty. Image after image rose before his eyes.... The dry pieces of bamboo spread like a carpet in bamboo groves in these hot months; a freshly-bathed young woman lowering her gaze at a ghat, standing under branches laden with kanchan flowers; messes and boarding houses in the city, clothes drying on the balcony, the babus all away at work, water running from a tap into a bucket at three in the afternoon....

In the last five years, how he had missed these little, familiar scenes and longed to see them, just once more! He had learnt to appreciate and understand his native land much better now, having been away from it for so long. Today, he was going to see it again—at seven o'clock in the evening.

The train left Ranigunj and sped on. Quite a long way away from Ranigunj, Apu caught sight of the river Singaron, dry in the summer heat and lost in a wide expanse of sand. Women from villages far away were digging the sand and filling pitchers with what little water they could find. One of them, possibly a farmer's wife, stood and stared at the train, her full pitcher under her arm. The sight made a thrill of joy coarse through Apu's heart. How long it had been since he had last seen a woman stand in that way, striking such a familiar pose!

Later, after they had passed Burdwan, Apu saw something else in the lengthening shadows of this summer evening. There was a pond. Its surface covered totally by lotuses, the flowers and the leaves hiding all the water beneath. Close to it was a thatched cottage; an ancient drumstick tree bent over the pond, most of its form rotten and decaying; and there was a heap of cowdung. Having spent the whole day passing through the dry and harsh landscape of Bihar and the Santhal district, looking at long stretches of their fire-red earth, this little dark lotus pond struck him as a symbol of the tender beauty and grace of the land he had left behind.

When the train pulled in at Howrah station, Apu felt quite taken aback, as if he had never seen so many lights, such milling crowds, or such a large number of vehicles before. While crossing the bridge, he glanced across at the sparkling, glittering metropolis, and felt enchanted. What were those? Motor buses? Why, they were not there before! What huge buildings there were in Calcutta, such an enormous number of people on its streets. Here was a flashing, illuminated advertisement on the top of a building—its colourful letters lighting up one minute, then going blank the next. Goodness!

Apu made his way to Harrison Road and took a room in a boarding house. Then he had a bath, which was most refreshing after all the smoke, dust and heat on the train. On returning to his room, he began playing with the electric light switch. Like a child he turned it on and off, time and time again. Every little thing struck him as new: each little object seemed strange.

The next day, he travelled all over the city, but could not find any of his old friends. The herbalist who used to live in Boubazaar had moved, and the old messes he used to frequent were now full of new people he did not know. Even the old tea stall on College Square had disappeared.

In the evening he went to see a play, simply in the hope of hearing a few Bengali songs. He bought an expensive ticket and got a seat in the front row. He took his seat, staring at all the other people in the audience with a mixture of excitement and curiosity. At the end of the first act, he went out to buy a paan. An old woman was sitting on the pavement outside, selling paan. 'Won't you have one, Babu?' she asked. Apu looked at her. There was a bigger, rather prosperous looking paan shop nearby. Everyone else seemed to have gone there. Apu felt sorry for the old woman, and bought a paan from her. Today his heart was full of affection for everyone he met, bursting with compassion. In his present frame of mind, he would probably have given the old woman ten rupees if she had only stretched out her hand and asked for it.

After the second act, when the curtain came down again, Apu rose and decided to get himself another paan from the same woman. On his way out, his eyes suddenly fell upon a man sitting at the back. He strode forward and greeted him: 'Sureshwar da, can you recognise me?'

It was the same Sureshwar, who had helped him so much when he had just started going to college. He was accompanied by a young woman. Sureshwar looked up at him and stared for a few seconds. Then he said, 'Goodness gracious, it's our Apurbo, isn't it?'

Apu laughed. 'Why, is that so hard to believe? I haven't seen you for *years*!'

'True. And you wonder why I found it difficult to believe it was really you? Your face has changed slightly, and you look more sunburnt, but you're as handsome as ever. Here, let me introduce you. Here's my better half; and this is my friend, Apurbo—poet, thinker, writer, traveller, what have you. So tell me, Apurbo, where were you all these years?'

'It might be simpler if you asked me where I wasn't … really, I've been to all sorts of places, quite far from civilisation. Oh look, the curtain's going up. I'll talk to you later.'

'Never mind the play, it's most boring. I'd much rather go out with you.'

The two friends went out. Apu offered Sureshwar a cigarette, then lit one himself.

'You found that play boring possibly because you often go to plays. It isn't anything new for you,' Apu remarked. 'If you could see it with my eyes, even a scene from the Ramayan put on by ordinary villagers would have seemed special. You know, Sureshwar da, a chameleon used to live near my house where I've just come from. It used to change its colour twice a day, and I used to make a trip just to watch it do so. That was my sole entertainment. I returned to the city only yesterday, after being in exile for five years.'

The play finished at half past nine. Apu came out with Sureshwar and his wife. They went to drop her at her parents' house in Maniktola. Then Sureshwar took Apu to a restaurant in Corporation Street. Having heard about Apu's experiences over the last few years, he said, 'Five years in a forest? Didn't you ever miss home?'

'Oh, yes. At times, I felt so terribly homesick … in the last couple of years, there were times when I thought I'd go mad if I couldn't go back home again.'

On the pavement outside, a group of Anglo-Indian girls were gliding by, laughing and chatting. Apu looked at them with interest. Who knew the sound of human voices could mean so much to a man? In the brightly-lit restaurant, there were people coming in and going out constantly. Outside, he could see a few English children playing in the house across the road in their neat and tidy little living room; motor cars sounded their horn, motorbikes shot past noisily, a cycle rickshaw trundled along with its bell tinkling. Apu stared at these, wide-eyed, as if he had not seen any of it before.

'Look at the star,' he said to Sureshwar. 'In the last few years. I saw that same star rise over tall mountains and dense forests. I saw it each night. But, today, when I saw it over the building of Whiteway & Laidlaw, it seemed new … different, somehow. What's the time now? Quarter to ten? At this time of night, over the last five years, I have always been alone, among trees and hills, hearing nothing but the cries of wolves and, just occasionally, the roar of a tiger. The loneliness! I couldn't describe it to you, not sitting here among so many people.'

Sureshwar told him about himself. He taught in a college somewhere in Chittagong. He wife was from Calcutta. They were here to attend her sister's wedding. 'I'd love to get away,' he confided, 'and have a taste of the life you just described. But I am married. Who knew marriage would tie me down so badly? Look, if you wish to make something of your life, do not get married. You're not, are you?'

Apu could not help laughing. 'What if your wife heard you talk like this?' he asked.

'No, no, I am not joking. Honestly, I am not the Sureshwar you last saw in 1915. Marriage and a wife, and the load of responsibilities have destroyed my youth, my strength, my dreams, my whole life. Oh, I still remember the day I got my MA degree. It was the end of winter, there were tiny new leaves on deodar trees, and a southern breeze had just started to blow. I came out of the convocation hall and went straight to a studio, still wearing my gown, and had a photo taken. I was so happy. I felt as if the whole world was at my feet ... I could do what I liked. There was so much I wanted to do. Do you know, I've still got that photo. I look at it sometimes, and I think of all that I wanted to be, and what I have become. Just a teacher in a small college in a small town, teaching the same subject year after year, getting involved in petty squabbles, trying to keep the principal happy, fighting with the wife, taking my son to a doctor, even worrying about my daughter's wedding! Don't laugh, Apurbo, I assure you it's no laughing matter.'

'Please, Sureshwar da,' Apu pleaded, 'why have you suddenly turned so sentimental? Let me get you a cup of coffee.'

'No, thanks. You see, I don't talk about these things to anyone. I told you because you'd understand. Others see me doing a job, getting a rise in my pay every year, so they assume I am all right. Nobody would ever imagine that I am dying—my spirit is dying, Apurbo!'

They left the restaurant and took leave of each other. 'You know what has been said,' Apu told Sureshwar, '*In each of us a child has lived and a child has died—a child of promise, who never grew up.* But life is a wonderful thing, Sureshwar da, one must never dismiss it as useless.... Anyway, I must go now. I cannot tell how pleased I am to have met you. When

340

I was new to this place, when I needed a roof over my head, you helped me out. I have not forgotten your kindness.'

❦

Apu slept until noon the next day. In the evening, he decided to go to Leela's house in Bhowanipore. For many years, he had had no news of Leela. When he saw the red brick house from a distance, his heart began racing faster in both hope and anxiety. Was Leela going to be there? What if she was? The last time he had seen her, Aparna was still alive. Eight years had passed since then.

The first person he met was Leela's brother, Bimalendu. He was no longer a young boy; his face looked different, and he had grown quite tall. It took him a few moments to recognise Apu. When he did, he welcomed him and ushered him into their drawing room. After a few minutes of routine small talk, Apu asked, trying to keep his tone as casual as possible, 'And what about your sister? Is she here, or with her husband?'

Bimalendu seemed taken aback. 'Didi?' he asked, 'er ... perhaps we had better go out.'

Now Apu felt decidedly alarmed. What was wrong? What had happened to Leela? A little later, standing on the pavement, away from the house, Bimalendu said in a low voice, 'You haven't heard anything about Didi?'

'No. She's ... she's ... still alive, isn't she?' Apu asked anxiously.

'Yes and no. It's a long story, Apurbo Babu, but I'll tell you everything since you're an old family friend. Didi has left her husband. He was a drunk, and quite characterless. He got involved with a Jewish girl from Bentinck Street, so much so that one day he even brought her home. You know Didi. A spirited girl like her wouldn't put up with such nonsense. So she called a taxi the same night, and left with her little daughter. Then, a couple of months later, her husband visited her and said he would take their daughter out to see a film. Well, he didn't. He took her away to Jabalpur to live with him, and refused to send her back to Didi, even for a short visit. Then ... then ... Didi did something that no one thought her capable of. Do you remember Heerak Sen? The barrister? You must have met him at some of our parties. Didi disappeared with him. She spent a year with him. I don't know where they lived, but now she has come back alone. She has left Heerak Sen, and is living alone in Alipore in a rented house. No one mentions her name in our family. My mother has gone to Kashi. She is not going to return.'

Bimalendu stopped speaking and remained silent for a few minutes, possibly to control himself. Then he added, 'Sen never meant anything to her, she just used him to settle scores. But ... anyway, I'd better go. You'll stay in Calcutta for some time now, won't you?'

Bimalendu turned to go, and at last Apu found his tongue. he caught his hand and said, a little unnecessarily, 'Listen. So Leela is living in Alipore?'

He had not meant to ask such a question, he knew it made no sense. But there was so much he wanted to know. What was he supposed to ask first?

'Yes,' Bimalendu replied, 'I can't tell you how stricken we've all been ... I went to our own house in Burdwan for Durga Puja, and it was the same story there. No one wants to have anything to do with Didi any more. Only our old maid started crying. She had helped raise Didi when she was a little girl.... Didi herself is not happy at all. I see her secretly sometimes. Each time she cries her eyes out for her daughter. Heerak Sen spent most of the money Didi had. Apparently, he had offered to take her to England. Didi belived him. She always did want to go to England. You knew that, didn't you?'

Bimalendu began walking away again. Apu clutched his sleeve once more. 'When do you go and visit her?'

'I don't go every day. Sometimes, in the evenings Didi comes in her car to the Victoria Memorial. I meet her in the open space in front of the main building.'

Bimalendu left. Apu started to walk, lost in thought, hardly noticing where he was going. There was a park by the road, where children were playing. Little girls were skipping, turning a rope high in the air. Apu went into the park and found a bench. He felt no anger towards Leela, nor any disappointment at her action. What he could feel welling up in his heart was a deep love, the kind of love he had never felt for her before. In the last eight years, Leela had become but a distant memory, almost unreal. Why, he could not even remember her face properly. Who knew in what secret recess of his heart all this love had lain hidden.?

He felt angry with her grandfather. It was he who had arranged this marriage. Who had asked him to marry her off to such a scoundrel? Poor Leela! Her life had been ruined by other people.

A few days later, he left the boarding house he was in and moved to another. In these few days, his financial resources had become somewhat depleted, and all his old problems had come surging back. He could not afford to take a single room, but sharing a room with two or three other men—all of them petty clerks—was now anathema to him. It was not that they were not good men, or that they treated him badly. It was just that Apu was far from familiar with the way their minds ran. He liked being alone, but that was precisely what his companions would not allow him to be. He might have just sat down on the balcony to think for a while, when Keshav

Babu would appear with his hookah, saying, 'Why are you sitting here all by yourself, Apurbo Babu? Haven't the Chowdhury brothers returned from work yet? By the way, have you heard what Mohan Bagan did today? No? Let me tell you....'

Calcutta was still the same, after all. He could see the same dust, the same smoke, the noise, the boredom, the insularity, the monotony with which each day repeated itself—nothing had changed.

He would have left the city by now, and gone back to where he had come from, but there was a problem. Mr Roychowdhuri had also returned to Calcutta, and was now busy trying to build a joint stock company. He had offered him a job here, but Apu was not sure that he could bring himself to sit behind a desk and do clerical work, especially after the last five years. Oh God, what was he going to do? If he did not accept this offer, how was he going to survive?

The last five years had taught him a few things that he knew he could not have learnt even in twenty-five years had he remained in the city. In the forest, he had learnt to dream new dreams about art; and, in the fading light of the setting sun, in the magic of the silent forest, in the empty, solitary plains, under the dark night sky, and in the long, sunny afternoons, when the breeze brought the fragrance of shaal blossoms, he had come to know the true meaning of life, having seen its deep, mysterious beauty.

In a noisy boarding house in Calcutta, it was impossible to recapture those magic moments. He needed total seclusion and silence to rebuild each image in his mind and his imagination. Where was he going to get that in Calcutta? The truth he had experienced miles away from here, that knowledge which had risen spontaneously like a shining star in the very depths of his being, was likely to remain hidden forever here, washed away in the great flow of life in the city.

He remembered he had vowed to capture with ink and paper the life he had witnessed, and all its joy and beauty. Until he had written it all down for others to read, he could not rest in peace. Suddenly, he recalled a particular day in the forest. Nature had taught him a strange lesson that day. He had been riding. He saw, in one corner of the forest, hidden among various other plants and creepers, one particular creeper that he could recognise. He had seen it before in Bengal. It was called telakucha. Apu looked at it with affection, it seemed to be a familiar friend in a foreign land. But the leaves on the creeper were dry. All it had was a half-ripe fruit, hanging from its top. Apu kept going back to it every day, and saw, day after day, how slowly and painfully the creeper died. The fruit grew bigger, rounder, riper; the green portion around its stalk turned bright red, like vermilion. But as the fruit prospered, the leaves turned paler still, and the stem began to shrivel.

One day, he saw that there was absolutely no sign of life left in the creeper. The fruit had ripened completely. Glowing red, soft and ready to be plucked, it was hanging lightly from the dead creeper, tempting whatever bird, monkey and squirrel that happened to see it. The creeper that had gathered warmth from the light which fell on it from ninety million miles away, and found other ingredients from the environment it lived in, to create this attractive, edible fruit, had fulfilled the purpose of its existence. It was only this ripe, red fruit that was the final culmination of the creeper's life. The bird or the animal that ate it would not thank the creeper. No one would ever sing its praises. Yet, its life had found fulfilment, in the creation of that red fruit. Even if it remained untouched, it would not matter. Even if it simply fell to the ground, it would give birth to other creepers, bear more fruit, feed more birds.

This little episode had shaken Apu, for his mind, at that time, had been particularly sensitive. It had made him wonder about himself. Was his life worth even less than that of the little telakucha plant lost in the forest? Did he have no aim, no purpose in life? Did he not have anything to give to others?

This question had come back time and again to haunt him, when he had spent long afternoons sitting on rocks in the shade of shaal trees.... Staring out of his tent at night, looking with wonder at the silent, starry sky, he had dreamt of the same thing. Kajal ... the face of his little boy came back to him often and gave him such inspiration! Then he thought of his future descendants—unborn yet, locked in the far distant future, but there they were, their faces soft and tender as the petals of a shirish flower. They, too, would have to face life and deal with nights of crisis, dark evenings of despair. *He* must stretch out a firm hand from across the ocean of time, to tell them how he had watched life unfold its mysteries, how the shining star of truth had risen in his own heart on grief-filled nights. He must record for the future generations every lesson he had learnt.

Apu watched his first manuscript grow and expand with the same affection and anxious anticipation with which a mother watches her child grow through laughter and tears, wondering—with a trembling heart—about its future. He often found himself thinking more about what his book would say, rather than going through the difficult process of actually writing it. Who would he write about? The poor people. He had to speak of them, he did not wish to write about others.

He had met such different people; in the streets, in markets, in villages, in the city, and on trains—ranging from holy men and teachers and singers to owners of shops, beggars, puppeteers, hawkers, even poets and writers. He would write about all of them.

Some time in the distant future, perhaps hundreds of years hence, when his name had disappeared and been forgotten like the blossom on the shaal trees that had appeared earlier in the year, or like the cobweb which had once grown in a corner of his room, may be, even then, some unknown soul would read his book—in the first light of dawn, or at dusk; in an open field, or on a river-bank; on a day of sadness, or a cold winter evening; or—perhaps—in the light of the stars, lying on dew-drenched grass, on a deep, dark and silent night.

Just occasionally, fear gripped him. What if no one read his book? Then he thought of the paintings in ancient caves. When those artists had drawn pictures of bulls, bisons and mammoths on the walls of those caves, could they have known that, one day, thousands of years later, their talents would claim recognition from the modern man? Or else why were scholars and travellers thronging the caves in Cantabria, the Dordogne and the Pyrenees mountains? The telakucha creeper in the forest had died. But it had given its life to create a fruit. Other plants would emerge from it, other lives would grow. The self-sacrifice of the first creeper would not go to waste.

His first book.... Anxiety and hope kept chasing each other in his mind, so many other thoughts crowded round. Never having had any experience in this matter before, he felt either startled by each thought, or deeply thrilled.

This was the history behind his writing.

৵◉৵

Apu had his first rude shock when he tried to find a publisher. He went from one to the other with his manuscript, but realised that no one was prepared to even speak properly to a new writer, let alone publish his work. At last, one publisher told him to leave his manuscript with them. Five days later, on receiving their postcard, Apu presented himself again, having taken care to dress well and polish his shoes. He had even borrowed a friend's glasses to add a touch of distinction to his appearance. He stood there with a trembling heart. Perhaps they were just amazed to find what a tremendous book he had written?

At first, the owner of the company failed to recognise him. Then, when he did, he simply called an assistant and said, 'Here, Satish, give this gentleman his manuscript. Look in the large drawer.'

Beads of perspiration broke out of Apu's forehead. Why did they want to return his manuscript to him? He turned a pale face to the owner. 'Er ... aren't you going to ...?'

The answer was 'no'. They were not going to spend any money on a new writer. However, if Apu himself could find five hundred rupees, it would be a different matter. Apu had never even seen so much money. Where was he going to find it?

The following morning, Bimalendu turned up at his house. Leela was going to visit the Victoria Memorial in the evening. She had specifically asked her brother to take Apu with him.

When Bimalendu returned in the evening, the two of them went to the park opposite the Memorial and waited for Leela. After nearly an hour, Bimalendu pointed to a yellow car and said, 'Look, there's Didi. Let's go, she'll park her car under that tree. The traffic police here are quite strict about parking.'

Apu's heart started beating fast. What was he going to say to Leela? What *could* he say? Bimalendu went ahead. Apu followed him. Leela did not get out of the car. Bimalendu spoke to her through a window, 'Didi, I brought Apurbo Babu with me. Look, here he is.'

Apu stepped forward. 'Hello, Leela. How are you?' he said with a smile.

Leela was still beautiful. The poet who had said that beauty itself was such a great virtue that those who possessed it needed no other, had indeed spoken the truth. Yet, she was not the same Leela. She had put on a little weight, and lost some of the youthfulness in her looks. She reminded Apu of her mother, Mejo Bourani. When, as a child, he had seen her in their house in Burdwan, this was how she had looked. Hers was not the kind of beauty that aroused unbridled passion. It was quiet, dignified, perhaps a little sad.

Now Leela looked like her—a goddess, her eyes filled with such deep sadness. Apu could not reconcile this figure with that of a woman who had created such a scandal by leaving home. Leela smiled at him and said busily, 'Oh, do come into the car, Apurbo. You've forgotten us totally, haven't you? Come on, let's go for a drive. Shobha Singh, to the lake!'

Leela sat in the middle, with her brother on one side, and Apu on the other. It was only during their childhood that Apu had ever sat so close to her. He kept looking at her again and again. Leela kept up a nonstop chatter, talking about the merits and demerits of various makes of cars, occasionally asking Apu about himself. When they reached the lake, Apu felt decidedly disappointed. *This* was the famous lake? Perhaps the babus of Calcutta were proud of it, but he could not see anything special. Even Leela seemed impressed by it ... poor Leela! She had not travelled much outside Calcutta, had she? Apu did not express his views about the lake for fear of embarrassing Leela. They spotted an empty bench under a coconut tree, and Apu and Leela got out of the car. Bimalendu went for another drive round the lake.

Leela turned to Apu with a smile. 'So tell me what you've been doing. I hear you went out to conquer the world?'

'I went to a place near Jabalpur, where your husband lives,' said Apu without thinking. Then it dawned upon him that it was a rather tactless remark, which might upset Leela. He changed the subject quickly by saying, 'What are those

349

things in the middle of the lake, like islands? Is it possible to reach them?'

'Only if you swim across. You're a good swimmer, aren't you? Anyway, now tell me about yourself, what you've been doing, and where you've travelled. I am so happy to see you today. Come to my house, we could have a cup of tea. You look sunburnt ... did you roam around in the hot sun quite a lot? Tell me, did you ever think of me?'

Apu gave a slight smile. He was not adept at uttering melodramatic or sentimental lines. In a situation like this, he always felt tongue-tied. After so many years, he was finally alone with Leela, sitting so close to her, yet he could find nothing to say. There was so much he had planned to tell her, but now not a single word would pass through his lips. Everything he had had thought of saying appeared laughably trite.

Leela broke the silence. 'Oh, I hear you have written a book?' she said suddenly. 'Won't you show it to me? I knew you would become a good writer one day, right from the time when we were children. Remember the stories you used to write? I knew it then.'

Then she made a proposal. Bimalendu had told her how difficult Apu was finding it to get his book published. Leela offered to meet all expenses. How much would it cost, anyway? She was prepared to pay every penny, she said.

This was totally unexpected. A sudden wave of joy swept over Apu. All expenses! Every penny? But he still could not utter a word. A second later, he felt an odd compassion and pity for Leela, just as he did in the old days. Leela too, had cherished such dreams. She had wanted to be a painter, and talked about it often. What was she doing now? Buying new cars, expensive lace from English shops, throwing her money away anyhow. There had once been a glowing fire in her, akin to the holy fire lit to invoke the gods. It had gone out, but the invocation had remained incomplete. Leela deserved sympathy from all who knew her. Poor, unfortunate Leela!

But her heart was still as generous as ever. She had stretched out a hand to help him the minute she heard he needed help, exactly as if she was his own sister. They were, after all, childhood friends—the purity of her affection for him had remained unclouded by any other emotion. Perhaps what she felt for him was similar compassion. She had seen his mother work as a cook in her house. Their abject poverty, and his utter helplessness, had probably touched her young, tender heart, and aroused sympathy and a deep understanding. These were the ingredients that went into making true love. Without these, love could captivate and intoxicate, but it could not offer the calm assurance of a permanent bond.

Everyone takes advantage of Leela's simple mind and generous heart, he thought. No, I can never exploit her. Never mind if my book doesn't get published.

❦

Apu was running out of money. A job was still hard to get. He went to see Mr Roychowdhuri, but he did not give him a straight answer. They were now drilling in the same area where Apu had worked, to look for manganese. Apu asked to be sent back there. After many repeated visits and several vague answers, Mr Roychowdhuri finally made him an offer: was he prepared to return to the same job on a lower salary? Apu felt so insulted by this that his face turned red, and he could feel his eyes smart. These people could make such an offer only because they knew he would agree to go back there, not for the money, but something else. To tell the truth, the question of money was not all that important to Apu. He would not swallow his pride just for a few rupees.

But....

It was early autumn. On the lower plateau, the first of the ebony fruit would have started to ripen, although higher on the mountains, it must still be raining. Deep in the woods, ripe cape gooseberry would have turned large areas bright yellow, enticing bears to come down after dark and gorge on them; parrots must still make an incessant noise all day; and higher on the hills, where the almond and the teak began there would be all the reetha trees, laden with bunches of fruit. If one looked carefully enough, it might even be possible to find clusters of late blossom on some of them. That huge forest, those dark starlit nights, that colossal expanse of empty grassland, that continuous, monotonous westerly wind, that bright, abundant moonlight, the endless freedom and the complete seclusion, were all calling him back.

Occasionally, when Apu thought of the steady destruction of the earth, particularly in Canada, Australia, New Zealand and Africa, he felt that one day nature would take her revenge. Every act of man's arrogance—the building of empires, the naming of mountains and lakes after kings and queens, the killing of animals and birds to promote trade, the destruction of glorious pine forests to open factories—every ruinous attempt would be crushed, every score settled.

Once, in the Chhindwara forest, Apu had been supervising the construction of a siding line for a copper mine. It was then that he had suddenly become aware of the enormous strength of the forest and the powers of nature. She was simply waiting; apparently lost in silent meditation like Shiva, all her fury curbed and controlled for the moment, but just waiting with infinite patience for the right time, and the opportunity, to strike.

❧

In spite of everything, Apu did not get the job. It turned out that, this time, it was not just Mr Roychowdhuri who could make the final decision. The other directors of the new company did not agree. Perhaps they were suspicious of Apu's motives for wanting to go back. Having worked there before, he might have learnt ways and means of stealing, or cheating the company. Besides, these new directors were human, too. Nearly all of them had a jobless nephew, or the son of a friend, to consider.

It occurred to Apu one day that instead of trying for a job, he could try again to get his book published. He began to send short stories to magazines. some got published, one even managed to earn a lot of praise, but no one paid him a penny. Then he remembered Aparna's jewellery. It was still with his father-in-law, he had not even thought of it in the last seven or eight years. If he sold some of it, that might give him enough money to get his book printed. Why hadn't this simple solution occurred to him in all these months?

He went back to see Leela a number of times, but did not raise this subject. All he did was read out the entire novel to her. She was very pleased, and did her best to encourage him, going so far as to make a rough calculation of how much money was needed to bring the book out. 'If it was someone else, I might have taken their help,' Apu thought. 'I cannot take any money from poor Leela.'

One day, his eyes fell on a small advertisement in the newspaper. It was of a chemist's shop; its owner was his old friend, the herbalist. Apu went out the same evening and found it in a little alley off Sukia Street. His friend was sitting outside his shop. 'You!' he exclaimed on seeing Apu, 'Hey, you're still alive!'

Apu laughed. 'I searched everywhere for you. Thank goodness I saw your advertisement today. How do you suppose I found you? Anyway, tell me what you've been doing. Judging by the furniture in your shop, you're not doing too badly.'

His friend made no reply. After a few moments' silence, he began talking of other matters. Finally, he said, 'Come, I'll take you to my house.'

It turned out to be a small, white two-storey building. There was a tin shed in the courtyard, where nearly ten men were busy packing or putting labels on various objects. At the far end was a tank, and another shed that served as a store. Apu went upstairs with his friend. There was a hall, with a room on each side, all done up nicely. A large clock stood in the corridor, ticking loudly. Apu's friend called one of his daughters: 'Bindu, go and tell your mother to make two cups of tea,' he said.

Apu glanced around curiously, 'Before that,' he remarked, 'I would like to meet Bou Thakrun. Can you get Bindu to fetch her? Or will she not deign to meet me, now that you are a wealthy man?'

His friend remained silent for a while. Then he said, almost to himself, sounding extremely sad, 'She's never going to meet you. Where will you find her? Romola and her mother have both left me!'

Apu could only stare at him speechlessly. 'Romola went in December,' his friend went on, 'and the following August, I lost her mother. I cannot even begin to tell you how we suffered. I was still steeped in debt, but we had to fight illness and death. She used to talk of you quite often. It's now five years since.... I had no wish to marry again, and for a long time I didn't, but about three years ago, I....' Then he asked his new wife to come and meet Apu. She came in with the tea and snacks. Dark but young and healthy, she appeared to be smart and clever. Apu's friend began talking of his business. Apparently, he was now making ink, and selling tea leaves in small packets, which were doing very well. Apu heard him in silence, trying to eat, but found it difficult to swallow. The food seemed to get stuck in his throat.

Later, as he took his leave, he said, 'Your new wife is certainly good-looking. She's also accomplished, isn't she?'

'Yes, she's all right, but very quick to answer back. You know what Romola's mother was like. She'd put up with anything. This one has no patience at all. What can I do, tell me? It's not as if I really *wanted* to get married a second time, but....'

Alone on the pavement outside, Apu's mind went back to his last visit to his friend's house. He could still see his wife clearly, standing with a flickering lamp in her hand at the door of their tiled house—so poor, without a single piece of real jewellery on her person, but a warm smile on her lips.

Six years had passed since that night, but it seemed like yesterday.

TWENTY FOUR

Kajal had grown older. Of late, the village teacher, Seetanath Pundit, had started to visit him every morning for lessons. In the evenings, Kajal was supposed to study by himself, but this proved to be something of a problem. Despite his grandfather's stern words, his eyes would close as soon as he sat down with his books, and he would fall asleep wherever he happened to be. If someone bothered to wake him up before dinner, only then would he get to eat with the other children. Otherwise, there was the additional problem of being asked to eat with his grandfather. Kajal dreaded this.

He had not yet learnt to eat tidily, without throwing grains of rice everywhere. His grandfather tried to teach him to eat properly. If he saw Kajal eating his rice simply with boiled potatoes, he would bark, 'Why aren't you mixing your rice with daal? Go on, pour some daal over your rice, and mix it nicely.'

At this, Kajal might hastily try to serve himself daal, his young hands trembling, and spill some on the floor. Some of his rice, too, would climb over the edge of his plate and fall on the ground. Grandfather would shout again, 'Oh God, this boy hasn't even learnt to eat his meal! Don't just stare, pick it all up.' Afraid and confused, Kajal would slowly pick up every grain of rice and place it back on his plate. But that was seldom the end of the story. Grandfather's irritation grew as other dishes appeared. '... And that bitter gourd? What did you leave that for? Never mind if it's now time to have the chutney. Put the chutney away, and eat your gourd.' Kajal hated bitter gourd, its taste made him feel sick. But he could hardly argue with his grandfather. Under his eagle eye, every single piece of fried gourd had to be eaten. By this time, Kajal was usually very close to tears. A great lump rose in his throat, making it hard for him to swallow.

When the meal finally came to an end, Kajal often went to his aunts and begged for a paan. On being given one, he quickly opened it to see what spices it was filled with. Then he pleaded again, 'Give me some more wood in this one, please Mamima? Just a little bit more?' By 'wood' he meant a stick of cinnamon.

'Cinnamon?' his aunts would snap. 'You want extra cinnamon every day. Such a self-indulgent boy—he has to go and look in the mirror, to see if his tongue's turned red!'

But, self-indulgent or not, what Kajal felt really passionate about was reading. He knew that Vishweshwar Muhuri, his grandfather's clerk, had quite a few books amongst his possessions. They told thrilling tales of how murderers and other culprits were caught. Besides these, he wanted to read *The Arabian Nights*. Oh, what stories it had, what pictures! He had found it on his grandfather's bed one afternoon, and leafed through a few pages. Sadly, though, Vishweshwar saw him and snatched it away, saying, 'Look at you! A child of eight, and he wants to read a novel! Do you know what your grandfather's going to do to you if he finds out?' But Kajal knew where the book was usually kept, in that big wooden chest in his bedroom upstairs. If only he could somehow get the key to the chest! He would stay awake all night to read it, and put it back before dawn.

Over the last few days, Sitanath Pundit had started to give him lessons in the evenings. His grandfather sat nearby, smoking his hookah. Kajal sat facing his teacher, and could see the open, empty space behind him to the north of the temple that stood within their compound. This space, from time to time, turned into a stage before his eyes. If asked, Kajal could not have explained how it happened. What he saw was never very clear; people appeared and events occurred in a hazy mist. But he felt as if he could see, in the fading twilight, all the princes and their followers from his grandmother's tales, stopping by a river whose name nobody knew. Princesses climbed into golden flying chariots and sped skyward, leaving behind trembling palaces.... Kajal forgot himself and leant forward, staring at the sky, feeling strangely depressed. At this precise moment, his teacher shouted, 'Look, look, Banerjee Moshai, see what your grandson is doing. I told him to write a few words on his slate, and he's simply staring into space. I've never seen such an inattentive child.'

'Why don't you give him a tight slap?' asked his grandfather. 'A pest, that's what he is. His father's not interested in him, and I had to be saddled with this wretch in my old age!'

It was generally agreed that Kajal had become very naughty indeed. He could not keep still for a second, nor could he stop talking. 'Look at your cousin, Dolu,' said Seetanath Pundit. 'He's sitting here quietly, isn't he, and

358

doing his sums? He's got something in him, and you, you're hopeless in arithmetic.'

'Dolu!' Kajal whispered, prodding his cousin with a finger, the minute the Pundit's back was turned. 'You've got something in you, have you? What is it? Rice? Daal? Khichuri? Would you like some khichuri, Dolu? Hee, hee, hee!"

More complaints were promptly made to his grandfather. As his punishment, Kajal was summoned and asked to spell the word 'catch'. He knew the correct spelling, but fear and anxiety made his stammer get worse, and he simply could not get out the letter 'c'. After a few moments of futile struggle, he gave up and began, 'K-k-a....' Immediately, a slap landed on his cheek with such force that his young, fair skin turned red like a pomegranate, the redness spreading to his ear. Kajal no longer felt afraid, just inexplicably hurt. He did know the spelling; was it his fault that the letters got stuck on his tongue? But he was not old enough to know how to protest, or speak in his own defense. His hurt got deeper, though he did not quite know who it was directed against.

It was around this time in his life that something strange happened.

Seetanath Pundit dabbled in astrology. Kajal had heard him discuss with his grandfather such things as horoscopes, positions of stars and calculations to determine the length of one's life. For over a year, he had overheard these remarks while doing his lessons, but had never ventured to open his mouth.

It was the middle of November. Winter had started, but had not yet become fierce. There were many date palms in the vicinity of the house. Most of the dates had just been harvested. The cool evening air was often heavy with the scent of fresh date juice.

One afternoon, Kajal's cousin, Aru, said to him, 'Brahmo Thakrun, I hear, is about to die. Everyone is going to see her. Want to come, Kajal?'

359

Brahmo Thakrun was an old lady who lived in the neighbourhood. She had been ailing for some time. No one knew exactly how old she was. She lived alone, and sold muri to make a living. No one could remember whether she had ever had any family. Highly irritable, she could not stand small children. Kajal had gone to her house a few times to buy muri; but if she saw him near her house, generally she shooed him away. 'You're a bandit!' she would say. 'Go away, and don't, for heaven's sake, step on those saplings!'

Now, when Kajal arrived at her house with Aru, he found that a lot of other people had already got there to see her in her little room. Kajal and Aru took a quick peep from the door. Brahmo Thakrun was lying on the floor. They could hardly recognise her. Her face looked gaunt and terrible, and her eyes had sunk deep into their sockets. Kajal's uncle was sitting with her. The local doctor was talking to a few people on the front verandah. It was generally believed that she would not last the night.

This surprised Kajal. He knew Brahmo Thakrun. He had seen with what ferocity she conducted her affairs—why, even his grandfather treated her with respect! But what had happened to her today? What had reduced her to that weak, helpless creature lying on the floor?

Brahmo Thakrun died before darkness fell. A sudden silence seemed to envelope the whole area. An unknown horror began lurking in every corner, about to spread, like darkness, and grasp everything on its way. It seemed to Kajal as if every face had fear written on it.

Dusk came early on this winter evening. Most of the neighbours got busy making arrangements for the funeral. Kajal's grandfather joined the others in the courtyard of the dead woman's house. Kajal followed him with hesitant steps, but could not bring himself to go very far. He stood in a bamboo grove at some distance from the house. Brahmo

Thakrun's house and courtyard were both invisible from here; nor was it possible to hear anything. The only noise came from the murmuring bamboo, as a sudden breeze swept through it. Kajal stood alone, his heart racing faster, his mind filled with a most peculiar emotion. It was not fear, but a sense of wondrous mystery. He saw a couple of bats fly off under cover of darkness. Usually, if he saw a flying bat at this time, he would chant a rhyme: 'Mister Bat, Mister Bat/what he ate/out he spat!' Today, the bats aroused no amusement in his mind, but heightened this strange sense of mystery.

This was, in fact, Kajal's first encounter with death. He was only five when his grandmother died; in any case, she had died in the middle of the night, and her body had been taken away before he woke. He had seen and heard nothing. This time, both the mystery and horror of death began to dominate his young mind. He did not have a lot of friends, so he was left on his own most of the time. The same thoughts kept going over and over in his mind. 'What if,' he thought one day, 'I, too, die like Brahmo Thakrun?' His limbs went numb with fear. It *could* happen, couldn't it?

With every passing day, his fear increased. Lying alone in bed, or sitting by the river on the steps of the ghat, he could think of only one thing: perhaps, one day, his own body will be brought here ... to be burnt on the riverside, like his dead grandmother and Brahmo Thakrun ...!

The very thought made his whole body go cold.

Kajal knew the year of his birth. His grandfather had got Seetanath Pundit to make a horoscope for him. Kajal had been present when the matter was discussed, but he did not know the exact date. All he knew was that it was a date in early February.

One afternoon, he slipped into the office where his grandfather's clerks worked. On a shelf were a number of old almanacs. He found the one for 1923, and began going through the dates in the first week of February. Suddenly, his eyes fell on the 5th, and for no reason at all, he began to feel convinced that it was a most inauspicious day. Whoever was born that day would never live long. Who knew, perhaps that was the day *he* had been born?

He asked his aunt that evening, 'When was I born, Mamima? Do you know the date?' Mamima had no idea, nor was she interested. Kajal found an older cousin. 'Do you know my date of birth, Potol da?' he asked. But Potol was only ten, so he could not help, either. His grandfather had the horoscope, but Kajal did not dare ask him. One day, he asked Seetanath Pundit, who promptly said, 'Why, what do you want the date for?' Unable any longer to keep his fears to himself, Kajal blurted out, 'H-h-how long will I live, P-p-undit Moshai?'

Seetanath Pundit stared at him, perfectly amazed. He had never heard a small child like him say such a thing. He called his grandfather instantly. 'Here, listen to this, Banerjee Moshai,' he said and repeated what Kajal had told him.

'Precocious brat!' exclaimed Shashinarayan Banerjee. 'He's worried about life and death, but he still hasn't learnt all his tables, has he? Go on, boy, tell me how much are twelve times fifteen?'

No one understood Kajal's fears. Sharp words from his grandfather did nothing to dispel them. Who else could he talk to? He was old enough to realise that there was no one in his house who would spare him even a few minutes to listen to him and offer him reassurance. If only ... if only he could see his father and talk to him! Surely *he* would understand?

A few days later, he came down with fever. This happened to him each year. Once the rainy season was over, Kajal went through a period of sporadic attacks of fever. As soon as he began to feel unwell, he would go upstairs and find a sheet or something to cover himself with. Then he would lie quietly in his bed, looking up only if he heard footsteps outside. He would then raise his voice and say, 'Mamima, I've got fever again. C-can you g-get me a quilt, please?'

He often wished someone would come and sit with him, but everyone was busy. No one had any time for him.

At first, when his temperature started to rise, the sensation was not altogether unpleasant. He felt lightheaded, as if he was in a trance. His eyes fell on little objects in the room— a big, black ant climbing up an iron bar on the window, a patch near the door, created by a mixture of paint and lime, that looked like a funny bearded face. Outside the window was a coconut tree, a bunch of coconuts half-broken and leaning out of it. Downstairs, his cousin Aru had started to clamour for a meal. But this pleasant feeling did not last long. As his temperature rose higher, his whole body burnt with fever, his limbs ached, his head felt heavy. If only someone would come and sit with him at such a time!

Outside the office, on the road-side, sat an old woman, who fried savoury snacks. Kajal was one of her regular customers. No amount of scolding or punishment had been adequate for him to resist this particular temptation. Only a couple of days after his temperature went down, Kajal made his way to her. At first, he simply sat and watched her dip pieces of various vegetables, even leaves of some plants, into batter and fry them. Then he spoke hesitantly, 'Will you please give me some of those? Those green ones? Look, here's the money.' The old woman declined. 'No, little one,' she said, 'you've only just recovered, haven't you? If I let you eat any of this, your aunts might get cross with me.' But Kajal continued to plead, until she gave in.

One day, Vishweshwar caught him. Kajal was standing by a pond, clutching his little packet of fried snacks, when the packet was snatched from his hand and thrown away. 'What a naughty boy you are!' Vishweshwar cried, 'you're eating this rubbish again?'

'What's it to you?' demanded Kajal.

Suddenly, Vishweshwar stepped forward, grabbed his ear and shook him. 'What's it to me? You want to know?'

Kajal flushed with rage and humiliation. This was the first time an employee of the family had dared to lay a hand on him. He cried out, his thin, childish voice rising in anger, 'You stu-stupid man! Why did you hit me?'

Vishweshwar gave him a tight slap. 'Why? I'll show you why. Come with me to the master, you'll see.'

Kajal lost his head. He screamed and shouted, calling Vishweshar whatever names he could think of. His cheek still smarted from the slap, his head reeled. He knew there was no one here who might defend him, or put the clerk in his place. So he ended by saying, 'Let my f-father come. H-he will t-t-each you a lesson!'

Vishweshwar laughed. 'Your father? You think I am going to hide in a corner because he might come one day? Did he come even once in these past five years?' Had he not been aware of his master's views on this particular son-in-law, Vishweshwar could hardly have made such a comment.

Partly in anger and partly in fear that he might be dragged to his grandfather, Kajal began running away from the pond, towards the coconut grove on the other side. 'Just you wait!' he kept shouting, 'just you wait until my Baba gets here. He'll settle you, he will!'

That evening, he sat by the river and thought about his grandmother for a long time. Would Vishweshwar have dared to raise his hand on him if she were alive today? What business was it of his if he had a few snacks?

What was that? A shooting star! His grandmother used to say each time you saw a shooting star, a new life was born on this earth. What happened if one died? Perhaps if he died, he would become a star in the sky.

A few months passed. One evening, something else happened to terrify Kajal. His aunt washed and cleaned a marble glass and gave it to him with instructions to place it on a table upstairs where other similar glasses and bowls were kept. This particular glass was his grandfather's. He drank sherbet from it every evening.

Kajal took it, and was going up the stairs when, somehow, the glass slipped from his hand, fell and lay in smithereens around his feet. Kajal's face went white, his heart seemed to stop beating for a whole minute. What a disaster! It was his grandfather's special glass. In despair, he picked up the pieces as quickly as he could. Afraid that someone might see if he threw them away, he took the pieces upstairs and hid them behind the big wooden chest that contained *The Arabian Nights*. But what was he going to do now? Someone was bound to look for the glass the following evening. What could he say then?

Kajal did not tell anyone what had happened. He spent the rest of the day worrying and fretting, but could not find any possible solution. If only the broken glass could be replaced somehow! Where could he find another one? While playing outside with a friend, he whispered to him: 'Is th-there a m-marble g-glass in your house?'

No, the friend could not help. Kajal grew increasingly desperate. At night, he thought of running away. Which way would he have to go to reach Calcutta? He would run away to Calcutta and find his father, long before the next evening.

But he could not do it. He spent a restless night, full of nightmares. When he woke in the morning, the first thing he did was to go and peep behind the chest to see if the broken pieces were still there. He began to avoid his aunt, in case she said anything about the glass. Late in the afternoon, Kajal glanced out of the window and saw someone go past on a bicycle. He forgot his worries for a moment and ran towards the hedge behind their temple to get a better look. Then something else caught his attention. A boat was moored at their ghat. A fair and good-looking man had just got out of it, carrying a bag in one hand and a walking stick in the other. He was standing on a step and talking to the boatmen. Kajal had only just started to wonder who he might be, when he finished talking and turned his face towards Kajal. For an instance, Kajal's vision seemed to blur. Then he slipped through the hedge, and began running down the path that led to the ghat. He had not seen that man for years, but had recognised him at once. That man was his father!

Apu had missed the steamer in Khulna. Had he not done so, he would have reached Kajal the previous night. He was asking the boatmen if they could call for him in two days, and take him back in time for him to catch another steamer. When he turned his head, he saw a handsome child running towards the ghat. A second later, he recognised him. Throughout his journey today, he had thought of his son and wondered how big he had grown, what he looked like, and whether he might remember him. He himself could not remember what the little Kajal had looked like. Now, looking at this attractive boy, he felt both pleased and surprised. When did that three-year-old child he had last seen turn into this good-looking, graceful young boy? He smiled at his son. 'Can you recognise me, Khoka?' he asked.

Kajal had, by this time, draped his arms around Apu's waist with absolute confidence. Then he raised his sweet face and smiled back, 'Of course! Didn't I start running the second

I saw you? Look, I ran from that hedge over there. Why d-didn't you come all these years, B-baba?'

An extraordinary thing happened to Apu. He had managed to survive for years without thinking of his child. But now, as soon as his eyes fell on him, a huge ocean of love began welling in his heart. How amazing, this child was his own! Without him, the child was helpless; without him, he was totally alone. How *could* he have neglected him all these years?

'What's in your bag, Baba?' Kajal asked.

'In my bag? I'll show you when we get home. There's a pistol for you—it goes bang bang—and there are some books with lots of pictures. And a rubber balloon.'

'C-can I tell you something, Baba? D-do you have a m-marble glass?'

'A marble glass? Why? What do you want that for?'

Kajal explained quickly. He was not afraid of his father. He knew Baba would understand. Apu laughed and stroked his son gently. 'Never mind, come with me. Nobody will scold you,' he said. At once, Kajal's fears and anxieties dissolved completely. It was as if he had found an infinitely powerful god, who had stretched his strong arms towards him, to offer him protection and shelter, and to say, 'Have no fear.'

Later at night, Kajal told Apu, 'I want to go with you, Baba!'

Apu was quite willing to take him back with him, but he himself had not settled down in Calcutta. Where would he go and live with his son?

'We shall see,' he replied. 'Look, why don't I tell you a story?' Kajal remained silent until the story was over. Then he repeated his request. 'You *will* take me with you, won't you? People here scold me all the time, and they beat me, too. If you take me, I'll do all your work for you.'

Apu had to laugh. 'Do my work for me? What kind of work would that be, Khoka?'

He began telling him another story. This time, Kajal fell asleep. Apu read for a while, then began to tuck him in. The sleeping child seemed so utterly vulnerable, so weak, and so totally dependent on others. Why, this young boy had not asked to be brought into this world! He and Aparna had created him. Now, if he simply left him to his fate again and ran away, would Aparna ever forgive him? But how could he take him away at this moment? Where could he go?

Suddenly, something he had read in book by Frederick Harrison came back to him. It was an epitaph on a tombstone in ancient Greece:

This child of ten years
Philip, his father, laid here
His great hope, Nikoteles.

Apu could see that child Nikoteles tonight—his face, his skin, beautiful as an angel, playing in an empty field, long, long ago. His hair was golden, his eyes bright. His loving memory was made immortal in that old graveyard in Greece. Today, Apu could feel in his own heart the emotions of the father who had laid his child to rest hundreds of years ago. Time was irrelevant; the human condition was the same everywhere, at any time. This was the first time he had felt such deep affection for his child.

The room Apu had been given was the old one. The bed was the same, the one on which he and Aparna had spent their first night together. Kajal was lying beside him, fast asleep. But Apu could not sleep. He stared out of the window, lost in thought. His new life, and new experiences over the last few years had dimmed the memories of the life that had once been his. Memories of this village and this house, in particular, had become very hazy indeed. For nearly nine years now, he had had no direct contact with anyone here. Perhaps that was why even this familiar room, the old bed, and the row of supari trees he could see outside the window, all appeared to be a dream. The moon had risen once again, just as it did before; the sound of keertan wafted up from the temple below, exactly as it had done in the past. But Apu was not the same any more. He had changed—completely and irrevocably.

◦◦◦

Apu returned to Calcutta alone. He sold most of Aparna's jewellery and got his book printed soon after Durga Puja. The only thing he could not bring himself to sell was the necklace Aparna used to wear frequently. He was more familiar with this piece of her jewellery than any other. When he held it in his hand, he could recall her face faintly. It came back quite clearly at times, but never for more than a second, or even less, before fading away. In that split second, it seemed as if she had turned her head in that old, familiar way and was facing him, a smile on her lips.

When he brought the first copy of his book from the bookbinders, Apu forgot his woes. This book would spell the end of all his troubles, he told himself. It would bring him fame and glory. His mind went back to Nischindipur and the life he had known there more than twenty years ago. He thanked his broken old home silently: 'No matter where I have been, I never forgot you.' Then he thought of all the people he had written about. The story he had told was really theirs. The pain and sorrow he had described had been felt by them. He had met them at different times, and different places, some might not even be alive today. He did not know where to find any of them but he was grateful to each. On this dark, silent night, his heart sent them messages of gratitude.

A few days later, Apu found a temporary job in a small office. At least for the next few months, things would be easier. He also found another part-time job as a private tutor. He had to, for he needed the extra money to pay for advertising his book. Very soon, his life fell into the same old routine: rushing out of the house at half past nine, and after a day's work at the office, making his way to the house of his two young pupils. The room that acted as a study was on the ground floor. The master of the house ran a business, which meant that most of the little room was often occupied by large packing cases, which were stacked high, sometimes touching the beams on the ceiling. Amidst these, his pupils—two little boys—sat on a mat spread over a wooden bed, and did their lessons. Usually, when Apu arrived at dusk, he found the room full of smoke from the coal stove that had just been lit.

Winter gave way to spring. Apu's book was not doing very well. He spent as much as he could on advertisements, sometimes going without meals to find the money, but it did not seem to work. The booksellers advised him to approach literary editors and critics to get good reviews published in journals. 'No one knows you, who will bother to buy your book unless it's written about?' they asked. But Apu simply could not do it. Go from door to door with his own book under his arm, begging for a review? No, he was not prepared even to think about it. If his book did not get sold ... well, so be it.

There was, however, something he did do. At night, he began writing another book. It had become almost an obsession. Whether he could find a reader or not, whether he sold his first book or not, he felt he had to go on writing.

He left the mess he was staying at and took a small room on the ground floor of a house. It meant paying eight rupees a month for it, but at least here he could be alone to write when he wanted, and for as long as he wanted. It was not that his roommates in the mess were not nice people, but their mentality, the narrowness of their vision, and their ignorance caused Apu great distress. He could perhaps get on better with people like Bishu and his friends in Chapdani, or Ajablal Jha in Amarkantak, for their way of life was totally unknown to him. It held a certain amount of interest, even fascination, because it was different from anything he had ever known. But the babus in the mess were not extraordinary like Jha. Apu found it difficult to have a long conversation with any of them. His new room offered little ventilation. The small window that faced south simply offered a view of the exposed bricks on the broken wall of the house next door. Nevertheless, Apu was glad to be alone. He could get on with his writing.

By the time he finished moving all his possessions from the mess and putting them in order in his new room, it was quite dark. It being a Sunday, he did not have to go out to teach the two boys in that smoke-filled, pokey little room, crammed with those packing cases that smelt of turpentine. Apu had a bath and could finally relax.

A few days ago, he had received a letter from Kajal. This was his first letter, full of misspelt words and rather untidily written. Apu took it out, possibly for the fifteenth time, to read it again. He missed his Baba, Kajal had written; would he please come and visit him soon, and bring him a copy of *The Arabian Nights*, and a lantern? Apu smiled. His son was quite mad. What would he do with a lantern? What a thing to ask for! He rose, switched the light on and wrote a reply to Kajal's letter. He would visit him the following Saturday.

All trains and steamers were packed on Saturday, as the following Monday and Tuesday were holidays. Once again, Apu missed the early steamer from Khulna. When he finally reached Kajal's village, it was late afternoon. He spotted his son waiting at the ghat, a big smile on his face. Kajal ran and threw his arms around him as soon as Apu climbed out of the boat. Then he raised his face and asked, 'Baba, where's my *Arabian Nights*?' Apu had forgotten all about it. Kajal turned tearful. 'You forgot? How could you do that, Baba? I wrote to you specially. And my lantern? Did you get it?'

'Tell me, Khoka, are you really mad? Why did you ask for a lantern?'

'It wasn't just any ordinary lantern. I wanted one with red and green glass shades, the kind you can swing from your hand. You didn't listen to anything I said, Baba! Can you get me a mirror?'

'A mirror? What for?'

'I want to see my ... my reshekflun ... no, no, reflection!'

❦

Aparna's elder sister, Manorama, was visiting her father. She was a good-looking woman; her face bore a discernible resemblance to Aparna. She was very pleased to see her brother-in-law. Speaking of her dead mother and sister brought tears to her eyes. After a very long time, Apu found himself being treated with genuine affection in this house. In the evening, he said, 'Come on, Didi, let's go up to the roof.'

It was quiet on the roof. It offered an unobstructed view of the river, which ran for many miles.

'Do you remember my wedding night?' Apu asked. Manorama smiled slightly. 'Yes,' she said, 'it seems like a dream. God knows how it all happened. I was thinking about it only the other day, sitting right here.... In fact, I didn't see you even once after your wedding. Thank goodness I happened to be around this time.'

Manorama smiled exactly like Aparna. Occasionally, the expression on her face reminded Apu of his wife, almost as if Aparna herself had returned from a forgotten world.

'You never even thought of me, did you?' Manorama complained. 'Please come to this didi's house for Durga Puja this year. And do give me your address.'

Kajal turned up unexpectedly. 'Baba, Baba, can you solve this riddle?' he asked.

'Which riddle?'

'When I fly out, loud and clear/all can hear me, far and near.'

Kajal's young face struck Apu as extraordinarily beautiful. Sometimes, he tilted his head and smiled happily as he spoke; then stopped, and smiled again, this time a little unsure of himself, and seemed just a little sad. The look on his face made Apu's heart ache with love.

He thought for a minute. 'A bird?' he ventured.

Kajal dissolved into giggles. 'A bird? Of course not. It's a conch shell. The sound of a conch shell, doesn't that go far and near? You don't know anything, Baba!'

The day before he was to return, Kajal whispered softly to him: 'Please, please take me with you, Baba. I just don't like living here.'

'I might as well take him with me this time,' thought Apu. 'No one takes proper care of him here, and he'll never get any education if I leave him in this village.'

The next morning, he got into a boat with Kajal. Aparna's trunk and an attache case had been lying around in the house for eight or nine years. Manorama added them to their luggage. She went to see them off at the ghat, and began crying again, repeating her request to visit her in Barishal.

The new rays of the morning sun fell on the broken walls of the temple. A faint, somewhat unpleasant smell rose from the river. A small fire had been lit on the river-bank, using dry twigs, to make sure pieces of red-hot coal were available at all times for his father-in-law's hookah. Coils of smoke rose from the heap. The air felt quite chilly. When he had arrived here all those years ago with Pranav, just to attend his cousin's wedding, could Apu have imagined for a moment that, very soon, this house and this place would become such an important part of his life? He could remember that day so clearly. The day before he arrived here, he had happened to hear a song in a gramophone shop, and had sung it to himself throughout his journey. Even now, if he hummed that tune, that particular day came back to him vividly.

TWENTY FIVE

❦

Apu first took his son to Monshapota. He had not
visited his old home for six or seven years. The next few days
were holidays; if he did not make use of those, he would not
get the time to visit Monshapota again for quite some time.

The little cottage was in a sorry state of disrepair. Apu
recalled having brought Kajal's mother here—the place
then had been as unclean, as uninhabitable. He went next
door to fetch the key and unlocked the front door. The
floor of his room was littered with straw, rats had dug
holes in the ground, cattle had broken through the fence
and damaged a portion of the verandah, the courtyard had
turned into a jungle.

Kajal stared at it all, wide-eyed, and said, 'Baba, is this
your home?'

Apu laughed, 'Yes, but it's your home, too. You've only

seen your grandfather's mansion, haven't you? This is your very own.'

The next morning he went to visit the Sarkars. What he heard there left him stunned. Nirupama was no more. She had left on a pilgrimage last winter and had been struck by cholera on the way and had passed away. Her old uncle said to Apu, 'Dada Thakur, now that you're an educated man, you prefer the city, don't you? If you came back to your village more frequently, you'd have heard. I still cannot believe what happened to dear Niru. All she wanted to do was go to a fair—in a holy place, some distance from here. You know how devoted she was, how much her puja mattered to her. So I let her go with some other neighbours. Three days later, we received word that she was dying, on the way to Shantipur, near a small shop. She had cholera, they said. All of us left at once, but by the time we reached her, she was just about to die. She couldn't speak, but she was still conscious. She recognised us. I could tell by her tears. They just streamed down her cheeks. You knew her, Dada Thakur, you saw how she always helped everyone else ... but when the time came, there was no one to help her. Those who'd gone with her simply ran away. The only person who tried to help was the man at that shop. Niru had been left in an empty, broken old hut nearby. No one called a doctor, she received no treatment. We lost her ... just like that.'

It took Apu a while to gather himself and return to his own house. 'Khoka!' he called from the courtyard. Kajal had gone to sleep after lunch, but had woken up now. He had found a pole with a hook, and was trying to get champa flowers from the high branches of a tree. But the hook had got caught on a lower branch. Kajal was tugging and pulling at it.

Apu found this spectacle amazing. It was the same tree Aparna had planted. In the last seven years, Apu had not been able to come and look at it; but even without any assistance from him, it had grown and had started to flower. How had it happened?

'Do you know who planted that tree?' he asked.

'Help me, Baba' Kajal replied, laughing. 'Can you pull that branch down? I've only got two flowers so far.'

'You've no idea, have you? It was your mother!'

But Kajal did not understand. The only woman he had known was his grandmother. Any mention of his mother left him quite unmoved. She was no more than an unreal, imaginary figure. He felt nothing for her.

Some of the old neighbours invited Apu to their house, all pleased to see him after such a long time. Many of them offered him advice on what he should do; one of them sent him milk, another offered a cartload of straw to rethatch their roof.

Later in the evening, Apu had to pass Nirupama's house again. He could not bring himself to look at it. The entire village seemed empty without her. 'Niru di,' he said silently, 'here I am with my child. Won't you come and see him, greet him, arrange a meal for him?' He found it difficult to sleep at night. Nirupama's smiling face kept coming back to him; he could still hear the plaintive tone in her voice. Wasn't there any way he could see her, just once more?

He and Kajal left the village the next day, and returned to Calcutta by the evening train. It pulled into Sialdah station after dusk had set in. Kajal grabbed his father's hand as he emerged from the station, staring, round-eyed, at all the lights, the tall buildings, and the people.

On reaching home, Kajal had a wash and changed his clothes. Then he stood outside in the street and began watching all the traffic going down the main road. He saw a hawker selling a snack called abak-jalpan. Kajal had never heard of it. His father had given him two paisa. He spent one of those now and bought some. He was truly amazed by its taste. What spices went into making this heavenly stuff?

Apu came to fetch him. 'You must never go out alone like that. What if you got lost?' he admonished.

Kajal did not mind. His nightmares were all over. Never would he have to hear his grandfather snap at him, go up the dark staircase alone, and put himself to bed; nor would he have to make himself swallow every grain of rice—even those that slipped off his plate—in case one of his aunts said, 'Go on then, waste as much food as you want. Why shouldn't you, it's being provided free by someone else, isn't it? After all, it's not as if your father pays for any of it!' Kajal was young, but these jibes about his absent father hurt him very deeply.

Apu found a letter waiting for him. He could not recognise the writing on the envelope. It had lain in his letterbox for five or six days. He opened it and read it quickly. A complete stranger had written this letter, simply to tell him that he had enjoyed reading Apu's book very much, he had been enchanted, and everyone in his family felt the same way. He had obtained his address from the publishers, and would like to meet him.

Apu read the letter two or three times. Here was proof, here was evidence, that at least one person had liked reading his book. He had always been rather fond of hearing praise, but for a long time none had come his way. His earlier habit of bragging had disappeared with age and experience, but even so, he showed the letter to his friends and colleagues with great joy.

The next day, Kajal saw the zoo, the Maidan and the museum. What intrigued him the most at the museum were the huge petrified shells of two tortoises, belonging to an extinct species. Kajal stared at them for a while, looking thoughtful. Then, as Apu turned to go, he clutched at his sleeve and said, 'Listen, Baba, suppose there was a fight between these two, who do you think would win?' Apu considered the matter seriously, then pointed at one of them and said, 'The one on the left, I think.' His words promptly removed all uncertainty from Kajal's mind.

But what appealed to him the most were large shoals of fish in the water in Gol Deeghi. Several other children were looking at the fish. Like them, Kajal bought a packet of muri and threw it into the water and watched eagerly as the fish came to eat it.

'Why don't you get a rod and catch some of them, Baba?' he asked. 'Look, there are so many, and such large ones, too!'

'Sh-sh,' Apu whispered. 'No one's allowed to fish at this lake!'

On their way back, Kajal saw a beggar sitting on the pavement. 'Baba!' he cried nervously. 'Give him a paisa, quick, or he's going to touch you!' It was his belief that every beggar in Calcutta had to be paid, or he would come and touch you. If he did that, you would have to rush home and have a bath … oh, it would mean a great deal of trouble.

Apu lost his job before the monsoons were over. For a long time now, he had not had to deal with such financial deprivation. Unable to put Kajal in a better school, he got him admitted in a free school run by the Calcutta Corporation. Even giving him milk every day became difficult. His book was not doing well at all; and his pockets were empty.

The only constant source of joy in his life was Kajal. He could glimpse a whole different world through him. Heaven knew how Kajal could find endless delight in playing simply with a couple of tin discs, two marbles, a mechanical toy and a few books. Since he was both restless and naughty, Apu had to leave him locked in the house when he went out. Sometimes it took him as many as four or five hours to finish his business and return home, but that did not appear to bother Kajal in the least. He spent all that time just staring out of the window and looking at the traffic on the road, or going through Apu's books to look at the pictures in them.

Life in the city was still a mystery to him. His eager young eyes picked out what would appear totally insignificant to the tired and jaded eyes of a grown up. Whatever he saw, he felt he had to share it instantly with his father. Sometimes, he pointed at a bird, and said, 'Look, look, Baba, that bird was carrying a twig in its mouth, then it struck against that parapet over there and the twig fell on the road. Look, it's still lying there!' At other times, walking down a road crowded with cars, buses and trams rushing past, he might spot a crow having a wash at a flowing drain. Delighted, he would point that out to Apu. While eating something, he would take a bite, then offer it at once to Apu if it was tasty. Apu accepted this offer, instead of telling him off, even when a half-eaten object was thrust into his mouth. He could not bring himself to discourage anything Kajal did spontaneously. It was for this reason that an easy friendship grew between father and son. Kajal had never found such an amiable companion before. In Apu's life, too, there had been no one so young, so trusting and willing to rely completely on him.

But what struck Apu more than anything else was his son's innocence. One day, they were out on a walk when suddenly Kajal said, 'Baba, listen! I've got something to say ... but I have to tell you quietly.' Then, glancing over his shoulder to make sure there was no one else within earshot, he added shyly, 'That cook in that hotel gives me so little rice every day. I feel hungry even after a meal. Will you please talk to him? Do you think he might listen to you and give me a little more?'

In the last few days, Apu and Kajal had been having their meals at a small restaurant in their lane. The cook had not deliberately neglected Kajal. The amount of rice he served him would have been adequate for any city boy of his age. But, having come from a village, Kajal was used to eating more. Apu nearly laughed at his words. Why did he have to make such a secret of something so trivial? Who would have heard him, anyway?

A few days later, Kajal gave him another shy look and said, 'Baba, can I ask you something?'

'Yes?'

'N-no, perhaps I'd better not.'

'Come on, what is it?'

Kajal came closer, and lowering his voice, said softly: 'Baba, do you drink?'

Apu was astounded. 'Drink? You mean alcohol? Who told you that?'

'Why, I saw you! Didn't you stop at that stall at the corner of our lane, and drink from a bottle? After you had a paan?'

It took Apu a few seconds to realise what he was referring to. Then he burst out laughing. 'That? That was a bottle of lemonade, you idiot. I didn't let you have any because that day you had a cold. I'll buy you some another day—it's like sweet sherbet, that's all.'

Kajal felt relieved. He had never seen bottles of lemonade being sold at paan stalls. For some strange reason, he had assumed that what those bottles contained was an alcoholic drink, and was amazed to see his own father buy such a bottle. He had felt too embarrassed to raise the subject before, but was now very glad to have the matter clarified. Apu bought him a bottle of lemonade that very day to remove the last shred of suspicion from his mind.

Life was not easy, but it did continue happily enough, until a letter from Leela's brother, Bimalendu, arrived unexpectedly.

He had asked Apu to go to Leela's house in Alipore as soon as possible. Leela was in trouble. Her money had almost run out. There was no help from her husband, naturally. No one from her own family was prepared to help, either. She had been disowned by all, except her mother and brother. The former sent her some money from Kashi, the latter saved what he could from his own allowance and passed it on to his sister. The real problem was that Leela had always had plenty of money to spend. She simply could not get used to counting her pennies.

She had changed considerably, Bimalendu had written. Not only was she depressed and listless most of the time, but she had also started to lose weight. Bimalendu had recently forced her to see a doctor. The doctor had diagnosed her ailment as phthisis. It was still in its early stages, but she would have to take great care.

However, things had taken a turn for the worse. Over the last couple of days, Leela's temperature had shot up alarmingly and she had turned delirious. There was no one to look after her except Bimalendu and a servant. They had stayed up all night and tried their best to nurse her. But now Bimalendu needed help, and knew of no one else he could turn to.

Apu had been so engrossed in his own affairs that he had not been able to visit Leela for a long time. Having received Bimalendu's letter, he did not waste another second. He reached Leela's house as soon as he could, to find her burning with fever. Her face looked red, and unnaturally bright. 'What am I do?' Bimalendu asked, his own face pale and drawn. 'No one from our house will come; and I am not going to ask anyone to help, anyway. Should I send a telegram to our mother?'

'What if she does not want to come, either?'

'Oh, she will. She loves Didi—but after what Didi did, Ma could not continue to live here. *She* will come, I have

382

no doubt about that. But the person Didi really wants to see is her daughter. Even last night, she kept crying out for her. But … bringing her here is impossible.'

'I see. There is, however, one thing that can be done. You wait here, I will go and arrange a nurse. What she needs is careful nursing and we men can't handle that.'

It was two or three days before their combined efforts got Leela on the way to recovery. One day, she even noticed Apu in her room, and asked faintly: 'When did you get here, Apurbo?'

In due course, Leela recovered physically, but she seemed to have lost her spirit. If she lay down, she refused to get up. If she went and sat somewhere, no one could make her move. She would not talk properly, or smile at anyone. She even began losing her hair. Her mother had arrived from Kashi, but was not staying in Leela's house. She had gone to her own, and visited her daughter every day for two or three hours, travelling in her motor car. The doctor told them to take Leela away for a change of air. That was the only thing that could cure her.

Apu arrived at her house one afternoon to find her sitting by a window. The sky was cloudy, there was no sun. It was difficult for Apu to come every day because Kajal could not be left on his own. Not only was he naughty, he was also remarkably naive about most things. Besides, Apu had to do all the housework himself. He might have got his son to help him, but he did not wish to take him away from his games and toys. 'Poor motherless child!' he thought often, looking at him, 'let him play and have what fun he can!'

Leela gave him a wan smile. 'Come in, Apurbo!' she said.

'Where are the others? Hasn't Ma arrived yet? And Bimal?'

'Sit down. Bimal has gone somewhere. The nurse is downstairs, possibly resting for a while after lunch.'

'So where did you decide to go? Dharampur? Who will go with you?'

'Ma and Bimal.'

Both fell silent after this. Then, suddenly Leela turned to Apu and said, 'Tell me, Apurbo, do you ever think of Burdwan? Do you remember our house?'

Apu wondered silently at the change that had come over Leela. Aloud, he said, 'Of course. I remember it very well.'

'You used to live in a room in a corner,' Leela spoke absently, 'and I used to go and visit you.'

'You gave me a fountain pen, remember? Fountain pens were new, quite rare in those days.'

Leela smiled. Apu made a rough calculation. 'It was almost ... twenty or twenty-two years ago,' he added.

After a few moments' silence, Leela spoke again. 'Do you know of anyone who might buy my car?' she asked. Apu's heart ached for her. He knew how precious the car was to Leela. Was she really in such dire need of money that she was thinking of selling it?

'I don't care what the others say,' Leela said abruptly, 'but even my mother thinks ... never mind. Will you take me somewhere, Apurbo?'

'Where?'

'Anywhere. To your Porto Plata. Don't you remember? You said you'd find a shipwreck and bring back gold from it? You read a story in a magazine, and so you made such a plan.'

Apu could recall it now. 'That's right. I am amazed *you* remember it.'

'I asked you how you'd find it. You said you'd buy a ship and set sail on the ocean.'

Apu smiled. Then he opened his mouth to say something about the futility of childish dreams and desires, but shut it quickly. Leela, too, had had so many cherished dreams. She had wanted to go abroad and become a famous artist. If he spoke lightly of the hopes and aspirations they had shared in their childhood, Leela might feel hurt. But she refused to drop the matter. A little later, she said again, 'Why don't you go now?' she giggled and added, 'go, go. Who but you can bring back gold from ... what was it? Porto Plata? Hee, hee, ... see, I still remember. Even after all these years, Apurbo, I have not forgotten. Will you have tea?'

There was something odd about the way she laughed, and her speech was incoherent. It pierced Apu's heart like a sharp arrow, and he realised that he had never felt so much love for her as he did at that precise moment.

'No, thank you, Leela. I certainly do not wish to have tea in the middle of the afternoon. Don't worry about it.'

'Apurbo, I haven't heard you sing that old song for such a long time. Will you please sing it now? *I am the restless one, I thirst for what is afar?*'

It was very quiet outside on this grey afternoon, except for a number of birds that were making a racket in a tree in the compound of a neighbouring house. Apu began singing. Leela turned her face away and stared out of the window again. Apu finished the song. Then, thinking it might make Leela happy, sang it all over again. But Leela did not turn back from the window. It seemed as if she was looking at some specific object, but was not really conscious of what she was doing.

A few minutes passed in silence. Suddenly, Leela spoke: 'Can you tell me something?'

There was something peculiar in her tone. It startled Apu. 'What is it? he asked.

'Why should one live? What's the point?'

Apu was not prepared for such a question. 'What do you mean? Why are you ...?' he began.

'Tell me!' Leela cut him short.

'I can't. I won't allow you to talk like this.'

385

'All right. Tell me something else, and I want the truth.'

'Yes?'

'What do people really think of me?'

Was it the same Leela? Who could ever have imagined she would one day ask such a question, sounding so pathetic, so vulnerable? Apu could see instantly how it had happened. The proud and spirited Leela could deal with anything, except contempt from others. And that was all she had received over the last few years. She had not realised its full implications until now ... and now that she had, life had lost its meaning for her.

A lump rose in Apu's throat. He strove hard to keep his voice normal and his tone casual as he made his reply. 'Look, Leela,' he said, 'I can't speak for others, but do you want to know what I think? I don't just think you are greater than me; I think you are greater than many. No one knows you well, no one bothered to try to get to know you. I often think that, too. I didn't just meet you yesterday, did I? I have known you since you were a little girl, so even if others misunderstand, I am not going to. I can never ...' he stopped.

He had never spoken to Leela like this. Taken aback, she opened her mouth to ask, 'Is that true?', but shut it without saying anything. The look on Apu's face told her the question was unnecessary. The next instant, impulsive as always, Apu did something else that he had never done before. He moved closer to Leela and, taking her right hand between both of his, turned her to face him. Then he stroked her flushed face with infinite gentleness and affection, pushing away the loose strands of her hair around her ears. 'We are childhood friends, Leela. We shall never forget each other, under any circumstance. I never did forget you, no matter where I went, or what I did, in all these years.'

A shiver ran through Leela's whole being. No one had given her what she had just received, no one had told her what Apu just did, not only in words but through the firmness of his tone, and the honesty in his unwavering gaze. Suddenly, she realised how much she had loved him, all her life, but especially from the day she had found him roaming, alone and unprotected, on a pavement near Lal Deeghi, after his mother's death.

Apu gave a start. Lost in his own thoughts, he had not realised when Leela had buried her pale and tear-stained face in his chest.

He left the room and came away. With every fibre in his body, he could feel a deep, tender love for Leela, the kind of love that makes one discard all thoughts of self. He would find a way to make Leela happy. She must never be sad again, nor find any cause to belittle herself. Never mind if everyone else left her; he never would. And yes, he would take her away somewhere. She might not live long if she had to go on with her life in the city, in her present state of health. The whole world might turn against him, but he would honour Leela's request.

Apu remained thoughtful all the way back to his house.

Three days passed.

It was eight o'clock in the morning. Apu had just had his bath, and was about to go out with Kajal for a walk, when a cousin of Leela called Arun rushed in. 'Please come quickly!' he whispered urgently, dragging Apu to a corner of the room. 'Didi has swallowed poison!'

What! Poison? Leela had taken poison? Apu couldn't believe it.

But what could he do with Kajal? Where could he leave him? 'Look, Khoka,' he said finally, 'you must stay in the house alone. I have to go out, something very important has come up. It may be quite late when I get back.'

Kajal agreed, but not before he had asked a dozen questions. What was so important? Where was he going? How long would it take? Apu answered as best as he could. Then he and Arun caught a taxi and reached Leela's house. Two other cars were standing outside. The old family physician, Kedar Babu, met them as they stepped into the house.

'How is she?' Arun asked hurriedly.

'Still the same. I have given her another injection. I am waiting for Colonel Hillcock.' In answer to Apu's question, he said, 'Sad ... it's all so sad. What she took was morphine. She took it some time during the night, but we do not know when. It wasn't until this morning that anyone realised what had happened. I've sent someone to fetch Colonel Hillcock. Until he gets here, well....'

Arun took Apu to the same room where, only three days ago, he had sat and sung a song for Leela. At first, Apu found it difficult to go into the room. He found himself shaking all over. The room was dark, and all the curtains were still drawn. There were not many people inside the room, but in the passage outside there were quite a lot of people, all from her grandfather's house. They were all moving quietly and talking in whispers. Even so, looking at them, it did not seem to Apu that something extraordinary had happened in this house. Yet, only a few feet away, there was someone lying in her bed, prepared to turn her face away from this world with complete indifference, and bid farewell ... when, once, she had been in love with life, hoping and craving for all the joys it could offer.

Leela was lying in the same bed by the window, draped in a light English silk quilt with a diamond pattern. She was unconscious, her face colourless, but her lips were slightly blue. One of her arms was hanging out. Apu put it back by her side. Swinging between life and death, Leela looked very beautiful. It seemed as if her features had been carved out of ivory. There was something ethereal about her beauty now. She looked, more than ever, like a goddess.

She seemed to be perspiring. Was that a good sign? Could it mean that she was out of danger? 'Why is she sweating?' he asked the doctor quietly.

'It's the morphine—one of its symptoms.'

Ten minutes passed. Apu went out of the room and joined the others in the passage. People kept going into and coming out of Leela's room. The only people missing were her grandfather, Mr Lahiri, and her mother. Mr Lahiri was away in Darjeeling, and her mother had left for Burdwan just the day before. Leela was truly unfortunate.

There were voices downstairs, followed by the sound of a car stopping outside. The English doctor had arrived. He came up the steps, followed closely by Bimalendu and Kedar Babu. Many among those present wanted to go into the room, but Kedar Babu stopped them. Colonel Hillcock left in less than ten minutes. 'Too late!' he said briefly before departing. There was no hope left.

Another half an hour passed. More people arrived. Where were all these people until now? Why were they here today, when it was too late? Too *late*!

Leela died at ten o'clock. Apu was at her bedside when the end came. She had been lying with her eyes closed. Suddenly, she opened them wide. Her pupils were dilated. She fixed her gaze on Apu. A tremor shot through Apu's body. Perhaps she had recognised him? But no, the look in her eyes was distant, dull, indifferent, abnormal. The next instant, she raised her eyes to the ceiling, then moved them towards the window behind her head, as if searching for something. Had she been normal, she could never have moved her eyes in such a strange fashion.

A second later, it was all over. Everyone left the room. Only Bimalendu gave a sharp, piercing wail, like a small child.

There was nothing left for Apu to do. He, too, came out and turned to go, a thousand questions in his mind.

Sin? Virtue? What were they? Who could define them? On whose yardstick could they be measured? Fools ... fools ... all these people were such complete fools! Who was going to make an assessment of Leela's character and proclaim whether she was good or bad? These perfect idiots?

Despite his prfound grief, Apu almost laughed out loud.

TWENTY SIX

Kajal's studies were progressing well. He had learnt a lot in the last few months. He read whatever he could, and began leafing through Apu's books when he finished reading his own. His father was very busy these days. Often, he went out for several hours. Kajal had started to do many of his household chores.

He had acquired a number of cats. When he had first arrived, there was only one. Now that number had risen to four. All of them came and surrounded him whenever he sat down to eat. None of them was interested in his rice, but each wanted a piece of fish. Kajal tried to steel his heart, vowing not to give anything to any one of them; then he began to feel sorry for the youngest kitten and offered it a little fish. This led to such violent entreaties from the others that it soon melted his heart. By the time all four were fed, Kajal himself had practically no fish left on his plate. A local boy called Anu had one day thrown a kitten out on the road. It would have got run over by the engine that went up and down the road. Luckily, however, the driver saw it and managed to stop the engine at once. Kajal had then found an empty wooden packing crate for the cats to sleep in.

Every night, soon after going to bed, he would say to his father, 'Tell me a story, Baba. Listen, I need to ask you something. Have you seen the driver of that engine outside? Do you think he can take it anywhere he likes?' The 'engine' was a steamroller. Kajal had been watching it, absolutely fascinated, for many days. He envied its driver. What fun it must be to have a job like that. He could start and stop it whenever he liked, and take it down the road and come up again as many times as he wanted. It even had a whistle. Sometimes, Kajal had seen it standing still, moving just one of its wheels. It could stay silent, but there was a rod in front of it which, if pressed, caused the whole thing to break into awful clanging noises.

One day, the even tenor of young Kajal's life was interrupted. Apu fell ill. Kajal woke to find that his father was still in bed, instead of sitting up and smoking. A little later, he looked at the clock. Ten o'clock ... but Baba was showing no sign of getting up. Suddenly, the world began to appear different. The sun was still shining, nothing in the lane outside had changed, yet nothing was the same any more in Kajal's little world. He had never seen his father so ill. Apu lay in a stupor the whole day, his temperature rising higher. In the evening, Kajal left him briefly to go out and buy some bread. Then, as it grew dark, he went out again, carrying their lantern, and filled it up at the local paan stall. He knew its owner, Paramanand.

When Kajal returned and lit the lantern, Apu was still in bed, his eyes closed. Kajal began to panic. He had never been in such a situation. What was he going to do? He went to check on his father a couple of times and called him. Apu responded only once, saying somewhat incoherently: 'The stove ... bring it, must light ... stove....' It probably meant that he wanted to light the stove to cook a meal for Kajal. It occurred to Kajal that Apu had not had anything to eat, either. Should he light the stove himself and make something for his father? But how could he, when he had never lit the stove before? He peered into it and discovered that there was no kerosene in it, anyway. So he went back to Paramanand, this time telling him of his predicament. Paramanand pointed out a new homeopathy dispensary next door. The doctor there was new, and happened to be free. He came with Kajal and Paramanand to see Apu, examined him and told Kajal to go back to the dispensary to fetch the required medicine. Apu, feeling just a little better, said, worriedly, 'No, he can't go back. It's dark outside ... and he's very young. Later, tomorrow perhaps ...?'

This annoyed Kajal a great deal. He was no longer a little boy, he had grown up. He could go anywhere, all his father had to do was let him. But no, he thought Kajal was still a baby. Kajal felt cross nowadays, particularly in front of others, if Apu treated him like a child or stroked his cheeks with affection.

The doctor and Paramanand left. Kajal took the stove outside on the verandah, but could not light it. Apu began calling him: 'Where have you gone, Khoka? What are you doing outside?' Oh God, why couldn't Baba trust him? Kajal went back to the room, and said, 'What will you eat, Baba? Shall I go and get you some biscuits?'

'No, no, you couldn't do that. I'm not hungry, I don't want anything to eat. Please, Khoka, just stay here and don't go out. You might get lost in the dark.'

Get lost? Ha! If he was allowed to go out, he could go anywhere in the world, all by himself. His father's words made him laugh.

The next morning, he went out and got the medicine from the dispensary. Then, on his way back, he bought oranges and a pomegranate from a fruit stall, and some warm milk from another. On seeing his son return with a pot of milk, Apu said, 'You didn't listen to what I said, did you? You crossed the main road to get the milk? Please don't do that again, the road's full of cars and buses ... where's the change?'

He had given Kajal a rupee for the medicine. Kajal had bought the fruit and the milk with some of the money left over, and spent a paisa on some savoury snacks which he simply could not resist. He returned the remainder to Apu. 'Get some bread,' Apu said. 'You can have milk and bread this morning, there's a good boy. I will cook you a proper meal later, all right?'

But that was not to be. His temperature began rising again in the afternoon. By the time dusk fell, he was virtually unconscious. Kajal locked the front door and ran to the doctor again. The doctor brought more medicines with him, and told Kajal to bathe Apu's head with cold water. 'Isn't there anyone else here?' he asked Kajal. 'Just the two of you? If he gets any worse, we'll have to send a telegram to your family in the village. Who else is there?'

'No one. I don't have a mother, or anyone else. Just my Baba.'

'Oh! That makes it more difficult. You're too young to handle everything. If things get really bad, he'll have to be moved to a hospital. Let's see how he does tonight.'

Kajal's blood ran cold. A hospital! He had heard somewhere that anyone who went to a hospital, never came back alive. Surely his father was not so sick that he had to be packed off to a hospital?

394

The doctor left. Apu was lying still, his eyes closed. By his bed lay half a pomegranate, and a few segments of an orange. Kajal had bought a bundle of spinach for Apu two days ago, knowing how much he liked it. It lay in a corner, dried and shrivelled. What if his Baba never rose again? Never cooked another meal? A huge lump rose in his throat, his eyes began to smart. He ran out on their little front verandah and wept silently, feeling utterly helpless. Please God, make Baba well again. Kajal would die if he could not see his Baba get up once more, and cook and eat and do everything he normally did. Please, please, God, let him get better soon.

He found the mat he usually spread on the floor when he did his lessons, and lay down on it. He kept the lantern burning in a corner, wondering whether it would last the night. He was still afraid of the dark, especially now that his father was neither moving nor talking to him.

What were those weird shadows on the wall? Kajal promptly shut his eyes.

❧

It was a month and a half since Apu's recovery. He did not have to be hospitalised, as it happened. The Banerjees who lived down the road came to his rescue. Their son was a good doctor, and they were a well-to-do family. On hearing about Apu's illness from his landlord, their son came himself to examine him. Then he gave him an injection, arranged for someone to stay in Apu's house to look after him, and took Kajal away to his own house to be fed. In the last few weeks, Apu and his son had grown quite close to the Banerjees.

It was mid-March. Apu had not yet found a job, but these days he occasionally earned a little money by writing. One morning, he was sitting with Kajal on the floor and giving him a lesson, when a bespectacled youth turned up at the door. 'Er … can I come in?' he asked. 'Are you Apurbo Babu? Namaskar.' He appeared to be in his early twenties.

'Namaskar. Please come in, sit down. Where are you coming from?'

'I am a student at the university. I have read your book, and so have all my friends. We were so impressed that I felt I had to meet you. So I took your address and … well, here I am.'

Apu felt delighted. This educated young man had liked his book so much that he had gone to the trouble of getting his address and visiting him. This had never happened before. The young man looked around briefly and said, 'Is this … I mean, do you live in this room?'

Suddenly, Apu felt embarrassed. The few pieces of furniture in his room were all old and shabby. The mat he was sitting on was torn. A few minutes ago, he and Kajal had had a bowl of muri. Some of it was lying on the floor. He decided to put the blame squarely on his son. 'You have become far too naughty, Khoka!' he exclaimed. 'Don't I tell you every day not to spread things around when you eat? And why did you have to leave that bowl near the door?'

Puzzled by this sudden admonition, Kajal protested, 'It wasn't me! Why, Baba, *you* took that bowl and….'

'All right, all right, now finish writing those spellings.'

The young man intervened. 'The thing is, Apurbo Babu, there has been a lot of discussion about your book. Will you be home this afternoon? The editor of *Vibhavari*, Shyamacharan Babu, would like to meet you. So, if it's all right with you, I'll bring him here; and there might be two or three others. Say, around three o'clock? Is that all right?'

Apu agreed. They spoke for a while, then the young man took his leave. Having seen him off, Apu turned to his son.

'Khoka?'

Kajal pouted. 'I am not talking to you.'

'No, no, don't say that. Please don't be cross with me, not now. What do you think we're going to do?'

'What about?'

'Look, let's not worry about lessons this morning. Get up now, there's a good boy, and help me clean this room. Put that torn shirt under the bed. The editor of *Vibhavari* is going to come here at three.'

'What's *Vibhavari*?'

'A magazine, it's the name of a very well-known magazine. Go on, go next door and get a bucket.'

By three o'clock, the room did not look too bad. Shyamacharan Babu and the others arrived a little after three. 'I am going to publish a review of your book in my magazine next month,' he said. 'It was I who discovered your book, you see. Do you have anything else? Short stories, or articles? Why don't you give them to me?'

Apu found a short story for him. It was published in the next issue of the magazine, together with an article on its writer. The editor sent him twenty-five rupees for the story, and asked for another one. Apu passed on the magazine to Kajal for him to read the article. 'Read it aloud,' he said, stretching himself on his bed. Kajal began reading, then stopped and exclaimed, 'Why, Baba, your name's written here! They're talking about you!'

Apu laughed. 'They have said a lot of good things about me, haven't they? And they'll say the same about you one day, if you work hard and pay attention to your studies.' The bookshops told him his book had started to sell really well after the article was published. He received three more letters from new readers. Each was full of praise.

One evening, he returned home to find Kajal doing his lessons. He hid his hands behind his back and asked, 'Khoka, guess what I've got in my hands?' Kajal got up and ran to

397

him. 'Show me, show me. What is it?' He took the packet from his hands and opened it quickly, staring at its content with a mixture of amazement and delight. It was a copy of *The Arabian Nights*, full of illustrations. Why, the one his grandfather had did not contain so many colourful pictures! He smelt the book quickly. No, it did not have that characteristic smel! that always came from old books. That was perhaps the only disappointing thing. Apu had brought himself a number of books and magazines, too. After a long time, his pockets had been full.

The next day, he received a letter from a Canadian friend called Ashburton, who was staying at the Great Eastern Hotel. Apu went to visit him in the evening. Ashburton was a man in his early forties. This was his second visit to India. He had come before to look for plants and trees in the Himalayas. He was also a painter. Having read his article in *The Staesman* on the Himalayas, lavish in its descriptions, Apu had met him at his hotel about two months ago, and got to know him quite well.

Ashburton was waiting for him. Clad in a loose flannel suit, he was tall and handsome, his eyes were blue, and his hairline receding. From his mouth hung a pipe. He rose as he saw Apu arrive and strode forward to greet him. 'Something rather wonderful happened yesterday,' he said. 'I have never had such an experience before. I went out of Calcutta with a friend in his car. In the evening, we happened to be sitting outside. There was a pond nearby, a temple on the other side, rows of bamboo and palm trees. Then, suddenly, the moon rose ... and I saw such a striking display of light and shadows! Honestly, I couldn't take my eyes away. I thought: ah, this is the East ... the eternal East! I'd never seen anything like that before.'

Apu smiled. 'And pray, who is the Sun?' he asked.

Ashburton burst out laughing. 'Look,' he said, 'I am going to Kashi. I want you to come with me, and I won't take no for an answer. Let's go next week.'

Kashi! How could he go there? Kashi was draped with so many memories ... such golden moments of his life had been spent there. He could not just go back any time, anyhow, and spoil it all. When he had been travelling, his train had passed through Mogulsarai. How his heart had yearned to see Kashi again, but he had not been able to get off there and make the short journey. How could he explain his feelings to someone else?

Ashburton went on: 'Why don't you come to Java with me? It doesn't rain enough in western Java, so the forest there is not very impressive; but if you saw the forest in eastern Java, you'd be enchanted, I'm sure. You like forests, don't you?'

Apu said nothing. His eyes fell on a painting. It showed Beatrice Dante. He had seen it before in Leela's house. 'It's one of Botticelli's, isn't it?' he asked.

'No. It was generally believed that Leonardo da Vinci had painted it. But now, some experts say it was done by Ambrazzo da Predice. Who told you it was Botticelli's?'

Leela had told him. Poor Leela!

At the end of the week, however, Apu had to give in. Ashburton proved to be extremely persuasive. On reaching Kashi, Apu left him at a European hotel in the cantonment area, and took an ekka to travel back to the main city. He took a room in a place called Parvati Ashram in Godhulia.

The girls' school near the corner of Godhulia was still there. His own school should not be far. It was in one of the many alleys in the area. But he could not find it. He did, however, recognise a house where a friend called Prasanna used to live. He saw a gentleman outside, buying a cucumber from a vendor, and asked, 'A boy called Prasanna lives in this house. Do you know him?' The man stared at him. 'Prasanna? A boy?' he asked in surprise. With a start, Apu realised that neither Prasanna nor he could possibly be seen as a boy any more.

'No, no, I mean … he would be of my age,' he explained hastily. Yes, it turned out, Prasanna did indeed live in that house, but he was out for the moment. Apu learnt that he was married, and had four or five children.

Still he could not find his school. No one knew where 'Shubhankari Pathshala' was. 'But I have been living here for ten years,' said one of the men he asked. 'I've never heard of it.'

'No, ten years isn't long enough. It was here twenty-two years ago, maybe more.'

'Then you must speak to Mr Basak. He's been here for the last forty years.'

Mr Basak's response was far more satisfactory. 'Of course I remember it!' he exclaimed. 'It was in a building owned by Hargovind Seth. There were verandahs on both sides. You had to go down a flight of steps to get to the school.'

'Yes, yes. There was a tank in front of it.'

'Right. Anand Babu used to run that school. He died nearly twenty years ago, and the school closed down after his death. How do you know about it, sir?'

'I was a student there, before I left Kashi.'

Apu went to the neigbhourhood where they had lived and found an old neighbour who could recognise him. 'Come in, son,' she invited, 'how is your mother?'

'She is no more.'

'Oh! She was a good lady … she cut her hand one day, trying to open a bottle of soda. Remember?'

Apu smiled. 'Yes, I remember that very well. My father was ill at the time.'

The neighbour called a younger woman. She was a widow, and appeared to be in her early thirties.

'Do you remember her?'

'Yes. She's your daughter, isn't she? She used to cry a lot. Every day, lying by a window ... I saw her crying most of the time.'

'Yes. I had lost my son, you see. She used to cry for her brother. Had he lived, he would have been about forty today.'

Apu took his leave, and made his way to Manikarnika Ghat. His father's body had been reduced to ashes at this ghat; but, for that reason alone, it was a holy place for him.

The next morning, he went to bathe at Dashashwamedh Ghat. Just as he was about to get into the water, he saw an old lady slowly going up the steps, a brass pot of water in her hand. He stared at her for a few seconds. Why, it was Jethima! Suresh da's mother, the very arrogant and snobbish lady he had visited a few times in Calcutta. After his humiliation on new year's day, many years ago, he had never visited her. Now, he followed her and touched her feet. 'Can you recognise me, Jethima? Do you now live here in Kashi?' he asked.

The old lady stared blankly at him for a few moments. Then she could place him. 'Apurbo? From Nischindipur? May you live long, son. Sorry I didn't recognise you immediately. I can't see very well now. Besides, living so far from home isn't easy, you see. This pot is so heavy, I can hardly lift it. Usually, my neighbour's daughter fills it for me, but she's been down with fever for three days, so....'

'I see. You mean you live alone in Kashi? Where's Sunil?'

Jethima put the brass pot down. 'In Calcutta. They're all in Calcutta. They just got rid of me. I chose Sunil's bride myself ... a girl from a good family ... but she turned my own son against me. I'll tell you everything if you come to my house, 3/1 Brajeshwar Gali, to the left of the temple, that's where I live. I'm all alone, there's hardly anyone to talk to. Suresh came at the time of Durga Puja last year, but he stayed for just two days. He couldn't stay longer ... you must come and visit me this evening. Promise me you will?'

'Yes, Jethima. Why don't you wait for just a few minutes? Let me have a quick bath. Then I'll carry your pot for you.'

'No, no, there's no need for that. It's very good of you to offer, but I can take it myself. Thank you for offering, son.'

Apu did not listen to her. He ran down to the river and finished his bath as quickly as he could. Then he returned, and took the heavy pot of water from her. Jethima, it turned out, lived in a small room on the ground floor of a building. Another old lady from Dhaka had rented the next one. Other rooms had been taken by a family from Bengal. It was the youngest girl in this family who usually helped Jethima fetch water from the river.

'Sunil was quite devoted to me,' Jethima told him. 'It was that stupid woman who poisoned his mind against me. She'd find any excuse to fight with me, you know. One day, she even told her children not to come to me and eat anything I had cooked. So I said, "Why, do you think I plan to kill my own grandchildren?" She said, what did I know of bringing up children, I was old fashioned, I mustn't meddle in her affairs. That is how it all started, and then I noticed my son would always speak in favour of his wife. So I said to Sunil, "Send me off to Kashi, I don't want to live with you." God knows what his wife said to him that night. In the morning my son seemed quite happy to pack me off! Can you imagine, son, after all that I did for my children....' Her voice trailed away. Tears poured down her cheeks.

'Why, didn't Suresh da say anything?' Apu asked.

'Suresh? Didn't I tell you about him? He was given some property by his father-in-law—in Rajshahi, or Dinajpur, or somewhere like that. So that's where he lives now. He doesn't bother to write either, even to find out whether his old mother is still alive or not. If he was in Calcutta, why, there wouldn't have been any problem at all!'

She found a few snacks for Apu, and continued to chat while he ate. '... Oh, by the way, I almost forgot to tell you. Someone else from Nischindipur lives in Kashi now. Remember Lila? Bhuvan Mukherjee's daughter?'

'Lila di? Why is she in Kashi?'

'Her brother-in-law has a job here. Poor girl. Her husband has paralysis, he's been confined to bed for seven years. They have a number of children. They live with her husband's brother, but she has to work day and night, like a slave. Go and meet her this evening, if you can. I'll tell you where she lives.'

Lila was Ranu's elder sister—the same Ranu who had played with Apu and Durga in Nischindipur, and had been a close friend, despite the difference in their social status. Apu could not wait until the evening. He took Lila di's address, and went to see her at once. The house had three floors, but was very narrow. The staircase was so dark that Apu had to light matches on his way up, although it was only two o'clock in the afternoon. A small door led to a small passage. A boy of about ten saw him, and asked him what he wanted. 'Does Lila di from Nischindipur live here? I'd like to see her.' A female voice from the next room asked, 'Who is it?', and almost immediately a slim, fair woman emerged and stood at the threshold. The saree she was wearing was not altogether clean; she had no jewellery except white bangles. Only her hair was thick, dark and beautiful. She appeared to be about thirty-seven. Apu had no difficulty in recognising her. He went over, touched her feet and said with a smile, 'Can you tell who I am?' Then, seeing that Lila di was simply staring at him, surprised, he added, 'I am Apu. I used to live in Nischindipur.'

'Oh, Apu? Hari kaka's son? Come in, sit down.' Lila sounded very pleased. She touched his chin affectionately, started to say something, then suddenly burst into tears.

403

Apu felt strangely moved, as if a soothing balm was slowly spreading through his whole being. Who but a woman from his village, someone who had known him as a small boy, could greet him with such open affection? As a matter of fact, Lila di had been the daughter of a rich man in Nischindipur. She was married when Apu was quite young. They had not known each other long; yet their childhood memories seemed to create an unshakable bond between them.

Lila di brought out a small carpet for Apu to sit on. He had to sit out in the passage, for Lila di did not have a room of her own. In spite of his protests, she got her son to fetch more eatables, and made him tea. Then she told him all about herself. Her oldest son had died at the age of fourteen. Her husband was incapacitated, so they had to depend entirely on his brother to look after them. Her brother-in-law was a good man, but his wife ... a tartar! Lila di was given every unpleasant chore she could think of. What was most sad was that there was no way she could go back to their house in Nischindipur. Her parents were no more, her brother Shotu was finding it difficult to make ends meet and could hardly be expected to give her any support. He had not received any education, spent most of the money their father had left, and was now running a small provision store in the village. Their large, sprawling house was derelict and uninhabitable in most parts. Moreover, he had married twice, and had two wives and their children to maintain.

'Why did he marry twice?' Apu asked, taken aback.

'Because he's a fool. Apparently, he had a fight with his first wife's father, and decided to take a second wife just to teach him a lesson. Now he himself is paying for it, trying to feed the whole lot. Besides, Ranu, too, is with him, you see.'

'Ranu di? Why is *she* still living in Nischindipur?'

'It's most unfortunate. She lost her husband seven or eight years ago. There was no one in her husband's family

404

who could take care of her, so she had to go back to Nischindipur. Her brother-in-law visits her sometimes, and she occasionally spends a few days with him and his family, but stays with Shotu most of the time.'

For a long time, Apu had been meaning to ask about Ranu, but had felt oddly hesitant. Now, at Lila di's words, his heart grew heavy. But they talked endlessly, both agreeing how wonderful it would be if they could go back to their village. 'How long has it been since you ate from a lotus leaf? Can you remember?' Lila di asked. 'People use shaal leaves here. Some shops have even started wrapping food in paper. My son brought some sweets the other day ... I told him to throw them away at once, no one in our village would even dream of using paper to pack food, would they?'

Lila di's words took Apu straight back to his childhood. It was true that food was almost always served on lotus leaves. He had forgotten about it. 'Why didn't *you* go back to Nischindipur, Apu?' Lila di asked. 'You're not a woman like me. There's nothing to tie you down, is there?'

'No. When I was younger, I used to think I'd return there with my mother, once I started to earn. That was her dearest wish. Even after her death, I thought of going back, but then ...' Apu stopped. He found it a little awkward to mention Aparna, but eventually told Lila di about his marriage and Aparna's death.

'How long did she live?' Lila di asked.

'Only a few years,' Apu replied, a little shyly.

'Why didn't you marry again?' asked Lila di. 'You're so young. I can still see you as a small boy, playing in our house. Really, you should marry again. Why didn't you bring your son? I'd have loved to have seen him.'

Then Apu met her husband, and children. Lila di invited him to lunch the next day. Apu arrived on time, but realised at once that Lila di's position in the house was truly not very different from that of a slave. She had to finish cooking for the whole family before she could cook something for him. As Apu watched her leaning over a hot stove, he could remember how beautiful she had once been. Now, there was virtually nothing left of her former beauty. When he looked closely enough, he could even spot a few strands of grey hair. Veins stood out in her workworn hands. Why had she taken on so much extra trouble simply for his sake?

'What can I do, tell me?' she said, when she could at last serve him lunch. 'My daughter is growing up fast. Soon, she'll have to be married. Who can help us except my brother-in-law? I have no choice but to put up with this.' She started crying again when Apu bade her goodbye. 'You must come again.' This time, Apu, too, found himself close to tears.

There was someone else in Kashi he had to see. It was Mejo Bourani, Leela's mother. She had her own house in Narad Ghat. It did not take him long to find it. Mejo Bourani seemed delighted to see him. As they sat talking, a young girl walked into the room. She was about seven-years-old, dressed in a frock. Thick curly hair framed her face. Apu did not have to be told who she was. So very beautiful, she had to be Leela's daughter. How was it possible for a human child to look like an angel? Affection, pain, and memories of the past welled up in Apu's heart so strongly that it almost brought tears to his eyes. 'Khuki!' he called, 'come to me, dear.'

Khuki smiled shyly and was about to run away, but Mejo Bourani called her back and made her sit near Apu. She now lived permanently with her grandmother. Her father had passed away last April, even before Leela's death. But Leela had not been informed. Her daughter looked exactly as Leela had done, at that age. Apu recalled the first time he had seen Leela, at a family get-together. She had recited a funny poem and made everyone laugh. He had spotted her before she had seen him. Little Khuki here was the spitting image of her mother.

'Such a lovely girl!' said Mejo Bourani sadly, 'but what's to become of her? I'll never be able to get her married. When people hear about her mother and what she did ... who doesn't know about it, anyway? ... who'll want to marry her?'

Apu bit back the words that rose to his lips. 'Don't worry about her marriage,' he said instead, 'getting her educated is more important, isn't it?' Silently, he thought, 'No, I won't say anything now. If my Khoka lives long enough, if he grows up to be worthy of her ... then I'll raise the matter.' Before he left the house, he called Khuki again. This time, she came to him without any hesitation, and stood close, looking at him curiously with her large, bright eyes.

⋆⟨◉⟩⋆

Apu spent what remained of the day with his friend, Ashburton, at Sarnath. By the time they returned to Kashi, dusk had fallen. Apu went back to Lila di's house to say goodbye. He had to catch a train the following morning to Calcutta.

The sincerity of Lila di's affection moved him deeply. She treated him as if he was her own brother, going down the stairs to see him off, touching his chin briefly in affection, when he touched her feet again. Then she gave him a few wooden toys. 'Give these to your son,' she said, tears brimming in her eyes. 'I bought them for him yesterday.'

On his way back, Apu thought: 'What a wonderful woman Lila di is! Poor woman, how she's suffering, slaving for other people! I did not say anything in so many words, Lila di, but I'll make sure you get to visit your village again, and see your own people ... yes, before this year is out!'

The next evening, travelling back by train, Apu became aware—not for the first time on the trip—of a new emotion.

407

He had never felt this before, certainly not so intensely. It was his concern for his son, and a deep longing to see him. In the last few days, he had missed him very much.

Kajal had been left with Mrs Banerjee, who was very fond of him. But had she been able to take proper care of him? Kajal was so naughty. What if he had gone out alone to the main road? Why, he might have been kidnapped ... or perhaps he had stolen out of the house and been run over by a car!

Had something like that happened, Apu tried to reason, surely the Banerjees would have sent him a telegram? Perhaps ... perhaps they had, but it had gone to the wrong address. So many other disasters could have befallen his son. Could he have gone up to the roof in the Banerjees' house to fly kites? That roof did not have protective wall. No, Kajal would not do that. Flying kites was an art he had not yet mastered. Still, the other boys in the house could have persuaded him to go up with them, couldn't they?

Only a little while ago, he had said to Ashburton that he wanted to travel abroad, to Java, Bali, Sumatra, to see the islands on the Pacific, see Africa. He would write a novel about the people in these lands. Europeans had described them already, but he wanted to see them with his own eyes, see how it all affected him—the endless grasslands of Uganda, the jungles of Kenya. Nights would be torn apart by the raucous cries of baboons, hyenas would laugh madly, excited by the smell of dead animals and their rotting flesh; in the afternoon, the mid-day sun would spread fire across all the open spaces, creating restless, trembling waves of heat, pale uneven lines fluttering across barren lands. Prides of lions would form circles and try to seek shelter under thorny bushes, hoping for just a little shade. If he went away, he could see it all ... he could make it happen.

But how could he, when little Kajal kept pulling him back? He did not wish to go anywhere without him. Kajal, his Khoka, young, innocent, naive ... there was so much he did not understand, so much he could not do. But he held the strings to Apu's heart in his small hands and pulled, pulled with all his might. How could Apu wrench those soft and gentle hands, and push them away? No, that was impossible. Never mind if he missed this chance to see the world.

The train sped on. Apu could see mango groves, ducks sitting by ponds, sugarcane fields being watered, wheat being threshed, and buffaloes returning home after a day's grazing. Gradually, the sun moved away to the west, and shadows became longer in the open fields. In the far distance, some of the hills, etched against the horizon, began to turn dark blue, and others black.

Possibly because of his meeting with Lila di, his mind kept going back to Nischindipur. Far away, long ago, a totally different life had flowed, through the melody of chirping birds in the mango and bamboo groves, through the fragrance of so many known and unknown flowers, through such grief and joy. That which had been an intimate part of his life had now turned only into a dream. The entire village, the sister he had known in his childhood, his mother, Ranu, the meadows, the woods, the river Ichhamoti, were all a part of a smoky haze, unreal and indistinct in his memory.

It was spring now ... the ground would be scattered with fallen leaves from bamboo stems. How often had he sat by his broken window, his mind full of childish fantasies, those days were so full of joy ... the cosy warmth of a kantha on a cool winter night ... all of it had been swept aside like flotsam in the endless ocean of time.

Only, sometimes in his sleep, he felt as if he could still hear the loud, stern cry of the village chowkidar: 'Roy Mosh-a-a-i!' Instantly, Nischindipur came to life; the spring of his childhood came down to bless the unclaimed, barren land next to their house. The woodlands filled with flowers, familiar voices spoke outside his broken window, a woodpecker hammering away at a coconut tree sent a secret message, soothing him even in his sleep. In his dreams, the first ten years of his life came back to him again, fresh and new.

The house could not be standing any more; perhaps even the rubble was about to be buried underground. There would be no sign of the broken window. Now, at the end of a long day, when the last golden rays fell on the trees in the woods, making their shadows grow longer, when birds like phingey and doel began calling, no happy child would wake from his trance by the window, and say to his mother plaintively, 'If the roof leaks again tonight, Ma, I will definitely go off to Ranu di's house tomorrow and sleep there. I am tired of staying awake each night!'

Apu remembered something else that made him smile.

About a year before leaving the village, he had found a large number of cowrie shells. They had been given to his father by one of his disciples. Apu had never seen so many shells together. Having found them, he felt as if he had suddenly come into enormous wealth. It did not matter if he lost in games again, and had to pass on some of these shells to his friends. His fund would last for ever. He put the shells in a round biscuit tin, and hid it in a niche high on the wall.

Then, somehow, he lost his interest in playing with cowrie shells. Besides, it was soon time for them to leave for Kashi. In all the confusion and excitement, he totally forgot about his tin of shells. He left with his parents, but that tin remained hidden in the high niche.

For many years, he did not think even once about his shells. He remembered them, for the first time, and for no apparent reason, one evening after Aparna's death, when he was sitting in the Eden Gardens, looking at the setting sun over the Ganges. Today, he thought of them again.

His cowrie shells! Hidden in a room on the northern side of their house ... now possibly ruined and totally destroyed. He could still see the tin ... the biscuits it had once contained had been tiny, absolutely miniscule, like spiders' eggs. One could get sixteen of those for a paisa. On the lid was a faded picture of a monster, with his mouth open wide. There it was, placed high, acting as a kind of symbol of his lost childhood. Behind it lay a bamboo grove, a wood of silk-cotton trees, the vast open field of Shonadanga, the cooing of doves ... and beyond that stretched the silent, dazzling blue sky of a totally enchanting April afternoon that he had left behind twenty-three years ago.

TWENTY SEVEN

❧◈❧

Soon after his return from Kashi, Apu was invited to a big party. The house had a large portico, and a big front lawn on which small chairs and tables had been arranged; in one corner stood a shamiana. The guests were all milling around. Apu noticed a marble tank, with a few white lilies in full bloom. There was a fountain in its centre, also made of marble. His hostess took him specially to show him this portion of the lawn, calling the tank her 'lily-pond'. The fountain had been made in Jaipur and brought all the way from there. She did not fail to mention how much it had cost.

Various arrangements had been made to entertain the guests. What Apu enjoyed the most were songs sung by a woman. He could not join the players at bridge, for he did not know how to play the game. But he pulled up a chair to watch the game until it finished. There were sandwiches, cakes, sweets, much talk and laughter, and more songs. When he left the party, Apu was in a very happy frame of mind. 'I was lucky to be able to attend such a party,' he thought on his way home. 'I would never have been invited if I hadn't written that book and become famous. I mean, this doesn't happen to everyone, does it? What a pleasant evening I've had! I wish I had Khoka with me!' He had decided against taking Kajal with him, as he was very likely to have fallen asleep. He had, however, wrapped a couple of cakes and placed them secretly in his pocket. He took them out and had a quick look to see if they were all right.

Kajal was fast asleep when he reached home. 'Khoka!' he called, stroking him gently. 'Wake up!' Kajal opened his eyes. He loved being stroked and caressed by his father. His lips spread in a mischievous smile, and he tilted his head, waiting for more. It seemed he could never have enough of it.

'Don't go back to sleep. Let's have a chat,' Apu told him. Kajal did not mind. Chatting with Baba was always fun.

'All right, Baba. I've got a riddle for you—'

'No, I can't solve all your riddles. You're too clever for me. Look, I brought you some cake, from the house of these rich people I went to visit. Get up!'

'Oh, I almost forgot. There's a letter for you, Baba. Under that book, over there.'

It was from Ashburton. He had written, 'What about the greater India across the seas? Will its contribution to civilisation remain confined to supplying slaves and labourers? People like you are sorely needed here. Most of these people are uneducated and ignorant. The missionaries are opening a school in Fiji. They are looking for a teacher who knows Hindi. Why don't you come out and work as a teacher for a while? Something else is bound to work out sooner or later. I realise you are not the type to settle down permanently to the life of a school teacher. Come as soon as you can, don't delay.'

Apu finished reading the letter, and remained thoughtful for a few moments. Then he said to his son, 'Tell me, Khoka, what would you do if I left you and went away? Suppose I left you with your grandfather? Couldn't you live with him again?'

Tears sprang to Kajal's eyes immediately. 'No, no, you can't do that! Your going to Kashi was bad enough. Three days, you said. And how long did you take to get back? No, I won't let you go anywhere.'

Apu said nothing more. Kajal did not realise just how different things would be if his father went away to join his friend. It would not be like going to Kashi. He could not be back in a matter of days. No, he could not do it. Who would take care of his son? Going away now was impossible.

When Kajal had gone back to sleep, Apu went up to the roof and sat alone in the dark. He could see a half-moon rising over a tall building on Circular Road. From the road below came the noise of the throbbing engine of a lorry. It was well past midnight. He had seen a similar moon rise before, over a hill that stood behind all the trees in the forest, at a spot where it rose like the hump on a camel's back and curved down again. Near that curve, down a slope, were rows of almond trees. Sometimes, during the day, the old leaves on these tree-tops took on a reddish glow. At this time of night, wild cockerels would start to call: cock, cock, cock!

He tried to imagine a world where there were no buildings, no Circular Road, no noisy lorries, no bridge parties, no lily ponds. Instantly, he could see woodlands stretching for miles, expanses of dried grass, ebony, teak, shaal, and endless wild flowers. There he was, back in this little room with a thatched roof, Ramcharit Mishir sleeping on the floor. The silent trees waited outside, and the dark night was turning pale as dawn broke. He could recall the freedom he had tasted then, the sense of mystery he had experienced while galloping down valley after valley, and his magical relationship with the sky and the stars, every dusk, and every night.

What kind of a life was he living here? Each day was the same as the other. Didn't he realise his life was being totally obliterated by his endless pursuit of a living, earning enough money to make ends meet, attending pointless bridge parties, and hearing meaningless chatter?

Apu went back to his room. Kajal had rolled to the centre of the bed in his sleep. Gently, Apu moved him to one side. How sweet he looked while sleeping!

Within a week after his return from Kashi, Apu had been asked to write novels for two leading magazines, *Vibhavari* and *Bongo-suhrit*. Both were well-known journals, their readership stretching beyond the confines of Bengal. Bengalis, no matter where they were in the world, liked reading them both. *Vibhavari* paid him an advance. *Bongo-suhrit*, it turned out, owned a press. They offered to publish another book by him at their own expense. His first book, in the meantime, had started to do so well that the bookshops which had never bothered to speak to him began to ask for more copies. Then, one day, a well-known firm of publishers wrote to Apu, asking him to meet them.

Apu made his way to their office in the evening. This firm was willing to bring out the second edition of his first book. What did Apu have to say to that? He thought it over. The first edition was almost completely sold out. The initial capital had come from Aparna's jewellery. The profits were all his own. If he agreed to let this firm handle the second edition, he would have to share the profits with them. However, it did mean that he himself would no longer have to run from shop to shop, chasing payments. Besides, the thought of being

415

paid a lot of cash held its own attraction. Apu agreed. A contract was drawn up and signed immediately. Apu would be paid six hundred rupees. For the moment, he was given two hundred in cash.

Most of it was in small notes. Apu found it difficult to hold it all together in his hands. What was he going to do with so much money? Had this happened to him before, he would have taken a taxi and gone for a ride, eaten at a good restaurant, or seen a film. But now he thought of Kajal before anything else. What could he get for him? Then, suddenly, he thought of Leela. How happy she would have been today!

Passing through a small lane, Apu saw a paan shop. It also sold sherbet. There were two or three bottles of syrup placed on the counter. The day was hot and sultry. Apu stopped at the shop for a glass of sherbet. A few seconds later, a boy and a girl arrived to buy something else. They obviously came from an ordinary, middle-class home, and possibly lived in the same lane. The girl appeared to be about seven; the boy was slightly older. She pointed at one of the bottles of syrup and said, 'Look at that green one, Dada. Must be nice.'

'He mixes it with all kinds of things, even ice. Look, there's the ice.'

'How much …?'

'Four paisa.'

By this time, the man in the shop had started to mix a glass of sherbet for Apu. The two children watched him eagerly, as he poured syrup out of the bottles and chipped ice. Then the girl turned to Apu. 'He'll give you some from that green bottle, won't he?' she asked, as if the green bottle was filled with some heavenly nectar. Apu began to feel sorry for these children. Perhaps they had never had a decent glass of sherbet. This cheap, sickly-sweet, coloured liquid was something special for them. 'Would you like a glass?' he asked. 'Go on. Two more glasses, please, of the same.'

416

The two children declined strongly. It took Apu a while to convince them that they need not be shy. 'Don't you have anything better than this?' he asked the shopkeeper. 'If you don't, can't you get it from somewhere else? I'll pay, whatever it takes.'

What his bottles contained, the shopkeeper assured Apu, was the best anyone could get in that whole area. In the end, he mixed them two large glasses of the syrup from the same green bottle, which the children drank with great relish.

Then Apu bought them a packet of biscuits and some cheap chocolates. The shop did not seem to have anything better. Even so, he went back feeling his money had been well spent.

❦

A couple of days later, on his way back from the Maidan, Apu had stopped for a minute in front of the shop of Whiteway Laidlaw, when a middle-aged man approached him. 'Babu,' he said, 'would you like a game of poker? I can take you to a decent place, there won't be any problem. Or, there are other games. Will you come?'

Taken aback, Apu stared at the man. His clothes were not all that clean, his face was covered with heavy stubble, his shirt was made of cheap tulle, a button was missing from its sleeve. His lips were dark—he clearly chewed a lot of paan. It took Apu only a moment to recognise him. It was Haren, the same boy who had tried to steal a book from their college library years ago. Apu had never met him after he left his college. By this time, Haren had recognised him, too. He stopped short, looking confused. Apu had never had such an experience before, but he realised how low his college friend had sunk.

'Forgive me,' said Haren, speaking before Apu could open his mouth. 'It's been a long time.... I did not recognise you at first.'

'Where do you live? Near here?'

'Yes. Taltola Lane ... why don't you come to my house? I have a lot to talk about.'

'Not today. I'll drop by next Monday, at around five, all right? Let me write down your address.'

'No, no. If I let you go now, I know you'll never come back. Come with me, please.'

Apu could not refuse. Haren's house turned out to be just one room, extremely untidy. A stale, musty smell greeted him as he stepped in. The room was packed with all the family's belongings. Haren made room for him to sit on a bed spread on the floor. The sheet, the pillows and the kantha were all dirty, the mat under the sheet was torn. In a corner were a few enamelled plates and glasses, and a lantern with a black chimney. Thin and dark little arms and feet poked out of the kantha. An older girl, of about eight, was sitting at a distance, on the threshold beyond which was a passage. The kitchen was possibly on the other side of the passage, where Haren's wife was cooking.

'Tepi, go and get a hookah ready for me,' Haren said to his daughter.

'You shouldn't ask your young children to prepare your hookah,' Apu remarked. 'Why don't you do that yourself?'

Haren raised his voice to call his wife: 'Where are you, come and meet my friend. He was my best and closest friend in college. There's no need to feel shy. Make us a cup of tea.'

Then Haren started to talk about himself. He had got married soon after leaving college, but his struggle with poverty had only got worse, especially now that he had so many dependents. He had tried his hand at many things—teaching, running a shop, supplying goods to other shops, working as a photographer—but nothing had worked. Apu had already seen what he was doing nowadays. Nobody in his family knew anything about it. What could he do, these days, with so many mouths to feed ...?

Apu did not like the way Haren spoke. There was something cheap and low class about the way he expressed himself. Perhaps he had simply grown accustomed to seeing the seamy side of life.

Haren's wife arrived. Apu's heart filled with pity when he saw her. She was thin and dark, the hair in front of her head had started to recede, she wore no jewellery except a few glass bangles. The alacrity with which she ran and made a cup of tea suggested that she thought their troubles were over, now that her husband had found his best friend and biggest well-wisher. When Apu finally rose to take his leave, Haren said, 'Look, if I can't pay my rent tomorrow, the landlord's going to insult me openly. Have you got five rupees?'

Apu gave him the money. As he was about to step out of the house, he saw Haren's wife whisper something to her son. The young boy stepped forward and said, 'Kaka Babu, I haven't been able to buy all my books. Will you please buy two of them for me? My teacher will scold me if I don't get them all.'

At this, Haren pretended to get cross. 'Books?' he said to his son. 'Don't be silly. Your Kaka's got better things to do than buy you books. The school's really stupid. Why do they change their books every year?'

'I haven't got any money on me just at this moment,' Apu explained to the boy. 'My pocket's empty.'

Haren came walking with him quite a long way. He had apparently seen a plot of land somewhere that could be cultivated. He needed two thousand rupees to buy it. Could Apu lend the money? Or he could become a partner, they could make a lot of money together.

419

This was the first time they had met after many years. How could Haren speak of such things on their first meeting? Apu returned home, feeling somewhat repulsed. What had his old friend from college turned into? A pimp for illegal gambling? In his youth, he had been a thief. God knew what else he had done for a living. Perhaps he would never be able to do any honest work.

Three days later, Haren turned up at Apu's house. He beat about the bush for a while, then began to talk about buying that plot of land again. Apparently, access to water would be a problem, so they would have to get a tubewell. How much was Apu prepared to spend on it? Before leaving, he said casually, 'By the way, Manik—my son—said you had promised to buy him his books.' Apu had certainly not made any such promise. Nevertheless, he gave some money to Haren.

After this Haren began visiting him frequently, bringing Manik with him at times. Manik and his family wanted to see a film. Could Apu give them the money? He did not have new shoes, or his baby brother needed new clothes, or one of his sisters wanted something else. A visit by Haren and his son usually resulted in Apu spending two or three rupees on them. Haren, too, found excuses to ask for money—either his rent had to be paid, or his wife was ill. One day, one of Kajal's toys went missing. It was the figure of a Japanese samurai, made of celluloid. Two days before its loss was discovered, Manik had come with his sister, Tepi. Kajal had seen Tepi play with the toy.

Two weeks later, Apu was invited to Haren's house for tea. The first thing he saw upon entering his room was the Japanese samurai, propped up against a lantern. If he said anything, Apu realised, his hosts would feel embarrassed. So he sat with his back to it, without looking once at the lantern, even when he got up to go. 'Never mind,' he told himself, 'perhaps Tepi couldn't help herself. I'll buy another one for Kajal.'

'Kaka Babu,' said Manik as he was leaving, 'Ma says why don't you take us to Kalighat one day? Let's go next Sunday, shall we?'

Apu had to agree. He ended up spending a small fortune on Sunday. He had to pay for a taxi, buy them snacks, toys, even a frock for one of the girls. Only Kajal, who had accompanied him, appeared to be very happy by this outing. This was his first visit to Kalighat.

Almost unconsciously, Apu thought of his friend, the herbalist, and his first wife. They, too, had been poor. But he had seldom asked for anything. On the contrary, they used to feel embarrassed if Apu tried to give them anything. Their affection had been so sincere, so completely selfless. He felt sad each time he thought about them.

He returned home that evening with Kajal, to find a young man of about eighteen waiting for him. Apu recognised him at once. It was Rasiklal from Chapdani, Mr Deeghri's son. Apu and his team of volunteers had nursed him back to health when he had typhoid. 'Rasik!' he exclaimed. 'How did you get my address?'

'I saw your novel, the one that's being published in *Vibhavari*. I got your address from them.' Rasik turned out to be rather shy. He blushed as he spoke.

'I see. Do come in and sit down. Tell me all about yourself. What's happening in Chapdani?'

'Do you remember my sister? It was she who sent me here. She said, if you ever go to Calcutta, do not fail to meet Master Moshai. She talks about you all the time. Why don't you come back for a visit?'

'Pateshwari? You mean she still remembers me?'

'Remember you? Didn't I just say she talks of you every day? It must be at least eight years since you left Chapdani, but Didi has certainly not forgotten you. Why, she even remembers what you liked to eat!'

421

'How is she? Her in-laws ...?'

'Her mother-in-law has died. So now there's really no one to harass her. She's got three children, it's she who runs the entire house. But they don't have a lot of money, so sometimes she finds it difficult to cope. She told me to buy chutney in a bottle. It costs ten annas, Master Moshai, how was I going to find the money? So I bought this small bottle of pickle for six annas. Nice, isn't it?'

'Look, I could buy you some pickle. What would she prefer? Mango? Or we could buy a bottle of Indian chutney. I don't think she'll like the English kind which has vinegar in it.'

'When will you come to Chapdani? Why don't you come today? If Didi learns that I met you, but did not take you back with me, she'll get very cross.'

'No, Rasik, I haven't got the time today to go anywhere. But I will go one day, tell Pateshwari.'

Apu went out with Rasiklal and bought more toys, games and packets of food, this time for Pateshwari's children. Then he went to see Rasik off at the station.

'You must come soon, Master Moshai,' Rasik urged, 'or my sister will make life very difficult for me!'

❦

The sky was such a clear blue today! It was cooler, too. Why did he always think of his childhood each time he looked at a blue sky on a March afternoon?

There was something else that he had noticed. When he was a child, each time he read a story or an account of a historical event, he could immediately see it all happening in his imagination, in the meadows, the bamboo and mango groves, and the river bank in Nischindipur. The bamboo

422

grove behind their house was packed with events from the Ramayan and Mahabharat. The broken two-storeyed house that belonged to Phoni Mukherjee, often acted as the palace of Dasharath. Even foreign characters appeared in his village. He could see Joan of Arc (of whom he had read in the *Bongobashi* magazine) with her herd of sheep in the kash-field near the river, or in the shadows of the silk cotton trees. Then he grew up, travelled to the city, learnt to read maps and was given lessons in geography. What he read as an adult no longer brought memories of Nischindipur to his mind, but any mention of the Ramayan or the Mahabharat inevitably made him think of the same woods, disused ponds and the wilderness surrounding them—grown hazy and unclear, they were still there, nothing could change them.

Now that he had settled permanently in Calcutta, Apu began to run into some of his old friends. Some were lawyers, others doctors. Janaki had become the headmaster of a government school, Manmatha was a successful attorney. He also met his friends from Diwanpur, Debu and Sameer. Debu was doing quite well in his job, but he wanted to become a building contractor and work independently. Sameer was an agent of a big insurance company. He had always been careful with his money. Now he was a rich man. Apu did not envy him, or anyone else, although his own struggle was not entirely over. Then he met Janaki one day. He had put on a lot of weight, and seemed to have lost the fiery spirit he was once known for. All he could speak of were his domestic problems. It seemed to Apu as if his friend had locked himself into a pokey little room and shut all its windows.

Manmatha remarked one day, 'I spend all day either in court, or working as the manager of an estate after five, which takes up at least three hours of my time every evening. Then I come back home, and there's more work. Sometimes, I don't even get the time to read the newspaper. Yes, I do

423

earn a lot of money, but even so, I think I was far better off as a student. Everything then gave me so much more joy ...!'

This made Apu think of himself. Why, he had been through such crises, such disasters, but *he* had not lost his zest for life. On the contrary, every day it seemed to flow with even greater exuberance. Why did the earth, the whole world, the universe appear coloured by such wondrous hues? Every day, the great mystery of life seemed to enthral and captivate him, making his awareness stronger and sharper.

He could sense the existence of another world. The visible sky, the song of a bird, the mere act of living, all bore only a hint of it. Just as an onion had a layer hidden under another, this secret world was hidden somewhere under all the mundane routine of everyday life, beyond the tangible world of body and mind. If he sat alone on a quiet evening, sometimes he could catch just a fleeting glimpse of it. A bridge had been formed with this world when his sister had died in his childhood. Then came the death of Anil, his own mother, Aparna and Leela. It seemed as if all his life he had tried to swim across a turbulent sea of tears ... only now could he see the palm-fringed coastline of this other world, dimly and faintly.

Today, sitting by himself on a bench in Gol Deeghi, he thought of Anil. Anil had once talked of taking over responsibilities from the previous generation. All his other friends had, each of them was now well-established. Only he and Pranav had not been able to settle down to any one thing. But did that mean he had failed in life? Was that the truth? What did his heart say?

His heart said something quite different. It told him what he had achieved in life was quite enough. He did not want wealth or power. Well then, what *did* he want?

It was not very clear. He only knew what he felt. At times, sitting on the roof in bright sunshine, inexplicable waves of rapture, overwhelmed and excited him. He lifted his eyes to the sky, as if he expected to hear a divine voice speak from it.

When he returned home from Gol Deeghi, Kajal was engrossed in a book. He looked up, starry-eyed, as Apu entered the room and said, 'What a wonderful story this is, Baba! Sit down, just listen to this bit....' Then he went on speaking. Lost in his thoughts, Apu did not pay the slightest attention. He could probably raise enough money to pay for his travel abroad, but where could he leave Kajal? Send him back to his grandfather? Why not? He could stay there for a couple of years, couldn't he? He would be back after that. After all, he was not going to go away for ever. Should he do that?

Kajal broke off, looking annoyed. 'You're not listening, Baba!' he complained.

'Of course I am. Go on, keep talking.'

'I don't believe you. You weren't paying attention. All right, tell me this: which garden did the white fairy first go to?'

'Er ... which garden? The white fairy? No, I can't remember. Tell me what happened before that, that'll remind me.'

'Very well, listen carefully,' Kajal replied, quite willing to start from the beginning. 'Now, the princess had to go and look for the root of a special plant, remember? (Apu had not heard a word.) So then the white fairy....' He went on, although Apu remained preoccupied.

Kajal's hair gave off such a lovely smell. Was it the smell of innocence? Apu found it difficult to take his eyes away when he looked at his son. How sweetly he smiled ... and those eyes ... he might be something quite unreal, not belonging to this earth at all ... any time, the moonlight-fairy might swoop down and whisk him off to the land of dreams. Restless he was, naughty and mischievous he was—but how naive, how vulnerable! How could he deceive his son? Kajal could not survive for a single minute without his father. What could Apu say to him to explain his going away?

'Khoka,' he said finally, coming out of his reverie, 'go and get some sugar. Let me make you some halwa today.'

Kajal was gone for only ten minutes when a commotion broke out near the corner of the lane. Apu went out to see what had caused it, and found people from the lane rushing out towards the main road. 'Someone's been run over by a lorry!' a man explained.

Apu ran with the others. There was quite a large crowd, each pushing and jostling the other, trying to get a closer look, Apu could see nothing. His legs trembled, his mouth felt dry. 'Who is it?' asked a voice.

'A boy ... tragic! He must have ... you know ... instantly ... his head's completely....'

'How old is he?' Apu gasped.

'About nine, I think. A good-looking child, from a good family, too. Poor thing!'

Apu opened his mouth to ask if the man had seen what the child was wearing, but could not bring himself to speak. Kajal had just rushed out wearing his new khaddar shirt. Suddenly, purely unexpectedly, life returned to his limbs. He could now feel an extraordinary strength. Perhaps this kind of strength comes only to those who love someone intensely. He had to go and find Kajal. Perhaps he was still alive? May be he was afraid? What if he was thirsty?

A taxi had stopped near a lamppost on the pavement opposite. The police were here already. The injured boy was being lifted into the taxi. Apu pushed his way through. When he emerged from the crowd, his eyes fell on something that nearly made him faint. Had he not unconsciously leant on the man standing next to him, he would probably have fallen. A little figure was standing in the knot of people gathered near the taxi. It was Kajal. He was standing on his toes, and trying—vainly—to see what was going on. Apu shot forward and grabbed his hand. Kajal turned frightened but curious eyes on him.

'What are you doing here? Come back home!' Apu exclaimed, and began dragging him away. His head was still reeling; his body felt as if it had received an electric shock.

On their way back home, Kajal spoke hesitantly after a while. 'Baba, in all that confusion, I dropped the money you gave me.'

'Never mind. You should have gone straight home. Who told you to stop and have a look? You're really impossible, Khoka!'

❧❧❧

Two days later, Apu was travelling in a tram, passing through Harrison Road, when he saw Ramdhan Babu, the old cashier in the office of Mr Seel. He got off the tram, and walked quickly over to join Ramdhan Babu. 'Can you recognise me?' Apu asked.

Ramdhan Babu raised his hands in a namasker. 'Apurbo Babu! After such a long time! You look a little different now. You were only a young man then.'

Apu laughed. 'Yes, I'm nearly thirty-five. How long could I have remained a young man? Where are you off to?'

To the office, where else? It's almost eleven, isn't it? I got a bit late today. Look, why don't you come and see us one day? You know, you might have been assistant manager today, if you'd stayed instead of leaving us so suddenly.'

It was past ten-thirty. Ramdhan Babu was dressed as before. Clad in a dirty kurta with torn sleeves, canvas shoes on his feet and an umbrella over his head, he was going to the same office where Apu used to work ten years ago. 'Ramdhan Babu,' he asked, 'how long have you worked in that office?'

'This is my thirty-seventh year,' he replied proudly. 'I've seen as many as five managers come and go, but I'm still there. No one can get rid of me.' Then he added with a smile, 'They increased my salary this year. I'm now getting forty-five a month.'

Just for a second, Apu's head reeled again. For thirty-seven years, this man had worked in the same dingy room, leaning over the same cash box, making entries with a pen in the same heavy ledgers, keeping a track of the Seels' household expenses, surrounded by the same familiar faces, hearing the same conversation—twelve months a year, every working day. He could not bear to even think about it. How could anyone spend almost his entire life in a dirty, muddy, lifeless, stagnant pool? The very thought made him sick. He knew, of course, that none of it was Ramdhan Babu's fault. He was a poor man, and had nowhere else to go. Why, had Apu seen anything different in the parties thrown by rich people? They were not petty clerks, but they, too, had lost sight of the true meaning of life in their pursuit of wealth, power and glamour. Their lives were as empty and monotonous, consisting of nothing but endless games of bridge, drinking, smoking and idle chatter about the same boring topics. It was enough to destroy all joy and exuberance of youth. It bred insularity, until it developed into a thick mist to block out the sun altogether. Their small, insignificant lives then ran anyhow, like a stream trying to trickle through heavy mud and slush. But Apu knew *he* had the power to save himself from such a fate.

Partly on Ramdhan Babu's request, and partly out of curiosity, Apu went back to his old office. Many of his old colleagues were still there. They received him warmly. Even

Mejo Babu, one of the owners, stopped by to talk to him. It was now eleven o'clock, but he had just got up. On the verandah outside the billiard room, a servant would soon start giving him an oil massage. Another brought him a silver hookah, its pipe covered by a piece of silk.

Then he met a young man he had once taught for a few days. He had been a small boy then. Apu remembered his face—innocent and unspoilt, his nature had been just as sweet. He was now almost nineteen. He came to touch Apu's feet. Apu felt considerably distressed to see that the boy had got into the habit of eating a lot of paan. His lips were dark, in his hand he carried a silver paan box, filled with paan and tobacco. He had failed the recent tests in school, he told Apu. Then he talked only of Hollywood films. Did Apu like Buster Keaton? What did he think of Charlie Chaplin? And Norma Shearer—oh, wasn't she just out of this world? Taking his leave after a while, Apu couldn't help feeling a great deal of compassion for his former pupil. How could he be blamed for anything? Even a great talent would have dried up in an atmosphere like this. He was but a helpless young boy.

'Are you going?' said Ramdhan Babu. 'Goodbye. Come and see us again.'

The lane outside was still strewn with dirty straw and rotten apples. The air was heavy with the stench of dried fish.

❧

That night, it occurred to Apu that he was not doing the right thing for his son. In fact, he was being most unfair. Kajal was still a child. These days of childhood were absolutely priceless. But what was he, his own father, doing? He was keeping him caged in a concrete prison, slowly killing his eager, young, imaginative mind. Day in and day out, the stifling monotony of his existence was destroying his perceptions. In his life, there were no woods and meadows, no rippling rivers, no singing birds, vast open spaces, boundless moonlight, or little joys and sorrows to be shared with close friends. And yet, Kajal was a beautiful, sensitive child. Apu had seen evidence of that, dozens of times.

He wanted his son to experience grief in his life, to grow up with that knowledge. To Apu, grief was like the magician he had read about in his childhood. The one who knew how to make gold. He was dressed always in torn rags, he carried a big bag, sported a long beard, and roamed on his own, not speaking to anyone. No one liked him; they said he was mad, and sent him packing if he came near. He went away and started working with metals, pumping his bellows, harder and harder.

Mad he might be, but he knew a secret no one else did. He could turn brass, and tin, and lead into gold. Very often, he did.

Slowly, thinking things over carefully, an idea began taking shape in Apu's mind. What if he returned to Nischindipur? Even if he could find no one else he knew, there would be Ranu di, his childhood friend. Besides, it was his duty to show Kajal his ancestral home before he went overseas.

The next day, he sent twenty-five rupees to Lila di in Kashi, with a letter saying that he was taking Kajal to see the village where his grandfather had lived. Lila di, too, should leave Kashi immediately with her brother-in-law as her escort, and make her way to Nischindipur.

TWENTY EIGHT

꧁◦꧂

Even when he had actually boarded the train, Apu found it hard to believe that he was going back to Nischindipur. Wasn't it simply a land he had seen in a dream when he was little? It had been wiped out ... faded into the past. All it had left was a faint, pleasant memory. Perhaps, truly, it had been no more than a dream. Nischindipur did not exist, either in the past or in the present.

They reached a place called Majherpara at one o'clock. Kajal had to jump down onto the low platform. Nischindipur did not have a direct rail connection. They would have to make their way from this station. It had changed a lot. The signal that rose above everything like the mast of a ship and had once caused him much wonder, had disappeared. A big jamun tree stood outside the main station. It had not been

431

there before. There was the madaar tree, under which his mother had cooked on the day they left Nischindipur for good. Two buses were waiting under the tree, looking for passengers. They were soon joined by a couple of old Ford taxis. Buses and taxis now ran straight up to Nawabgunj, he was told. Somehow, Apu did not like the idea. Kajal, a product of modern times, said eagerly: 'Shall we go by that motorcar, Baba?' Apu told him to get into the taxi, and loaded all their luggage, still feeling strangely dissatisfied. How could he go down the old, familiar path in a car? The smell of petrol in this vast, open countryside seemed an oddity, totally incongruous.

It was almost mid-April. Spring was at its height. Apu stared, enchanted, at the thick clusters of flowers by the road. His childhood was so closely linked with this mid-day sun, and the smell of these ghetu and akondo flowers. He had forgotten the tender beauty of springtime in his homeland.

Here was the Betravati. Could there be another river with such a sweet, melodious name, anywhere in the world? On the other side of the river was a bazaar. A petrol station stood close by the river, a big advertisement for Dunlop Tyres displayed prominently. The bazaar had changed, too. The number of brick buildings twenty-four years ago had been far less. Nischindipur was only two miles away. Apu found someone to carry their luggage, and decided to walk the rest of the way. In his time, bullock carts could be hired; but now, with the advent of buses and taxis, they had disappeared. 'You want to go down the track that goes past Dhoncheypolashgachhi, don't you?' asked his coolie. Dhoncheypolashgachhi? He had not heard the place mentioned in all these years; in fact, he had totally forgotten the name. Oh, what a pleasure it was to hear that beautiful name after so many years!

They reached Shonadanga in the late afternoon. A lake called Modhukhali stretched along one side, filled with lotuses.

Shonadanga was another expanse of open land, that had always enchanted him. He had travelled far and wide, but nowhere had he seen a meadow that held such magic.

Then, in the distance, he could spot the leafy top of the famous banyan tree, as if it was sunk in the horizon. Bandits used to hide behind it once, to attack unsuspecting travellers. Beyond it lay Nischindipur. Slowly, the tree got bigger, and then they left it behind. Apu's heart raced faster, all the blood in his body seemed to be rushing to his head. A strange feeling was starting to make his limbs go numb.

The open field came to an end. Here were the mango groves that lined the path running down to the river. Apu dropped his handkerchief, using it as an excuse to gather a little soil in his hand when he picked it up, and touched it to his forehead. 'This is your grandfather's village, Khoka,' he said to his son. 'Do you remember his name?'

'Of course. Shri Harihar Roy.'

'No, not Shri. Say Ishwar Harihar Roy. He's no more, so you add 'Ishwar' before his name. I told you before.'

❧

He met Ranu di the next evening. What preceded their meeting was quite interesting. Ranu told him what had happened.

She had no idea that Apu had returned to the village. On her way back from the river, she saw Kajal near a bamboo grove, walking alone. Ranu stopped short, feeling quite confused. When she was a child, Harihar Roy and his family used to live in a house behind that bamboo grove, not far from the ghat. They had left the village many years ago. Wasn't this young boy his son, Apu—the Apu she had known in her childhood? But how could that be? She pulled herself together and looked closely at the boy. No, it was not Apu. Yet, he appeared to be the spitting image of the young boy she used to play with. She could never forget how little Apu had looked at the time when they had left the village.

'Who are you visiting, Khoka?' she asked.

'The Gangulis.'

The Gangulis were rich people. They had several relatives in Calcutta. Perhaps this boy was one of them. What an amazing resemblance he bore to her childhood friend! It was incredible.

'Are you Kadu Pishi's grandson?' Ranu went on. Kadu was the eldest daughter of the Gangulis.

Kajal looked at her shyly. 'Kadu Pishi? No, I don't know anyone by that name. My grandfather used to live in this village. His name was Ishwar Harihar Roy. I am Amitabh Roy.'

A wave of joy and amazement swept over Ranu. For a few seconds, she could not speak. Then a cold hand clutched her heart. 'Your father ...?' she began breathlessly.

'I came with him yesterday. We went to stay with the Gangulis last night. Baba is sitting in their front room right now, talking to a lot of people.'

Ranu took Kajal's beautiful face in her hands, and lifted it. 'You look so much like your father, Khoka. Your eyes are exactly like his!' she said affectionately. 'Go and call your father. Tell him your Ranu Pishi wants to see him.'

Apu walked into her house just before dusk, holding Kajal by his hand. 'Where are you, Ranu di? Can you recognise me?' he asked. Ranu ran out of her room, and stood staring at him. 'What made you come back?' she said after a while. 'And why did you decide to stay with the Gangulis? Since when did *they* become your own people?' So saying, she burst into tears, very much like her sister in Kashi.

Apu, too, stared at her. The last time he had seen her, she was fourteen. Where had that young girl gone? She had

434

lost the grace she had had in her early youth, although she was still beautiful. But, dressed as a widow, the woman standing before Apu seemed a stranger. How could she bear any relation to his childhood friend?

More surprising was the change in their house. Ranu's father, Bhuvan Mukherjee, had been quite wealthy. There was nothing left of the eight or ten granaries Apu had seen as a child, or the big temple and the adjoining area where Durga Puja used to be held. Most of the rooms on the western side were in ruins. The whole house wore an air of despair.

'What are you looking at?' Ranu said, her eyes still full of tears. 'Everything's gone. My parents died, and so did my uncle and aunt. Shotu has no education, he couldn't get a job or do anything else. So he began selling off all the property we had.'

'Yes, I'd heard that in Kashi. Lila di told me.'

'Lila di? You met her in Kashi? When? When?'

Apu explained quickly. Ranu was delighted to hear that her sister was going to be back soon. The two had not seen each other for years.

'Why didn't you bring your wife? Where is she?' Ranu asked.

'In heaven,' Apu replied lightly.

'Oh! When did...? I see. And you never married after that?'

The same evening, a fair started in the village. It was a special fair called Charak Mela. Similar fairs used to be held when he was a child, but nothing seemed the same any more. Apu realised with a shock that if things seemed lacklustre, it was only because his own mind and outlook had changed. He had lost the enthusiasm, eagerness and excitement his mind had felt twenty-four years ago. Now his role was simply that of an observer. He had started to judge and question, without even realising it. Besides, all his old friends had gone.

435

There was no one left to share his memories with. Only old Chinibash remained. He used to sell sweets. Apu found his stall of fried snacks at the fair.

Twenty-four years ago, he had left Nischindipur with his parents the day after this special fair. Memories of that particular day came flooding back with amazing clarity. How could this happen, Apu wondered, when they had, until now, been buried under so many events of a whole new life?

It grew dark. Small children began returning from the fair, laughing and chatting, some clutching flutes, others colourful toys. They dispersed, some going down the track that ran through Shonadanga, some made their way to the river to catch a boat, and others went back to the village. Twenty-four years ago, the children who had gone past just like this, playing their flutes and eating their sweets, were now busy adults. Some were no more. But their offsprings were still doing what they had done, deriving just as much joy. Their days were as full of innocent pleasure, as free of responsibilities. Silently, Apu thanked whatever power it was that had just shown him this side of life.

❦

Lila di arrived from Kashi towards the end of April. She and Ranu hugged each other, both crying copiously, 'I have to thank you for this, Apu!' Lila di said. 'If it hadn't been for you, I could never have come back here.' She had brought a lot of toys for Kajal from Kashi, as well as things to eat. She handed them over to Apu, then set about meeting all her old friends, and going all over the village.

In the evening, Apu took his son for a long ride in a boat down the Ichhamoti. There were boats moored at every ghat; some, adorned with shells, had come from the south. There

were smaller boats, too, smeared with tar. The wind brought
its smell ... that old, familiar, forgotten smell! A thick growth
of vegetation covered the slope going up from the river bank,
the grass and the undergrowth almost touching the edge of
the river. The water, in places, was dark and absolutely still,
as if its depths were immeasurable. He spotted labourers
from the north, watering vegetable patches by the river, large
hats made of palm leaves on their heads. Meadows stretched
on both sides, flowers bloomed amongst reeds. Date palms
abounded, with bunches of ripe dates hanging down. There
were termite mounds, cranes taking flight, nests of kites on
the top of silk cotton trees. Kajal pointed at a tree and said,
'Look at those fruits! What tree is it, Baba?'

Apu did not reply. He was still trying to take in the magic
of the open countryside. He had not seen it for so many
years. It was spreading through his veins like a powerful
intoxicant, overwhelming his senses. It whispered a secret
message in his ears. He could hear it, but how could he
explain it to anyone else?

'This is a nice place, isn't it, Baba?' Kajal added.

'Why don't you stay here, Khoka? If I left you here with
Ranu Pishi, you could stay with her, couldn't you? Suppose
I had to go away?'

'No, never. How can you even talk of leaving me
anywhere? I want to go with you, Baba.'

Apu said nothing more. He went back to staring at the
water. The Ichhamoti had always been like a mother to him.
He had grown up by her side, the music in the breeze that
blew from her had been soft and soothing like a mother's
lullaby; it had nurtured his impressionable young mind, just
as a mother nurtures her child. It was here that Apu had
learnt to dream of travelling, of seeing distant lands, of sailing
across the great oceans, surrounded by nothing but surging
waves. All his dreams and desires had taken shape on the

banks of the Ichhamoti, looking at her gushing waters, particularly after heavy rains, when she rose and swirled as if she might burst her banks. She reminded him of the land he had read about in one of his English books, somewhere beyond Cape Nun—from where no one returned. *He who passes Cape Nun, will either return or not.* Turning his admiring gaze on the overflowing river, he had thought: 'Oh, what a mighty river she is!'

He was not a little boy any more. He had seen rivers larger and far more forceful than the Ichhamoti—the Ganga, Sone and Narmada. He had seen sunsets on their waters, witnessed a spectacular display of colours. The Ichhamoti now seemed a much smaller river. It was as if his poor, dear mother from his humble home had been swept aside by wealthy and glamorous women from elsewhere; her simple cotton saree and glass bangles, on a festive day, could never compare with the others' heavy silks and priceless jewels.

Even so, how could he ever forget his Ichhamoti?

Apu could not stay indoors in the afternoon. The warm breath of the March afternoon brought so many familiar scents—of dry bamboo stalks, half-open ghetu flowers, the sunburnt earth, the blossom on neem trees, and so much more. When he was small, a warm afternoon like this had often driven him and his sister out of their house, urging them to roam in the open—in the fields, the woods, and by the river. It had the same effect on him today. The whole village slept, but on this silent afternoon, like a mad man, Apu went walking up and down the village paths, and the high grounds covered by fresh flowers. It did occur to him that the joy he felt now was not the same as the joy in recalling childhood memories. It was still there, but its nature had changed. In the past, it was as if gods and goddesses from heaven came down on such afternoons, in the shadows of the bamboo groves. Now, Apu took himself to the riverside and simply lay for hours on the fragrant grass, resting his head on his arm, thinking of nothing in particular, just staring at the brilliant blue sky. Sometimes, he buried his face in the grass and said silently: dear motherland, the nectar you had me drink when I was little is what has seen me through all these years, in all my grief and pain. That has been my only source of strength. It was in the shadows of your woods that all my dreams were once born. Give me that strength again, mother, I beseech you!

He felt very sorry for city-dwellers—entire communities, each member of which lived in the city, never stepping out of its confines. Had they ever seen the sky changing colour across that field covered with reed? Had they heard the call of a dove, deep in the wood, on a silent autumn afternoon? Had the quiet celebration of a deep blue, wild aparajita flower ever touched their heart when they were young children? They had never sat on the verandah of a small hut and watched the moonlight flicker on coconut leaves. They were truly unfortunate!

⋘◉⋙

Apu felt very moved by the care and affection he received from Ranu. She was in charge of her brother's household. Childless herself, she looked after her nieces and nephews. At her request, Apu and Kajal had had to move to her house from the Gangulis'. Kajal had already become quite devoted to her. For some reason, Ranu appeared to have assumed that Apu was fond of drinking tea, just because he now lived in

439

the city. Nobody drank tea in her house, but Ranu sent Shotu to the big market in Nawabgunj and got him to buy, with her own money, cups and saucers and everything else required to make tea. She did her utmost to produce a cup of tea for Apu, twice a day, at the right time. Funnily enough, Apu had never been a great drinker of tea, but he did not wish to point that out to Ranu. 'Make the most of it,' he told himself. 'Where on earth will you find anyone to take such good care of you?'

The next few days remained grey and dull. One evening, Apu realised with a start, that the sky had cleared. He came out and sat on the front verandah. Here was an evening straight out of his childhood. When he had first left this place, living in an alien land, his young heart used to long for such evenings. Then it became a faint but fond memory, and then it disappeared altogether. Now, however, he could remember waking up on such an evening when he was a little boy, feeling oddly disturbed by something he could not quite understand, and bursting into tears. His mother returned from the ghat, picked him up and tried to comfort him. 'Don't cry, Khoka,' she said. 'Why are you so sad? Yes, yes, of course I understand. You've lost all you had, haven't you? Well, never mind. Look at that bird. Look, there it goes!'

Ranu was going to fetch water from the well. Apu stopped her and said, 'Remember Ranu di, the games we used to play in the evenings? You, Didi, me, Shotu and all the others?'

Ranu laughed. 'I see. Is that what you have been thinking of? Of course, I remember our games, and the garlands we used to make with bokul flowers. I don't see many children today making garlands. In fact, I don't even see as many flowers as I used to. Everything's changed.'

On her way back from the well, she said, 'Tell you what, Apu, I have an idea. Your father had mortgaged his mango orchard, hadn't he, and taken money from us? Why don't

440

you take that orchard back from Shotu? It's yours, anyway. Shotu is only going to sell it off.'

'Yes that's what my mother had wanted me to do. She had mentioned it a few days before she died. It's a good idea, Ranu di. I will find the money to buy it back.'

Every evening, Ranu spread a mat on the verandah, to sit and chat with Apu. They spoke of old times more than anything else. 'Remember the swarm of locusts we got once?' said Apu one day. Yes, they remembered. A widow from the neighbourhood had joined them that evening. Apu had been a small boy when she had first arrived in the village as a new bride. 'Do you remember where you stood when you entered your house after your wedding?' Apu asked her.

'No, son. All that happened in a different life. How should I remember?'

'I'll tell you. You stood just outside the cowshed at the bottom of your courtyard, on a stone slab soaked in milk and alta.'

'Oh yes, that's right. How strange that you should remember everything. It happened so long ago.'

Apu remembered various other things everyone else had forgotten. The name of a very beautiful female relative who had come to attend a wedding eluded everyone. 'Her name was Subasini,' Apu said.

'Yes, I remember now. Subasini is what she was called,' Lila said, surprised. 'How did you manage to remember it? You could not have been more than eight or nine when you saw her.'

Apu smiled. 'There's something else I could tell you about her. She wore striped sarees, stripes on a red background.'

'Good heavens, that's quite right!' exclaimed the widow. 'When she visited us, she was in her early twenties. That must have been at least twenty-six years ago. What a memory you have got!' Apu remembered her because until she appeared, he had not seen such a beautiful woman. He could still picture her taking part in all the wedding festivities.

Each evening in the village brought its own magic. After spending a month here, Apu felt convinced that nowhere, despite all his travelling, could he have seen such beautiful evenings. When the sun began to set in a clear sky on cloudless days, the last of its red-gold light lingered on the top branches of every tree, making them look as if handfuls of vermilion had been spread all over them. Where else could he find such evenings, laden with a fragrant message from the blossom on wood-apple trees, filled with the plaintive calls of birds? The whole area abounded with wood-apple trees; everywhere he went he was greeted by the same sweet scent.

A few weeks later, one evening in mid-May, thick, dark storm clouds rose from the north-eastern corner of the sky, spreading quickly to remove even the last vestige of light. Then a high wind began sweeping across the whole region. It was the first Kaal Baisakhi of the season. The sight was a familiar one. In his childhood, the army of blue-black clouds over the swaying bamboo had aroused an inexplicable excitement in his heart. They had brought a message of hope, and spoken of many things besides, but the child who stared at them with fascination could not always grasp their meaning. Today, the clouds, the swinging stems of bamboo, and the evening were all still the same; but the child and his world were no more. Whatever joy the sight of the storm brought him was really the joy of reliving old memories.

Not for the first time since his return to Nischindipur, Apu pondered on this. When he looked back, he could still recall the rapture these woods held, the golden afternoons, the chowkidar's cry in the dead of night, the hoot of the white owl, the call of an imaginary, mysterious land beyond the horizon. But all that was in the past. Those birds had died. The moon that used to dance on the wavering branches of coconut by the little house with a thatched roof, flooding the young heart of an imaginative village boy with waves of a nameless ecstasy, had lost its radiance. And that boy? He had gone, too. Almost twenty-five years ago, he had left with his family one afternoon, never to return. The prints of his small feet, left behind on the path that ran through those bamboo groves, had been wiped clean, a long time ago.

He and his sister had had such hopes and dreams. Were they ever fulfilled?

Poor, naive children!

Almost every evening now, clouds gathered in the sky and a storm broke. Apu said to Ranu, 'Ranu di, shall we go out and look for mangoes?' Ranu laughed. Apu took Kajal to their new, reclaimed orchard and invited the entire village to fill their baskets with the windfalls. It gave him a great deal of pleasure to see the whole place fill with little figures—running, shouting, busy and excited. Many years ago, Durga had been accused of stealing the fruit that belonged to other people, and harshly reprimanded. She had tried to hide her pain behind a bright smile, and quietly slipped out through a hedge of prickly pear. She had been only slightly older than Kajal. Apu had not forgotten.

What was he going to do with an orchard, anyway? In his mango orchard, he would allow every poor child to come and go as he liked, collecting mangoes to his heart's content, with no one to stop, scold, or insult. The little girl, standing behind that hedge, would peep through the prickly pear and grin happily.

In all these weeks, Apu had not been able to step into his old house, although he had had to pass it every day on his way to the river. One evening, he went alone, and quietly walked in, picking his way through the wilderness that had once been their courtyard. There was no sign of the house. All he could see was a heap of broken bricks, surrounded by a thick growth of plants and creepers. The bamboo that grew behind the house had grown much taller in all these years, and were now leaning over where the house had once stood. The setting sun played on their top branches.

Only the compound wall was not wholly destroyed. On the western side, Apu found the little niche in the wall in which he used to hide his precious possessions—marbles, a grapefruit that he used as a ball, and cowrie shells. But it was set so low in the wall! When he had used it, it had always appeared quite high; he had had to stand on his toes to reach it. Further down the wall, he had carved the figure of a 'ghost' with a penknife. It was still there.

The house next door was similarly abandoned. As a matter of fact, this whole neighbourhood had lost its inhabitants, very few people now bothered to walk this way. Here was the spot where he and Durga had once had a picnic. Thorny bushes now made the area totally impassable. In the plot of land next door stood the same wood-apple tree, under which, at the age of nine, he had often imagined Bhishma from the Mahabharat lying on his bed of arrows. The thick blossom that covered its branches added something special to the balmy evening breeze.

Apu thought again, with amazement, of the low niche in the wall. His mind kept going back to it. How small he must have been when he had used it, for it to have appeared high. Perhaps he had been as little as Kajal.

A funny scent came from a creeper somewhere. He had forgotten it in all these years. When one lived away from home, one might think of everything else, but it might not always be easy to remember smells. This was something he had realised only since his return to the village. A few days ago, he had been greeted by the smell of the ripe fruit on a banyan tree, which had taken him back instantly to an evening in his childhood. His father was out to buy tar from

444

a local shop, carrying Apu on his shoulder. In his hand was an old-fashioned lantern, a candle burning inside. He had picked up a water lily while passing a pond, and given it to Apu. The smell of the ripe fruit brought the whole scene back in a flash. Although it still seemed hazy and unreal, Apu could see the faint light from the lantern, the long stalks of bamboo in the semidarkness.

Close to the wall was a huge date palm, weighed down with its load of fruit. Apu remembered it as a much smaller tree. Durga used to chop one of its branches sometimes, and tie a rope to it to pretend it was a cow. How big and tall it had grown!

Here ... the back door had been here. But now there was absolutely no sign of it. This was the spot where he had once stood and thrown away the little golden box Durga had stolen. But there were other objects he could recognise. The bowl used to feed their cow was still there, under their jackfruit tree, full to the brim with rotten bamboo leaves and other rubbish. His father had once got a pile of bricks to strengthen their compound wall, but never managed to find the money to do it. Those old bricks were still lying where they had been heaped in the shade of a bamboo grove. Years ago, his mother had kept an earthen pitcher on a shelf. It had fallen, and now sat half buried in the ground. But that niche in the wall ... Apu simply could not get over it. It was still intact, as if it had been built only yesterday. How had it managed to survive? What good was a niche in the wall, amidst such decay and dereliction?

On the high ground next to their back door, his mother had planted a drumstick tree, only a year before they left. In these long years, it had grown old; now no one bothered to collect its fruit. The last rays of the sun fell on the tree, giving it a rather sad, pathetic air. The shadows grew darker, and the air heavier with the same strange smell from that creeper. Apu shivered.

It was not just a smell. With it and with this fading light, came memories of his mother's voice, brimming with affection; his sister's tales; his father's music, the poverty all around him— but even that was sweet, so full of warmth.

A dove called somewhere in the wood. Apu turned startled eyes once more on the drumstick tree, bathed in the soft glow of the evening sun, and thought: it can't be true. Surely these wild plants, and all this rubble, were just a dream? Any minute now, his mother would return from the ghat, freshly bathed and wearing a clean saree. Then she would spread out her wet clothes on the bamboo rack in their courtyard to dry; and then, lighting an oil lamp under their tulsi plant, she would look up, see him, and complain, with a touch of surprise in her tone: 'Apu, have you only just got back? What took you so long?'

The site where the main house had once stood was littered with pieces of broken earthenware. Apu felt very moved by these. He began picking them up. So much of their lives were linked to these—all their sorrows, and all their joys. He found a piece of a green glass bangle, the kind usually worn by small girls. Perhaps it was one of Durga's. He picked it up. A few minutes later, he found a broken bottle. His mother used to keep coconut oil in a similar bottle. Perhaps it was the same one? He stopped at the sight of something else. In the corner where their kitchen had been, a karahi still sat where it had been left. It had rusted, its handles had dropped off, but having sunk into the ground, it had not moved an inch.

When they had finished their last meal here, his mother had placed that used karahi in that corner, twenty-four years ago. The people who had used it had almost all disappeared, but that metal pan had stood its ground, all these years.

So many thoughts chased each other in his mind. How was it possible for one man to understand the intimate details of the life of another? To outsiders, this whole area was no more than a piece of useless land, a veritable depot for mosquitoes, without meaning or significance. How could they imagine how closely every tiny object here was related to the joyous moments in the life of a young and innocent boy?

Thirty, fifty, a hundred ... thousands of years would pass. This village would be gone, perhaps even the Icchamoti would disappear. A new civilisation would start, under a totally new regime, the like of which no one dared imagine. The might of the British would be confined to the pages of ancient history, and a new language would replace the one spoken at present. Even then, three thousand years hence, storms would rage towards the end of May, birds would sing, and the moon would rise just as it did today. But who would think of the little world of a small village boy, who had lived three thousand years ago, and the joy he had felt by the smell of rain, and gusts of wind? Who would record his hopes and aspirations, aroused by the cool evening breeze? Would an account be kept of his thoughts when he played in the woods in the autumn, or returned home after a long absence to be refreshed by a drink from his mother's hand? Or when he woke at the end of a long afternoon and heard the sweet notes of a nightingale's call? Would anyone write about his feelings on a rain-swept night?

There would be new boys, and new girls, to read the message of joy a Kaal Baisakhi might bring, in that far distant future. Where would those new children come from, which heavenly path would bring them to this world?

Apu left his old home and came out. Then he looked back once more. The approaching dusk had cast a strange, pitiful shadow all over the place. It seemed as if the broken and abandoned house had been waiting all this while for someone's arrival on such an evening—but it was now old, tired and exhausted, even indifferent. All the life had gone out of it; it no longer cared.

Apu thought again of that niche in the wall. How had it managed to remain undamaged, when the people had all gone?

Nischindipur had gone, too. Yes, there was still plenty that reminded him of his childhood, but he could no longer live here permanently. He had learnt to question and judge, and compare. Now his vision and attitude were entirely different from those he had left behind. Some of them had been his playmates, but in the last twenty-five years, none of them had left the village. Many had land and property here, so they had never had any reason to step out. Their minds had stagnated at the point at which Apu had left them. He no longer had anything in common with them.

Besides, with the exception of Ranu, most of his closest friends had gone. Even Potu, who used to visit him in Diwanpur, had moved elsewhere. Only the women in the village offered him some comfort. Ranu di, Lila di, the old widow, and some others, seemed genuinely happy to have him back after so many years. There could be no doubt about the sincerity of their feelings. It was most satisfying to talk about old times with them for they appeared to have remembered all the minute details of the times gone by. They had clung to these little, trivial things possibly because their lives ran within such narrow confines.

Apu had realised one thing very clearly. What he had learnt in life through his grim struggles would have remained unknown to him, had he owned land or property in the village and stayed on, without a care in the world. If he left the country now and went overseas, he would go with a special insight, something he would never have acquired if the last twenty-four years had been spent right here. There was a time when Nischindipur had been his, he had earned it as an intrinsic part of all the joys and sorrows of his life. Today, through his experience of grief and happiness in his later life, he had earned the right to be a part of the world outside.

These thoughts occurred to Apu one silent evening while bathing in the river. It was still very hot, there was no breeze. The moon was about to rise—it was the day after a full moon. He thought of the women who used to come to the same river to fetch water. Some of them were now middle-aged, others had died. The koels, that used to sing on rapturous spring afternoons in his childhood, had been replaced by their descendants, who still filled the air with their song amidst the fresh young leaves in the bamboo groves. Only his sister had not moved anywhere. She was still lying quietly under the old chhatim tree in the village cremation ground. She had not grown older, nor lost her youthful looks. Her glass bangles, and the bag she used to fill with old, dried fruit, were still intact. She was the eternal child. On lonely, dark nights, she stole into that quiet corner of Apu's being, where the innocent and unspoilt mind of a young boy lay buried under the knowledge, experience, work and ambition of adulthood. With tears in her eyes, she searched for the child who had been her faithful companion, all those years ago.

For twenty-four years, at dawn and at dusk, the sun had spread its golden rays on her final resting place; dark clouds on rainy nights had bathed it in heavy downpours; flowers had bloomed over it in different seasons. She had loved each of these things. Perhaps that was why she had remained here, unable to leave any of it.

449

TWENTY NINE

❧

Towards the end of June, Apu had to go back to Calcutta. It took him nearly a month to finish his business. The monsoon was in full swing by the time he got back. Before he left the city, however, the last couple of days remained dry, bright sunshine alternating with cool, grey clouds.

In the last few days, Nischindipur had changed a little. The trees looked more green and fresh, young creepers hung low from some of the high branches. It was another sight that took him back to his childhood. When he looked around, he saw the same wild flowers that always bloomed at this time of the year, and bunches of familiar fruit on many trees. A particular flower—the locals called it ghetkol—spread a rather pungent smell in the evening, so much so that women covered their faces when they passed a bush. Each sight and every smell was so utterly familiar, yet he had forgotten it completely, until his return to the village.

It was around this time that, one day, when the rice fields were looking bright green with their new crop, Apu had a remarkable experience. It was hot and sunny, and past three o'clock. He was walking down a path through a wood, at the back of the village. It was lined by thick, dark-green bushes. A small yellow bird kept flitting about, from one young bamboo shoot to another.

A narrow track ran through the wood, created by dozens of feet treading on the grass. The dazzling sun shone through the big trees, making their young leaves look almost transparent, A sweet smell came from some unknown bush. Suddenly, Apu's eyes fell on this track and he stopped abruptly.

Here, right here, was the entire world of his childhood. Perhaps some god had cast a spell, and wiped out twenty-five years of his life. Precisely at this time of the day, before lengthening shadows could claim the sunny afternoon, he and Durga used to roam in the woods, looking for ripe fruit, sweet berries and even birds' nests. Miles could not measure the distance travelled, there were no vehicles to take him back. Perhaps there was an invisible path, somewhere on this earth, which could carve its way through time, unbeknown to man. One look through the thickets transported him at once to the world left behind twenty-five years ago. This blue sky, this deep wood and this golden joy-filled July afternoon had once made up his entire universe. What lay outside it was something he did not know and, at that time, did not much care about. Here was enough happiness, enough rapture, enough mystery and excitement.

It was as if he had found the source of eternal youth. His mind could bathe at this invigorating spring, time and time again, to regain all the lost exuberance and bouyancy of spirit. All the greenery around him, the abundant sunlight

451

and the singing birds, almost made it possible to hear the voice of his sister, calling from the far end of the track.

Apu simply stood and stared, transfixed. There were no words to describe his feelings. His eyes began to brim over. Which god had heard his prayer? His purpose of returning to Nischindipur was fulfilled, at last.

Today, he felt convinced that his childhood was indestructible. That lost world was still there, somewhere within his own being. All it needed was perhaps the song of a particular bird, or the scent of a flower, to make it come rushing back to him. For Apu, it was a spiritual experience. It flooded his heart with a sense of beauty and whispered a special message of freedom, every time it came to him. But that mysterious world could only be felt, and perceived during moments of silent meditation.

His son, Kajal, was now an inhabitant of this world. It was for this reason that Apu tried so hard to keep his imagination alive. That was why he had taken him away from his materialistic grandfather. His young dreams must never be crushed under the dead weight of materialism. Let him find his own world in the bamboo groves, open fields and flowering bushes of Nischindipur. Let him build a special link with the solitary river bank where nothing grew but reeds, where Apu had once caught glimpses of his own invisible world which, in his childhood, had been his only precious possession.

Nischindipur
10 August

Dear Pranav

I had not heard from you for a long time, nor did I know where you were. But recently, I read in a press report that you had given a lecture on communism in a court. That was how I learnt of your present whereabouts.

Perhaps you don't know that I have returned to my village after a very long time. I am not going to be here for much longer, but I am coming to that later. I brought Kajal with me. He remembers you very well. You had looked after him when he was ill—he has not forgotten how you bathed his head when he was burning with fever.

I must share with you the thoughts that have filled my mind lately. I have been thinking much about the meaning of life, and now feel convinced that what constitutes 'life' is simply one's feelings, hopes, imagination and dreams. After my arrival here. I learnt to look at life anew. Nowhere, except in the forest near Nagpur, did I get the chance or the time to ponder on such matters.

My life has been blessed with such joy-filled days. How can I ever forget the day I went with my father to look at an old indigo factory, or the day Didi and I ran to find the railway track, or the day before my wedding when we sat on the roof in the evening? Or the dark and rainy night in Monshapota when Aparna and I stayed awake all night in our small thatched house. These days and nights that stand out in my memory have given me not just joy, but the strength to face life with all its uncertainties. Such joy does not come from great wealth, or even fame and success. It is as generous and impartial as the sun with its warmth; it creates no distinction between the rich and the poor. My mother often derived as much pleasure on seeing me return from a dinner with an extra packet of food, as rich women do on buying a new car. My sister, too, felt just as ecstatic if she found a creeper hanging heavy with a ripe fruit in the wood, or a bunch of berries.

Even if I live for a thousand years, I do not think I could ever forget the excitement of travelling alone to another village to visit an aunt. I could not have been more than nine at the time. I have read of Arctic explorers who spend a fortune to go out on winter nights, either under snow flurries, or under a sky wrapped in the northern light and a mysterious, pale yellow moon. They go across frozen rivers. They walk in the silent, snow-laden pine and silver-spruce forests, and hear wolves howl in the distance. But I doubt if the thrill they experience can match that of a nine-year-old boy, travelling on his own for the first time, barefoot, down a sandy track, in the shade of silk cotton and other trees, on to a place he has not seen before. I have been to so many different places since then, but nowhere have I felt that first exhilarating sense of liberation I experienced on my first journey alone. If my mind keeps harking back to those moments, how can I blame it?

What I have now realised, dear Pranav, is that in life, grief and joy both bear equal significance. Life itself is the greatest romance—the mere act of living is a romance. Even the most trivial, insignificant and monotonous life ever lived is a romance. I did not know it until now. It was my belief that roaming restlessly, being on the move all the time was what life was all about. Now I have seen that that is not the case.

The human spirit can have such a wonderful adventure, experiencing all the happiness, sorrows, hope and disappointment that life brings with it. But to appreciate it truly, one needs a special insight. That can be gained only through a perception of the heavenly beauty that such a mystery-filled journey can offer.

Having returned to my village, I have witnessed the true meaning of life and seen this beauteous side to it. Never before have I been able to take such a close look at my own life. Lying alone in the wonderful, undisturbed peace and quiet of hot, sunny afternoons, I have been able to recapture my childhood; gone back to the shadows under banyan trees in vast fields that stretch right up to the horizon; and heard the flute of the shepherd boy. All of it has shown me a glimpse of that other everlasting world that lies beyond.

But there is something that puzzles me. Can you tell me why most people seem devoid of curiosity, or an ability to express wonder? To be able to feel wonder is a very special gift. A person who is not moved, or surprised by anything may as well be dead. I have seen people—big and powerful people in the city—spend all their time on such small, insignificant matters. Living itself is an art. To succeed in the business of living, one must know this; or become bankrupt very early in life.

At least a few minutes must be spent every day in silent meditation over this. I realised this during my days in the forest. Oh, I cannot describe to you the sheer joy I felt when I went to sit on a rock in the shadows of the shaal trees every evening! In my heart, the existence of the other world became very real—that which transcends the cycle of birth and death, that which is for ever. It is a world bigger even than the one described by Einstein or De Sitter.

What I learnt in the forest has been reinforced here. I have seen how easy it is to get a great deal of pleasure from ordinary things. Wealth, fame and glory? That is so trivial. The little things are all I want to live for, all I want to remember. Where else would I find such deep, dark shadows, such trees, such heady fragrance of ripe dates, the blossom on wood-apple trees, or simply the joy of reminiscing? I could spend a thousand years here, and still not get tired of any of it.

Did you know about Leela? You may have heard me mention her a few times. She is no more. It's a long story, but whenever I think of her, I think of Aparna, and I feel grateful to both. Remember reading in the Bible, *'And I saw a new Heaven and a new Earth'*? These two women gave their lives to make me realise the significance of these words.

Perhaps I should tell you now: I am going overseas, possibly to Fiji and Samoa. A friend of mine is making arrangements. At first I could not decide where I might leave Kajal. There was no question of taking him back to his grandfather, although one of his aunts did write to say they were all missing him, and their house seemed empty without him. Nevertheless, I would not even consider sending him there again. There is an old childhood friend in Nischindipur. I have decided to leave Kajal with her. I know he will be well looked after. If I had not found her, it would have been impossible for me to travel anywhere, least of all overseas.

Today, it is trayodashi. In just two days, we will get a full moon. The sky is absolutely clear. In just a few minutes, everything is going to be flooded with moonlight. I wish you were here to see it. There is

456

so much I want to share with you. But I could never repay what I owe you, my friend. Had it not been for you, Aparna would not have come into my life. Perhaps you will never realise what a great loss that would have been for me.

Your friend, for ever,

Apurbo.

THIRTY

✦

One afternoon, Ranu said, 'Apu, you owe me something.'

'Really? What do I owe you?'

'You had started writing a story in my notebook when you left for Kashi. You're going to have to finish it now.' Apu was amazed. 'You kept that notebook all these years?' he asked.

Ranu smiled. 'Very well,' Apu added. 'What I write now gets published in magazines. I will not let your story remain incomplete. But tell me, what on earth made you keep it?'

'If you must know,' Ranu replied, still smiling, 'it was only because I knew in my heart that one day we would meet again, and you would *complete* that story for me.'

'Thank God for a friend like you, Ranu di!' Apu thought

to himself. 'When I am reborn and I go into my next life, please God, let me find another friend like you.' Aloud, he said, 'Really? Where's that story, then? Show it to me.'

Looking at his own childish handwriting was most amusing. 'Look!' he said to Ranu, 'Just look at this. Seven misspelt words in a single page!'

Ranu laughed with him. He looked fondly at her. All his life, in every woman he had come across, he had seen the same affection and compassion. Perhaps it was partly because none of them had remained very long in his life. He had known Aparna for only a few years. His relationship with Leela had been untouched by the conflict, self-interest and tensions of one's daily life. The same applied, in varying degrees, to Pateshwari, Ranu, Nirmala, Nirupama and Tiwari-bahu. Apu did not mind. He realised how fortunate he had been to have found the kindness and support of these women when he needed it, in the life he had led in the past, like flotsam, flowing with time. He did not regret not getting to know them better. Closer and more frequent contact might well have resulted in a discovery of their weaknesses. Certainly, Apu did not want that. He would simply remain forever grateful to all womankind for what he had received from them.

Apu had to return to Calcutta again for a few days in September. During his stay there, he read in the papers that a number of Indians, just returned from Fiji, were staying at a guesthouse run by the Arya Samaj. He went there as soon as he could. There was no one immediately available on the ground floor to talk to him, but someone told him to go upstairs.

A young man in his early thirties met him and asked him in Hindi what he wanted. 'I heard you were just back from

Fiji, so I came to meet you,' Apu replied. 'Will you please tell me all about life in Fiji? I do so want to go there.'

The young man was a missionary, working for the Arya Samaj. He had been to East Africa, Trinidad, Mauritius and several other places. He gave him their address in Fiji: Post Box 1175, Lautoka. 'My home is in Ayodhya,' he said. 'When I return to Fiji, we can both travel together.'

It was half past ten when Apu left the guest house. He went back to his house, but could not stay there for long. It felt odd without Kajal there, although there seemed to be evidence of Kajal's presence everywhere he looked. There was the window where he used to stand and look out on the street; there was a nail on the wall he had fixed himself, to hang a tin horn; there, in that corner, he often sat on a stool and ate muri from a bowl, swinging his legs. No, Apu could not stay there without his son. He felt suffocated in the empty house.

In the evening, he roamed a little, trying to collect some of his payments, and got four hundred rupees. He was going to leave Calcutta once more, this time to sail across the seas ... who knew if he would come back again ... Viti Levu, Vanua Levu, New Hebrides, Samoa! The deep blue coral sea on one side, and on the other an endless, boundless ocean, stretching to the South Pole. Small huts by the waves, all made of coconut fronds; hard, rocky mountains sharply dividing the land, every inch of it bathed in brilliant sunshine. His days as a traveller were about to start again, in a new country, under an unknown sky.

Later in the evening, Apu decided to visit some of his old haunts again. He even went past the house where he used to live before his mother's death. He had not visited that area for many years.

He stood under a gas lamp for a few minutes, lost in thought.

A slim, young man, possibly no more than twenty, was standing on the pavement opposite, staring uncertainly. He had only recently arrived from a village, and was unfamiliar with the ways of the city. A little shy, even a little foolish, he had probably not had enough to eat all day, for his face looked pale. Apu knew him. That young man was called Apurbo Roy. Thirteen years ago, he had lived in a house in this lane, and suffered endless humiliation at the hands of an owner of a restaurant, just for a handful of rice. Homesick and missing his mother, he had sometimes drawn marks on that outside wall to count the number of days left before he could see her again. Next to that jamrul tree, on that damp, dank wall, perhaps those marks were still visible.

It grew darker and as soon as the gas lamps were lit, the image of the young man vanished. Apu returned to his empty house and sat alone on the roof. What turbulent emotions his mind was filled with! The moon had risen already. It occurred to him that the same moon was shining on his little house in Monshapota; the open space before his thatched bungalow in the forest; his overgrown and abandoned home in Nischindipur; by the window of the room he and Aparna had shared in her father's house; on the courtyard in Pateshwari's house in Chapdani, and the compound of the boarding house in Diwanpur, where he had spent the last few years of school. The thought of all these places he had known in the past suddenly brought back such a host of memories that he began to feel quite overwhelmed. Truly, how strange life was, how mysterious, how varied!

This time, on his way back to Nischindipur, Apu could not bring himself to walk even part of the way after getting off the train at Majherpara. That would delay him unnecessarily. He wanted to reach his son as soon as possible. He had been away for six weeks. Now he was desperate to see Kajal. It made him think of his own father. He, too, had

461

left his children often enough when Apu was small, and yearned just as eagerly to see them after a long absence from home. Apu could now understand fully the longing in a father's heart, but in a certain matter he was more fortunate than his father. In his childhood, there was no alternative to walking. Now, he could get into a bus and reach Nischindipur in an hour. The only delay occurred at the ghat at Betravati.

❧

It was three o'clock by the time Apu reached his village. A little before it got dark, he went out with Kajal and sat on the front verandah. Ranu and Lila joined them, as did a few others from the neighbourhood. It was almost the end of October. The sun would set in a few minutes. From the plants and creepers around Ranu's house rose a soft, sweet smell.

What a strange brilliance the sun had on this late autumn afternoon! Under the dark blue sky, the bamboo grove behind Ranu's house glittered in its golden light, the pointed end of each stem glowing like a spear. Little birds sat on some of them. Bats had started to fly. In the wood behind the compound wall stood a number of wild plum trees, great bunches of unripe plums hanging from their branches.

It grew dark. The sound of conch shells could be heard from every household. Was one sounding also from his old, ruined home? His father used to be away for so long, seldom able to send money, even for Durga Puja. How his mother had suffered ... and his sister had died without proper treatment. But why did such thoughts come into his mind at this time?

The others left one by one. Kajal took out his books to study. Ranu got up to start dinner. 'Come and sit here by the kitchen,' she invited.

462

'I feel so comfortable chatting with you, Ranu di,' Apu remarked. 'I don't like the way the boys in the village talk.'

'I see. Would you like some muri? Wait, I'll get you some. Then I'll make tea, as soon as the milk is boiled.'

'Ranu di, that brass pot over there ... you had it in your house when we were children. Isn't that right?'

'Yes, my grandmother got it from Puri when she was a young girl. Tell me, Apu, can you remember Durga's face?'

Apu smiled. 'No, Ranu di. Sometimes, I think I can, but only vaguely. I can't tell you how much of it might be just my imagination.'

Ranu sighed. 'It seems like a dream. Her entire life ...!'

Apu thought silently: 'If I were to die now, Kajal, too, would forget my face!'

'Mama!' called Shotu's daughter. 'We saw an ailopalane today. Flew over our house.'

'Yes, Baba,' Kajal put in. 'I saw it too. Went right over that tamarind tree.'

'Really, Ranu di? An aeroplane?'

'Yes, that's true. I don't know the English name for it ... one of those machines that fly. The noise it made!'

So a seven-year-old girl in Nischindipur was now able to see an aeroplane? His sister's last wish had been simply to see a train. Apu could never forget it.

❦

The next night, he went as usual for a walk by the river, after the moon rose.

Many years ago, he used to sit under a particular thorny bush in the evening and try to fish. Now that whole area was thick with similar bushes, it was impossible to locate the old one.

So much had changed. To Apu, the river Ichhamoti was a symbol of this continuous flow of life. So many trees grew by its banks, so many birds flew over it, so many ghats lined its banks. Year after year, century after century, flowers had bloomed and withered here, gleeful children had arrived with their mothers to bathe in the water, fishermen had cast their nets ... and then, when their lives, spent amidst tears and laughter, came to an end, their mortal remains were swept away by the rippling waters. Mothers, children, men and women ... so many had arrived and departed, travelling down the road of time. Yet, the river appeared to have remained the same—gentle, quiet, familiar and harmless.

These days, every time he was alone, Apu found himself thinking of the spiritural significance of everything he saw around him. He knew there was a different world hidden behind the one that was both visible and audible, behind the trees, the flowers, the light and the shade. Having seen the same objects every day, however, having been raised amidst them, it was not always possible to see, or even feel, the existence of this secret world with all its mysteries and complexities. It reminded him of his friend, Ashburton, who used to say: 'There is a different side to India that you do not know about. It's only because you were born here, and overfamiliarity with what you see every day has spoilt your vision.'

The sky now looked much darker. The green meadow under it, and the bamboo grove in the distance, how different they seemed tonight, as if an unseen hand had drawn a strange picture, ethereal, unreal, unworldly in its quality. The old familiar world had suddenly changed into a land where perhaps only the gods lived ...!

It was as if nature had a language of her own. During his days in the forest, sitting on the rocky bank of the river Bakratoa, under a shaal tree at midday, looking at the huge, leafless tree in the far distance, silhouetted against the blue sky, his mind had filled with thoughts that, at other times, would not occur to him at all. Below the mountains there had been trees bearing wild fruit. They, too, had seemed eager to speak a message. This was the language of pictures. Nature used it, too. Now, in the clumps of dry grass around termite mounds, and in the rows of bamboo far away, she seemed to be saying similar things, arousing the same emotions in his heart. Apu could understand this language well. That was the reason why he could feel such rapture and derive so much inspiration when he walked alone in silent meadows and empty fields, or in the woods. What he felt in his heart was the true joy of life. Dry leaves and twigs under his feet, green bushes by the river, wrapped in a red glow, thickets and clusters of wild flowers—all of these nurtured his soul, gave him substance for silent meditation.

On these quiet evenings, sitting by the Ichhamoti and looking at the radiant clouds gathered in the deep blue sky, thoughts of the other, greater world came to him. As a child, he had dreamt of distant lands while sitting under that thorny bush and trying to catch a fish. Now his awareness had risen far above the confines of childhood, soaring high on wings of light. Just thinking about it brought him joy at times. It did not matter if he went nowhere, did not visit any foreign country. The world of which he was a citizen was neither small, nor trivial. All calculations here were based on millions of light years. Constellations hid in the darkness here, galaxies formed their own worlds. Worlds in the invisible ether, where expanses were beyond the imagination of man, where nothing was held back by a finite shape ... it was to that infinite, ever-expanding, indestructible cosmos that he belonged. It was there that he had been born.

Being alone now inevitably meant feeling the presence of this other world. He felt as if the whole universe was throbbing with joy; waves swept from it across a blue ocean of ether—

465

at dawn, midday, or dusk—to break over his entire being, filling it with boundless joy. He realised now that not only had his awareness expanded immeasurably, but it had acquired a whole new dimension. On a silent October afternoon, when his mind thought tenderly of similar enchanting afternoons spent in his childhood, he could sense that his present awareness which was sharper than before could take him anywhere—perhaps to some unknown, beauteous land, which might have been kept from him, hidden by the monotony of a humdrum existence.

Sitting by the river in the gathering dusk, Apu could even view death in a different light. It seemed to him that the wheel of life and death, through the ages, had always been turned by the hands of a divine artist. He knew how to place one after the other, in what form, and in what order. There might be discrepancies, but even that was part of the complete process, the art of creation on a much higher scale.

Six thousand years ago, he himself might have been born in ancient Egypt. Who knew what joys his life might have been filled with, growing up amongst ordinary people, with his parents and siblings and friends, playing among the papyrus-reeds, on the bright, sunny banks of the Nile?

Or perhaps he had been born by the Rhine, in the mansion of a wealthy aristocrat. He would have spent his life in medieval splendour, in the green shadows of oak and birch, surrounded by beautiful women.

He might return to this earth thousands of years hence. Would he remember this life? Who knew, he might not return at all. This time, he might be born as a star and find a whole new life, like that first star of the evening, winking faintly over the banyan tree.... How many times had he come back to this earth already, from life to life, from death through death? He felt as if he could see the path quite clearly, the path he had travelled from the distant past, stretching far into the future. There were other Nischindipurs, other Aparnas, other Durgas. But it was down this very path of life and death that his tired yet buoyant spirit had embarked on its journey. What a wonderful journey it was—in joy and life; youth and exhilaration; virtue and grief; pathos and peace. All of this came together to make up a greater form of existence, of which this life on earth was only a small part. Perhaps to dream of it was no more than soaring on a flight of fancy, who could tell? Who knew which god turned the wheel of this greater life?

Perhaps there were other beings whose creative urges, unlike those of man, were not confined to art, or music, or poetry. They created different worlds, revealing themselves through the rise and fall, joys and sorrows of their inhabitants. Who could tell to what higher system of evolution they belonged? What made them express their unbelievable artistry through the galaxy, in every planet and every star? Who knew them?

An indescribable surge of joy, hope and anticipation rose in his heart. It was this sense of a vital and immortal life that made him aware of the bitter smell from the dry and sunburnt branches and wild creepers around him; and hear the swish of the teals' wings in the blue sky above. No one had the power to deprive him of his life. He was neither poor, nor sorrowful, nor insignificant. This was not the beginning, nor the end. He was a traveller of all times, his never-ending path taking him closer every second to the far, the distant and the unseen, through a colossal blue expanse, the myriad stars, the Great Bear, the Milky Way, and the Andromeda galaxy. The world he was making his way to was untouched by death. Like the great ocean Newton had talked about, it was there for all to find, complete and untarnished. May the journey of every man through this path of infinity be unhampered and without obstacles, in every age, through all eternity.

Apu walked slowly to their ghat. Many, many years ago, on a similar night, the village deity, Vishalakshi Devi, was said

to have appeared before a man called Swarup Chakravarty,
What if she now appeared before him?

'Who are you?'

'I am Apu.'

'You are a good man. What would you like?'

'Nothing, Devi, except the childhood I had spent here in
the woods, by the river and in the shadows of the bamboo
groves. Ten years of innocence, eagerness and unending
dreams. Can you give those back to me?'

> '*You enter it by the Ancient Way*
> *Through Ivory Gate and Golden.*'

⁂

It was midday. Ranu went looking for Kajal. She could not
always control him, he refused to stay still. One minute
he was in the house, the next minute he was gone, no one
knew where.

He asked her every day, 'Pishima, when is Baba coming
back? How much longer is he going to take?'

Apu had said to her before leaving, 'Ranu di, I am going
to leave Khoka with you. Please keep him here, and don't
tell him where I've gone. If he cries for me, try to take his
mind off things. Only you can do it.'

'How can you do this?' Ranu had cried. 'How can you
deceive him like that? He'll believe what you tell him because
he's innocent and he trusts you. What if he was more clever?'

Apu had said something else. 'Ranu di, I have to show
you something before I go. There's a spot outside our old
home, near where the back door used to be, where a golden
box is buried under the ground. You need to dig only a little.
It's been lying there for years. If I don't return at all, and

468

if Khoka lives ... and grows up, give that box to his wife when he gets married, for her to keep sindoor in it. I don't want Khoka to have a very easy life; there's no need to put him in school right away. Don't stop him if he wants to go out. Only make sure you are with him when he goes to the river to bathe. He cannot swim, he might drown. He's a little unsure and afraid of certain things, but don't try to remove his fears by telling him what exists and what doesn't. Who can vouch for anything, anyway? It wouldn't be right to impose any rigid views on him, whatever they might be. Let him grow up with an open mind and make his own decisions.'

Apu knew Kajal's fears were simply a result of his inventive imagination. It was these imaginary fears that would act as the source from which would come all the joy and romance in life. He wanted his child to grow up close to nature, and prayed that all his evening and nights would be coloured by the same sense of wonder as his had been.

His passion for travelling had taken Apu away from home again. He had been gone for more than six months. Who knew, perhaps he had set out to fulfil Leela's last wish, and was looking for gold in a shipwreck in Porto Plata?

Ranu's brother, Shotu, was also very fond of Kajal. He had changed dramatically from the naughty, even cruel, little child he once was. Life had taught him a hard lesson, and made him turn to God. He dressed like a Vaishnav, wearing his hair long, and a garland round his neck. On returning from his shop every evening, he played a drum and sang devotional songs. Apu had paid him seventy rupees to reclaim his mango orchard. In addition to that, he had borrowed another fifty from Apu to pay for supplies to his shop. Ranu did not know about this. She would never have allowed him to borrow that extra money, if she had any idea.

Kajal was most interested in birds. He had never seen so many. His grandfather's house had been in a village, too; but it was far more congested, there had not been so many woods, or such wide, open spaces. At night, while he lay in bed, all the fields and trees outside seemed full of ghosts and spirits and monsters, jackals and wolves ... he snuggled closer to Ranu. But, during the day, all his fears disappeared. It was a good time to look for birds' nests and eggs. Ranu had warned him many times of the danger in slipping his hand into nests built by the river. Sometimes, snakes lurked in them. Kajal did not listen, and felt brave enough to venture to the riverside in search of nests, without Ranu's knowledge. But his courage failed invariably, as soon as it got dark.

This afternoon, he was out roaming among the bamboo behind Ranu's house. Winter was over, it felt quite warm in the midday sun. The breeze brought a funny smell. His father had pointed out various trees, and taught him the names of birds; so he knew where to find creepers of wild pepper, laden with fragrant blossoms. There were other creepers, too, that peeped over bushes, swinging low like snakes.

He had never stepped inside the old and derelict house of his forefathers. Apu had shown him where it was, but not allowed him to go in, possibly because it had turned into a jungle. Now Kajal felt most curious. He had to go and take a closer look at it.

There was a high mound. Kajal looked around quickly, then climbing over it, pushed his way through a barrier of thick vegetation. Then he found himself in the old courtyard. There were bricks everywhere, and stems of bamboo. Couldn't he find birds here? No one ever came this way. Who would know where their nests were hidden?

A bird called out: *tukli, tukli*! It was a basantabouri. His father had taught him how to recognise that call. But did that mean there was a nest nearby, or was the bird simply sitting on a branch?

Kajal raised his face and scanned the branches of all the big trees in the vicinity. A gust of wind rose suddenly from the wasteland and sped towards Kajal, as if bearing words of welcome. All his ancestors—Biru Roy, his great grandfather; Harihar, his grandfather; his grandmother, Sarbajaya; his aunt, Durga, and all their unknown predecessors seemed to rise at once to receive him with warm smiles, to say: 'Here you are, you have come back to us at last. We see ourselves in you, you represent us today. You have our blessings and our love. May you be a worthy son of our family.'

But that was not all. From the shadows of the woods rose Sahadev, carrying a pitcher of water: from the wood-apple tree rose Bhishma from his bed of arrows; then out came the brave Karna; Arjun with his Gandiv bow; the driver of his chariot, Sri Krishna; the defeated prince, Duryodhan; the hapless Bhanumati; the tearful Janaki on the bank of the river Tamasa; the beautiful princess, Subhadra, at her swyamvar sabha, garland in hand, eyes cast down, walking slowly; and many other figures from the two epics. Together, they beckoned and smiled at him. 'Here you are!' they said, stretching their arms. 'Come back to us again. Don't you know us? Think of those afternoons spent by your broken window, those intimate exchanges ... we know you well. Come back to us ... come ... come ... come ...!'

Ranu's voice sounded at once, 'Khoka, you naughty boy, what do you think you are doing in this jungle? Come out immediately, I tell you!'

Kajal emerged, grinning broadly. He was not in the least afraid of Ranu. He knew she loved him very much. After his grandmother died, no one except his father had showered such affection on him.

Ranu looked at him and thought suddenly, 'Apu used to look exactly like this when he was up to some mischief!' Little Kajal's face wore an identical expression.

The unvanquished mystery of life, travelling through every age—how gloriously it had revealed itself again!

Kajal's father had made a small mistake in thinking his childhood was lost for ever. After an absence of twenty-four years, the innocent child Apu had returned to Nischindipur again.

❦

Glossary

aata

custard apple

alpana

delicate and intricate patterns drawn on the floor or on walls with rice paste, on auspicious occasions

alta

red liquid with which women adorn their feet

annaprashan

an auspicious occasion when a child eats its first spoonful of rice

aanchal

the flowing end of a saree

arati

invocation of a god or goddess, usually with an oil lamp

Aryavarta

The area (almost the whole of north India) where the Aryans had settled

babu	the Bengali equivalent of 'Mr'. Added to first names as a mark of respect
barasinga	a species of deer
bokul	small white flowers
boro	a kinship term used in Bengal, meaning the eldest, or the first-born
boti	an implement used in Bengali kitchens to peel and chop vegetables. It is a sharp blade fixed to a wooden plank
bou	literally, a bride. A daughter-in-law in a household is often called 'bou'. 'Boro bou', for instance, would indicate the first or eldest daughter-in-law
boudi/bou thakrun	brother's wife. A friend's wife is often called either boudi, or bou thakrun
bourani	a term of respect for a daughter-in-law in a household, used particularly by domestic staff
chhatim	large tree with digitated leaves
chhatu	ground barley or maize
daab	a green coconut
dada/da	elder brother. 'Da', short for 'dada', is added to first names to indicate that the person addressed is seen as an elder brother. Even close friends, if they are younger in age, would add 'da' to a man's name to denote repect. Hence Apu is Apurbo da to his friend Debu
dada thakur	another term of respect; 'thakur' indicates that the person addressed is a Brahmin

dadu	grandfather
dak bungalow	a place for travellers to stay overnight
didi/di	elder sister. The female equivalent of 'dada'
didima	grandmother (mother's mother)
doha	couplet in Hindi
Durga Puja	Bengali Hindu equivalent of Christmas. It is the most important religious and social occasion in Bengal. Durga is a goddess with ten arms, seen as mother who would protect her devotees from all evil. 'Puja' is to worship. It lasts for five days and is celebrated usually during the month of October.
ekka	a horse carraige drawn by a single horse
gamchha	a coarse, hand-spun towel
grihalakshmi	literally, a goddess of home, i.e., a woman who is as beautiful and gracious as a goddess in one's home.
halwa	a dessert, made with semolina, sugar and ghee
Janamashtami	the birthday of Lord Krishna
jamaibabu	sister's husband
jethima	the wife of one's father's elder brother
jatra	a stage entertainment which has been popular in Bengal for centuries. The play is accompanied by instrumental music and has interludes of singing,

	dancing and improvised buffoonery. The female parts were played by boys
Kaal-Baishakhi	severe storm that takes place in Bengal between mid-April and mid-May
kantha	an embroidered bedspread
kash	tall grass with downy end. Similar to pampas.
kaviraj	A doctor who practises ayuraedic or herbal medicine
keertan	devotional songs
khichuri	a special dish in which rice and daal are boiled together
khoka	a little boy. Many young boys are addressed as khoka
kojagari	literally, 'to keep awake'. It is a special occasion at which the goddess Lakshmi is worshipped. One is expected to keep awake all night to invoke her
Lakshmi	the goddess of wealth and prosperity
mama	uncle (mother's brother)
mamima	the wife of one's mama
mashima	aunt (mother's sister)
mejo	a kinship term meaning 'the second'. It follows 'boro', i.e. the second child is called 'mejo'. The title 'Mejo Bourani' is used for the wife of the second son in the family
moshai	a term of respect for a man
muri	rice crisps (puffed rice), usually mixed

	with mustard oil and spices and eaten as a snack
muriwali	a woman who sells muri
Paan	betel leaf
pishi/pishima	father's sister. A close female friend is seen as a sister. Hence Ranu, to Kajal, is like Apu's sister, and is called pishi
polash	bright red flowers
prasad	the offering made to a god or goddess, which is later distributed among devotees
puja	the act of invoking a god, or offering prayers
reetha	soap-nut
saboo	sago
sambar	a species of deer
sanyasi	a man who has renounced the world
Saraswati	goddess of art and learning
shaal	valuable timber
shikar	hunting
sindoor	vermillion, usually worn in the parting of a woman's hair to indicate that she is married
sloka	couplet in sanskrit
supari	betel-nut
swayambar sabha	in ancient times, princesses were allowed to choose their own husbands. Kings and princes who wished to be

married to a particular princess, gathered together. The princess walked past the suiters in the gathering, and was told how well each man was qualified. She was then free to put a garland around a man's neck, to indicate who she had chosen to be her husband. This gathering of suitors was called a 'swayambar sabha'

syce	a groom for a horse
teli	one who sells oil
thakurpo	the younger brother of one's husband
Vijaya Dashami	The last day of the Durga Puja when the Goddess is immersed in water. A day of celebration